Ashes of the Rift

The Riftreach Series

Book One

Aurora Sandelands

Created with Vellum

Content Warning:

This book includes depictions of graphic violence, explicit sexual activity, a scene involving attempted sexual assault, captivity, psychological manipulation, emotional abuse, and themes related to trauma, grief, and death. Reader discretion is advised.

Dedication

For my husband—thank you for showing me a love so beautiful I had to write it down. To the max, baby.
Papa, for giving me everything I need and more.
Colleen—thank you for always, always, always believing in me. This book was no different.
Mama and Tom, for always pushing my creativity to the next level.
Grandma Becky, Grandma Vicki and Grandpa Heinz.
Lilyah, when you're old enough to read this, never forget that me and Dad love you so much.
To my aunties and uncles. Angela, Kendall, Holly.
To Zack—my mentor in art and patience.
And to all my other friends, blood relatives or chosen family:
Thank you.

Shafts of thick black smoke twirled, spiraled, yawned toward the sky with open arms, drinking the cool night air as fuel. The flames ripped over the timber of my home, leaving nothing but ash in its wake. I was caged in my fathers arms, being silently whisked away from danger. I listened to my mothers tortured screams on the wind. She was trapped inside, bathed in flames. I listened until the screaming stopped.

Chapter One
Evandra

"The Rift, an enigmatic and eternal force woven through the fabric of our realm, serves as both the wellspring of creation and the harbinger of chaos. The Rift itself exists beyond mortal perception, a primal energy that courses through all things and whispers its secrets to those attuned." —Magic of Edralis: An Introduction to Magical Creatures and Riftborn, p. 1

It was the morning of my 24th name day, and I sat atop my dusty yellow comforter in my cramped attic room, lost in thought. The remnants of last night's dream clung to me as they so often did. It was almost always the same—unless I was too exhausted to dream at all, which, more often than not, seemed to be the case.

In my dream, I was always a child again, cradled in my Papa's arms as we fled from the roar of wild flames. Over the years, I'd come to believe it wasn't just a dream but a memory—a fragment of the night my mother died. Though I could have sworn something felt different last night. Somewhere in the flame, there was a presence… ancient, aching, like it knew me. And stranger still—it felt like it was waiting. Like a thread pulled tight across time, humming in the dark, not yet tied… but tethered.

I glanced out my sole bedroom window at the town below. On mornings like this, when the dew clung thick to the rooftops, and the sunlight made the leaves sparkle, Winshire almost looked magical. Almost. But magic was long dead—or so we were told. This whole place was dying. It had been for years.

The tiny, ever-quiet town of Winshire lay tucked in the heart of the Aberdeen Kingdom, forgotten amid the vast, rolling grasslands. A handful of crooked dwellings and a sagging inn stood precariously as though centuries of wind and time might topple them at any moment. Half the town clung to a creeping pine forest, the other faced the endless grasslands. A narrow road snaked its way toward the distant Castle City, but few ever ventured through Winshire. After all, there was nothing worth stopping for.

Somewhere out there, beyond the grasslands and thick woods on the edge of town, the world was alive. And I was stuck here, serving ale and making beds for men who barely remembered my name.

The Nestlers Inn existed in the heart of town. It was the business Papa had taken on after my mother had died, hoping it would provide us both a future. By the time I turned thirteen, I was already helping out wherever I could. In those early years, Papa—Philip to everyone else—was still active, managing the inn as best he could. Though, now, as time wore on and his health began to fade, he retreated more often to the attic with his books or to wander the garden. I didn't mind one bit. At nearly seventy, he had earned these years for himself. Besides, I had always been someone who valued solitude.

I worked tirelessly to keep the inn standing. Tending the bar, turning the beds, and cooking meals day after day. Despite the fact it was essentially rotting from old age, it smelled of home. The scent of my cooking paired with the rich, earthy aroma of Papa's signature ale.

Shaking myself free from my thoughts, I wandered down the dim, empty corridors, floorboards creaking beneath my feet as I made my way to the tavern to begin another day.

Nameday or not, business didn't wait, and I doubted anyone else in town would have much to say about the occasion. Papa, however, never forgot. Even with money tight since mother died, he always found a way to mark the day, no matter how small.

The tavern was the beating heart of the inn, its two-story timber frame giving it a sturdy charm despite the wear. Toward the back, the bar and kitchen stood ready for the day's work. Eight well-worn tables filled the room, each scarred with years of use, while a large stone hearth dominated the space, its chimney stretching high into the ceiling.

I found Papa seated in one of the two tired chairs by the hearth that morning, holding a small package in his lap.

"Good morning, papa!" I smiled as I pranced over to him, giving him a small peck on the cheek. He chuckled and swept me up into a gentle hug.

"Happy Nameday, my girl." He smiled up at me through his thick round glasses, passing the crudely wrapped gift into my hands. I could tell his arthritic knuckles bothered him as he pressed down the messy folds. My heart warmed at his apparent effort. "Well, go ahead then!" He urged me on.

As I tore the paper away, my breath caught. The book beneath was like nothing I'd ever seen. Its green leather binding gleamed, textured with soft, overlapping scales. Gold-edged pages glimmered in the firelight and the cover was embossed with images of dragons mid-flight and beasts locked in battle. The title read: Magic of Edralis—An Introduction to Magical Creatures and Riftborn.

Edralis... Edralis... Where have I heard that name before? I glanced up at my father and noticed his knowing smile.

"Is this..." My voice faltered as I ran my fingers over the scaled spine. "Is this *contraband*?" I whispered the last word.

Papa chuckled softly, but his eyes were serious. "It's knowledge. And knowledge should never be forbidden. But technically... yes."

My heart raced as I hugged the book to my chest. "Thank you, Papa," I whispered, throwing my arms around his neck. He patted my back, his hands trembling slightly.

"It was your mother's," he said quietly. The words hit me like a gust of wind. I knew he rarely parted with anything of hers. I looked at the book again, my throat tight.

"What is Edralis?" I asked as I stroked the gold-lined pages of the book.

"It was the kingdom's name before Aberdeen's reign," he explained, watching me closely.

Of course. Edralis—the name whispered in half-forgotten stories, buried in the songs no one dared to sing anymore. The weight of the book suddenly felt heavier.

"I..." My voice dropped to a whisper. "I shouldn't have this."

"You'll keep it hidden," he said firmly. "Just as your mother did."

I nodded urgently, tucking the book under my arm. My father understood my fascination with magic, no matter how forbidden it was. The urge to devour the contents of the banned book was overwhelming, but there was work to be done. The inn wouldn't run itself, and despite my name day, the regulars would expect their lunch and ale on time. I hurried and slid the book into my nightstand before returning to my daily duties.

The day dragged.

I served the usual faces: the old farmers, slowly nursing papas ale from a worn tankard, the blacksmith muttering about who knows what, and the lone wanderer who barely spoke a word. My mind, however, was miles away—upstairs, tucked into the pages of my new book.

When the last customer finally left, I kissed Papa on the cheek and slipped upstairs, my heart pounding with anticipation.

In the safety of my attic room, I curled up by the window, the scaly tome cradled in my hands. The golden title glinted in the fading light as I opened the cover. A faint scent of dust and aged parchment wafted up, filling the air around me.

There, in the upper corner of the first page, was a name written in delicate script:

Morwenna Dawnshade.

My mother's name. Her handwriting.

I ran my fingers over the letters, hoping to feel some trace of her in the ink. But all I felt was the cool, smooth surface of the page.

I turned to the first chapter.

An Introduction to Creatures and Magic Wielders, Known as Riftborn
By: *Edwaurd Thistlebellow*

Magic was foretold to have begun at a time when Gods walked the earth among men. They shared their lives and shaped the world with their divine power. During this time, known as the Ages of Divinity, the Gods sought to leave a lasting mark upon the earth. To do so, they bestowed upon certain humans the gift of magic, transforming them into the First Magi, individuals capable of wielding powers that defied the natural order.

Beyond gifting magic to mortals, the Gods also created creatures imbued with extraordinary powers —beasts that embodied their divine aspects and served as guardians of the world's hidden mysteries.

As the Gods withdrew from the physical realm during the period known as the Rift, magic remained, shaping the foundations of civilization. The First Magi and these magical beasts became the inheritors of a world where divine power lingered, but its originators had faded into myth. Thus, the study of Thaumatology began, tracing the threads of divine power back to those ancient days, seeking to understand the gifts left behind by the Gods.

Hours slipped by as I read. Each page pulled me deeper into a world I had only dreamed of—a world of beasts that defied nature and humans who wielded impossible power. I read of Blade Dancers, healers and Hellwrought. Of dragons and magical people called Riftborn, of civilizations shaped by forces I could hardly imagine.

I was utterly consumed, lost in reading as the moon slowly crossed the sky. When the first rays of sunlight began to filter through the evergreens outside my window, I realized I hadn't slept. My body was heavy with exhaustion, but my mind was alight with sorrow and awe.

How could the king outlaw something so beautiful? How many lives —how many mothers —had been erased for this silence? To hide this knowledge?

I slipped under my comforter, my thoughts churning with rage. The last image I saw before sleep claimed me was of a crimson dragon soaring through a golden sky, free and untamed.

Sleep brought my usual dream, but this time, something was off. I was slung over Papa's familiar shoulder, jostled by each hurried step as the air was thick with heat. The fire roared around us, but something new caught my attention.

When peering into that too-familiar flame, a dark, cloaked figure looked back. He was tall and broad-shouldered, his presence radiating power, urgency, strength. His face was obscured, his features swallowed by the oppressive shadows, I could see his lips moving—frantic, desperate— but no sound reached me. I knew he was trying to tell me something. Something I already felt, even if I didn't understand it.

A strange sensation filled me, some sort of pull as if my bones were iron and he was a magnet drawing me in. My confusion quickly turned to dread as I realized I was being whisked away from him. I strained against the arms caging me, desperate to get closer to the man in the flames. But the arms held me firm, unyielding.

The dream blurred, and I woke with a start as the morning light crept further across my walls. My heart was pounding, the magnetic pull of the figure lingering in my chest like an echo.

Chapter Two

Eldrake

The path snaked endlessly before me, a dark ribbon winding through the suffocating black of the night. Rain lashed at my face, the cold seeping into my bones despite the heat simmering under my skin. My horse's hoofbeats clattered rhythmically against the slick cobblestones, steady and unrelenting. Somewhere behind me, Fen and Felix's horses echoed the rhythm, their sounds muted by the downpour.

Why did this woman have to live in the middle of fucking nowhere?

What if she refused to come with us?

The thought tightened my grip on the reins. Commander's orders had been clear—she had to come to Riftreach. There was no room for negotiation. The Uprising's survival depended on it.

I cursed under my breath, the memory of his words gnawing at my pride. "Use any tactic necessary, Captain. Charm her if you must." As if I was nothing but a cock for hire. I'd sooner drag her back in chains than play the fool in her bed.

A growl rose unbidden from my throat, drowned out by the thunder rolling overhead. I cracked the reins, urging my horse faster. I was Captain of the Riftborn Uprising—a soldier, a leader, branded in fire and trained in war. Not some *seducer.*

I was here to save our people, to bring her back by whatever means necessary.

But not that. Never that.

I pushed the thought away, focusing on the steady rhythm of my horse's gallop. The darkness ahead was unbroken, a void that seemed to stretch forever. Somewhere beyond it lay the woman who, unknowingly, held the fate of the Uprising in her hands.

She'd better be worth all this trouble.

Another crack of thunder split the sky, and my horse let out a snort of protest, its hooves slipping slightly on the uneven cobblestones. I steadied the reins, muttering a quiet apology to the beast. It wasn't its fault we were out here, chasing shadows and hopes.

Somewhere in the distance, I heard Fen shout something to Felix; her voice lost to the storm. It didn't matter. I knew what I had to do. Failure wasn't an option. Not for me. Not for the Uprising.

The rain stung my face, sharp and cold, but my heightened temper made the feeling almost unnoticeable. I was tired. Bone-deep, soul-deep tired—the kind that doesn't come from fighting—but from carrying everything. But there was no room for that anymore.

I didn't care how far into the wilderness this mission took me or how stubborn this woman was. I would bring her back.

And I would do it on my terms.

Chapter Three

Evandra

"To the Riftborn, the Rift itself is more than mere energy; it is a living essence, a boundless reservoir from which they draw powers that reshape reality itself." —Magic of Edralis: An Introduction to Magical Creatures and Riftborn, p. 3

I traced absentminded circles on the oak bar with my rag, the wood beneath my fingers worn smooth by decades of use. My thoughts drifted somewhere distant, far beyond the stale confines of the inn. The copper bell above the door chimed, pulling me back to the present.

I glanced up, expecting the first customer of the day. Instead, I was met with a sight that immediately flooded me with irritation.

"Hello, Evandra," came the familiar, oily voice.

Colin Junior.

He strode in with his usual entitlement, his polished leather shoes clicking against the floorboards in time with the tap of his decorative cane. His crooked, practiced smile was plastered across his face, but behind it was no warmth.

"Colin," I replied, not bothering to mask the irritation in my tone.

"There's that charm I love," he said, his voice laden with sarcasm.

I rolled my eyes, letting the gesture speak for me as I continued pretending to wipe down the bar. Colin Junior was one of the few men in Winshire close to my age, which might have been appealing if he weren't such an unbearable ass.

His father, Colin Sr., was the owner of The Winshire Stables, which was the primary source of work in town and the only thing (if at all) that put us on the Aberdeen Kingdom map. Or so the Colin's seemed to think.

The business bred and broke horses for The Royal Army, which gave them an ego the size of the kingdom itself. As children, Junior and I had been friends—or as close to friends as two kids could be when one was insufferably spoiled. But somewhere along the way, he'd traded mud pies and tadpoles for coins and condescension.

"Eva, be a dear and fetch me a drink," he commanded, leaning his cane against the bar and sliding onto a stool. His grin was full of self-satisfaction. I turned to pour him an ale, biting back one of the many insults I had prepared. His pointed jawline and well-tailored coat did little to distract from the emptiness in his pale blue eyes. For a fleeting moment, I almost wished he were better—someone worth the company.

But no amount of loneliness would make Colin Junior tolerable.

I set down his mead as he launched into a monologue about a new horse that would be "the king's prize mare" and "fetch mountains of gold," I let my mind drift away as he prattled on. My gaze wandered to the window, a usual reprieve from his droning voice— but this time, something felt off.

The woods across the street were silent. No sparrows flitting between the branches, no squirrels darting across the mossy floor. The familiar sunlight filtering through the canopy was absent, replaced by an unnatural darkness that seemed to seep from the trees like ink. My stomach twisted.

"Evandra? Are you listening?" Colin snapped, his voice cutting through my unease.

"Uh, yeah. Great about the horse," I mumbled, already stepping away from the bar. My dress brushed against the stools as I moved quickly between the empty tables and out the front door.

The cobblestone street was eerily still as I crossed it, my eyes locked on the tree line. The woods had always been my haven, my escape. But today, they loomed like a predator waiting to pounce. I had to investigate.

I stopped at the edge, the familiar scent of earth and pine doing little to calm the chill creeping up my spine. The trees seemed alive, their twisted branches leaning toward me, whispering a warning I couldn't understand.

The sunlight that should have dappled the mossy floor was gone. In its place was shadow—thick, impenetrable, and suffocating. It wasn't just darkness. It was... alive.

Alive and... Watching me.

My breath quickened as I backed away, unwilling to turn my back on the void. By the time I reached the inn, I was practically running.

I caught my reflection in the window and froze. I hadn't really *looked* at myself in days. My dress—once a soft, lovely blue—was stained and patched. I wore tangled red hair in a bun and deep bruises under my eyes. Exhaustion was etched across my face.

Then I saw it.

Behind me, in the woods, a figure stood a few feet into the forest. A shadow clung to it like a living thing, bleeding into the surrounding trees, consuming what little light remained. I couldn't make out its features—only its presence, dark and oppressive. A chill skated down my spine.

I whirled around so fast I almost gave myself whiplash, but saw... nothing.

The figure was gone, swallowed by an unnatural void. I stared into the forest for what felt like an eternity, my pulse racing, searching for the figure. Though, even if the figure had vanished, something in the air still felt wrong - like the silence was watching me. After a moment, I turned and hurried back inside, the copper bell above the door jingling weakly in my wake.

"Did you see that?" I blurted, breathless.

Colin barely looked up from inspecting his nails. "See what?"

I hesitated. Realizing he'd never believe me, or worse, tell his father to have me shipped off to castle city to be committed, "Never mind." I muttered, grabbing his glass and topping off his mead.

"Anyway, Eva," he began, his tone too casual, "I'm sure you're wondering why I came here this evening. The truth is, we've known each other for a long time. You're not seeing anyone. I have prospects. It just makes sense, doesn't it?"

I sighed, bracing myself. Gods, this man never gave up! "Coli—"

"Just think about it," he interrupted, flashing me the same practiced grin. His egotism took me aback. "I'll stop by in a few days. Maybe we can get a drink somewhere that isn't... this place." He gave a judgmental glance around the room.

Before I could respond, he was gone, the bell chiming in his wake. I stood there, staring at the door, wondering if I even had a choice.

The rest of the evening slipped by in a blur. I tried to immerse myself in preparing the next day's meals, hoping the familiar rhythm of cooking would quiet my racing thoughts. Typically, it was one of my favorite tasks—a chance to create, to let my soul sing as I painted with spices and flavors. I never followed a recipe, just trusted my instincts to guide me instead.

Tonight, I was slow-cooking a roast with sweet potatoes and pears, the rich aroma of sage, onion, and garlic filling the kitchen. Sweet and savory notes mingled in the air, a symphony of comfort. But no matter how much I tried to lose myself in the task, I couldn't shake the unease creeping over me.

The dark windows at the front of the inn seemed to watch me. Once familiar, now they felt like empty eyes, peering into my space, exposing me. I shivered, the weight of an unseen gaze prickling at my skin.

Who—or *what*—was out there?

It was being ridiculous, I told myself, shaking off the sensation. I stirred the pot absently, the scent of sage and pear doing little to soothe me. The stillness beyond the glass continued to press inward, making the once-cozy kitchen feel like a stage. My heart thudded in my chest as I forced myself to focus on the meal, but my hands moved slower, more deliberate.

Darkness had fully settled by the time I finished my preparations and set the roast in the crackling stove to cook overnight. I piled up a plate with bread and cheese for Papa, grabbed a small lantern, and hurried up the creaking stairs to his attic room, relieved to leave the oppressive gaze of the kitchen. Reaching his ancient door, I knocked gently, not wanting to disturb him if he was already asleep. The pressure of my knock caused the door to creak open slightly, and the familiar sight inside brought a faint grin to my face.

Papa sat slumped in his worn chair by the fire; his head tilted back, mouth agape as quiet breaths escaped him. Beneath the deep cracks and creases that lined his mouth and nose, echoes of the man that raised me lingered—a sharper jawline softened by time, a spark in his tired eyes that hadn't entirely dimmed. I still saw the man who read me stories of magic and kingdoms every night until I was old enough to read them for myself.

He had worked tirelessly to provide for me after the fire, sacrificing so much. It warmed my heart to think that now, in some small way, I could return the favor.

After making sure the blanket was tucked snugly around him, I slipped out of his room, taking one more short glance behind me. This part of the day was mine. No strange men, no shadows in the trees. Just the scent of my cooking and the quiet rise and fall of Papa's breath. I locked up the inn for the night, my footsteps echoing in the silent halls. By the time I reached my bed, the unease from earlier had faded, replaced by an eager anticipation.

I wasted no time pulling out my new book, the scaled cover cool under my fingers. Settling into the comfort of my dusty yellow blanket, I devoured another chapter, each word feeding a hunger I hadn't realized I'd carried for years.

Excerpt from On the Nature of Beasts and The Riftborn
by *Professor Ameryn Valdain*

In the annals of our world's history, few beings inspire both awe and trepidation like the Beasts—humanoid creatures that embody the union of mortal and magical essence. Unlike humans, whose magic is often channeled through their blood and innate senses, the Beasts are born with their powers woven into their very flesh, as if they are conduits for the arcane.

Physiologically, Beasts bear traits reminiscent of legendary creatures: wings akin to those of skyward drakes, horns that spiral like the ancient earth-rending wyrms, and eyes that shimmer with the light of aether. These features are not mere ornamentation but serve as focal points for their innate magic. Wings grant them flight and wind-based sorcery, while horns are believed to act as conduits for more destructive magics, such as fire and lightning. The shimmer in their eyes, often described as a "Star-Glow," hints at an ability to see beyond the veil of reality, perceiving realms and energies beyond human understanding. Unlike humans, who must study for years to master even simple spells, the Beasts draw upon their powers with the same ease with which they draw breath, making them both formidable allies and dangerous foes. Pure embodiments of The Rift- that we, as mere mortals, can scarcely comprehend.

After hours of devouring the pages, I lay down, willing my restless mind to calm, though it refused to settle. Images from the book lingered behind my eyes—the men with horns and wings, their forms both majestic and terrifying.

My thoughts drifted, unbidden, to my reflection earlier in the window. How plain I seemed compared to the creatures in the book, compared to the Riftborn who once were. I was unremarkable, just like everything else in this town. And then there was Colin—my only suitor — *if he could even be called that.* He was the only one who'd ever shown interest in me, though for reasons I doubted were entirely noble.

I wondered if this was all there was for me. A life of solitude. *What if I never left this place? What if no one came for me?* Forced to live a life as forgettable as the town I called home.

Then, my mind returned to the trees. The figure. The way it had stared at me, its presence lingering long after it disappeared into the darkness. The thought sent a shiver down my spine, and I pinched my eyes shut, trying to push it away. But fear gave way to something else—something deeper, heavier. A sudden ache swelled in my chest, and I felt tears spill from my closed eyes. My life was dreary enough, and I couldn't even wallow in that dreariness in peace—some shadow had to come along and ruin even the quiet of my sorrow.

I cried for the Riftborn, for how something so beautiful could be erased so cleanly from history. I cried for all the parts of the world I would never know. The tears came quietly, but they came for some time, soft and unrelenting, until exhaustion overtook me. At last, I drifted into sleep, the weight of my sorrow trailing me into my dreams.

The fire roared behind us, its crackling voice echoing through the chaos. I was tossed over the familiar shoulder. I felt the heavy thud of footsteps beneath me, each step jarring against my fragile frame. Fear pressed down on my chest, too heavy to allow me to look up.

But slowly, hesitantly, I peeked over the broad shoulder carrying me. The place I once called home was disappearing, swallowed whole by the flames. The golden glow of its timbers turned to blackened ash, and embers swirled in the air like fireflies. A gust of wind swept through, carrying with it a storm of ash and smoke that filled my lungs. It burned with a searing intensity as if somebody had rammed a fireplace poker down my windpipe.

The scene was agonizingly familiar, a terrible memory etched into my soul. I'd seen this before—every night, I think. But this time, the pain was sharper, the air heavier. I began to cough, my body heaving violently in a desperate attempt to expel the acrid taste from my throat. For a fleeting moment, I wondered if this was how my home had felt: consumed by fire, carried away by forces beyond its control.

Then, a voice broke through.

Low, beautiful, and rasping, it breathed my name.

Evandra...

I froze. No one spoke to me in my dream. Ever. The voice was dark, unnaturally deep, and it reverberated through me like the rumble of distant thunder.

The familiar smell I had clung to—a warm, comforting scent that was wholly my father—shifted. It was gone, replaced by something new. Spice and incense lingered in the air, rich and heady. It was a scent I thought I recognized, though I couldn't place it. Familiar, yet strange. But there was more. Beneath the spice and incense, something sharper cut through—a coppery musk that clung to my senses with a metallic tang. *Blood.*

My breath hitched as I realized the man carrying me was no longer my father. He was someone else, someone unknown yet somehow intimately familiar. The sensation of being held shifted, the embrace at once protective and unnervingly alien.

The flames raged on behind us, but it was his presence that consumed me now.

I gasped, jolting upright as the feeling of thick smoke was still palpable in my lungs.

My chest heaved, my fists tangled in my damp bedsheets, a thin sheen of sweat slicking my skin. The bright sun streamed mercilessly through the window, its warmth a cruel contrast to the cold dread pooling in my gut. My head pounded, a sharp, relentless ache like a knife twisting behind my temple. The dream lingered, vivid and unshakable.

The figure's face... Something about it had pierced through the haze, jerking me awake as if pulled from drowning.

I stumbled from my bed. Every muscle was sluggish, and I braced myself against my vanity. I splashed cool water on my face, letting the shock of it chase away the lingering fog of the dream. My breath steadied as I peered down into the basin. For a fleeting moment, my reflection stared back at me from the rippling water, pale and tired, but then—a sharp pain lanced through my skull, sudden and blinding. A flash—not in the room, but *behind* my eyes. I stumbled back, pressing my palms to my temples, my eyes clenched shut. The glint lingered for a heartbeat—bright, impossible, beautiful—and then vanished, leaving behind a faint shimmer in my vision and a thrum low in my chest. Like something ancient had stirred. Like something had seen me.

Star-Glow. The words from my book echoed in my mind. Eyes that shimmer with aether. Vision beyond the veil. I clutched the edge of the basin, struggling to make sense of it. Could exhaustion do that? Could stress conjure something so vivid—so real?

My heart pounded. I stood there, dripping and trembling, staring at my reflection like it belonged to someone else. I shook my head, forcing the thought away. Exhaustion, I told myself. That's all it is. Just a dream. Just stress. Just... a moment. But as I turned away from the mirror, a shining glint still danced faintly behind my eyes. And something deep in my chest stirred.

I quickly pulled on a dress from my wardrobe, one I knew was unflattering but blissfully comfortable. It was the sort of morning where comfort was all I could manage.

Shakily making my way to the tavern, I was met halfway down the stairs by the savory aroma of my roast, the rich scent immediately calming my senses.

As soon as the hearth came into view, my eyes darted instinctively to the forest through the window. It remained unchanged: dark, foreboding, and still too quiet. My flesh prickled and caused my hair to stand on end. I tore my gaze away. Maybe I *hadn't* imagined what I saw yesterday.

Papa was already seated at one of the tables, his thick glasses perched on his nose as he thumbed through a book. The firelight flickered across his weathered face, the familiar sight anchoring me for a moment.

"Good morning, Papa," I said, swinging around to plant a kiss on his cheek. "Thank you for my gift. I love it."

"You're welcome, my girl," he replied, his eyes still fixed on the book in his hands.

He wasn't a man of many words, but the sly grin tugging at the corner of his lips said enough. I paused for a moment, my gaze flitting between him and the darkened tree line beyond the window. The trees were as ominous as ever, their shadows creeping closer in the morning light.

The day passed with some semblance of normalcy until the copper bell over the door rang its familiar chime.

"'Ello, Miss Evandra." came the thick northern lilt I knew well.

I turned to see Mr. Trebuie hanging his felted hat and coat on the rack near the door.

"Hiya. Lunch?" I called out.

"Yes, please!" He said, settling into his usual corner seat by the window. I brought him a steaming cup of tea and a plate of roast and bread. Setting it down, I sank into the chair across from him, eager for a distraction.

"How are things? Feels like it's been a week or two since I've seen you." I said, resting my chin on my hand.

"Oh, aye. Had to ride up to Castle City for supplies," he replied between bites. "Heard some strange talk while I was there." He stated. I raised an eyebrow.

That flicker of unease returned—the same one I thought I'd shaken off after last night.

"Castle City always has its fair share of strange," I said, trying to sound dismissive, though I leaned forward without meaning to. "What is it this time?"

His expression darkened as he leaned closer, lowering his voice. "Three politicians. Inside the Castle gates. Tore to shreds, like wolves got to 'em. But 'ere's the strange bit: no animal made it past the guard. No prints. No blood trail. Nothing." A cold rush flooded my chest. I set the teapot down with more force than I meant to.

"You're saying... it wasn't an animal?" I clarified slowly.

Trebuie shook his head. "I doubt it. Those men were no saints—crooked as a broken wheel, the lot of 'em—but this wasn't some random attack. Felt like retribution, if you ask me. The kind you can't explain." He took a sloppy bite of his roast, some of the brownish gravy dribbling down his chin.

"Something strange is happening lately," I murmured, mostly to myself. The figure in the woods flickered back through my mind.

"Well," Trebuie added, sitting back with a satisfied sigh, "that's why me and the missus never moved to the city. Too much sin draws too much trouble if you ask me." He loudly sipped his tea. I nodded before excusing myself.

As the day dragged on, I couldn't shake his story from my mind. Strange attacks, the darkness of the woods, my dreams shifting for the first time, and the figure I'd seen watching me all wove themselves into a single, nagging unease.

By nightfall, the tavern was quiet. Papa sat in one of the chairs by the hearth, his book open in his lap. I approached hesitantly, clearing my throat.

"Papa... Can I ask you something?" I began slowly, still unsure if I should share what I'd seen. He nodded, his gaze fixed on the pages in his hands. I lowered myself into the chair beside him, clasping my hands tightly in my lap. "Have you ever seen anything... strange in the forest?"

For a moment, he didn't respond. The silence stretched, and I caught the faintest tension in his jaw before he finally spoke. "No," he said at last, his tone sharp and clipped. "Though I'm not always paying attention."

The answer felt too quick, too careful. Papa wasn't one to lie to me, yet something about the words seemed... rehearsed, as though he'd said them before. His eyes flicked toward me, then away, and for an instant the firelight caught on something like sorrow in his gaze. He pushed his glasses up the bridge of his nose and sighed, setting the book aside with deliberate calm.

"Eva, my dear, listen closely." His voice lowered, steady but carrying a weight I couldn't name. "In my seventy years of life, if I've come to understand anything, it's this: no matter how harmless something may appear, there is always a shadow lurking within. Some shadows are buried so deeply that no one should ever uncover them." He hesitated, just a breath too long, before adding, "And sometimes it's better that way."

I studied his face, but his eyes had fixed on the fire, as though afraid of what I might read there.

"The forest and the grasslands beyond Winshire stretch farther than anyone has dared to map," he went on. "There are things out there the world chose to forget—things better left forgotten. If you're seeing shadows in those woods, my advice is simple: stay away. Don't go looking for answers." His tone hardened. "Some truths do more harm than good."

The words lingered in the air like smoke, heavy and strange, and for a moment they felt less like a warning and more like a confession. Little did he know, my nightmares had already begun to conjure such things.

I furrowed my brow, unsettled, and then—just as the heaviness became unbearable—a small smile tugged at the corner of his lips.

"Boo!" He turned to me as I jolted, laughing his deep, rolling laugh. I managed a smile, but the sound rang hollow. Behind his humor, I could still hear what he hadn't said.

Chapter Four

Eldrake

We set up camp in the woods just outside her village, Fen casting a shadow ward to cloak us from sight. The magic wove a veil around us, blending our camp seamlessly into the surrounding forest. Anyone who passed would see nothing but darkness and shadow. I leaned casually against an old oak, gazing toward the inn.

Describing it as ramshackle would be putting it kindly. The place looked as though a stiff wind might blow it over. "Ramshackle Inn," I muttered under my breath, smirking at the thought. Maybe she should call it that instead.

My eyes fixed on the window, and there she was. Firelight caught her in its glow, outlining every curve, every careless motion as though the world itself wanted me to see her. She moved about, unaware, yet I could not look away. To anyone else she might have seemed ordinary—a fleeting shadow behind glass—but not to me. In that moment she was inevitable, a truth written into the marrow of my bones.

The Rift in her was undeniable, its presence pulsing faintly even from this distance. It brushed against mine like a breeze through silk—subtle, but impossible to ignore. It danced on the edges of my senses, a beacon I could feel through the cool night air.

Well, there's no doubt that's who we're looking for.

How her father had managed to keep her hidden here for so long was a mystery. To tuck someone so powerful away in a place like this—forgotten and out of reach—it was almost ingenious. *Almost.*

I glanced back toward the others at camp, the faint flicker of Fen's ward shimmering as she fine-tuned it. Felix set up our tents, his usual silence hanging heavy. The two of them had settled into an easy rhythm, but I couldn't shake the sense that this mission wasn't going to go so smoothly.

Now, standing in the shadow of the pines, the quiet intensity of her Rift brushing against my awareness, I understood why the commander had insisted on her importance. I understood why he'd sent me. But as I watched her, her patterns were as ordinary as the inn itself. A flicker of doubt stirred.

Did she even know what she was?

I watched her weave among the guests she served, her smile lighting up the space like the only flicker of warmth in the otherwise dreary town. It was clear she loved her work—or at least she was trying to convince someone—maybe herself—that she did. But there was something in her eyes, something elusive and haunting. Sadness, perhaps?

The light from the hearth shimmered off her hair, catching the copper tones in its soft waves. My gaze drifted lower, taking in her frame. She was curvaceous, her figure full and natural. There was an undeniable allure to her, one I hadn't expected.

I clenched my jaw, shifting my weight against the tree. I told myself I wouldn't use charm as a weapon. But the longer I watched her, the more that line began to blur. She was beautiful, yes, but more than that—*she was captivating.*

I shook my head. *No. I am a Captain who has spent my whole life training to be respected; I will not use my cock to manipulate a woman.* I will simply tell her the truth, she will respect the mission and come willingly. Besides, I wasn't blind. I'd noticed the way Fen's eyes lingered on me during quiet moments, the subtle flirtations she thought went unnoticed.

Since she and Felix had been assigned to my task force years ago, I'd learned two things: Fen was as sharp as the blades she wielded, and she didn't take kindly to rivals—real or perceived. And I wasn't stupid enough to piss off a blade dancer. Nor get tangled up with one.

Boisterous laughter broke through my thoughts, pulling my attention back to the inn. Through the window, I saw her—the small gathering inside hanging on her every word, their faces lighting up before erupting into laughter again. She had a natural charisma, the kind that drew people in, making them want to be a part of her world.

Then, a breeze swept through the trees, carrying with it a smell that hit me like a punch to the gut. Whatever the hell she was cooking, it smelled divine. Sweet, savory, earthy—it was enough to make my stomach twist in envy. It smelled incredible.

Fuck sleeping in the woods. If she was the key to everything- we need to be closer. And, I'm hungry.

Chapter Five

Evandra

"The Shadow Ward is a veil woven from the Rift itself, bending light and thought alike to conceal its subject in darkness." —Magic of Edralis: an Introduction to Magical Creatures and Riftborn, p. 130

The last of the dinner rush had faded into the quiet hum of the hearth, and I was wiping down the tables, the repetitive motion second nature to me. The copper bell above the door chimed, cutting through the stillness. I groaned, not wanting to work anymore for the night- as I glanced up.

Three figures stood silhouetted against the doorway, their arrival altering the air in the room as though the temperature had dropped. They didn't move at first, their presence was both deliberate and unsettling.

My eyes moved to the first figure, a woman of breathtaking beauty. She was tall and willowy, her leather armor hugging her lithe frame like a second skin. Her black hair was cut sharply at her jaw, framing a face that was both elegant and cold. Her eyes, feline and calculating, flicked around the room with an expression that gave nothing away. She was completely unreadable, and her beauty felt like a knife to the gut.

The second figure stood a step behind her—a shorter man with a round face framed by golden curls. Despite his boyish features, there was a sharp intelligence behind the spectacles perched on his nose. His fine clothing, rich with embroidery and tailored to perfection, spoke of wealth, nobility perhaps, though he carried himself with a casual ease that suggested otherwise.

Then my eyes fell on the third figure, the man standing slightly ahead of the others. My breath caught in my throat the moment I laid eyes on him.

I knew that face—that presence.

Not from memory- but from the place where dreams become prophecy. I felt my mouth fall open, and I couldn't bring myself to close it. My mind raced to keep up as I drank in every last detail of him, each one more vivid than the last. He was large—easily over six feet—and built like a warrior. His leathers clung to his broad frame, worn smooth in the places that flexed with muscle. Every detail of him exuded strength and danger, an impression only heightened by the belt bristling with knives and swords slung low on his trim waist. His presence was magnetic, commanding, as though the very air bent to his will.

All three of them wore felt wide-brimmed hats and dark woolen cloaks, each adorned with an identical silver emblem depicting a dragon mid-flight that glinted ominously in the firelight. I gripped my bar rag in my hand, my knuckles white, as my pulse thundered in my ears. I had no doubt—this was not a coincidence.

My heart pounded against my ribs, wild and erratic like a caged animal desperate to escape. These strangers were unlike anything I had ever seen, their presence both mesmerizing and unnerving. My legs felt unsteady beneath me, and for a moment, I worried I might faint and embarrass myself entirely.

Then it hit me—the *scent*. It drifted across the room, faint but unmistakable: spice, incense, and the metallic tang of blood. My breath caught as the memory of it surged forward, vivid and undeniable. It was the same exotic aroma from my dreams, as hauntingly familiar now as it had been then.

I stood frozen, unable to move or even breathe, as the man from my dreams stepped forward. His movements were slow and deliberate, almost like he was trying not to startle me. My eyes tracked him helplessly as he reached up, grasped the brim of his hat, and pulled it away with a graceful ease that made my chest tighten. My heart, already racing, stumbled unevenly, and then it stopped altogether.

Thick waves of chestnut brown hair tumbled to his shoulders. His features were sharp and commanding; his high cheekbones and square jaw softened slightly by the dark scruff decorating his face as though he hadn't shaved in days. Then, I landed on his eyes.

They burned silver. For a breathless moment, all I could do was stare. This wasn't a trick of the light. It wasn't lantern oil or illusion.

It was real.

Star-Glow.

The Rift is real.

My father's stories, the outlawed histories, the burned books—it had all been true. A forbidden thrill surged through me, quickly chased by something sharper: fear. If someone saw this, if the wrong eyes found us—

"Hello," he said simply, nodding in my direction.

My eyes widened, and I felt my cheeks blaze with heat. I must have looked utterly ridiculous—wide-eyed as a startled doe—but I couldn't stop myself. Out of the corner of my eye, I thought I caught the shorter man snickering, but it was a distant distraction compared to the overwhelming presence of the man standing before me.

"Um..." I stammered, staring at him, my feet rooted. My mouth went dry as panic swelled in my chest. I couldn't bring myself to say anything more or move closer, too bewildered by his presence to think clearly. I cleared my throat, forcing the words out.

"H-how can I help you, sir?" My voice cracked, and I cursed myself silently for wearing my most unflattering dress today. He stepped forward, his boots landing heavily on the wooden floor, the sound reverberating through the quiet room.

"We need three rooms, madam," he said, his voice impossibly deep, almost inhuman.

Each syllable seemed to linger in the air as if daring me to refuse. He loomed over me, his imposing frame filling the space between us. His Star-Glow eyes burned with an intensity that was both mesmerizing and unsettling, but it wasn't just their brilliance that held me captive. There was a scar running over his left eye, jagged and stark against his tanned skin—skin that spoke of long days under the sun, far from the shelter of any roof.

I swallowed hard, my heart pounding. He was intimidating, to say the least, and not just because of the weapons he carried. Those eyes—haunting and otherworldly—spoke of such power, the kind that could unmake someone with a single glance.

Was he a criminal? He had to be. And yet, I couldn't bring myself to turn him away. The thought of refusing him was abhorrent to me for some reason. Though if the King ever found out I had harbored a Riftborn...

"Rooms are 40 pence per night," I managed to squeak, my voice barely audible. He didn't break eye contact as he reached into the tight pocket of his riding trousers, pulling out two gleaming gold coins. The movement was deliberate, unhurried, and somehow more unsettling for its calmness. With his free hand, he gently grasped my arm and placed the coins into my open palm, his fingers lingering against mine for a moment too long.

He leaned closer—not to threaten or seduce, but as if drawn by something neither of us could name.

"Keep the change," he murmured.

My breath came out ragged. The space between us felt charged as if the air itself had thickened. His scent enveloped me, leaving me light-headed and foggy. Still staring at me, he stepped back.

"T- Thank you," I breathed, clutching the coins so tightly that my knuckles turned white again. My heart raced, my thoughts spiraling. Was I dreaming? I couldn't be; I felt too aware of the weight of his gaze, the lingering heat of his touch, to believe this was anything but real.

Trying to regain some semblance of composure, I sidestepped him, my shoulder brushing awkwardly against his massive frame as I moved around him.

"Follow me to your rooms, Mr...?" I asked, keeping my tone steady as I ascended the stairs ahead of the three mysterious strangers.

"You can call me Eldrake," he replied, his low voice vibrating through the space between us. My heart fluttered at the way he said it, slow and deliberate like the name itself was a secret meant only for me.

"What an interesting name," I said, forcing lightness into my tone, though my mind was anything but steady. As I led them up the stairs, I caught a murmur behind me.

"Keeping it professional I see," someone whispered, followed by a soft snicker.

Heat flushed my cheeks, and I quickened my steps, eager to focus on anything other than the inexplicable tension crackling in the air. At the top of the stairs, I opened the door to my favorite room, the canary-yellow walls warm and welcoming in the flickering candlelight.

"This is yours," I said, stepping aside to let him in. The room was cozy but straightforward, the large bed dominating the space save for a small wardrobe in the corner. A sprig of fresh dogwood still rested atop the armoire, the soft smell mingling with the waxy glow of the newly lit candle in my hand. I glanced at Eldrake, his towering frame almost too large for the small room. I wondered if he could even fit on the bed.

He stepped inside, his gaze thoughtfully assessing the space before turning back to me. Those intense eyes met mine once more, and I felt warmth flood my cheeks as I looked up at him. I had never been shy before; my reaction to him was... bewildering. There was something about him—something undeniably intriguing. I'd seen countless strangers come and go, but he possessed an inexplicable energy that set him apart. And then there was the Star-Glow. Oh— *and* the unsettling certainty that I'd seen him in my dreams.

A subtle smile played on his lips, revealing slightly imperfect teeth that were just slightly too sharp and only added to his rugged charm. My heart leaped into my throat, and a sudden heat blossomed within me, leaving me momentarily breathless.

"Thank you, Miss...?" he prompted, his deep voice sending a tremor through me.

"Eva," I managed to whisper.

"Thank you, Eva," he replied, nodding gently before closing the door between us. I stood there, frozen, staring at the worn wood grain as I tried to make sense of what had just happened. My fingers tingled where the coins had pressed into my palm earlier, the lingering memory of his touch refusing to fade. A faint shuffle of movement brought me back to the present. I turned to see the other two guests waiting patiently, though their expressions couldn't have been more different.

"I'm so sorry," I said quickly, my cheeks flushing again as I realized how rude I had been. "What were your names?" I asked, offering an apologetic smile.

The strikingly beautiful woman's jaw clenched. "Fen," she said curtly.

"My name is Felix," the shorter man offered with a warm smile, his golden curls framing a pair of kind eyes. At least he seemed friendly.

I led the two to their rooms before drifting back to my own, my steps feeling weightless, my thoughts too tangled to register the path I'd taken. By the time I collapsed onto my bed, I could hardly recall how I'd gotten there. I lay staring up at the ceiling, the quiet of the inn pressing around me, but my mind was anything but still.

He was just a floor below me.

The thought sent a shiver through my body, and I couldn't shake the image of him.

My fingers twitched at the idea of them grazing across his skin, mapping every line of his body. Heat flared low in my belly as my mind lingered on his thick lips.

"As if a man like that would ever want me," I muttered into the quiet.

Chapter Six

Eldrake

I CLOSED the door to my room with a soft thud and immediately smacked my palm to my forehead.

Gods, I'm an idiot.

I tried to play it cool. Probably just scared the shit out of her. What was I thinking, leaning in like that? Whispering in her ear? I cringed at the memory.

Smooth, Drake. Real smooth.

I'd never been exceptionally gifted when it came to women. Some found my rank or bloodline appealing, but it was always superficial. Eva didn't know about any of that, though. She didn't know who I was or why I was there, which made the interaction feel... different. More... authentic. And apparently, that meant I didn't know how to act like a normal human being. Or, half-human being, at least.

Sighing, I turned my attention to the room she'd put me in. It was clean and well-kept, though ancient enough that every creak in the floorboards seemed to whisper its age. I felt bad about calling her inn "ramshackle" earlier. It was clear she cared about this place—every corner of the room spoke of love and attention to detail.

My fingers brushed against the delicate petals of the dogwood flower on the armoire, its presence a small but meaningful touch. She put that there. I thought of her wide, amber eyes gazing up at me earlier, the way they seemed to shine even when she was trying to maintain composure. Even with walls between us, I could feel her rift, pulsing and powerful.

I inhaled, catching the faint scent of her lingering in the air. Light and sweet, like lavender and honeysuckle, subtle but impossible to ignore. My pulse quickened, and I felt a rush of blood rush south.

I shook my head sharply. Nope. Not going there.

I was here for a mission, not... that. Whatever that was. I sat on the edge of the bed, trying to meditate with my hands on my knees and exhaling slowly.

Stay focused. Focused, Eldrake.

I'd barely sat down when a knock at my door pulled me out of my spiraling thoughts. In a few quick strides, I reached the door and cracked it open, only to find... no one?

"Down here," came a voice.

I glanced down to see Felix standing a good two feet below me, his usual unamused expression in place.

"Oh. Sorry," I muttered, stepping aside. "Come in."

With a little hop, Felix perched himself on the edge of the bed, crossing one ankle over the other like he owned the place. He regarded me with a pointed look, saying nothing—letting the silence do all the work.

"...Yes?" I finally prompted, narrowing my eyes.

"Care to explain what the hell that was?" he asked, his voice thick with disapproval. I felt a flicker of heat rush to my cheeks. Gods above, the Captain of the Rebellion does not *blush.* Felix didn't miss a beat. "Because last I checked, our great Captain of the Rebellion had no time for—what was it again?—*'cheap seduction tactics, so far beneath me, I'd never stoop so low, rah, rah, cue the flexing.'*"

I pinched the bridge of my nose. "Are you done?" I deadpanned.

"Never," he said sweetly, tilting his head, curls bouncing.

"First of all, watch it, *Doctor.*"

"And secondly?" he prompted.

"Secondly," I said, "through my skilled observation, I realized she may be too attached to this place to leave without... a little extra persuasion." It was a lie, of course. The truth was, whatever plan I'd had didn't survive long after seeing her. But Felix didn't need to know that.

He snorted, unconvinced. "You do know my sister's been interested in you for years, right?"

"Yes, Felix. I'm aware. And I'm not interested in Fen," I replied firmly, tugging my damp tunic over my head and tossing it aside. The cool air hit my skin, and my scaled shoulders flexed in relief.

"Tragic," he sighed, all false melancholy. "She'll write a ballad."

"Besides, I'm a professional. I wouldn't court someone in my squad."

His smirk twitched wider, eyes glittering. "Ah, but Eva's not *technically* in your squad."

I groaned. "Get out."

He slid off the bed, chuckling as though he'd just won a private game. "Good to know where the line is, Captain. I'll keep score."

Even as he left, I couldn't shake the echo of his words. I'd buried so many feelings over the years I thought I'd forgotten how to have one. But here she was—kicking the lid off the damn box.

Chapter Seven

Evandra

"Beasts of the Rift" display extraordinary resilience, unusual forms, and a natural inclination toward Rift energy, making them uniquely resistant to typical magics." —Magic of Edralis: an Introduction to Magical Creatures and Rift-born, p. 12

My mind buzzed with questions, each one louder than the last. Why were those three here, in my tiny town, in my inn of all places? There was something about them—about him—that didn't add up.

Then, I got a brilliant idea. A painfully stupid, *brilliant* idea. The next thing I knew, I was padding barefoot down the darkened corridors toward the rooms I'd lent to the mysterious strangers. The faint light of the moon poured through the arched windows, casting soft patterns across the walls. My pulse quickened with every step, my heartbeat pounding so loudly in my ears that I was sure it would give me away. *I'll just say I'm getting water.*

As I approached his door, I slowed, pressing my ear to the wall just beside it. The low murmur of male voices reached me.

"We have to be back to Castle City in ten days' time, Drake," Felix's tone was measured but firm. "And three of those are just the ride. We don't have time to dilly-dally."

Castle City? My brow furrowed. *Why are they going back there?*

"I understand that, Felix," that unmistakable growl- Eldrake. "I will make sure the mission goes well, and we get what we came for. By any means necessary." There was weight behind that last sentence, the kind that sent a jolt of unease ripping through me.

"Well, that's already been made evident," Felix replied, his tone tinged with something I couldn't place—disapproval, perhaps?

What are they talking about? My mind spun, trying to piece together what little I'd heard. Then, I caught the faint sound of footsteps approaching the door. My stomach dropped.

Without thinking, I darted into a small broom closet just a few feet away, pulling the door shut as quietly as I could. I held my breath, straining to hear through the thin wood.

"Good night, Captain," Felix said, his voice now just outside the door. The door clicked shut, and silence followed.

Captain. So Eldrake was their leader. Hot.

I leaned back against the closet wall, my head spinning with the scraps of conversation I'd overheard. They were on a mission. They were going back to Castle City. And Eldrake... wasn't just a leader. He was a *Captain*. But a Captain of *what* exactly? I knew he couldn't be in the Kings army- he was Riftborn.

The thought sent a thrill through me, and I pressed a hand to my chest, trying to steady my racing heart. What kind of mission brought a *Riftborn* Captain and his companions to a place like Winshire? Whatever it was, I had a sinking feeling it wasn't good. And yet, despite the unease swirling in my chest, I couldn't stop the faint, ridiculous smile tugging at my lips.

As soon as the corridor fell silent, I slipped out of the broom closet and padded back up to my room, my heart still racing. Once inside, I shut my door quietly and sank onto my bed, trying to make sense of what I'd overheard.

What are they after? I wondered, staring up at the cracked ceiling. Could it be my book? The thought sent a shiver through me, though whether it was fear or excitement, I wasn't sure. Or was it something else entirely—some hidden piece of contraband buried here in Winshire?

I hugged my knees to my chest, my mind spinning with possibilities. Whatever it was, it was important enough to bring a Captain and his squad to this forgotten town. Important enough for "any means necessary."

This was exciting—terrifying, yes, but exciting. For the first time in what felt like forever, something was happening. Something bigger than the monotony of the inn, the endless routines, and the quiet, unchanging days of Winshire.

Some time passed of me just laying on my bedspread, trying to will my thoughts to quiet down. The restless energy wouldn't let me sit still. I decided to go for a walk to try and settle my mind.

I crept downstairs once again, barefoot, letting the hush of the late hour settle around me. The ancient rugs below my feet were rough with age, and the shadows of the moonlit trees painted the wooden walls. The inn was silent—Papa asleep, the hearth embers soft and low. But the corridors beyond the kitchen still held a strange pull. I wasn't sure what I was hoping to find. Just air, maybe. A minute to think without the weight of it all pressing on my chest. The hall curved ahead in quiet shadow. I turned the corner—and nearly smacked straight into a wall of muscle.

My heart jolted. "Gods—!"

A hand caught my elbow to steady me. "Easy."

Eldrake.

He released me quickly, but the place where he'd touched my arm still tingled. He stood half in shadow, shirt loose, hair slightly damp. The air shifted around him like it didn't know how to behave.

"Should I be worried you're stalking my halls like a ghost?" I said, trying to sound steady and casual. My voice came out a little breathier than I liked.

His silver eyes scanned me, unreadable. "I could ask you the same question."

"I couldn't sleep."

He nodded once, and for a moment, neither of us moved. The silence pressed in—heavy, humming. Then he tilted his head, the faintest curve tugging at his mouth.

"You smell like pears."

I blinked. "What?"

"The roast. From earlier." His lips quirked. "It stuck to you. Smells good."

"Oh." Heat prickled up my neck. "Thanks. I was... cooking."

"I noticed." He took a step closer, voice low. "You always cook like that?"

"Like what?"

"Like you're trying to conquer the kitchen."

My arms crossed before I thought about it. "Is that supposed to be an insult or a compliment?"

"That depends." His eyes glinted. "Did you win?"

A laugh escaped me—sharp, nervous. "Still standing, aren't I?"

His gaze dropped, lingering on my bare feet against the wooden floor. When he looked back up, his expression had changed—softer, almost reluctant, though his voice was firm.

"You interest me." His eyes locked on mine, and the air between us shifted, charged with something unspoken, dangerous. My chest tightened, ribs aching with the effort of holding still. Then, just as quickly, he stepped back—a single pace, enough to shatter the moment like glass.

"You should be careful, Eva," he said quietly. The warning was real, but there was something else in his voice, too—like maybe he wasn't talking about the inn at all. He turned and walked away, disappearing down the corridor without another word. I stared after him, heart pounding.

What the hell was that?

My thoughts churned for what felt like hours, spinning over the endless possibilities of what their mission could be. Finally, exhaustion crept in, dragging my eyelids down. The last thought I clung to before sleep claimed me was the memory of Eldrake's eyes, burning like starlight in the dim light of the inn.

I woke with an unusual sense of enthusiasm, a lightness that carried me from my bed to my wardrobe. For once, my dreams had left me alone. I pranced across the creaking floorboards, opening the wardrobe doors with a flourish as I debated what to wear. My hand lingered on a little yellow dress tucked toward the back, one I'd only worn a handful of times.

It was beautiful, but I'd always deemed it too revealing for work. Today, though, I hesitated.

Seeking attention, are we? That little judgmental voice that lived in the back of my head whispered.

I cursed myself, pulling the dress from the wardrobe. It was simpler than I remembered, but still striking. The neckline dipped a little lower than I was used to, and its hemline stopped just above my knees—far shorter than the modest, ankle-length gowns I usually wore. The heavy linen clung to my curves as I held it up, the fabric buttery-soft against my skin. It wasn't inappropriate, exactly, but it was far from prudish.

The little voice scoffed. *Why are you doing this?* A dress from my name day ten years ago wasn't going to catch the attention of a man like Eldrake—especially not when that stunning woman, Fen, stood at his side.

I shook my head, biting back a wry smile. *Gods, what am I doing?* Still, I slipped into the dress, smoothing the fabric over my hips. The soft yellow felt warm, like sunlight, and for a brief moment, I let myself enjoy the small indulgence. Even if it was silly, today felt like a day worth wearing it.

At least I wouldn't look quite so embarrassing. In fact, I want to look like something more than myself. Maybe even... *beautiful*. I tugged a brush through my bouncing red curls. Instead of throwing them into the usual messy bun, I let them fall loose, framing my face in soft waves.

My excitement carried me down the stairs into the bright kitchen, where I busied myself preparing breakfast and tea as I would for any guest. The scent of warm bread and chamomile filled the air, but the three strangers didn't emerge from their rooms.

"Smells amazing!" Papa's cracking voice called from the stairs, startling me so badly that I nearly dropped the kettle.

"Gods, Papa! Are you trying to kill me!?" I teased, though I couldn't quite mask my disappointment that he wasn't who I was hoping for.

He chuckled as he descended, his old bones creaking with each step. "Did I hear you up last night?"

"Yeah, we actually had a few guests check in late," I replied, my eyes drifting to the closed doors upstairs as I served him his breakfast.

All day, my mind raced with thoughts of the three. Drake's piercing Star-Glow swirling with molten silver, and his towering, muscular frame haunted my every other thought. I found myself hoping, wishing, that his door would open and I'd get another chance to speak with him.

I made excuses to wander past their rooms throughout the day, listening for even the faintest sign of movement. Each time, I held my breath, straining to hear anything, but was met only with silence. I cursed myself for being so unprofessional, basically stalking my guests like some infatuated fool.

Frustrated, I threw myself into my usual tasks —cleaning and cooking — to keep my mind occupied. The rhythm of sweeping the floors and the gentle flicker of the candles burning around the inn usually lulled me into submission, but today, the routine only heightened my restlessness.

I put a tray of baked chicken and fresh carrots in the oven and finally allowed myself a moment to sit down, sinking into the well-worn chair by the kitchen window. Outside, the dreary weather mirrored the storm of my thoughts. I absently toyed with the strands of my apron as I stared into the gray sky.

Until now, I'd never really thought about what I wanted for myself —or even if I wanted anything at all. I'd always imagined I'd run this inn until I was old and gray, just like Papa had planned. But was that his dream for me... or mine?

I'd never visited the castle- or seen the mountains to the west. I'd never ridden a horse, watched the sun dip below the horizon, or laughed until I cried. I'd never... loved. *Made love.*

The ache of it pressed against my chest like a weight.

There has to be more than this.

I sighed and rose to my feet, shaking off the thought. Dreams, big or small, wouldn't change the reality of my life. I tied my apron tighter and returned to my chores, letting the familiar routine pull me back into its grasp.

For now, this was my world. And I'd accepted it.

The tavern had mostly quieted by evening. Only a few regulars lingered, nursing their drinks while the fire snapped low in the hearth. I wiped down the counter, half-lost in the rhythm, when a door creaked open. Then they entered together.

Three cloaked figures descended from the upstairs rooms—silent, purposeful, the weight of their presence pulling every gaze in the tavern. Wide-brimmed hats and low hoods shadowed their faces, dimming whatever sharp light might have betrayed them. They crossed to a small round table near the fire, their cloaks sliding from their shoulders and draping over the chairs. Eldrake took the seat with his back to the wall, Felix beside him, Fen on the other side like a shadow anchoring them in place.

From across the room, they looked like the beginning of a story: a blade, a scholar, and a shadow.

My pulse quickened. My feet moved before my mind caught up, carrying me across the floor with a cloth in hand as if I had business there. *What am I doing?* I was already halfway to their table, pretending to wipe down wood that didn't need cleaning, when Felix looked up first, a smile already softening his face.

"Miss Evandra," he said warmly, as though greeting an old friend he hadn't seen in years. His tone carried just enough flourish to make it sound like he might kiss my hand if I offered it.

I offered a nod, suddenly aware of the sweat gathering at the back of my neck. "Can I get you anything? Tea? Ale? Something stronger?"

Eldrake didn't speak. He watched me. Quiet. Still. His gaze didn't burn—it settled like he was cataloging every part of me and hadn't yet decided whether I was important or not. *Gods,* I could feel him staring. My skin buzzed like it knew something I didn't.

Felix leaned back in his chair, curls catching the firelight, and lifted his brows with a charming lilt. "Ale would do nicely, darling. Something frothy enough to make me forget these two brood like it's a profession."

"I'll bring a round," I said, trying to sound professional, though my voice wavered more than I liked. When I returned with a tray of mugs, I set them down carefully—first for Felix, then Fen, then Eldrake. His fingers brushed mine as he took the handle, deliberate or not I couldn't tell.

"Careful," he murmured, voice low. "Wouldn't want you spilling on me." Heat prickled at my cheeks, but before I could fire back, his gaze flicked downward—just for a second, catching at the neckline of my dress. My stomach flipped. *Gods.*

I glanced away too quickly, only for my eyes to land on the line of his thighs beneath the table, the fabric of his trousers pulling taut as he shifted in his chair. We both snapped our gazes back up at the same time. His jaw tightened; I knew my face was crimson.

"Right," I managed, forcing my voice steady. "I think I can manage a mug." The faintest curve tugged at his mouth, as though he knew exactly what had just passed between us. Not quite a smile. Not quite mockery.

Felix cleared his throat and gestured to the empty chair beside him. "Now that we're settled, do be kind and sit with us. Save me from staring at their long faces all evening." He pulled out the chair himself, eyes twinkling with mischief. I hesitated. Fen's eyes flicked up to me. Sharp. Measuring. She didn't say a word, but the message was clear: You don't belong here.

"I suppose I could sit for a moment," I said and took the seat. The moment I did, I realized how loud my heartbeat was.

"So, tell me," Felix began once I'd sat, leaning in as if we were already conspirators, "how does a girl like you end up running a place like this?"

"A girl like me?" I raised an eyebrow. "What exactly does that mean?"

He shrugged. "I mean—you hardly strike me as the *'tavern wench'* type." He made air quotes with a flourish, the smirk tugging at his lips betraying the tease.

I laughed—genuinely this time. "We got the inn when I was a little girl. Papa's getting older so I do what I can." I said with a shrug. I could feel the glances from the regulars and townsfolk eyeing me and the mysterious strangers.

"Ah. Obligation." His voice gentled for just a beat, then quirked back into mischief. "It suits you far too well. Though I'd wager you were destined for grander things than polishing mugs and roasting turnips."

"Isn't that why you're all here?" I asked lightly. "An *obligation*?" Fen's jaw ticked. Eldrake's gaze flicked to me again, unreadable.

"No," Drake said simply. "Not... entirely."

His voice was low. Not cold—just controlled. Every syllable felt like it had been weighed before it was spoken. I held by breath. I wasn't sure why. Maybe it was how still he was. Like he could strike or vanish at any moment—and either would make perfect sense.

"What brings you to Winshire, then?" I asked, trying to keep my voice steady. "We don't get many visitors."

Eldrake didn't answer. Instead, he looked at me with that silver stare —his Star-glow, I realized again—and I felt the weight of it behind my ribs.

Felix stepped in. His Star-Glow was fainter. Subtle. Sort of like a swirling ocean, hidden behind his deep blue irises. "We're passing through. Supply run. Maps and mules and mead, you know."

I nodded but didn't believe him. Not after what I'd overheard. I turned slightly toward Eldrake. "You don't talk much, do you?" His lip twitched—almost a smile.

"Only when I have something worth saying."

"And do you?"

His smile flickered, sharper this time. "Maybe. Depends if you're worth saying it to."

Heat rushed to my cheeks. *Gods. That was flirting. That was actual flirting. With me.* My brain scrambled for words, for air, for *anything*. *Eldrake just—he actually—was he flirting with me?!*

Felix's eyebrows lifted, the ghost of a smirk tugging at his mouth. Fen's gaze cut sharp as a blade unsheathed. Eldrake's faint smile faded as quickly as it had come, but his eyes lingered, steady and unrelenting. Being seen like that was unsettling—not for what I was doing, but for what I *was*.

Suddenly, the room felt too warm, the fire too close. I pushed back from the table. "Well. I should go check the roast."

"Of course, darling. Wouldn't want the kingdom's finest cooking to char itself on our account." I didn't dare glance at Fen, but I could feel her stare following me, cold as steel, all the way back to the kitchen.

The kitchen was warm, but it didn't calm me. I moved on instinct—checking the roast, slicing bread, stoking the hearth—anything to distract myself from the burning behind my ribs. My thoughts wouldn't settle. Every word from that table replayed in my head, and Eldrake's voice echoed louder than the rest. Steam rose from the kettle as I poured hot water into the mugs, the scent of spiced tea curling around me.

My hand trembled slightly, but just enough to betray me. The mug jerked, sloshing hot liquid across the front of my dress. I gasped, instinctively clutching the fabric just above my chest, where the tea had soaked straight through the thin linen.

Fuck, Gods, that's hot. That's—nope, that's definitely my burning my tits.

I scrambled for a towel, patting at the fabric uselessly, the soaked linen clinging to my skin in all the wrong places. The yellow dress had already been a bold choice. Now, it was practically transparent, putting my whole bodice on display. Then, I heard footsteps approaching the kitchen.

Ugh, Papa always had shit timing.

I turned—too fast—still clutching the towel to my chest. I froze. It wasn't papa.

Eldrake stood in the doorway, backlit by the faint fire of the hearth. He didn't speak. His gaze flickered briefly over my full breasts, spilling over the top of my now transparent dress, warm and wet from where the tea had soaked through the fabric—just for a breath—but I felt it.

I am going to die. Right here. In this kitchen. Buried in a puddle of spiced tea and humiliation.

"I, uh—spilled on myself," I said, with what I hoped was a casual laugh and not a wheeze. His eyes met mine again. Calm. Controlled. But the corners of his mouth twitched. Barely.

"I can see that. You alright?" he asked, voice low.

"I—yes. Perfect. Just... wet. Er, from the tea." *Fuck.*

He nodded once, gaze lingering for half a second too long before drifting toward me.

"I didn't mean to intrude," He said gently.

"You didn't," I said quickly. "You're... welcome. To be here. Or whatever." My face was on fire. My chest *actually* was on fire. My brain had packed its bags and left the building.

He stepped forward, slow and deliberate. He reached past me—his arm brushing mine as he picked up a dry rag from the counter—my heart felt like it was in my throat. His gaze locked on mine, unwavering as he stepped even closer, and for a second, I forgot how to exist. I could feel the heat rolling off him, smell that now-familiar blend of incense and rainwater, sharp and clean and entirely *him*. The scent curled around me, making the air feel heavy as if I'd stepped into something sacred and dangerous.

He pressed the cloth gently to my chest, his hand steady but cautious. Not lingering, but not impersonal, either. He was just... drying tea.

But he was touching me.

My heart thudded against my ribs like it wanted out. His eyes never left mine—not even as the cloth moved in slow, deliberate circles, the pressure feather-light but unbearably present. Every brush of fabric sent sparks skittering across my skin. When his gaze finally dropped, just briefly, to my lips, I felt my whole body lean toward him without meaning to. My skin burned under the towel. My thoughts scattered.

He held the towel there a beat too long. Not moving. Just... breathing. Like he was weighing something behind those molten eyes—something impossible to say out loud, then, just as suddenly as he'd stepped into my space, he stepped back. The distance was jarring.

Cold, somehow.

"May we have the same rooms again this evening?" he asked, his tone now cool and businesslike, though his voice still carried that same impossible depth.

I blinked, momentarily disoriented. It was only when he turned slightly that I really saw his teeth—mostly human, but his canines were just a touch too long, slightly pointed. Predatory.

"S-sure," I stammered, still rooted in place.

"Thank you," he said, pausing as he reached the door. He turned his head slightly, his eyes landing on my spill once more.

The moment he was gone, I sagged against the counter, towel clutched to my chest like a lifeline. My skin still burned. My mouth was dry. I was pretty sure my brain had dissolved somewhere between his hand on my tits and his eyes on my mouth.

Oh. My. Gods.

It wasn't just attraction. Not just heat or embarrassment. It was like something in me had been pulled toward him—not just my body, but something deeper. Like a rope had been quietly tied between us and was now slowly, steadily pulling taut.

I touched the place where the towel had pressed against my skin, then let my hand fall away—good Gods, I thought, heat flooding through me again at the memory of his touch.

That man is so unbelievably sexy.

I finally made it to my chambers for the evening. As I closed the door to my room, something twinged low in my stomach—not nerves, not desire. Something warmer. A ripple beneath the skin. Like the air inside me flexed. I pressed a hand to my ribs, startled. It was a sensation I'd never felt before, but I pressed it down and called it exhaustion.

I sank into my bed, the worn mattress creaking beneath me. Sleep felt like an impossibility as my mind refused to quiet. Every second of my encounter with Eldrake in the kitchen replayed in vivid detail, his towering presence and the way his heat pressed into me. I closed my eyes, letting the memory wash over me. I could still feel the warmth of him, the way he looked at me, different from before. More primal. My body responded immediately, a flush spreading from my cheeks down to my chest and peaking at my breasts as the memory morphed into fantasy.

I imagined what it would be like to feel his hands on me, the strength of his fingers trailing over my skin with deliberate intent. The heat rolled through me in waves, growing stronger as I pictured my hands on his chest, exploring the hard muscles hidden beneath his leather. My breath quickened as the image of him pulling me against him and filling me completely consumed my thoughts. Skin on skin, heat, and passion coursed through my mind like a fire I couldn't extinguish. His touch, his lips, his weight pressing against me—it all felt so vivid, so real, and yet so maddeningly out of reach.

Before I could stop myself, my hand slipped beneath the thin fabric of my nightgown, seeking the source of the ache that had been building since he leaned over me that first night. My fingers brushed against my soaking wet skin, and I gasped softly, the slickness evidence of just how deeply he had affected me.

This time, there was no hesitation, no holding back. I paused, just for a breath—stunned at how much I wanted this. At how my body had never felt this alive. My fingers ventured further than they ever had before, exploring the sensitive heat between my thighs. I bit my lip as I pressed deeper, finding the spot that made my body shudder with anticipation.

My hips arched into the touch as I began to move, my fingers thrusting slowly at first, then faster, as the waves of pleasure built with each motion. My breath came in ragged gasps, his name echoing in my mind like a mantra.

"Eldrake," I whispered, my voice laden with need.

I imagined his hands in place of mine, his body against mine, his low voice murmuring my name as he claimed every inch of me. The thought sent me spiraling, the tension coiling tighter and tighter until it snapped, sending a flood of ecstasy through my body.

I cried out softly, the sound swallowed by the darkness of my room as I collapsed inward on myself, trembling from the release.

"Eldrake..." his name left my lips again in a breathless moan, lingering in the quiet as I lay there, spent and still yearning. The intensity of it left me dazed, my heart pounding in my chest as I stared up at the ceiling. The heat of my fantasies began to fade, replaced by a quiet ache—not just for his touch, but for the connection I knew I could never have.

I sighed, curling into the blankets and letting the exhaustion finally claim me, though the memory of him stayed with me, etched into every corner of my mind.

Chapter Eight

Eldrake

I slammed my door shut, the sound reverberating through the small room, and threw my hat and cloak onto the desk. My boots hit the floorboards hard as I paced, fists clenching and unclenching.

That dress. That Godsdamned dress.

The way it clung to her curves, the way her hair framed her face when she wore it down. The way she looked up at me with those wide, amber eyes— completely unaware of what she was doing to me. My jaw tightened as blood rushed south, my body reacting before my mind could rein it in.

I groaned, running a hand through my hair. *I'm crushing. I'm crushing HARD.* This was bad. Really bad. I was the Captain of a Rift-born squad, for Gods' sake. I didn't get *crushes*; I executed missions. I led. Fought. I didn't spiral over a redhead in a yellow dress.

I'd seen beauty before. I'd had it. Left it. Burned it behind me and walked away. But this was something else. Something I couldn't walk away from.

My jaw ached. I'd been clenching it so hard I hadn't noticed. I braced my shaking hands against the desk. I'd been so disciplined for months. No distractions, no indulgences, no women. It was supposed to make me sharper, stronger. Instead, it had left me… lonely and… frustrated.

And now? Now, all I could think about was her. My draconic bloodline wasn't helping, either. Passion, dedication, lust—our emotions ran hotter, deeper, and more consuming than most. For a while, pouring all of that intensity into the rebellion had been enough, but now… I wanted her. I wanted to taste her. I wanted to burn for her and blame her for the flames.

I dropped onto the edge of the bed, head bowed. My chest rose and fell with shallow, useless breaths. I stared at the floor, but all I could see was her—standing in the kitchen, soaked, breathless, close enough to touch.

The scent of her still lingered in my senses—spiced tea, warm skin, honeysuckle. And when I looked up, I saw the dogwood she'd tucked into the vase.

My mouth quirked—just for a second. But the smile vanished as I circled back to the moment in the kitchen. *Gods, I hope she wasn't afraid. She looked afraid. Had I overstepped? I had asked permission to touch her, hadn't I? But what if she felt like she had to say yes? Fuck.* The thought sent a pang of guilt straight into my gut.

I pressed the heels of my palms into my eyes, trying to banish the image from my mind. But instead, it brought her back even more vividly —her bodice soaked with tea, the fabric clinging to her skin and becoming translucent, highlighting the peaks of her hardened breasts.

Gods, her breasts, shining and damp… Her breath shallow as I stood so close…

"Fuck," I hissed, the ache in my trousers impossible to ignore. My cock throbbed, hard and hot, straining against the leather. I hadn't let myself feel like this in months, and now it was her. Only her.

Growling under my breath, I shoved the covers back and collapsed onto the bed. My hand slipped past the waistband of my trousers, fingers wrapping around myself, the need blinding. I closed my eyes and let her fill me—her softness, her scent, her quiet fire. Her gaze made me feel like I wasn't just something illegal, but something… *worthy*. Something *wanted*. I stroked with a steady rhythm, breath catching, hips rising toward the friction like I could claim something I didn't deserve.

Evandra...

Her name echoed in my mind as I came, the release slamming through me like a breaking wave. I gasped, arching into it, the tension uncoiling in a rush that left me dazed—and then, for a split second, something else.

The Rift inside me pulsed—sharp and hot, like a heartbeat that wasn't mine. A shimmer stirred just beneath my skin, electric and foreign. Not pain. Not power. Something aware. It vanished as quickly as it came, but it left a mark. *That was weird.*

I lay there, breathing hard, staring at the ceiling. But even as the heat subsided, the guilt and yearning remained, curling tight inside my chest like smoke.

"Gods help me," I muttered into the silence, staring up at the ceiling.

This mission just got a hell of a lot harder.

Chapter Nine

Evandra

"For every Rift gift bestowed, there is a shadowed cost, a debt that must be repaid in ways only the Rift itself can decide." —Magic of Edralis: an Introduction to Magical Creatures and Riftborn, p. 13

My tired eyes finally fluttered open after a night of restless, fragmented sleep. I sighed, rubbing at the dark circles beneath my eyes like I could rub last night away. I thought about our moment again. The intensity. His hand had been so steady. So careful. Like I was something fragile. I hated how much I liked it.

I finally rolled myself out of bed, and I chose a gown that was neither as dreadful as my blue one nor as flattering as the yellow one, unfortunately. The fabric, a muted lavender, pinched neatly at the waist and the material was trimmed with delicate white lace at the hems.

It was respectable. Which was my aim most of the time... but now that he was around, I found myself wishing it wasn't. It was simple, practical, and, I hoped, enough to make me feel somewhat presentable.

Once I was satisfied with my hastily pinned messy bun, I made my way downstairs, determined to keep myself busy. Trying anything to keep my thoughts from circling back to him. But it was no use. Our moment in the kitchen replayed in my mind with maddening clarity—the way his deep voice had softened, the heat of his gaze, the overwhelming presence of him standing so close. It had felt too real, too *intimate* to be entirely in my imagination. I shook the thoughts away as I stepped into the dining room, rag in hand, ready to wipe down the tables. My resolve faltered the moment I noticed the door to his room was still closed. *He was still here.*

I busied myself with breakfast and cleaning, the familiar motions meant to steady my spiraling mind. But I was hyper-aware of every sound, every creak of the floorboards, every rustle of movement from that side of the inn. My eyes darted to his door more often than I cared to admit. Still, the quiet stretched on, and the only sounds were the faint clink of dishes and the steady sweep of my rag against the wooden tables. Yet, I couldn't shake the feeling that something lingered in the air, something tethering me to that closed door and the man behind it.

At one point I debated knocking—telling myself it was a reasonable thing to do, maybe to check if he needed anything. But every time I considered it, my stomach twisted. I didn't want to seem desperate. Or, worse, be caught in my own awkwardness.

My mind spun in endless circles. *Should I? Shouldn't I?*

To busy myself, I cleaned the banisters on the balcony outside his room, swept the steps leading up to the hall, and dusted the sconces near his door that hadn't been touched in months. All the while, my thoughts were entirely consumed by him. I felt ridiculous, like a silly schoolgirl again, mooning over a man who had barely spoken a handful of words to me.

By the time dinner rolled around, I meandered into the kitchen, the dimly lit space offering some semblance of peace. The air was cool, the faint smell of herbs and flour lingering from earlier. I found myself staring at the counter, at the spot where he'd had me pinned just last night, dabbing at my breasts with a towel.

"*Dabbing at my breasts*," I muttered under my breath, rolling my eyes at myself. "Really doesn't sound sexy," Maybe what I'd thought was tension, something tangible and electric between us, was just my own loneliness playing tricks on me.

I wiped the sweat from my brow with the hem of my dress and set about preparing dinner. I chopped herbed potatoes, sautéed buttery vegetables, and slid a fresh chicken into the hearth to roast. The rhythmic motions helped calm me, but my thoughts refused to settle. I grazed and tasted the food, wondering if the glances, the touches, the whispers I'd replayed in my mind meant anything at all.

Was it real? Or was it just my imagination running wild, desperate for attention?

I stared into the small fire in the range, the flickering light casting shadows across the room. Maybe he was just a regular guest, polite out of habit, and I was the lonely innkeeper too eager to make something out of nothing. It wouldn't be the first time I'd misread a moment.

Next time we interact, I'll act normal. Calm. Like he isn't the Captain of my thoughts.

As I assembled a tray, I felt my resolve waver. The tray was simple, yet I'd carefully arranged every detail. A generous portion of food because—well, he was huge. A bottle of wine with a glass to the left of the plate and to the right, a small glass vial holding a single stem of dogwood I'd plucked earlier. I stood there for a moment, staring at the tray, my heart thundering in my chest.

It's soup. I scolded myself. *You're not delivering a love letter.*

Taking a deep breath, I carried the tray up the stairs, balancing it carefully. As I stood in front of his door, I hesitated. My hand hovered near the wood for a moment before I gave a slight, tentative tap.

"He's just like anyone else," I whispered to myself. *I definitely didn't touch myself while thinking of him last night...*

The thought sent heat rushing to my cheeks, but before I could spiral further, a voice came from the other side.

"Come in," his deep voice bellowed from within the room. The sound shot through me like a bolt of lightning, sending a hot spike straight to my core. I steadied my breath, turned the door handle with my free hand, and peered inside. The room was quiet and dim, and all three of them were packed in. *Damn.*

Eldrake sat nearest the window at the desk, boots planted wide, elbows on his knees. Felix lounged sideways across the narrow bed, looking far too comfortable and lazily turning the pages of a book. Fen stood near the dresser, arms crossed, back straight as a sword. She turned first—and smiled. The kind of smile that didn't reach her eyes.

"Aw, did you make that yourself?" Fen asked, her tone a delicate dagger.

"Uh, yes," I said.

She arched a brow. "How sweet. A little seasoning. A little seduction." A pause. "Or was that part unintentional?"

My face flushed hot. "Just soup."

"Of course," Fen said lightly. "Though next time, I'd go with the yellow dress. It makes a... stronger impression."

Eldrake stood abruptly and his chair loudly scraped the floor.

The motion silenced the room. He didn't speak, but the air around him seemed to shift—like tension crackling between storm clouds.

"That's enough," he said finally. His voice wasn't loud, but it landed hard.

Fen tilted her head, eyes narrowing—but said nothing more.

Felix, ever the diplomat, chuckled softly. "Eva, you've saved us. Truly. I was starting to think the Captain might gnaw his own arm off before morning." I gave a nervous little laugh and set the tray down on the desk.

"Just thought you might be hungry," I said. Eldrake's stomach betrayed him with a loud rumble that echoed in the otherwise quiet room.

"Oh, go on, darling," Felix chuffed, leaning back with his mug. "Eat before you terrify the poor girl with all that brooding. We'd all like to keep our fingers."

Eldrake moved then—slow and silent like a predator shifting toward prey. He picked up a spoon and dipped it into the bowl of stew. I braced myself for stoicism. A low, satisfied moan escaped his lips, deep and guttural. My heart skipped a beat at the sound. I'll die if I never hear that sound again. I forced myself to stay composed, brushing a loose curl behind my ear.

He took a bite of bread next—and shoved nearly the whole thing in. Chewed aggressively.

Swallowed.

"Food like this is... *dangerous*," he said, looking up at me from beneath his thick lashes. The words were flat, but heavy—like there was reverence in them.

I laughed under my breath, shocked. "Is that a compliment?" his mouth was still full, but he nodded.

Felix leaned toward me with an impish grin, lowering his voice as though sharing a scandal. "That, my dear, is as close to a compliment as you'll ever wring out of him."

"I heard that," Eldrake said without looking up. It was the first moment I'd seen him human. Not the cold, coiled thing at the table. Just a man. Tired, hungry, and slightly unhinged about root vegetables. I watched him in fascination, the contrast of his perfect, statue-like physique and his almost feral appetite utterly captivating. I wanted to know what else might undo him like this. As he shoveled another spoonful into his mouth, a small giggle escaped me before I could stop it. I moved toward the door.

"Well, enjoy."

"You should stay," Felix said lightly, a wicked glint in his eye. "He might propose after another bite or two."

Fen snorted.

"I really shouldn't," I muttered, hand on the doorknob.

"Thank you," Eldrake said, voice lower now.

I looked back. He was watching me again—but softer. Less calculating. Still intense, but... different. My stomach flipped.

"Actually, Evandra," Felix's voice stopped me mid-step, polite but firm, "a word, if you would. Don't worry—I promise it's not about soup." He sat up, patting the edge of the bed beside him with just enough flourish to make it feel like an invitation rather than a command. His molten gold eyes, usually so full of mischief, burned with something far more deliberate.

"Um..." I hesitated, glancing between the three of them. Their unnaturally striking features unsettled me, as if I were staring at something too perfect to be real. "I—I should get back to work. I can bring more food if-" my voice wavered as I tried to excuse myself, but their eyes—intense, expectant—told me they had been waiting for this moment.

"Please?" Felix urged as he sat up and patted the edge of the bed beside him. His molten gold eyes were serious now- burning with something I didn't recognize.

Swallowing hard, I slowly closed the door behind me. My feet moved before I had a chance to second-guess them. As I approached, I caught Drake still chewing, spoon halfway to his mouth.

"Gods, this is good," he muttered thickly, grabbing the wine and drinking straight from the bottle. I bit down a smile despite everything.

Felix gave me a knowing look, one brow arched. "You see? A miracle. You've turned him into a man of feeling, Eva. If he starts reciting poetry next, we'll know you've bewitched him."

"Glad you like it." I smiled.

"Look, Evandra," Felix began slowly, the playfulness sliding away. His gaze locked on mine, all warmth and no smirk now. "We haven't been completely honest with you."

"What do you mean?" I asked, my voice barely above a whisper. Unease crept into my chest, tightening like a vice.

"We actually knew a bit about you before we came here," he admitted. I looked at him warily, my stomach twisting, waiting for him to continue. He hesitated, glancing at Fen, who was casually picking at her nails and looking utterly disinterested. "I know this may come as a surprise to you, but we were... associates of your mother," the words hit me like a slap to the face. Even Eldrake, who had been shoveling food into his mouth moments ago, froze, his eyes flicking toward me at the mention of my mother.

"My mother?" My voice cracked as I knitted my brows, hurt and suspicion clear in my expression. "Is this some kind of joke?" I stood abruptly, the room blurring around me as anger and disbelief boiled in my chest. "How *dare* you—"

"Please, listen." Eldrake's voice interrupted, soft but commanding.

I looked at him. There was something in his expression, something raw and pleading, that made me pause. Slowly, I sank back onto the edge of the bed, my hands trembling in my lap.

"How much do you know about your mother?" Felix asked gently.

"I..." I searched my memories, grasping for something concrete. "I know she worked for the royal court somehow."

Fen scoffed, rolling her eyes. There was a pause, heavy with unspoken tension. Felix exchanged a glance with Fen and Eldrake before nodding toward him.

Eldrake leaned forward. "Your mother was part of the royal court, at first," he said. "But she wasn't human. Not fully. She served as an ambassador between the humans and the Riftborn—until King Aberdeen outlawed magic and ordered us to be hunted." My heart hammered. "She went into hiding with the rest of us," Eldrake continued, "but she feared staying in Riftreach would draw the King's wrath down on everyone. He wouldn't stop hunting her, and she refused to put the city at risk. So she fled... until the King finally tracked her here, and ordered her killed. Her Rift was too powerful. He was afraid."

"*No.*" I whispered.

"She helped stop a genocide," he said. "Her power turned the tide in a battle the King wanted to be forgotten. That's why they erased her. That's why they burned her."

"The fire..." I said, voice breaking. "It was an accident."

Felix shook his head gently. "No, darling. The fire was the King's doing. Not fate. Not chance. His cruelty."

"Stop," I snapped, standing again. "Stop talking about my mother like she was—like she was *Riftborn*. My father would have told me!"

The three of them exchanged a look. *Pity*. Fen finally looked up. Her voice was sharp and unflinching.

"Why do you think your father hid you in this shit-hole town your whole life?"

My chest was hollow. My voice cracked.

"I- Excuse me," I rasped. "I need—" I didn't finish. I turned, flung the door open and ran. The slam echoed down the hall.

I threw open the door to my dull, familiar attic room, the hinges groaning in protest, and collapsed onto the bed. The old mattress sagged beneath me, sending a puff of dust swirling into the air as I landed. I didn't care. Tears poured down my face, hot and relentless, blurring my vision as I gasped for breath between sobs.

My chest heaved. My mind spun in an endless loop of disbelief, anger, and grief. I sobbed for my mother—not because I believed them—not yet—but because she wasn't here to tell me the truth herself. I ached for her voice, for her guidance, for the truths I'd never gotten to hear from her lips. Instead, there was only silence where answers should have been.

I sobbed for my father, for the man I trusted. The man who always seemed so open, so kind. Had it all been lies? Was it for my safety—or his own selfish reasons? I didn't know, and that cut deeper than I cared to admit.

I buried my face in my pillow, muffling my cries, but the pain refused to be stifled. My whole life- this town, this inn. No choices, no say in the matter—just the life my father decided for me. And now I was learning that life was built on secrets.

My fists clenched around the edges of the pillow, trembling with frustration. There was a whole world out there, vast and beautiful that I'd never seen. A world I hadn't even allowed myself to dream of until now. And yet, here I was. Alone. Ignorant. A mess of emotions I couldn't sort through.

I sat up slowly, wiping at my tear-streaked face with shaking hands. The room felt colder than usual, its plain walls closing in on me. Mechanically, I changed into my silken nightgown, letting the soft fabric glide over my skin. It was the only luxury I allowed myself, and tonight, it felt like a hollow comfort. I climbed back into bed, curling into a tight ball beneath the blankets.

My tears had slowed, but the ache in my chest lingered, sharp and unrelenting. I hated this. I hated the way my life had turned into something I barely recognized. Hated the secrets, the lies, and the strangers who had upended everything with their cryptic revelations. Most of all, I hated the loneliness—the way it clung to me like a second skin, leaving me hollow and adrift.

The earth blurred beneath me, moving far too quickly as though some force beyond myself was carrying me. My breath came in sharp bursts, and a fire raged inside me—an inferno so fierce it drowned out everything else. It wasn't just anger. It was primal, consuming, coursing through my veins like molten blood, roaring in my ears until the world around me became a haze.

I was running. But I wasn't myself. I was taller, stronger. My heart was not my own, but it was familiar. Brambles tore at me as I hurtled through the darkened wood, the sharp tang of fear flooding my senses. I could smell it—my prey's terror. It clung to the air, thick and pungent, igniting something savage within me. Ahead, a flash of white. My focus narrowed. My pulse thundered. My legs, impossibly strong, launched me forward with terrifying speed. The air tore past me, and the branches whipped at my skin, but I felt nothing.

The scent hit me again, sharper this time, and I knew I was closing in. Then, with no conscious thought, I was on it—on him. The world turned red. My claws—talons, I realized—slashed through his flesh, rending it apart with brutal efficiency. My hands, my fingers, were no longer human. They moved with an unrelenting purpose, shredding pink tissue and spilling crimson blood in rivers. A sound rumbled deep within me, guttural and feral, echoing through the woods. It was the growl of an animal, but it carried the weight of human rage—a horrible sound, one that made my stomach churn even as it reverberated in my chest.

Then, through the sea of blood and viscera, I saw it. A face. Colin's face.

His eyes were wide with terror, his features frozen in death- permanently twisted in horror so pure it burned itself into my mind. I tried to stop, tried to pull myself away, but I was trapped—helpless—watching as this monstrous form tore him apart. My claws ripped through him with savage precision, and his expression froze in that final, terrible moment of realization.

I wanted to scream, to wake up, to flee from the nightmare. But I couldn't move, couldn't look away. I was locked inside this creature's eyes, forced to witness the carnage, the overwhelming, unrelenting violence. *I was watching death.*

I gasped myself awake, bolting upright as though the nightmare were still chasing me. My chest heaved, the air in the room thick and suffocating. My hands instinctively went to my face, rubbing at my eyes with trembling palms as I tried to gather my bearings. The room around me was cloaked in darkness, faint moonlight filtering through the cracks in the curtains. My breath came in shallow, uneven gasps, and my heart pounded against my ribs like a storm surge. Sweat clung to my skin, the damp fabric of my nightgown sticking to my back and chest. My pulse didn't feel like mine. My skin buzzed like it remembered someone else's grief.

I stared at the shadows dancing across the walls, my mind racing.

What the hell just happened?

The dream—it was unlike any I'd ever had before. For the first time, I hadn't been reliving that horrible fire, trapped in some hazy memory. This was something else entirely.

I hadn't just seen Colin's death—*I'd felt it.* I felt the rage, the bloodlust, the savage need to hunt and destroy. The image of his face, twisted in terror, burned itself into my mind, refusing to leave.

"What's happening to me?" I whispered into the darkness, my voice shaky and small. The timing... it couldn't be a coincidence. It can't. My thoughts spiraled as I clutched the edge of my blanket.

There's no way HE didn't have something to do with this.

My mind latched onto Eldrake, unable to stop thinking of his haunting presence. Since his arrival, everything in my life had shifted—it had twisted into something unrecognizable. First, the stories about my mother, the revelations about the Riftborn... and now this? It was too much. Too perfectly timed. Too impossible to ignore.

I clenched my fists, my nails digging into my palms as I struggled to calm my racing heart. But— even as the logical part of me tried to dismiss the thought, I couldn't shake the feeling that somehow, some way, Eldrake was connected. I exhaled sharply, my breath trembling as I buried my face in my hands. I need answers.

Throwing the comforter off my legs, I swung out of bed and slipped into the cool darkness of the inn. The air was still, the quiet of the night pressing against my ears. It had to be the middle of the night now, but I didn't care. This couldn't wait.

I padded down the halls with careful steps; the aged wood cool beneath my bare feet. I didn't bother with a candle; I knew every hall, every creak in the floorboards, every turn in this old inn like the back of my hand. My movements were precise and silent so as not to wake my father.

Nervous sweat continued to coat my skin. I told myself I had to do this. For answers—about my mother, about Colin, about the nightmare that had me questioning everything. But as I neared his room, I couldn't ignore the knot of nerves twisting in my stomach. I stopped in front of the door, the faint scent of dogwood from the flowers I'd left earlier still lingering in the hallway. I hesitated, pressing my ear against the wood. Nothing.

This is insane. I stared at the grain of the wood like it might answer for him. My hand hovered near the door, uncertain. *What if it wasn't him? What if I imagined it?* No. I didn't. I know it was him.

I didn't bother wiping the sweat from my skin. I needed answers more than I needed dignity. Summoning what little courage I had, I rapped lightly on the door, the sound barely more than a whisper against the stillness. For a moment, nothing. Then, faint shuffling. A muffled groan. Heavy footsteps moving toward the door. The handle turned, the door creaking open just enough to reveal him.

Eldrake stood in the dim light; a loose linen shirt, trousers slung low on his hips, hair tousled from sleep. He blinked at me, eyes bleary and half-lidded, and scrubbed a hand over his jaw like he was trying to wake up a second too late. His familiar scent hit me like a wave—spice and rainwater but now mingled with the warmth of sleep. There was something softer about it, something dangerously intimate.

He blinked again. "Eva?" he looked confused. And sleepy. "Are you okay?" My mouth went dry, and for a moment, I forgot why I was there.

"Not really." I managed, my voice barely above a whisper.

He studied me for a long moment, his expression unreadable, before stepping back and pushing the door open wider. "Come in." he said, his tone low and steady, and the sound of it sent another shiver through me. I caught his eyes, tracing the length of my figure as I drifted past him, suddenly aware of how little I was wearing. The dampened silk of my nightgown clung to my every dip and curve. His gaze lingered for a moment too long, and my heart leaped in response.

"I'm sorry to wake you... Part of me didn't entirely think you slept, to be honest,"

"You'd be surprised," he murmured.

"I saw... something." I said quickly, because if I didn't, I'd forget how to speak. I turned to him. "I saw someone die." his expression didn't shift, but the air between us tensed. "I was inside this... body," I said. "I felt everything. The forest floor. The panic. Colin will be killed," A silence stretched between us, heavy and trembling. "It hasn't happened," I said, softer. "Not yet. It was like... like *knowing* a thing before it unfolds. I keep seeing his hands. The dirt under his nails. The —" I stopped.

Then, unexpectedly: "Who's Colin?"

I blinked. "Uh- A man from town who... it's—ugh—complicated."

He hesitated, gaze flicking away for half a second before settling back on me. "Oh. Are you two...?"

My face went hot. "Oh! No. I mean... kind of, but—Gods, no."

The question hit with more force than it should have. Was he *jealous?* He studied me a moment longer. His face was unreadable, but something in him eased—barely. The moment hung, unspoken, until he shook it off with a breath and looked away.

"I see," He turned toward the desk. But not before his eyes flicked again— this time to where the silk of my nightgown stretched taut over the hardened peaks of my breasts— then away fast, jaw tightening.

"I'm not sure what you saw, Eva, but you're not safe here." His eyes flicked to the curtain, to the dark window beyond, as if measuring the night. "We caught a watcher on the ridge at dusk. A warden's man. Fen scattered him. She found the mark he left." He moved to the desk and picked up a square—thin charcoal rubbed into a folded scrap of paper. He opened it. A symbol, clean and ugly, stared back. A slash through a circle. "Aberdeen's. They're getting close."

My mouth parted. "How... What is that?"

"They can sense the Rift," he said quietly. "You're Riftborn, Eva. You inherited it."

I shook my head. "Wha— what? What does that mean?" I trailed off, not understanding what was happening.

"Your mother didn't die in an accident." I froze. "She was one of us," he said. "She was powerful. She led operations that saved hundreds — thousands of lives. And when the King realized what she was... he sent men to burn her alive."

I stared at him, vision tunneling. "No. That's not—"

"She fought for us," he said, sitting on the end of the bed. "Until the end. She was a hero." Something inside me cracked.

"Your mother was special, Eva." I stilled. "She had the gift of prediction. They called her The Seer. And it seems our commander was right —not only that she had a living heir, but that you've inherited her power," *The Seer*. The words sank like stones in my chest.

"There aren't many of you left," he continued. "You're rare. And you're hard to track," he smirked faintly, the humor brief and sharp. "Probably because you can all see us coming," he paused. "Except you, of course." I almost smiled back. Almost.

He turned serious again. "Felix, Fen, and I were sent to retrieve you."

"Retrieve me?" I snapped. "Like a lost dog?"

Drake grimaced, raking a hand through his hair. "Poor choice of words. I'm trying." I waited. "Look, Eva—your mother wasn't just powerful. She *was* the Uprising. She could see the King's movements before his generals made them. She saved so many of us. She was the reason many of us are still alive," he looked down, shoulders tense. For the first time since I'd met him, the mask cracked. "And without her," he said, his voice softer, "we're falling apart. Soon, there may be no Rift left to protect."

I sat next to him on the bed and stared into the candlelight. Everything felt unreal. "I don't believe this, Eldrake." I said, voice shaking.

"Call me Drake," he said softly.

His gaze flicked to my lips. Just for a second. Then down— again. I shifted in place, the motion causing our thighs to brush against each other. The contact was electric. We both froze. I heard him expel a ragged breath, his chest rising and falling as though he were steadying himself.

It's criminal this man ever wears clothes.

We sat too close, the edge of the bed dipping beneath our weight. I tried not to notice the heat of his thigh brushing mine—but then I saw it. Just above the waistband of his trousers, where the fabric slouched low, a faint shimmer caught the candlelight. Crimson ridges, small and sharp-edged, fanned just along his hip before vanishing beneath the cloth. My breath caught. Scars? No—too patterned, too deliberate. I dragged my gaze away before he could notice, cheeks burning. I didn't dare ask.

I looked back at his face—and saw him watching me like he didn't know whether to kiss me or run. He blinked, then straightened—retreating behind his command.

"The more you practice your gift," he said briskly, "the farther you'll be able to predict. Not just in distance, but in clarity. You may even develop abilities beyond foresight. Our archivist can guide you. But we need to leave soon," the shift was jarring. Captain Eldrake was back. Calculated, cold. The man beside me—Drake—was gone.

Though, I couldn't ignore the way his thigh still lingered against mine, as if neither of us dared to move away first.

I narrowed my eyes. "What?! I never said yes!"

"You were never meant to stay buried here."

"No offense," I snapped, "but I'm not a package to be picked up and delivered. I need to think. I—" I stood and headed to the door, heart pounding.

"Wait," he said. I turned, but he was already crossing the room in three long strides. He stopped inches from me, caging me between his body and the wall. My breath caught. His voice was low, fierce. "For what it's worth, I know you're meant for more than this," the words hit harder than they should have. "Please," he said. "We need you." He reached up, brushing a curl behind my ear. The gesture was so gentle, so unexpected, it knocked the air from my lungs. Then he stepped back. Back into his role. Back into armor. He opened the door for me.

I left in a daze. I stumbled out, my legs barely carrying me as I made my way to my bedroom, my thoughts a swirling tempest of emotions.

Meant for more than this... save us.

His words echoed in my mind, tangling with the heat of his gaze and the lingering warmth of his touch. I felt him like a brand beneath my skin—too close, too much, too fast.

He needed me.

The thought sent a shiver through me. Eldrake—this larger-than-life figure with molten eyes and a commanding presence—had looked at me as though I held the key to something greater. To him, I wasn't just the lonely innkeeper's daughter or a forgotten girl in a nowhere town. To him, I was important. *Vital.*

I sank back onto my bed, staring up at the ceiling. My heart raced, excitement thrumming in my ears, and for the first time in what felt like forever, a glimmer of possibility sparked within me. Could it be true? Could I really be more than this—more than what this little inn and forgotten town had made me? The idea tugged at something deep inside, a quiet yearning I hadn't dared to acknowledge before.

I thought of Eldrake's words, his touch, the way he'd looked at me. And for once, I didn't feel insignificant. I closed my eyes, letting the warmth of that thought settle over me like a blanket. For the first time in a long time, the world beyond these walls didn't feel so far away.

Chapter Ten

Evandra

"Human-beast hybrids, like that of the Dragonblood, are believed to be the result of Rift magic mingling too deeply with the primal essence of creatures, forging a union of man and beast. In some cases, this transformation was a punishment for Riftborn who sought forbidden powers; in others, a blessing for those chosen by the Rift itself." —History and Annals of the Rift, p. 23

I sat at the farthest corner table in the tavern, my fingernail tracing the knots and grooves in the aged wood. It was a futile attempt to keep my mind occupied, to push away the dissatisfaction with the event that was about to take place. Last night, the encounter with Drake burned behind my ribs; today, I have a date with Colin.

The air felt heavy, the room too quiet despite the hum of conversation from the other patrons. I couldn't stop my thoughts from drifting back to the dream. Colin's shredded features, the visceral horror etched into his face, the relentless tearing of claws. Was it truly a vision of the future or just a twisted nightmare born of my fear and confusion?

I sighed, shifting uncomfortably in my seat. If I felt like I had a choice, I wouldn't be here. But in Winshire, choices were often a luxury. Refusing Colin Junior's advances outright was one thing, but standing him up tonight? That was another matter entirely. You didn't offend the wealthiest family in town without consequence, and those consequences wouldn't just fall on me—they'd fall on my father, too.

So here I sat, waiting for Colin to make his grand appearance, trapped between obligation and revulsion. Eldrake's face flashed across my mind. His molten silver eyes, the way his scales shimmered in the candlelight, his rough voice low and commanding. I imagined how those scales would feel against my bare skin, the texture of them brushing over me. My fingers on his broad chest. I gasped, heat pooling low in my belly, and I shifted again, trying to quell the thoughts.

This was ridiculous.

The copper bell above the door rang, jolting me from my reverie. My heart sank as Colin strode inside, his presence a sharp contrast to the heat and intrigue of my imaginings.

"Good evening, Evandra," he greeted me in that nasal tone of his, his voice grating against my nerves. He sauntered over to me, his slim frame outlined in what was unmistakably a new, tailored white suit. The candlelight reflected off his slicked-back blonde hair, giving him a polished, almost artificial sheen. His blue eyes bore into me with an intensity I couldn't describe as anything but... entitled.

"Hello, Colin," I replied, forcing my voice into something resembling civility but failing to mask the chill beneath it. He extended his elbow toward me, a gesture so practiced and stiff it felt like a command. Reluctantly, I slid my hand into the crook of his arm, silently steeling myself for whatever this "date" would entail.

We stepped outside, the cool night air brushing against my skin as we walked down the cobblestone street. The inn faded behind us, and I kept my eyes on the uneven stones beneath my feet, my mind already bargaining with itself.

An hour, I told myself. I'll listen to him talk for an hour, maybe offer a quick peck on the cheek, and then he'll let me go home.

The thought brought me no comfort. No matter how I spun it, I felt trapped, my chest tightening with every step. As Colin droned on about something—likely his father's business or his imagined grandeur—I tuned him out, my thoughts drifting once more to Eldrake.

Would I see him again tonight?

The idea sent a flicker of warmth through me, a strange and fleeting hope amidst the monotony of Colin's presence. But for now, all I could do was endure.

"You couldn't have dressed up a bit?" Colin sneered, his eyes raking over me with barely concealed disdain. "My, Eva, it looks like you've just woken up." I rolled my eyes, biting back a retort. He wasn't worth the effort.

"How was your day?" he asked, his tone forced, as if he were attempting polite small talk but couldn't be bothered to hide his condescension. I couldn't help but compare his oily grin to Drake's molten silence...

"Fine," I said shortly, shrugging. "Yours?" I could at least manage simple conversation, though my lack of enthusiasm must have been apparent. That was all the invitation he needed. He launched into a long-winded ramble about his prize horse again, his voice grating against my ears like nails on stone. I'd banked on him doing most of the talking—less effort for me—but I quickly regretted it. I had nothing to say to him. Nothing I *wanted* to say to him.

I cursed myself again for agreeing to this farce of a date. I tried to tune him out, though the occasional phrase managed to break through the haze of my disinterest.

"He wasn't even wearing cufflinks!" I caught, his voice laced with indignation, as though the absence of cufflinks were a personal affront to his existence. I rolled my eyes again, suppressing a groan. Irritation. It seemed to be the only emotion he could elicit from me. What was I even doing here, trudging alongside him, when my mind was spinning in circles of *DrakeDrakeDrake?*

We walked a half mile down the moonlit street, passing familiar landmarks that should have felt comforting but only reminded me of how small my world had always been. The general store and the tailor's shop stood silent; their shutters closed tight against the cool night. Mr.

Peters's chickens clucked softly in their coop, nestled beside the burnt rubble of what was once my childhood home. My chest tightened at the sight, but I quickly looked away, unwilling to let the past pull me under.

Finally, we passed the doctor's house, its windows were dark, signaling that even he had retired for the night. Colin's voice droned on beside me, filling the empty spaces with his complaints and self-important musings. By the time we reached the bench at the edge of town, it felt like an eternity had passed.

The bench overlooked the babbling creek that marked the border of Winshire, its gentle whispers the only sound breaking the oppressive silence. Beyond the creek, the forest loomed—just as dark, just as silent as the woods on the east side of town. I tilted my head back, letting my gaze drift up to the glittering sky. But no matter how beautiful the night was, no matter how serene the creek or how vast the sky, my thoughts kept returning to one place. One person.

"And that's why she makes a better show horse than anything." Colin concluded, his voice tinged with self-satisfaction.

"Wow." I said flatly, offering only the barest acknowledgment.

"You're a good listener." he said, turning toward me with a sleazy, practiced smile that he likely flashed all the girls. I returned his look with my best thin-lipped grin that felt like it looked like a scowl. I hoped it conveyed just how little I cared. My gaze flicked to his upper lip, where a faint, wispy mustache perched awkwardly. I hated it.

Colin leaned in, his intentions clear, and my body responded before my mind could fully register what was happening. *Is he going in for a kiss!?* I instinctively recoiled, leaning back as his cloying cologne assaulted my senses—a sickly mix of musk and something overly sweet. He hesitated, his face twitching as he pivoted, pretending he'd simply been brushing a stray hair from my cheek. He didn't acknowledge the rejection, though the stiffness in his movements betrayed his bruised ego.

My Gods, he's insufferable.

A breeze swept past, cold enough to raise goosebumps on my skin. The air around us was unnervingly silent, the usual sounds of the forest absent. I glanced around, my ears straining, but there was nothing—just Colin's incessant voice.

"So, *Eva*, how's Philip?" he asked, his tone overly casual as he peered at me, his use of my nickname deliberate and grating. I stared straight ahead, determined not to meet his gaze. I knew if I did, he'd take it as an invitation to try and kiss me again.

"My father is fine," I replied tersely, my voice sharp. "And my name is Evandra. To you, at least."

"Look, *Evandra,*" he drawled, over-enunciating the name as though mocking me. "Just for a moment, set your prejudices aside and think about what it would be like to be married to the richest and most important man within a 25-mile radius," he purred, leaning closer, his bony hand landing too high on my thigh.

My body stiffened in revulsion. His pale, spidery fingers gripped me possessively like I was something he'd already claimed. "Doesn't that mean anything to you?" he continued, a smirk curling his thin lips. "I know you'd clean up nice if we got you some decent clothes," he leaned in further. Slowly. Deliberately. His nose grazed the side of my neck as he inhaled deeply.

My stomach turned. His cologne singed the back of my throat.

I stood abruptly, knocking his hand away. "Get away from me!" but before I could put real space between us, his fingers clamped around my elbow, painfully tight. I gasped as he yanked me back toward him.

"Think of what I could give you," he hissed, his breath hot and sour against my cheek. His grip tightened. "And all you'd need to give me in return..." His other hand slid beneath my skirt, fingers brushing the soft skin of my inner thigh. "...is you."

My breath hitched. I froze.

No. No, no, no—

His eyes raked over me—my dress, my messy hair, my tired face. He sneered. "It's not like men are lining up around the block to court... *this*."

Hot tears began to blur my vision. Humiliation. Disgust. Rage. And before the pain of his words could settle, my hand moved on instinct.

CRACK.

I slapped him hard— my palm stinging as the sound echoed through the trees. He staggered back, stunned. I saw confusion. Then fury. But I didn't flinch. "This date is over," I spat, my voice low and shaking with fury. "Don't come near the inn again." I turned and walked away fast, trying to outpace the sob rising in my throat.

Don't let him see you cry.

I couldn't go back—not like this. Not to Papa. Not to Drake.

When I spotted the shed on the Doctors property, I ducked inside, slamming the door with shaking hands. The dark enclosed me like a cocoon. And then I broke. I slid down the wall, knees to my chest, sobbing into my hands. My whole body trembled as the fear and revulsion poured out of me.

I cried until I couldn't breathe. After a little while, I forced myself to stop and glanced around, wiping at my damp and puffy face. My eyes adjusted slowly to the dimness.

That's when I saw it. A shadow shifted on the far wall, just behind a pile of hay. My heart seized in my chest. Before I could react, a clammy hand clamped over my mouth, shoving me roughly against the wall. My head struck the wooden boards with a sickening thud, and white-hot pain bloomed behind my eyes. A cold, sharp edge pressed against my throat, its threat unmistakable. A knife.

This isn't real. It can't be real.

But then I caught that revolting and unmistakable scent. My eyes flew open.

"*Colin.*" I hissed, my voice muffled beneath his hand. His features twisted with a wicked grin as he pressed closer, his breath hot against my cheek. I tried to scream, but the sound was muffled beneath his hand. The pressure of the blade against my throat increased, silencing me further.

"I told you." he said, his voice low and venomous, "I always get what I want." He inhaled deeply, his nose brushing against my neck. I recoiled, but his grip only tightened, pinning me harder.

His free hand slid under my skirt, the cold blade never leaving my throat beginning to sting and draw thin beads of blood. "I decided I needed to teach you a lesson." he sneered. "No one turns me down, Eva. And how convenient you ran right in here," tears streamed down my face as I struggled. "Oh, don't cry," he mocked, his voice syrupy sweet. "You'll ruin the mood."

His hand reached lower, and the metallic clink of his belt buckle nearly broke me. My stomach churned, bile rising in my throat.

"You're *scum*," I hissed through clenched teeth.

"Oh, come on, Evandra." he purred. "It could be worse."

I froze as his hands roamed further, his touch revolting and violating. My mind raced—images of Eldrake, my mother, and the rebellion flashing before me. I thought of all the things I hadn't done, all the life I hadn't lived.

No. Not like this.

Something inside me snapped.

Fueled by pure adrenaline, I stomped down hard onto his foot. My wooden heel hit bone. He screamed, his grip faltered— just enough. I drove my elbow into his ribs with all my strength. He staggered back, cursing loudly.

"You bitch!" he snarled, his face contorted with rage.

He lunged at me, the knife glinting in the dim light. I braced myself, but just before he could strike, a deep, guttural growl echoed from outside the shed. The sound was inhuman—raw and primal, vibrating through the wooden walls and into my very bones.

Another growl followed, this time more distinct.

"*Run*." The voice was low. Ragged. *Familiar.*

Caught off guard, Colin's blade missed its mark, slicing into the thick muscle in my shoulder instead of my throat. Pain exploded across my body as blood began to gush from the wound. I screamed, clutching my shoulder, my vision swimming. The growl came again, louder this time. Whatever was outside the shed was close—and it was coming.

I scrambled to my feet, my legs trembling beneath me, and burst out the opposite side of the shed. My feet hit the ground hard, echoing with a dull thud as I tore into the woods. The trees blurred around me, the brambles clawing at my legs and dress as I raced through the darkness. I ducked under low-hanging branches and vaulted over exposed roots, moving as though the forest itself was guiding me. My shoulder throbbed with every stride, the pain sharp and unforgiving, but I didn't dare slow down. The rage hadn't left me. It buzzed behind my ribs, wild and coiled. Something in me had changed.

The air was cold and damp, filling my lungs like ice as they heaved with each breath. The smell of earth and leaves wrapped around me, grounding me even as panic threatened to take over. Before I could fully process how far I'd come, the woods opened up, and I stumbled back onto the main road, my heels clacking against the cobblestones. My lungs screamed for air, my vision swam, but there it was—home.

The inn loomed ahead, its familiar crooked sign swaying gently in the breeze. Relief surged through me as I threw myself at the door and pushed it open, nearly collapsing onto the tavern floor. Felix was already there, waiting for me.

"Oh Gods. Hurry!" His voice was sharp, but his hands steady as he caught me by the good arm. "Sit, sit—before you topple and make me look bad." He half-guided, half-dragged me into one of the old creaky chairs, his curls bouncing with the effort.

He knelt beside me, inspecting the wound with quick, practiced movements. His golden eyes flicked up, softened. "All right, darling, let's see what we're working with." Without hesitation, he grabbed either side of the tear in my gown and ripped it wider. I gasped.

"Apologies," he said quickly, a faint smirk tugging at his mouth. "I don't usually undress women in public, but you're bleeding everywhere, and I am a professional."

My laughter almost made me forget for a moment what had happened, even as the pain flared. He pressed a clean linen cloth to the wound, and I hissed, biting down on the cry. His eyes darted up again. "I know, I know. Breathe. Hate me later, yes?"

Then his pupils disappeared, golden light filling them until they burned like the sun. The glow radiated from him, beautiful and terrifying. His curls caught the light like a halo. I froze as he placed both hands over my shoulder. His body jerked once, his head tipping back as though struck by an unseen force. Heat spread through me, flooding my veins with soothing fire. My pain ebbed, my thoughts softened.

When the light dimmed, Felix slumped forward, catching himself on the arm of my chair. He was pale, but smiling faintly, breath shallow. "There. Good as new. Don't you dare tell the Captain I nearly fainted—I'll never hear the end of it."

I stared at my shoulder, the pink scar where the wound had been. "That was... incredible."

"Healing's my Rift," Felix said simply, voice light again, though exhaustion pulled at his edges. He patted my cheek, gentle as a feather. "Someone has to keep the Captain's ass in one piece. Can you imagine him trying to stitch *me* back together? Disaster. Utter disaster."

"The Captain...?" I echoed, my mind drifting unbidden. The word slipped out before I could stop it.

Felix's smile curved, tender and amused. "Yes, love. That tall, broody one who can't seem to stop staring at your ass." The unexpected honesty pulled a laugh out of me, small but real, and for a moment the pain didn't feel so heavy.

"Ah, that's better," Felix said softly, relief flickering in his golden eyes. "Don't you go slipping away on me, darling. Not after I just put you back together." He lifted a cup of cool water to my lips. "Sip. Slowly. That's a good girl." But even that wasn't enough to keep me tethered. The room tilted, edges blurring.

The last thing I remembered was Felix's voice, warm and insistent, as he held onto me like he could keep me anchored by charm alone: *"Stay with me, Eva. You're far too pretty to die on my floor."*

Chapter Eleven

Eldrake

I SLAMMED the inn's door open with enough force to rattle the frame, my chest heaving as I scanned the room. My eyes found her immediately. Evandra was slumped over in one of the rickety chairs, her usually vibrant hair a dull halo around her pale face. Her purple dress was soaked in blood— the fabric clinging to her shoulder where the crimson stain was darkest.

"That *motherfucker*!" I roared, the words tearing from my throat before I could stop them. The rage inside me was molten iron, boiling over with each second I took in her limp form. I crossed the distance in three strides and fell to my knees at her side, my blood-covered hands hovering uselessly above her, shaking.

"She's not moving," I said, hoarsely. Panic clawed at me, hot and feral. "Is she... is she dead?" My chest tightened, my heart pounding so hard it felt like it would split open. She couldn't be dead. She couldn't be. The mission was one thing, but the thought of her lifeless—it felt like someone had driven a blade straight through my ribs. A small hand gripped my shoulder firmly, snapping me out of my spiraling thoughts. Felix.

"She's going to be okay, big guy," Felix said, his voice calm but sure, golden eyes soft as he pressed a steadying hand to my shoulder. "She lost too much blood, passed out—but I stitched her up. She just needs rest." His lips curved in a small smile. "Breathe. She's not leaving you yet."

"Ahem. Good," I said gruffly, willing my voice to steady. "I was just... concerned for the sake of the mission. That's all." I tried to casually stand up and act like I wasn't panicking.

From the corner, Fen leaned against the wall, her arms crossed, unimpressed. Her eyes rolled skyward. "Right..." she muttered, the skepticism thick in her voice.

Felix's golden eyes flicked up at me, concern threaded with a spark of amusement. "You're welcome, by the way. Gods, Captain, I nearly drained myself putting her back together. A little gratitude wouldn't kill you." He gestured at the gore caked across me, wrinkling his nose. "Honestly, look at you. I hope you don't expect me to mop that up too."

I stilled, the memory flashing through my mind like lightning. Colin's smug face. His reeking cologne. Eva's blood on his hands. The way his body crumpled when I tore him apart. I should feel guilty. I didn't. Not yet. Maybe I never will.

"She was attacked," I said shortly, my voice like iron. "By Colin."

"Colin?" Felix repeated, brows shooting up. "That ridiculous little peacock? With the hair oil?" His tone turned sharp.

"The bastard forced himself on her," I growled. "I was outside the shed where he attacked her. I could smell his cheap cologne—and her blood."

Fen pushed herself off the wall, her arms dropping. Face sharpening. "And you...?"

I didn't answer. I didn't need to. The silence was heavy, broken only by the crackle of the fire in the hearth.

"Fuck." Felix blew out a breath, dragging a hand through his curls. "Of course you killed him." He glanced toward Eva, his expression softening, protective. "Good. Bastard didn't deserve to breathe the same air."

"Men like him don't deserve to breathe." I said, final. No apology. No one argued.

My gaze returned to Evandra. She stirred slightly, a soft whimper escaping her lips. The sound tugged at something deep inside me.

"She needs rest," Felix said gently, almost like a lullaby, his gaze lingering on her pale face. "She's safe for now, but if she wakes and sees the pair of you looming like ravens, she'll faint all over again. Let me sit with her awhile."

Without thinking, I bent down and scooped her into my arms. She fit there too easily. Her head lolled gently against my chest, and I hated how much that steadied me. Her warmth seeped through my blood-soaked leathers.

"What are you doing?" Fen asked, her tone half-curious, half-annoyed.

"Taking her to her room," I said simply.

"Of course you are," she muttered, rolling her eyes again.

Behind me, Felix chuckled under his breath. "Careful, Captain. If you carry her like that every time she swoons, she'll start doing it on purpose." His smile was tired but fond, and it was the first thing that made the fire in my chest ease.

I carried her up the stairs with care, following her scent to what could undeniably be her room, each step slow and deliberate. I laid her down on the narrow bed, the frame groaning beneath the weight of her. The room was small. Too small. Plain shelves, thin curtains, a scatter of books and little trinkets she'd tried to make mean something. It wasn't enough. The walls pressed too close, holding her in like she belonged here. She didn't. I could see her in velvet, with firelight painting her skin, a window thrown wide to something bigger than this town. A place that matched her. I pushed the thought away before it could settle.

She stirred again, her lips parting slightly as if to speak, but no words came. She looked fragile in the dim light, but even in her broken state, she radiated something unbreakable. As I turned to leave, I hesitated, my hand resting on the doorframe.

"I won't let anyone hurt you again," the words hung in the air as I stepped into the hallway, closing the door softly behind me.

Chapter Twelve

Evandra

"Among the rarest Rift-given abilities is the Sight of the Other—a gift, or curse, allowing a Riftborn to slip their vision into the eyes of another, seeing the world as they do. Those marked by the Sight are rare and seldom spoken of, known only in whispers and distant legends."
—Index of the Rift and magical Beasts, P. 5

I gasped myself awake—again. A habit that was becoming far too frequent and far too exhausting. My chest heaved as I tried to gather my bearings. The motion startled Felix, who had been dozing lightly in the chair beside my bed.

"Gods, you scared me," he muttered, rubbing his eyes before turning his sharp gaze on me. "And not in the fun way. How are you feeling, darling?"

"W-what happened?" I asked, my voice scratchy as I pushed myself up slowly. Pain flared from my shoulder, sharp and unforgiving, and my head throbbed like a drumbeat.

"You're in your room, Miss Eva. Don't try to move your shoulder," Felix said, his tone both gentle and firm. "I stitched you back together as best I could—miracle worker, truly—but your body still needs time." He reached out, his small hand resting lightly on mine. The pale morning light gilded his golden curls, and for a moment he looked more like an angel than a gnome.

Then memories came crashing back. The shed, Colin, the growling in the dark, and my frantic run through the woods crashed over me like a wave. I flinched, my free hand clutching at the blanket. Before I could ask any more questions, heavy boots pounded up the stairs. The door flew open.

Drake.

He filled the doorway, his eyes locking onto mine. For a fleeting moment, I thought I saw something soften in his expression. Relief? Concern? It was gone almost as quickly as it appeared, replaced by the mask.

"She's fine, Eldrake," Felix said, mildly annoyed. "No need to tear the door off its hinges." Drake ignored him, crossing the room with deliberate steps. He perched carefully on the edge of my bed, his weight making the mattress dip slightly.

"I'm glad you're feeling better," he said, his voice low and steady.

"Thank you," I murmured, managing a small smile.

"Please," Felix cut in, leaning back with a wicked smirk. "Don't let him fool you. He's been pacing holes in the floor since he carried you up here. I nearly had to tie him down—or sedate him, which I was honestly tempted to try—just to stop the questions." my cheeks burned as the words sank in. He carried me? And I *missed it*? Damn.

I stared at him, trying to imagine the moment—his strong arms cradling me, his warm scent wrapping around me. And I missed it?! I cursed myself silently for being unconscious through all of it.

"I was concerned for the mission," Drake said gruffly, his jaw tightening.

Felix snorted. "Yes, yes, *the mission.* You'll forgive me if I don't swoon over that excuse."

I watched Drake, trying to decipher his expression. His stoicism wavered for just a breath, and I thought I caught a flicker of something genuine.

"Really," I said softly. "Thank you. Both of you. I don't know what would've happened if—"

Drake shook his head, cutting me off. "It doesn't matter what *could've* happened," he said firmly. "You're safe now," the way he said it —like it was a promise—sent a strange warmth blooming in my chest.

Then it hit me.

"The growl," I whispered. "I heard it... It was you. You told me to run."

His molten silver eyes locked onto mine, still, unreadable.

"Might as well own up, Captain," Felix said, his voice carrying a note of dry amusement. I looked at Drake expectantly, waiting for an explanation. His square jaw tensed, his gaze flickering briefly to the floor before meeting mine again.

He cleared his throat. "I may have been... trailing you."

"What?" I blinked. "You were following me? Why?"

"Strictly to assure the safe delivery of you to Castle City," He said, defaulting to full military cadence.

Felix rolled his eyes dramatically. "Strictly professional, mm? Darling, you've been staring at her like she's the last glass of wine in the kingdom. Don't insult us."

Drake shot him a glare that could've melted steel but softened as he looked back at me. "When I saw what that piece of shit was doing to you..." He paused, visibly struggling with the words. "...I lost control."

My breath caught. "And now," Felix interjected, his warmth cooling to something sharper, "one of the richest families in town has a dead son. We'll need to leave with Eva half-healed and a pack of hounds sniffing at our heels. Not exactly the subtle exit we'd hoped for." the words hung heavy in the air, crashing over me like a wave. My mind reeled, piecing together what Felix had said. I turned to Drake, who was now hunched slightly, looking more guilty than Godlike.

"Wait," I said slowly, the realization hitting me like a blow. "You... you killed him?" Images from my vision flooded back into memory.

Drake's jaw tightened, his silver eyes flicking away from mine for the briefest moment. He looked nothing like the unflinching warrior I'd come to know. There was a vulnerability in him now, a crack in his otherwise unshakable armor.

"I had to," My emotions churned violently—shock, anger, and something dangerously close to relief and gratitude warred inside me. Part of me wanted to comfort him, to reach out and ease the guilt etched into his features. But he'd just admitted to taking a life, and I didn't know how to feel about that.

Felix broke the silence, his tone matter-of-fact. "We need to leave, Eva," Felix said, already on his feet, shoving things into a satchel with quick, precise hands. "Tonight, under cover of darkness. Before this turns into an even uglier scandal." I tried to move my injured shoulder, testing its range and was immediately met with a sharp, searing pain that forced a hiss through my teeth. I looked between Felix and Drake, their tense expressions mirroring the gravity of the situation.

"I understand," I said finally, my voice quieter than I intended. Drake and Felix exchanged a look— tense, grim.

Then—more footsteps thundered up the stairs, and the door to my room burst open once again. Fen stood in the doorway, her dark eyes wide with urgency. "They found the body."

Drake stood immediately, his hand instinctively dropping to the hilt of one of the daggers strapped to his side.

"We need to move," Felix said, his voice losing all trace of its usual levity as he crossed the room in two strides. Even his warmth had its limits. Drake turned back to me, his expression softening just enough to break my heart. "Rest, Eva. We'll be back."

He placed a reassuring hand on my knee, his touch grounding me in the midst of the storm of uncertainty. Then, just like that, he was gone.

I rested for a few more hours, the ache in my shoulder a dull throb that refused to let me fully relax. It must have been early afternoon when the creak of my chamber door pulled me from the haze of restless sleep.

"Eva? Doctor Whitehand is here to see you," my father said softly, standing in the doorway with a sullen expression.

I blinked groggily, assuming the doctor had come to check my shoulder. I grabbed my robe and slippers, wrapping myself against the chill, and made my way into the hall. I was halfway down the stairs when a thought hit me: no one else knew about my shoulder.

Dread twisted in my gut. The faint murmur of hushed voices grew louder with each step. As I descended, I saw them. Dozens of people from the town were packed into the dining hall, all whispering and shifting like coiled snakes. At the center of it all, Mr. Smith— Colin's father.

His black suit was crisp, his shoes polished to a mirror shine. Too polished. Like a man clinging to dignity when his world had already broken. His eyes were bloodshot, rimmed raw, his jaw tight as though he were holding himself together by sheer force of will.

"What's this about?" I asked, feigning ignorance. I descended the last few steps with deliberate calm, my voice steady despite the storm brewing inside me. Every head turned.

"Evandra." Colin Senior's voice was smooth, but the edge of it cracked, grief leaking through. "Nice to see you," he said, the lie thin and brittle. He swallowed hard before continuing, each word like glass in his throat. "Doctor Whitehand found my son's body in the woods behind his house this morning."

A ripple of gasps spread through the crowd like a wave.

Colin Sr.'s hands clenched at his sides, trembling faintly. He stepped forward, his eyes narrowing as though anger could eclipse the grief swimming there. "And Colin mentioned that you and he were to have a... date last night." His tone curdled into condescension, venom layered over something ragged. My heart thundered in my chest, but I kept my face carefully neutral. "Did you happen to see anything... untoward?" he asked, his voice raising slightly to draw the attention of everyone in the room. Every pair of eyes bore into me now, the weight of their stares pressing down like a physical force. I could feel the tension in the room shift, suspicion sharpening the air.

"What happened to your shoulder?" he asked pointedly, his gaze dropping to the sling Felix had placed me in. My blood chilled. I cursed silently, willing my face to remain impassive. My mind raced, trying to come up with an explanation that wouldn't implicate myself—or worse, Eldrake.

"I tripped." I said finally, my voice calm but firm. "There was a loose board in the kitchen, and I fell."

Colin Senior's lips curved into a frosty smile, though it didn't reach his eyes. "How unfortunate," he said, his voice dripping with insincerity. "Still, it must've been a shock to hear about poor Colin." I forced myself to hold his gaze, even as unease crawled up my spine. Whatever game he was playing, I wasn't about to let him win.

"Now, wait just one minute!" My father's voice barked through the growing murmur of the crowd, sharp and indignant. He stood behind the bar, his hands gripping the worn wood as he addressed the gathering. "The doctor said the injuries were consistent with an animal attack —and what about those strangers in town?" He turned to look at the room. "You think it's more likely to be someone you've known since birth— or someone you know nothing about!" He looked directly at me, his eyes pleading for support, begging me to back him up.

My heart lurched in my chest. My thoughts raced. I couldn't let him —or anyone else—draw attention to Drake, Fen, and Felix. The room was a powder keg, and one misplaced word would strike the match.

I stepped forward and raised my voice to be heard above the din of the crowd. "How about before we go throwing accusations around, we stop and think?" I said quickly. Every face turned toward me. My pulse thundered in my ears, but I forced myself to stay calm. "Mister Trebuie was just telling me about animal attacks in Castle City," I continued, drudging up the first thing I could think of. "Savage, unexplained killings. Maybe it's related. Maybe whatever did that traveled here," the murmurs grew louder, the crowd shifting uneasily as they processed my words.

But Colin's father wasn't having it. He surged forward, his face twisted with fury. "I know it was you, wench!" he spat. "You're lucky my boy gave you more than a passing glance!" The insult hit like a slap. Gasps echoed, and the room erupted once more, voices rising as accusations and opinions flew back and forth.

"You watch your damn mouth!" my father shouted, stepping out from behind the bar and pointing a shaking finger at Colin Senior. "You don't get to speak to my daughter like that!"

"And what are you going to do about it, old man?" Colin shot back, his tone dripping with disdain. Their voices clashed, the tension in the room reaching a fever pitch. Others joined in, shouting their own opinions and suspicions. It was chaos, pure and raw. And while they shouted, and blamed and postured— I slipped quietly toward the stairs. My movements were quick but deliberate. My heart pounded as I climbed, every step taking me farther from the fray below.

At the top, I pressed a trembling hand to my forehead, trying to make sense of it all. One thing was clear: Drake was right. We had to leave tonight. If we didn't, Colin Senior would bring in the Kingdom's officials. A formal investigation would follow, and it wouldn't just endanger Drake and his companions. It would expose everything—about them, about me.

The rebellion.

I entered my room and shut the door behind me, letting out a breath I didn't know I'd been holding—only to spin around and find Drake, Felix, and Fen already inside. I jumped, my hand flying to my chest.

"Gods, how do you do that?" I asked, my voice tinged with exasperation. I brushed past them, heading straight to the window. Peeking through the curtains, I watched as the townsfolk slowly filed out of the inn, their voices still carrying faintly from below.

"You get used to it," Fen said flatly, lounging on my bed like she owned the place. Her long, crimson-painted nails perfectly matched her full lips. Her feline face wore its usual air of detached disdain, but her beauty was undeniable—sharp cheekbones and piercing eyes. The contrast between her pale skin and jet-black hair was striking. I paused, feeling a pang of envy. How could Drake not be interested in her? Unless... *he was.* The thought made my stomach twist uncomfortably, though I quickly pushed it aside.

"What happened!?" Felix's voice snapped me out of my thoughts, sharp but laced with warmth. He was already stepping toward me, curls bouncing, his golden eyes wide and worried. "Tell me everything."

I took a steadying breath, glancing between the three of them. "Colin Senior was here, along with the rest of the town. They knew he and I had a... a date last night." My eyes flicked—against my will—toward Drake. Heat crept up my neck. "One I definitely didn't *want* to go on," I added quickly, the words tumbling out faster than I meant them to. "Nevertheless, they're suspicious."

Felix groaned dramatically, throwing his hands up. "Perfect. Just what we needed. A grieving mob with pitchforks and nothing better to do than gossip."

Fen grimaced. "Wonderful."

"And then my father," I swallowed— "*helpfully* reminded everyone about our three mysterious guests," my gaze lingered on Drake, who cursed softly.

"You just had to kill him, didn't you?" Fen's voice was sharp, cutting through the room like a blade. She shook her head, her eyes narrowing as they fixed on Drake.

He stepped forward. "He saw me, Fen. What would you have me do? Let him live and run to the Kingdom with our names?"

Fen pushed off the bed. "How about sticking to the original plan? Take the girl. Get back to the city. No games. No Delays. But no, instead, we're lingering in this depressing little village, pretending she has a choice!"

Pretending I have a choice. Her words hit harder than they should have. I turned to Drake, searching his face for some kind of reassurance, but he refused to meet my gaze.

"That's enough," Drake snapped, his voice was thunderous. His expression was steely as he glared at Fen, his massive frame radiating tension. "I acted as captain of this unit and made a call."

Fen's smile was sharp as glass. "A call you made with your cock,"

Before the silence could curdle, Felix stepped smoothly between them, his curls haloed by the dim light. "Fen," he said softly, but his tone carried a rare firmness. "That's not fair. He saved her life. Yours too, indirectly, unless you fancy explaining to the King why someone saw a riftborn almost commit murder. You don't have to like his methods, but don't you dare belittle them."

Fen's jaw ticked. Her eyes flicked to Felix. For once, she didn't speak. Just a sharp exhale through her nose before she shoved past me and stormed out the door.

I stood frozen, my mouth slightly agape, watching her retreat. Drake's expression was unreadable as he moved to follow her. He paused in the doorway, his hand briefly clenching the frame, but he didn't look back. The door clicked shut behind him, leaving me and Felix alone.

I blinked hard, feeling tears welling up in my eyes, hot and stinging, threatening to spill over.

"Hey, hey," Felix murmured, stepping closer. He patted my good shoulder gently, then squeezed my hand with his smaller one. His smile was crooked, apologetic. "Don't take her daggers too deeply, darling. She throws them at everyone. Complicated doesn't begin to cover her." He tilted his head, his molten gold eyes softening. "But you? You're not the problem. Don't you believe that for a second."

He lingered long enough for me to feel steadied, then sighed, releasing my hand. "Now, dry those pretty eyes before the Captain walks back in. If he sees you crying, he'll tear the door off its hinges—and I'm the one who has to deal with the repairs."

Despite everything, a weak laugh bubbled out of me. Felix grinned, satisfied, then slipped toward the hall. And just like that, I was alone again.

Absolutely everything that had happened in the last twelve hours had left me more emotionally and physically drained than I'd ever thought possible. I now stood alone in my dimly lit room, the faint golden glow from the lamp on my nightstand barely keeping the darkness at bay. The weight of it all pressed down on me, suffocating in its intensity. I was a murder suspect in the eyes of my neighbors, an unknowing linchpin of a rebellion I hadn't asked to be part of, and—of all things—a Riftborn. Magic coursed through my blood, apparently, though it felt more like poison than a gift.

Oh, and I was nursing a stab wound.

I caught sight of myself in the cracked mirror above my small vanity. My pale skin seemed even more ghostly in the faint light, my hair a tangled crown of red fire, and a tear-streaked face. I carefully reached up with my good arm, tugging at the robe draped over my shoulders. It slipped free, revealing the silk beneath and the faint pink scar— Colin's final mark. The sight made my stomach twist, a bitter cocktail of fear and anger churning inside me. The sling on my arm looked pitifully out of place against the delicate silk of my nightgown, the fabric clinging to me in ways that felt both comforting and suffocating.

I didn't have the energy to get beneath the comforter. Hell, I barely had the energy to stay upright. My body felt heavy, my limbs like lead, and the ache in my shoulder throbbed in time with the erratic beat of my heart.

With a weary sigh, I sank onto the bed, the cool fabric of the sheets brushing against my skin. I stared up at the ceiling, tracing the faint lines of cracked plaster. Tears pricked the corners of my eyes, unbidden and unwelcome. I didn't know who I was anymore. I didn't know if I'd ever really known. Was I Evandra, the quiet innkeeper of Winshire? Or was I something *more*—something dangerous, something powerful?

I exhaled shakily, the weight in my chest pressing harder as I replayed the events of the day. Colin's face in the shed—Drake's growl in the darkness. I didn't know what scared me more—what I'd seen or what I felt.

With a final, shuddering breath, I let my eyes drift closed. Sleep came slowly, pulling me under like a reluctant tide, leaving me exposed on the surface of my own restless thoughts. For now, I could only surrender to the void.

A light tap pulled me from the familiar depths of my usual dream—the one where Mama dies. My eyes flew open, and I lay still, my breath caught somewhere between the dream and waking. I sat up slowly, the ache in my shoulder reminding me of everything that had happened. The absence of any light filtering through my sole window told me it must be late at night. The air felt different, heavier somehow.

Tap. Tap.

I blinked toward the door, heart still hammering from whatever half-formed nightmare had dragged me awake.

Another tap. Lighter this time, but insistent.

I slid from the bed, the night air licking over bare thighs as my nightgown swayed against them. My hand hovered over the handle, chest tight with hesitation. I already knew who it was.

I cracked the door.

Drake.

He filled the doorway—barefoot, tousled, and only half-dressed. His shirt clung to him like it had been pulled on in a hurry, the collar askew, sleeves pushed up. His trousers hung low, sitting loose against the sharp cut of his hips. A lock of damp hair clung to his temple.

"Hey," he said, voice low. "I couldn't sleep." Neither could I. My mouth had gone dry.

"Um, come in."

He stepped past me, all heat and smoke and leather, the door shutting behind him with a soft click that felt far too loud. My skin flushed beneath the thin silk of my gown. It clung in the wrong places. Or maybe the right ones.

We stood there, the quiet stretching, the space between us narrowing by the second. His gaze dragged over me—lower than it should have, slower than it should have—and when his eyes met mine again, they were darker.

"You look..." His voice caught. "Warm."

I tilted my head. "Thank you?"

He didn't smile. Not fully. His eyes were too busy devouring me.

I didn't sit. Neither did he.

Our breath mingled in the short distance between us. My fingers twisted at my side, and his gaze flicked down again—trailing from my hands to the soft peaks of my breasts under the fabric, and then lower still. Heat flared in my core.

Then he stepped forward. I didn't move. Another step. I held my breath. His hand came up—slow, deliberate—as though I were something fragile. He brushed a strand of hair behind my ear with the backs of his fingers.

"I wanted to see you," he said.

"Here I am." I giggled awkwardly.

"I didn't mean your face."

My throat tightened. The room was suddenly too warm, my skin too aware.

He moved closer, his hand finding the small of my back. His other hand hovered near my hip, not touching—yet. My breasts brushed his chest with every breath. His heat soaked into me.

"You're making it really difficult to remain professional," he murmured, his tone low and strained.

"You should go," I whispered, though it lacked all conviction.

"I know." His hand slid lower, over the curve of my ass, slow and sure. His grip was firm—possessive, like he had every right. "I'm not going to."

I swayed into him, hands finding the hard lines of his shoulders. He was trembling faintly. Or maybe I was.

"Tell me to stop," he whispered.

"No."

"Please."

"No."

He groaned, pressing his forehead to mine, breath ragged. His lips ghosted mine—once. Twice. Not kissing. *Tasting.*

Then, finally, *finally*—

His mouth found mine.

It was soft at first. Testing. A single breath's worth of restraint before it deepened, open-mouthed and hungry. His hands mapped the sides of my thighs, fingers pressing into soft skin, dragging the hem of my gown higher. My breasts ached against his chest. His tongue teased the edge of my lips—seeking more. I gave it.

I melted into him. Into heat and hardness and fire. Into the sound he made when I bit gently at his bottom lip. Into the shudder that wracked him when I pulled him closer, hips tilting toward his.

And then—

Knock. Knock. Knock.

Eldrake froze, every muscle in his body going rigid. "Fuck," he hissed, eyes wide, voice low and ragged.

He pulled back—just enough that the loss of his warmth made me shiver—and immediately started fussing, adjusting himself with one hand while running the other through his hair in a futile attempt at composure. Then, without a word, he strode to the window and planted himself beside it like a man deeply invested in the mysteries of the moon.

Unfortunately, the tension in his shoulders and the unmistakable bulge in his trousers told a very different story.

Knock knock.

I scrambled, yanking the hem of my nightgown down with shaking hands, trying to smooth out both the fabric and the storm still rioting beneath my skin.

KNOCK. KNOCK. KNOCK. Sharper this time.

"What?!" Eldrake snapped, still facing the window, his voice a barely restrained growl as he tried—and failed—to tame the situation in his pants.

"It's Felix," came the muffled reply through the door.

Eldrake unleashed a string of curses involving *"timing," "that Gods-damned gnome,"* and something about *"needing five more minutes."*

I sat frozen on the edge of the bed, heart still hammering like a war drum, heat still coiled low and furious in my belly. I cleared my throat and called, "Come in," forcing my voice into something resembling casual indifference.

The door creaked open.

Felix stepped inside—sharp-eyed and all business—until his gaze swept the room and hit the invisible wall of tension still humming like a struck chord. His eyes ping-ponged between me—flushed, sitting straight as a board—and Eldrake, still posed like a moody statue looking out the window.

"Well," Felix said finally, golden brows arching. "Unless *logistics* now involves flushed cheeks and rumpled hair, I'd say someone owes me a better excuse."

"Y-yes... like I said we were discussing... logistics," Eldrake replied, tone clipped and entirely too formal for a man who had just had his hand on my ass. Still, he didn't turn around.

Felix folded his arms, lips twitching. "Felix's mouth twitched. "Mm. Yes. The same *logistics* you mentioned ten minutes ago, no doubt. Fascinating topic. Thrilling. That must explain why you look like you've been mauled by a particularly enthusiastic barmaid." His gaze slid deliberately to Eldrake's mussed hair, then down—pausing just long enough to make heat bloom all over my face. "The stable boy's gone," Felix added, as though it were perfectly normal to be delivering this news while standing in a storm of lust. "If we're going to leave without bloodshed, it's now or never."

Eldrake let out a grunt—noncommittal and vaguely threatening.

Felix tilted his head, golden eyes glinting. "Everything... alright, darling?" he asked, but it wasn't clear if he meant me or Eldrake. Probably both.

Finally, Eldrake turned to face him. Chin high. Hands on hips. The kind of stance that screamed *I am innocent* while his shirt clung in places it had no business clinging.

Felix blinked. Tilted his head. Sniffed the air, just once. His mouth twitched like he was holding back laughter.

"Tell me, Captain," he drawled. "Are you wearing cologne? Or is that just the scent of shame?"

Eldrake's nostrils flared. "No."

"Mm." Felix's eyes narrowed, but the smile he fought back was wicked.

My face went up in flames.

"We ride in one hour," he said smoothly, then added under his breath as he backed toward the door: "Try to keep your trousers on until then." The door clicked shut.

I exhaled. Eldrake didn't move.

"Logistics?" I muttered.

He sighed, scrubbing a hand down his face. "I panicked."

He lingered, still standing like a war general at the threshold—hands on hips, jaw tight, the room thick with the ghost of everything that hadn't happened but *very nearly had*. His gaze found mine, and something unspoken passed between us. Something that sizzled. Then, without a word, he crossed the room.

I straightened, pulse skittering. I didn't know what to expect—an order, maybe. A dramatic monologue. Possibly an apology and a running leap out the window. Instead, he reached up, fingers brushing a curl from my cheek. And then he kissed me.

Not like before. Not that desperate, molten thing that had nearly destroyed both of us. No, this kiss was *soft*. Gentle. *Suspiciously wholesome.*

It lasted only a moment—barely long enough for my brain to catch up—but it lingered. Warm. Careful. Sweet. Too sweet.

By the time I fully processed it, he was already pulling away. "Pack your bags," he said, voice low and unreadable.

And then he turned and left. Just like that. Door closed. Gone. I sat there for a moment, blinking, lips parted slightly. Still holding my breath like he might come back and *finish the damn job.*

What *was* that?

Too tender to mean nothing. Too brief to be a promise. Just... baffling. Emotionally destabilizing. Possibly illegal in some kingdoms.

Eventually, I flopped backward onto the bed with a groan, palms smashing over my face. His heat still clung to my skin. My lips still tingled. My thighs were having an existential crisis.

"I'm going to die a virgin."

Chapter Thirteen

Eldrake

I followed Felix, who was stomping his way back to his chambers like he was going to commit murder. He threw open the door to his room without a glance back, and I hesitated briefly before stepping inside. It struck me immediately how stark and plain his quarters were —no color, no charm, just four walls and a single window overlooking the alley. My room had been painted a cheerful canary yellow, filled with fresh flowers in a little vase, and had a view of the garden. Warm. Bright. Her touch evident in every detail. I grinned despite myself.

She'd given me the best room in the inn. She didn't have to do that.

"What do you think you're doing?" Felix's sharp tone cut through my thoughts like a dagger. He spun to face me, curls bouncing, golden eyes blazing with rare fury.

"What do you mean?" I replied, playing dumb, even as I braced for whatever he was about to throw at me.

"With *her,* you scaly menace!" he jabbed a finger toward the hallway as though Evandra herself were standing there. "Seriously, Drake—if brooding in corners wasn't bad enough, now you're *making out with the mission?*"

"I'm simply following the Commander's directions, *Doctor,*" I emphasized his title with a pointed tone, reminding him of my rank. "Ensuring she comes with us by all means necessary."

Felix let out a scandalized gasp, one hand flying to his chest. "By all means necessary? Saints above, listen to yourself! What's next, a proposal over porridge?" He said coldly. "She's already agreed to come with us! Not only that, she's now a *murder suspect.* We have leverage. You don't need to—what, *seduce* her?"

I clenched my jaw. "I'm not seducing her," I said, which was technically true. I'd been the one seduced.

Felix sighed, pinching the bridge of his nose. "Get your Dragonblood under control, Eldrake. She's not just some girl—she's the Uprising's best chance. If you get distracted or, Gods forbid, bored—"

"I wouldn't," I snapped, but it came out raw. I could still see the fear in her eyes, the blood soaking her gown. The way she looked at me after I told her what I'd done. "I'd *never* hurt her."

Felix studied me, eyes softening, his tone gentler now. "You're falling for her."

I hesitated. "I like her," I admitted. "She's... kind. Fierce. Honest. She's not like anyone I've ever met." I exhaled, the words sticking like thorns on my tongue. "I've even started to wonder if this is what love feels like."

Felix's head fell back with a groan. "Gods save me from Gods-damned dragons."

I blinked. "Excuse me?"

"You've known her for four days," he said flatly, spreading his hands.

I opened my mouth. Closed it. Four days? That... can't be right. "She made me the most incredible soup," I said, as if that explained anything.

Felix's eyes widened, horrified. "Soup? Soup?! Well then, darling, I suppose you'll be announcing the engagement at breakfast."

"She *looked* at me."

Felix clapped a hand over his mouth and let out a muffled, strangled noise somewhere between a scream and a laugh. "Oh saints, I need a drink. A strong one. And possibly a head injury."

"Still." I crossed my arms. "That doesn't mean it's not real."

Felix groaned into his hands, dragging them down his face. "Please, for the love of reason, just let her survive two more days before you go full tragic dragon lover. Castle City first, romance novels later."

I scowled. "Fine," I muttered.

Felix gave me a long, assessing look before finally nodding. "Good. Now get out before I say something truly cruel."

I turned and walked out, closing the door behind me. But even as I stepped into the quiet of the hall, I couldn't stop thinking of her—her voice, her fire. The way she looked at me like I was worth saving.

Four days or not, the truth was undeniable. I was falling for her. And Godsdamned, that's going to make everything so much harder.

Chapter Fourteen

Evandra

"Mating rituals between hybrids and humans are rare, bound by customs steeped in both primal instinct and human tradition. The hybrids, with their dual nature, engage in elaborate displays—often rooted in the behaviors of their beastly side—yet tempered by human intelligence and restraint." —An Excerpt From A study of Beasts, Chapter 12

After cooling myself off from our encounter and trying, with little success, to push Drake out of my mind, I began gathering what I thought I'd need for the journey ahead. Excitement thrummed in my chest, a wild, restless rhythm that seemed to shake the very foundation of who I was. For the first time in my life, I was leaving Winshire—leaving the inn, the only home I'd ever known. The thought sent a shiver of both anticipation and fear down my spine.

I piled a small assortment of belongings onto my bed: a hairbrush, a few of my least stained gowns, and my pillow, worn flat and threadbare from years of use. Gods, what I wouldn't give for something finer to wear on this grand "adventure." Then came my most treasured possession: *Magic of Edralis: An Introduction to Magical Creatures and Riftborn*. Its scaled cover gleamed faintly in the moonlight as I placed it atop the growing pile. I traced the title with my finger, knowing it held secrets I was still far from uncovering.

I glanced at the heap of belongings and frowned.

Shit, I don't have a bag.

After a pause, I slipped from my chambers and padded quietly across the inn, into the cool, musty basement storage. My candle flickered as I scanned the shelves, landing on a sack of potatoes. Dumping the spuds onto the floor, I examined the burlap sack. It was dirty and embarrassing, but it would have to do.

Back upstairs, I shoved my meager belongings into the makeshift bag, tying the top with a length of frayed twine. Not exactly the image of a woman about to change the world, but this was my reality. Threadbare and cobbling courage together from scraps. I tightened the sling around my shoulder, still tender despite Felix's miraculous healing, and gave the room one last look.

It struck me then—this might be the last time I'd ever stand in this space. My little attic room, with its slanted ceiling and warped floors, had been my sanctuary for so long. I stepped closer to the window, the buttery moonlight pouring in and illuminating the worn edges of my life. The faint scent of the kitchen below—roasting meat and old spice —mingled with the must of the walls.

I brushed my hand along the edge of the rickety vanity, pausing to catch my reflection once again in the cracked mirror. My braid rested neatly over my uninjured shoulder. My face was pale but resolute. And for the first time in my life, there was something else in my eyes.

Hope.

With a deep breath, I turned back to the room and took it all in one last time—the weathered bookshelf, the patchwork quilt Mama had sewn, the corner where I used to sit and read stories until the candle burned low. Each detail etched itself into my mind as I promised myself I wouldn't forget. This place had raised me. It had sheltered me. It had shaped me into the woman who now stood ready to leave it behind.

As I exhaled, the weight of nostalgia lifted just enough to let excitement take its place. I adjusted the strap of the burlap sack, squared my shoulders, and stepped into the hall, closing the door gently behind me.

I gingerly made my way down the creaky steps, letting the soft glow of my candle push back the shadows that filled the empty corridors. I took my time, each step deliberate, savoring the familiar sensations of this place that had always been my sanctuary. The worn and rough rugs beneath my feet carried the weight of generations before me, their fibers comforting yet bittersweet. The ancient structure groaned softly, its creaks and whispers a lullaby I had known all my life. My heart grew heavier with each step as if I were saying goodbye not just to a building but to a part of myself. I suppose, in a way, I was.

Finally, I reached Papa's door. The wood creaked softly as I eased it open, revealing him sound asleep in his hay-stuffed bed. His peaceful form was cocooned beneath a patchwork of knitted blankets, his face softened by slumber. He looked like a swaddled infant, so small and vulnerable compared to the man who had been my whole world.

Like someone I wasn't ready to lose.

I stood still in the doorway, the flickering light of my candle casting a warm glow over him. Memories flooded my mind. The two of us sipping tea on the front porch. Hours spent by the massive hearth in the tavern, where he'd read me fables of the Rift and its mythical beasts. I thought of the safety of his arms around me when the world felt too big. He had always protected me, even from myself.

Tears pricked the corners of my eyes. Though he had never given me the choice to leave this inn, I understood now that his choices had been born of love. He thought he was protecting me, shielding me from a world that he knew could be unkind, cruel even. But now I was choosing for myself. And that choice would break his heart.

He will never forgive me. The thought struck me like a dagger, sharper and deeper than any wound I'd ever known. It wasn't anger that frightened me—it was the hurt. The betrayal he would feel when he woke to find me gone. The thought twisted painfully in my chest, making it hard to breathe. I wanted to touch him, to tell him I loved him, to promise I'd return one day. But I knew I couldn't wake him. The goodbye would shatter us both.

Instead, I lingered in the doorway for a moment longer, imprinting the scene into my memory—the blankets rising and falling with each soft breath he took, the faint murmur of the inn settling in the night.

With trembling fingers, I crept across the room to his side table and placed the note I had written on the worn surface. I quietly stepped back and let my eyes linger on the words:

Papa,
You have done well to light my path, but now it is time for me to carry my own torch.
I love you with my entire heart, and though you may not see it now, I'm doing this for you. For Mama.
I will return someday. When, I do not know, but I promise you'll be proud of me.
Always your little girl,
Evandra

I stood over his peaceful, sleeping face a few moments more. My heart ached with the weight of not knowing when I'd see him again—not knowing if he would forgive me—not knowing if he'd still be here when I returned. But I had a destiny to fulfill. For him. For Mama. For me. I blinked away the last of my tears and straightened my spine, forcing myself to stand tall. I had to be strong now—strong enough to carry the torch he had lit for me, strong enough to walk into the unknown.

With one last lingering look, I whispered, "I love you, Papa," and slipped silently out of the room, leaving behind the man who had been my whole world and stepping into the one I was destined to save.

My palms were clammy as I sat in the dimly lit dining room, my favorite spot in the whole inn, waiting for the moment I'd leave it all behind. Anxiety thrummed in my chest like a caged bird, a strange blend of excitement and sorrow. I traced the familiar knots in the worn wooden table, committing their every swirl and groove to memory. This might be the last time I'd sit here—the last time this inn would feel like my world.

Finally I caught sight of movement through the window. My heart leaped as I saw them—Drake, Felix, and Fen—riding up to the front of the inn, their mounts kicking up small clouds of morning dust as they approached. Of course, Eldrake's horse was as impressive as he was. It was black as shadow, with a thick, flowing mane and a powerful build that demanded attention. The creature must have stood a full head taller than me, with hooves that struck the ground with a command. Its coat gleamed faintly in the soft, early light.

My eyes shifted to Felix, and I couldn't help but stifle a giggle. He rode an unimpressive gray pony that matched his small frame perfectly, the creature plodding along, trying desperately to keep up with Drake. Beside him, Fen's mount was a painted mare, her white and golden patches striking against the earthy tones of the forest backdrop. The sunlight glinted off her mane, making it look like molten gold, cascading in waves down her neck.

Finally, my eyes landed on the fourth horse, and my breath caught. A purely white mare, her coat so pristine it seemed to shimmer as though made of moonlight itself. She moved with a grace that bordered on ethereal, her tail and mane flowing like spun silk in the faint breeze. The morning sun cast a soft glow over her, making her appear less like an animal and more like a creature born from a dream.

I rose from my seat, my legs unsteady. The white mare was meant for me—I knew it the moment I saw her. My heart ached with the weight of leaving, but the sight of her stirred something deep inside me. The world beyond Winshire was calling, and for the first time, I felt ready to answer.

I suppose they don't know I've never ridden a horse.

I stood, taking one final look around the inn that had been my home for the last 14 years. Every worn floorboard, every mark on the walls, every memory seemed to call out to me, begging me to stay. But I knew I couldn't. With a deep breath, I turned and stepped outside to face my companions.

"What the hell is that?" Fen's gruff voice cut through the quiet, stopping me in my tracks.

"What's what?" I asked, looking down at myself, my voice uncertain. I wore a plain, white cotton dress—well, it was once white. Years of wear had left it faded and dotted with minor stains, but it was clean and the best I had. Clutched tightly to my chest was my makeshift potato-sack satchel, bulging with my hastily packed belongings.

Fen stared at me for a long moment, her dark eyes narrowing before a wry smirk tugged at her lips. "Is that a potato sack?" she asked, incredulity dripping from her tone. "Gods, you really are from Winshire."

I froze, cheeks blazing. Felix tilted his head, squinting at the burlap sack like it might insult him next. "Oh, darling... a potato sack? Truly?" His voice softened, more fond than cruel. "Well. It's not ideal, but we're short on time and long on problems, so—it'll do."

I chanced a glance at Drake. That damned sly grin of his was back, tugging at the corner of his lips, and it made my heart flutter in the most frustrating way.

"Let's go," Felix continued, nodding toward the white mare waiting for me. I approached the shimmering creature with awe, running my hand down her silky neck before gripping the horn of the saddle. With some effort, I slipped one foot into the stirrup and gave a mighty hop. My hands scrambled for purchase, but my leg didn't quite make it over. I dropped back to the ground, readjusted, and tried again. And again. And again.

Each attempt was a little more desperate than the last. My curvaceous body heaved with exertion as I hopped, the mare stomping and whinnying in apparent disapproval. At last, I gave one final, ungraceful kick and managed to haul myself into the saddle, my round bum landing with an audible thud. I straightened myself, smoothing my dress as though nothing at all had been amiss, and turned to face the trio with what I hoped was a look of quiet dignity.

Fen, however, was burying her face in her hands, her shoulders shaking with laughter. Felix let out a small, pained sigh. "Well. Points for persistence. We'll work on grace later." he said, doing his best to sound encouraging but not quite hiding his disbelief. Drake, on the other hand, stood silent, his lips pressed into a thin line—but the rest of his face betrayed his amusement. I could see the effort it took him not to laugh.

"Evandra, love," Felix said carefully, golden brows arched. "Have you truly never ridden a horse before?"

"Nope," I replied plainly, sitting a little straighter in the saddle.

"Isn't it obvious?" Fen quipped, her laugh cutting through the early morning air.

Without another word, the trio flicked their reins and set off down the cobblestone street. I mimicked their motions, awkwardly guiding my mare to follow. The rhythmic clip-clop of hooves echoed around us as we passed through the familiar streets of Winshire.

The journey ahead was daunting—terrifying, even—but as we left the edges of the town behind, a strange sensation began to bloom in my chest. It wasn't the panic I had expected, nor the sadness of leaving my home. No, it was something different entirely. My heart beat fast, adrenaline coursing through me. My lungs felt full like I could finally breathe.

I realized, with a thrill of excitement that shot up my spine, that this unfamiliar feeling was freedom.

Our horses approached the gate at the edge of town, its weathered wood standing as the last marker of the life I was leaving behind. I gently pulled back on the reins with my good arm, signaling my mare to slow. The party sensed my hesitation and came to a halt.

Eldrake turned to look at me; concern etched into his striking features. The breeze caught his dark hair, sweeping it away from his face. In the pale moonlight, he looked almost otherworldly atop his magnificent black steed, like something out of a fable. His woolen cloak had fallen away, revealing the powerful musculature of his thighs as he clutched the animal, his form exuding strength and command. I felt a pang of vulnerability—how small and out of place I must seem next to him—and yet, there was a pull. A feeling that I'd follow him into hell itself if he asked.

"This is the furthest I've ever come before," I admitted, my voice quiet as I looked out over the field that stretched beyond Winshire's limits. It shimmered faintly in the early dawn, its golden hues still kissed by the dew of the night. It felt like standing on the edge of a precipice, staring into the unknown.

"We must ride now, Evandra. They'll realize we're gone soon." Felix's voice from the front of the group broke the quiet, urgency lacing his words. Eldrake's attention remained on me, offering a steady, assuring presence. He gave me a slight nod, the kind that told me I was stronger than I believed. I nodded in return, inhaling deeply as I loosened my reins and urged my mare forward. The horse responded with a gentle trot, and soon, we were riding beyond the town I had always known into a world I had only ever dreamed of.

For a while, we rode in silence. The rhythmic clip-clop of hooves mingled with the rustling breeze as my companions allowed me the space to adjust. The morning air was crisp, carrying the faint scents of earth and freedom. My mind, however, was far from calm.

I couldn't stop thinking about Papa. I pictured him waking to find my note, the panic spreading through him as he searched the inn for me. I imagined him shouting my name, desperate to stop me, only to realize it was too late. A pang of guilt tightened in my chest, but I forced it away. I couldn't turn back now.

After some time, I realized Eldrake was watching me. His gaze was soft yet intense as if he were trying to read the emotions etched across my face. I must have looked as conflicted as I felt. Summoning the strength to reassure him, I offered a small, tired smile, silently telling him I'd be alright. He seemed to understand, his lips curving into a faint, approving grin before turning his attention back to the road ahead.

The sun began its slow ascent, casting its golden light over the endless wheat fields that flanked us. The shimmering hues danced like fire in the breeze, painting a picture of serenity. Each hoofbeat from my horse sent a jolt of pain through my injured shoulder, anchoring me to the present.

I looked ahead, letting my eyes settle on my new companions. They were silent as we rode, their faces etched with concentration or perhaps preoccupation. I found myself drawn to the large sword slung across Eldrake's back. Its sheer size made it look almost comically out of reach for someone like me, but in his capable grasp, it seemed perfectly at home. The leather of the handle was worn and smooth from use, a testament to years of battles fought and won. How many lives had been taken by the shining tip of that blade? How many knights had fallen before him? The thought sent a shiver up my spine.

I entertained myself for a while by imagining Eldrake in the stories my father used to read to me when I was a child. In my mind, he was the mysterious, handsome protagonist, cutting through endless foes with ease, slaying monstrous beasts without so much as a flicker of fear.

His silver eyes gleamed with determination as he fought not for glory but to save me, his fair maiden. The thought brought a smile to my lips, though the irony wasn't lost on me. In this life, it was allegedly my powers that were meant to save him.

As the hours stretched on, the morning dew began to lift, rising like faint ghosts from the golden wheat fields that bordered the dirt path. The cicadas' buzzing formed a steady hum, joined now and then by the soft, sorrowful calls of mourning doves somewhere in the distance. The sun rose higher, casting warm light across the expansive flatlands. I couldn't help but smile as I took it all in. It was so beautiful. I kicked myself for waiting this long to leave and see it.

The flatlands stretched endlessly in all directions, the horizon merging into a haze where earth met sky. The forests of Winshire were far behind us now, replaced by this open, sprawling sea of wheat and wild grass. I'd heard whispers from travelers at the inn that it took a whole day to cross the flatlands by horse.

After a while, I grew bored of my own thoughts, but the questions burning at the back of my throat refused to fade. I wanted to bombard my companions with them. Who am I, really? Who was my mother? Who sent them to find me, and what exactly is this rebellion? And what about him? Who was Eldrake, truly?

The three riders ahead of me remained silent, their postures rigid with focus. I didn't dare disturb them. Instead, I closed my eyes, imagining Castle City and what its streets hold for me.

However, instead of conjuring rooftops or market stalls... something else answered. I strained my mind, trying to make sense of the picture in my head, but the harder I focused, the more I felt like I was sinking. A flicker came first— a shimmer. I felt it before I saw it, as if I were drifting backward into water, the image on the surface just beyond reach. I didn't resist. I let the current take me, and suddenly, I was no longer on horseback.

The vision was vivid and overwhelming.

I hovered high above an enormous cavern, its walls glittering with veins of glowing stone. A hidden city clung to the rock like it had grown there—hundreds of wooden and stone homes perched along ledges and ridges, webbed together by swaying footbridges. There was no sun, and yet the light glowed golden and warm, radiating from lanterns that floated and flickered like stars.

I gasped.

Children raced along the wooden paths, their laughter rising like music. Horned women leaned over balcony gardens. A man with ocean-blue skin lifted a toddler high above his head as they both squealed with delight. Wings shimmered in the darkness. Smiles bloomed everywhere. This place wasn't just surviving. It was thriving.

And then— A scream tore through the air, sharp and gut-wrenching.

My head snapped toward the sound, and I saw them—shadows spilled over the walkways—soldiers bearing the crest of King Aberdeen, charging like a dark tide.

My chest tightened as I watched the blue-skinned man fall first, gutted where he stood, his entrails spilling onto the ground as he wailed in agony. A horned child screamed—then her head rolled across the boards. Her mother's anguished cries echoed, mingling with the clatter of swords and the roar of flames. I tried to scream. My throat wouldn't work. My limbs wouldn't move. I was a ghost in my own mind, forced to watch as the child's head rolled across the wood.

Mothers begged. Fires roared. A woman threw herself onto a soldier's blade, shrieking, clutching her child behind her. It didn't matter. The soldier ripped them apart anyway.

I sobbed. Hands clawed at my face—but they were only illusions. My real hands wouldn't move. I couldn't close my eyes. Couldn't escape. Couldn't breathe.

Please, please let me wake up—

The vision snapped again.

Suddenly, I was looking at myself—from outside my own body. I saw the wheat fields, the tree line, the road beneath us. Drake's gaze. His panic. He shouted, leaping from his horse with inhuman speed as I began to slump in my saddle. I saw my body tumble.

The ground rushed up to meet me. Agony bloomed in my shoulder as I hit the earth. Everything turned white, and then I was back. My own lungs. My own eyes. My own pain. And Drake's face hovering over me, terrified.

"Evandra! What happened?" His voice cut through the spinning world like a blade. I tried to focus on him, his presence grounding me even as my vision spun.

Tears welled in my eyes as the memory of the vision flooded back. "It was... so horrible," I whispered, my voice trembling. "The children..."

His jaw clenched. He turned sharply as Felix and Fen galloped back to us. Felix dismounted first, falling to his knees beside me. His hands moved gently over my injured shoulder, searching for the damage.

"What did you see?" Drake's voice was steady but tinged with worry.

"I saw... an underground city," I began, closing my eyes to recall the details. "There were Riftborn everywhere, living peacefully." I choked on the next words. "But then the King's men came... they butchered them," tears spilled freely down my cheeks now. "The children... the women... I could hear them screaming."

Drake's face darkened, his eyes glinting like molten steel. "Riftreach," he murmured, exchanging a grave look with the others.

Felix leaned forward sharply, curls bouncing, golden eyes intent. "Darling—did you sense time? Was it memory... or warning?" His voice was gentle but edged with urgency.

I shook my head, still trembling. "There was no sky. No sun. I couldn't tell. Just death."

Fen's jaw tightened. "Then I ride ahead." She was already moving toward her horse.

Felix threw up both hands with a disbelieving laugh. "Absolutely not. What do you think you're doing, galloping off like some martyr? Riding Castle Road alone?" He was already moving toward his pony.

Fen shot him a scathing glare. "Felix, the girl needs a healer. You know I can handle myself." She gestured to the assortment of daggers and swords strapped to her belt. "Captain?" she asked, turning to Drake, who was still crouched beside me. Drake's gaze flicked between me and Fen. Reluctant. Sharp. "Go," he said. "But take the high ridge and stay out of sight."

Felix muttered something colorful under his breath but didn't argue further. He adjusted his pony's reins with unnecessary vigor, golden curls catching in the wind as Fen mounted and charged off.

Drake turned back to me, his voice softer now. "Can you ride?"

I nodded, though the movement made me dizzy. With his help, I managed to get back on my horse, gritting my teeth against the pain. Every step of the journey would hurt, but the image of Riftreach's destruction burned in my mind. I needed to get there to understand why the Rift had shown me this.

We rode for a long time in silence. The fields stretched endlessly before us, golden and swaying, their beauty stark against the vision still echoing in my skull. My pulse hadn't fully calmed. I couldn't shake the sounds—the screams, the blade against that child's throat.

My fingers tightened around the reins.

I glanced at Drake, riding steady at my side. He hadn't said a word since helping me up. His jaw was tight, eyes narrowed against the sun—but I could tell his mind was still back there with me. Still seeing what I'd seen.

I swallowed thickly. "Thank you. For catching me."

He looked over, something unreadable flickering in his eyes. "Don't mention it."

The wind shifted, rustling the wheat around us. I let the silence stretch, let my mind settle until the rawness dulled just enough that I could breathe again. My body still throbbed, but the weight in my chest had lessened. I needed a distraction.

"So, where did you find my horse? She's beautiful," I asked, reaching out to pat the mare's silken neck. Her coat glimmered in the sunlight.

Drake cleared his throat, glancing sidelong at me with a sheepish look that immediately raised suspicion. "Well... I may have *borrowed* her."

I raised an eyebrow. "Borrowed?" My jaw dropped. *"You stole Colin's horse!?"*

"She was tied up. Saddled. Ready to go," he held up a hand. "That's not stealing. That's reassigning. And she clearly likes you better."

"Drake," I said slowly. "You stole a dead guy's prize mare."

"She's fast and reliable, and you needed a horse," he said flatly as if this justified everything. "It's not like he had future plans."

Ahead of us, Felix barked out a laugh. "You're fucking ruthless." He gave me a grin over his shoulder, golden curls bouncing in the sunlight. "Darling, only you would end up with a stolen nobleman's mare as a parting gift."

I groaned, heat rushing to my cheeks. "Don't call it that."

"Too late," Felix said airily, giving the horse an approving look. "Prize mare, tragic backstory, dramatic entrance—it's practically poetry. So very *you*."

Drake's lips curled into that familiar sly grin, and I couldn't help but feel both exasperated and amused. He looked so unapologetically pleased with himself.

"What are you going to name her?" Drake asked after a moment of silence. His voice softened, his usual sharp tone replaced with something almost thoughtful.

I hesitated. My hand stroked the mare's silken neck. The name surfaced before I could stop it. "Morwenna," I said finally. "Wenna for short."

Drake tilted his head, curious. "Hmn. Why Wenna?"

"It was my mother's name," I said softly, patting the mare's neck again. As if she understood, Wenna let out a chortle, her ears flicking back to catch my voice.

Drake nodded, his expression unreadable for a moment. "I like it," he said simply.

We rode in silence for a time after that, the rhythmic sound of hoofbeats filling the quiet. I let my gaze drift to the horizon, the golden fields shimmering in the sunlight, the endless expanse feeling both liberating and daunting. My thoughts began to wander to memories of my mother, but before I could lose myself completely, Drake spoke again.

"Do you miss her?" His voice was gentle, almost hesitant, like he wasn't sure he had the right to ask.

"Yes," I admitted, my voice barely above a whisper. "Every day."

He nodded solemnly, his gaze fixed on the path ahead. "I miss my parents, too."

The unexpected vulnerability in his tone made me look at him, studying his face as he stared forward. "What happened?" I asked softly.

His jaw tightened. "My father was Riftborn. My mother was human," his voice dropped. "The King's men murdered my father during the first purge. I was just a kid. My mother went into hiding. I haven't seen her in years."

The weight of his words settled over me like a heavy blanket. "Drake, I'm so sorry," I said, wishing I could say something more meaningful.

He shrugged, but there was nothing casual in the tension across his shoulders. "It's why I fight."

I felt the sincerity in his words, the resolve in his tone. I felt the sincerity in his words, the resolve in his tone. But something tugged at me. Riftborn. That word again. Yet even after all this time, he had never said what his Rift truly was. My gaze drifted over him—the way his broad shoulders caught the light, the faint shimmer I'd glimpsed once at his collarbone, almost like scales beneath the skin. A memory flickered: the strange heat radiating from him when he stood too close. His teeth almost resembling fangs. Questions pressed at my lips, but I swallowed them back. Not yet. "We'll stop him," I said firmly, surprising myself with the strength of my conviction.

Drake finally turned to look at me, his eyes meeting mine. There was a flicker of something there—gratitude, maybe. Or hope.

"We don't have another choice." I replied without hesitation.

For the first time, Drake smiled—not his usual sly grin, but something softer, something genuine. "You're something else, Evandra."

Heat rose to my cheeks, and I quickly looked away, focusing on Wenna's steady gait beneath me. "She really is amazing," I said my voice barely above a murmur.

"She suits you," Drake replied, his voice low, his gaze lingering. And for the first time in days, I felt a little more like myself. Maybe even someone stronger.

As the day gave way to dusk, the forest around us seemed to exhale with life. The towering trees swayed gently in the breeze, their whispers threading through the undergrowth. The golden light of the setting sun cascaded through the leaves, creating a shimmering mosaic of shadows and amber hues. The air smelled of pine and damp earth, grounding me enough that I almost felt safe. I inhaled deeply, letting the serene environment steady me.

The sound of the horses' hooves slowed, and I noticed Drake had stopped his horse atop a large stone by the riverbank. He surveyed the area, his sharp eyes scanning for any sign of threat before he dismounted with practiced ease. "We will camp here," he decided.

I followed his lead, sliding off Wenna with a bit less grace. My legs were stiff and wobbly after hours of riding. I led her to the water and tied her to a nearby bank. She dipped her muzzle and drank eagerly as I stoked her neck.

Drake was already working, his powerful hands lifting heavy stones to form a fire pit. The veins on his forearms bulged slightly with the effort, and I couldn't help but watch. He had more grace than someone his size should. It was clear that building the structure was a matter of muscle memory like survival was his art.

After he was satisfied with his work, he strode to a nearby tree, removing his wide-brimmed hat and cloak. He hung them on a branch, the moonlight catching on the crimson scales that peeked out from his collar. Without saying a word, he returned to the campfire and settled onto a log, his long legs stretched out in front of him.

"Evandra, may I look at your shoulder?" Felix's voice broke the peaceful quiet, and I turned to see him gesturing toward the fire. His golden curls caught the last rays of sunlight, giving him an almost angelic glow. I nodded, and he motioned for me to sit.

Felix's hands hovered over briefly before he began. His small fingers, surprisingly strong, pressed gently around the wound, causing a sharp sting to radiate through me.

"Sorry," he murmured, his voice soft with genuine concern. Then, he closed his eyes, tilting his face toward the sky. A soft glow began to form within him— just like before. Warmth surged through my shoulder as the pain dulled and then vanished, melting away beneath his Rift.

"Better?" he asked, his boyish face lit with a small smile.

"Much," I replied, flexing my shoulder cautiously. "Thank you, Felix."

He nodded and stood, Felix gave a little flourish of his hand, as if dismissing thanks before walking toward the pile of supplies. Without hesitation, he began pitching the three tents we'd brought with us. For someone so slight, he worked with brisk efficiency.

I glanced at Drake, who was tending to the fire, feeding it small twigs to encourage the flames. His Star-Glow caught the flickering light, making the silver seem even more intense than usual. Despite his calm exterior, there was a tension in the set of his jaw, a weight he carried that I couldn't yet decipher.

"You're good at this," I said, nodding toward the growing blaze.

Drake's lips twitched into a faint smile, his gaze still fixed on the flames. "You learn quickly when the wild is all you have." I let the silence return.

I let the peaceful sounds of the forest wash over us—the gentle crackle of the fire, the soft rustling of the trees, and the distant murmur of the river. The sky had settled into a velvety blackness, its expanse dotted with shimmering stars that cast a gentle, cool glow over our camp.

Eldrake broke apart a loaf of bread and handed each of us a chunk. I took a small bite, savoring the simplicity of it, though the autumn wind nipped at my skin. I moved closer to the fire, letting its heat seep into my bones. Each ember's glow was a reminder of safety and warmth, but now and then, a wisp of smoke curled into my lungs, choking me and drawing my thoughts back to my nightmares.

"Are you cold?" Drake's voice pulled me from my thoughts. I looked up, startled by the softness in his tone. He wasn't giving orders now; he was watching me. "You're shivering," he observed.

"A little," I admitted, rubbing my hands together. The fire's heat was a comfort, but it couldn't quite chase away the chill that had settled into me. Drake rose, crossed to the tree, and returned with his cloak. Without a word, he draped it around my shoulders.

The fabric was thick and surprisingly soft, its scent unmistakably his —a mix of leather, rain, and something spicy and warm. It filled my senses, making my thoughts foggy. I pulled it tighter around me, trying to ignore the flood of heat rising within me that had nothing to do with the fire. He settled beside me on the log, sending my heart into overdrive.

I have to pull it together.

"Thank you," I murmured, looking down to avoid his gaze. My fingers toyed with the edge of the cloak as I fought the urge to lean into him, to feel his warmth fully envelop me.

The air between us felt charged, and I needed to break it before my thoughts betrayed me entirely.

"So," I started, clearing my throat. "How did the three of you meet?" My voice sounded strained even to my own ears.

Felix perked up instantly, scooted closer to the fire, and poked at it with a stick.

"Commander Julian decides the teams," he began. "But Fen and I... Well, we've known each other since we were kids."

"Really?"

"She found me," Felix continued, his tone softer now. "I was seven, starving, barely clinging to life in some half-burnt house. Fen was thirteen. Brought me food every day until I could walk again."

My brows rose. "That doesn't sound like her."

A low sound rumbled from Drake—half grunt, half laugh.

Felix's golden eyes warmed, though his smile was wistful. "No, she doesn't exactly scream nurturing, does she? But I wouldn't be here without her. She'd sneak bread into my hands even when it meant she'd go hungry." He tilted his head. "She'll slit your throat if you cross her, but she'll starve before she lets me."

The confession stole my breath. "That's... amazing."

"We didn't have much choice," Felix added with a one-shouldered shrug, pulling me back to him. "Both being Riftborn meant we were on our own early. We were hunted. Our parents..." He hesitated, his voice catching slightly. "...were either executed for what they were— or for hiding children that were."

I winced, the weight of his words sinking in. "Felix, I'm so sorry."

He waved me off, though his grin was a touch forced. "Don't be. We're survivors, love. That's why this fight matters. Not just for us, but so no child has to grow up the way we did."

Drake shifted, feeding another branch to the fire.

I stared at him, awed. For all his smirks and teasing, there was a fierce resilience under his warmth.

"But that's also why Fen and I are never split," he added, letting the moment soften again. "She's the Sword Dancer. I'm the healer. Standard pairing. She cuts, I patch."

Sword Dancer. I had read about them. Wielders of weapons that fought as if they were alive, controlled by unseen forces. Capable of fighting with deadly precision and unpredictability. Deadly elegance. They were some of the most formidable warriors among the Riftborn—and some of the most dangerous. I tried not to imagine her cleaving someone in half with a flick of her hand. The thought sent a shiver down my spine, though it was accompanied by a pang of envy. She was everything I wasn't—strong, confident, and breathtakingly beautiful.

Felix caught my expression and grinned, teeth flashing. "Don't worry, darling. She terrifies everyone. You're in good company."

I let out a short laugh. "Not exactly easy to get along with."

Felix smirked knowingly, stirring the fire. "Ah, but once you chip through the walls? She's not half bad. Still terrifying, mind you. But worth it."

Across from us, Drake made a low sound—half grunt, half laugh—as he adjusted the wood in the fire. "She's been that way since I met her," he said, voice low. "Blade first, words second."

Felix shot him a look over the firelight, lips twitching. "And yet you still haven't bested her in sparring."

Drake's silver eyes glinted in the flames. "Because she cheats." The corner of his mouth tugged, just slightly.

The fire crackled softly, its glow flickering across the surrounding trees, but my mind was far from the serene setting. My companions were quiet, which I appreciated; it gave me space to wrestle with my spiraling thoughts. I stared into the flames, watching as embers floated upward and dissipated into the cool night air. My decision to leave Winshire played over and over in my mind. Was I insane? Stupid? My father would certainly say so. But there was something about the way these three looked at me, the urgency in their eyes. The desperation. It told me this was more than just a reckless leap into the unknown. It felt... *right.* Like this was where I was supposed to be.

Yet the doubts lingered. My chest tightened as the memory of Colin's death resurfaced. I could still see it through Drake's eyes, feel the raw fury coursing through him as he tore Colin apart. I knew it was self-defense—justice, even—but the fact that I was smitten with the man who had so brutally killed someone unsettled me. I cursed myself for the thought; yet another part of me whispered that Colin deserved it. He had tried to hurt me, and if Drake hadn't been there...

A shudder ran through me. The sounds of Colin's flesh ripping and bones snapping reverberated in my ears, overlapping with the horrifying screams from the underground city in my vision. The child's severed head tumbling across the blood-soaked ground flashed before my eyes, and I flinched. My hands gripped the edge of Drake's cloak tightly as if grounding myself in the present could silence the horrors in my mind. It didn't. I squeezed my eyes shut and shook my head violently, willing the images to fade. Nothing worked. My heart pounded in my chest, and my stomach churned with unease.

"I should sleep," I said suddenly, my voice breaking the stillness. Sleep was my only escape, though I knew it would come with its own form of torment.

Drake's gaze shifted to me. He nodded once, his expression unreadable. "We all should," he agreed, glancing at Felix. The healer rose, stretching his small frame before murmuring a soft goodnight.

Drake remained seated for a moment longer, his eyes locked on the fire. I wondered if his mind haunted him like mine did. He finally stood, brushing the dirt from his leathers.

"Goodnight, Evandra," he said quietly, his deep voice a calming rumble. For a moment, I thought he might say more, but he only turned and walked to his tent.

"Goodnight," I whispered after him, though I wasn't sure he heard me.

The silence of the forest felt oppressive now. The warmth of the fire no longer comforted me, and the shadows it cast seemed too alive. I wrapped the cloak tighter around myself, inhaling his familiar scent as I made my way to my tent. I eased myself down onto my bedroll, my body protesting after the long day of riding. My joints ached, my shoulder throbbed, but I was relieved to find that the bedroll, though modest, offered more comfort than I expected. It was just a simple layer of stuffed pelts on the hardened ground, but it cradled me enough to take the edge off the day's fatigue.

My eyes were heavy, but my mind refused to quiet. The fire's glow still flickered through the seams, but its warmth felt distant, like the home I'd left behind. I lay on my back, staring at the dim ceiling of my tent, breathing in the crisp, pine-scented air that filtered through the fabric. Outside, the forest was alive. The soft rustle of leaves in the night breeze, the chirping of crickets, and the occasional hoot of an owl created a symphony of wilderness. I closed my eyes, trying to lose myself in the sounds, but my thoughts were louder.

I sighed deeply and closed my eyes, hoping for sleep to take me. Even if it meant falling into another nightmare, it had to be better than the waking horrors playing endlessly in my mind.

Then, I heard it—soft footsteps outside my tent. My breath caught, and I froze. My heart raced. Was it the King's men? Had they found us? Every nerve in my body was on high alert, and I held my breath, praying I'd misheard. The steps grew closer, and the flaps of my tent rustled. My heart thudded painfully in my chest as a shadowed figure emerged.

Drake.

The tension in my body loosened when I saw his face, his shirtless frame bathed in the faint moonlight that spilled through the entrance. Before I could speak, he brought a finger to his lips, motioning for silence. The sight of him stole what little breath I had left.

"It's just me," he whispered, his deep voice soft and reassuring as he knelt beside me. His presence filled the small space of the tent, commanding it entirely. "How are you feeling?" His tone was quiet but warm, filled with concern.

I propped myself up on my good elbow, trying to read his expression in the darkness.

"Fine, considering," I murmured. I wanted to ask why he was here, but something about his demeanor stopped me. His nearness sent my senses into overdrive, clouding my thoughts.

Drake didn't respond immediately. He sat back slightly, his massive silhouette barely discernible in the dimness. "I left my mother to join the Uprising many years ago," he said after a long pause. His voice was steady, but there was an undercurrent of vulnerability I hadn't heard before. "I remember how difficult it was. I imagine you're going through something similar."

I blinked at the sudden intimacy of his words. My voice wavered. "Yeah. It's not easy."

"No," he agreed. Silence fell between us again, heavy but not uncomfortable.

"Can't sleep?" I ventured, my voice barely louder than a breath.

He shifted closer, his knees brushing the edge of my bedroll. "Something like that," he murmured. Then, to my surprise, he lifted his hand and gently brushed his fingers against my cheek. The unexpected tenderness of the gesture sent a shiver down my spine.

"You've already saved lives today," he said, his thumb grazing my lower lip in a way that made my breath hitch. My heart pounded, and I was sure he could hear it. His hand lingered, warm and firm against my skin, sending tingles down my spine.

I... I'm happy to help," I stammered, my voice trembling under the weight of his gaze. The way he looked at me made my thoughts scatter, his silver eyes intense yet unreadable. I wondered if he'd been as consumed by the memory of last night as I had been. Was that why he was here? His nearness made my skin flush, and my lips tingled where his thumb had just brushed. I wondered if he was here because he couldn't stop thinking of last night either.

He leaned in slowly, his lips brushing mine in the quiet darkness. I held my breath as his hand cupped the side of my face, his touch firm yet gentle. The moment his lips pressed fully against mine, a blaze ignited within me, spreading warmth from the tips of my toes to the crown of my head. His kiss was soft at first, testing and exploring, but it quickly grew deeper and more urgent.

I raised my hand to his face, the stubble on his cheek scratching against my palm. I held him there as though he might vanish if I let go. His weight shifted, and he laid down beside me, his body aligning with mine, every point of contact sending sparks through me.

His hand trailed from the nape of my neck to my shoulder, then down to my waist, pulling me flush against him. The heat of him, the press of his lips, the scrape of his teeth—it was intoxicating. He tilted my head gently, guiding my lips open to meet his. I felt his breath, hot and uneven, as his tongue swept across mine, igniting sensations I'd never known. A soft sound escaped me, and he responded with a low, primal growl that sent shivers cascading down my spine.

"Is this okay?" he murmured, his voice rough and husky against my ear.

"Gods, yes," I whispered, the words tumbling out before I could stop them.

His lips captured mine again, this time with more fervor. One hand tangled itself in my hair, tugging just enough to make my scalp tingle, while the other moved deliberately over my waist and up to my chest. He kneaded the curve of my breast over the thin cotton of my dress, and my body arched instinctively into his touch. After a moment, his calloused fingers dipped under the fabric and found my bare skin.

When his rough palm grazed over the sensitive peak of my breast, I gasped against his mouth. He pinched it gently, rolling it between his fingers, sending waves of pleasure coursing through me. His lips left mine to trail down my neck, his stubble scraping deliciously against my skin as his kisses grew more insistent. I couldn't think, couldn't breathe, couldn't do anything but feel.

My hands fisted in his shirt, tugging hard, pulling him closer until the thin fabric slid upward. I shoved it over his shoulders in one frantic motion, desperate for more of him, for the heat of his skin against mine.

And then I froze.

The firelight caught along the ridges of his chest—not scars, not skin. Scales. Crimson, faintly iridescent, fanning across his chest and shoulders, running down the cut of his biceps like molten armor.

I gasped. My fingers hovered, then brushed the hardened texture, tracing the ridges in awe. "What—?"

His jaw flexed, but instead of answering, his mouth kept moving down my throat as though nothing had changed. I shivered as my fingertips slid over the plates, unable to stop tracing them.

"Be careful touching me like that." His voice was low, ragged, when he finally pulled back just enough to speak.

"What are you?" I whispered, breathless, as his teeth grazed my earlobe.

"Dragonblood." Just one word, muttered like a confession.

Before I could even begin to process it, his lips returned to my neck, his teeth scraping, his heat overwhelming. He eased me onto my back, hands trailing down to my hips, pulling me under.

I moaned at our contact. He paused—just for a breath—as if collecting himself, before brushing his lips down my throat. The sound that left him was half-growl, half-groan. "Shhh… we don't want to wake Felix," he teased, his grin evident even in the darkness. It was a smile I hadn't seen. He was no longer hiding behind his toughened facade. This smile was genuine. Sweet.

The ache between my thighs grew unbearable. I shifted, trying to get closer, to feel more of him, but my bedroll constricted me. I kicked at it frantically until I was free, earning a quiet laugh from him. He rolled onto his side to face me, the darkness softening the hard lines of his face. His hair fell over one shoulder, brushing my cheek as he leaned in again.

This time, his kiss was slower, more deliberate, as though he wanted to memorize every inch of my lips.

"You're unlike anyone I've ever met, Evandra," the sound of my name rolling off his lips was divine. "I just can't stay away from you," he whispered into the crook of my neck as his hand drifted down my side, tracing the curve of my waist and hip before slipping under the hem of my dress. His fingers grazed my bare thigh, and he paused, letting out an uneven breath. "May I?" he asked softly, his voice barely a whisper but filled with raw hunger.

I nodded, unable to form words. My head was reeling. His fingers slid higher, exploring until they found the wetness pooling between my thighs. His touch was electric, sending jolts of pleasure shooting through me as he massaged the sensitive bundle of nerves at my center. I gasped, biting my lower lip to suppress the moan that threatened to escape.

"Gods," he groaned, his lips brushing against my ear as his free hand returned to my breast, kneading and teasing. Each stroke of his fingers built a fire in my core, a tension that tightened with every movement. When he slipped two thick fingers inside me, I gasped again, this time louder. He stilled for a moment, letting me adjust to the stretch before beginning a slow, deliberate rhythm.

Pleasure rippled through me, and my hips moved instinctively to meet his thrusts. His thumb circled my sensitive bud in perfect time with his fingers, drawing me closer and closer to the edge. My breathing grew ragged, my hands clutching at his shoulders as I tried to hold on.

I looked at him with desperation, and he knew my completion neared. The tension in my body snapped, and I fell over the edge, my walls spasming around his fingers as wave after wave of ecstasy crashed over me. I bit down on my lip to muffle the cry that tore from my throat, but he clapped a hand over my mouth just in time, silencing me completely.

"Fuck," he muttered, his voice tinged with awe as he slowed his movements, drawing out my release. His fingers left me, and I whimpered at the loss, my body still trembling.

He lay back beside me, his chest rising and falling heavily. I turned my head to look at him, my lips curling into a satisfied smile. "That was nice," I said breathlessly, unable to articulate the depth of what I felt.

"Yeah... totally," he said, the corner of his mouth quirking up in that lopsided grin I was quickly falling in love with.

Chapter Fifteen

Eldrake

Nice?! Fucking nice?! What the hell does that even mean?! Was I not good enough?

I lay flat on my back beside her, staring at the tent ceiling, the word echoing like a Gods-damned curse. My cock was still hard as stone, and all I could think about was how perfect she felt.

Soft and wet, the way her body trembled under my touch, the way she clenched around my fingers—Gods, how would that feel wrapped around my—

She shifted, interrupting my thoughts, and before I could process it, she rolled over, draping a small, delicate hand across my chest and resting her head against the scaled side of my shoulder.

She wanted to... *cuddle?*

I froze, uncertain. Women didn't do this with me. They didn't stay. They wanted my body, my strength, my title—then they left. That was the unspoken agreement: a quick tumble, no strings, no attachments. No one had ever wanted to stay, let alone curl up against me as though I were something worth holding onto.

Her breathing was soft and steady, brushing warmly against my neck. She fit so perfectly against me, her more petite frame curling into mine like she belonged there. My heart was pounding, not with lust this time, but with something far more dangerous. I stared down at her fiery hair spilling across my chest, catching faint glimmers of moonlight from outside the tent. My hand moved on its own, resting gently over hers, and I let out a long breath.

This felt... good. Too good. It felt natural, as though my entire life had been leading up to this moment. And that terrified me.

My mind churned against the peace she brought me, dragging me back to reality. You're a Captain, I reminded myself, my inner voice harsh and unyielding. You're sworn to the Uprising, to the cause. Nothing else matters. No one else matters. I couldn't let myself get distracted—not by this, certainly not by pretty, squishy, red-haired women.

But then I thought about her eyes. Those wide, amber eyes looked at the world with so much wonder that it made me feel like I was seeing it for the first time. She noticed the smallest things—the sparkle of sunlight through the trees, the intricate patterns on a single leaf. How she'd agreed to come with us, leaving behind everything she'd ever known, simply because we asked for her help. No hesitation, no conditions.

Her kindness, her heart—it felt like something worth protecting. Like she was worth protecting, I pulled her closer, letting her warmth seep into me as though she could melt away the jagged edges of my soul. Maybe this wasn't a distraction. Perhaps this was what I needed.

They say when a Dragonblood bonds, it's eternal. Dangerous. World-shifting. The word popped into my head—*bond*—unwelcome and sharp. No. That wasn't what this was. She was just a pretty redhead with soft skin, kind eyes, and a laugh that made my chest ache. That's all. Just a woman. Not fate. Not mine. Gods, I was already so fucking doomed.

My lips quirked into a lazy grin. *And, well... her ass didn't hurt either—Gods, that ass.*

I snorted softly at my own thought, careful not to wake her. She shifted again, tugging the edge of the bedroll over our legs, and her scent filled my lungs—sweet and intoxicating. I felt my eyelids grow heavy. My body, for the first time in years, felt truly at ease. Maybe I didn't need to leave just yet. Ten more minutes. Ten minutes of pretending I could have this—this warmth, this peace, this woman.

The loneliness of my own tent could wait. For now, I let myself fall into the quiet comfort of her presence, my arm tightening protectively around her as my eyes closed—*just ten more minutes.*

Chapter Sixteen

Evandra

"To touch the Rift is to reach for the Gods and come back marked. Those who survive its embrace do not remain unchanged—no matter how pure their hearts. The question is never what the Rift gives you. It is what it takes in return." —Magic of Edralis: an Introduction to Magical Creatures and Riftborn, p. 12

My eyes fluttered open slowly, the cool morning air brushing against my skin. For once, I hadn't dreamed. The absence of those haunting visions felt like a reprieve—a silence I hadn't realized I craved. I turned my head and felt the soft pressure of warmth against my cheek. I almost gasped when I saw him—Eldrake, still asleep, his strong chest rising and falling steadily beneath my cheek. His scaled shoulder felt surprisingly smooth and warm against my palm. How did this become my reality?

I traced his features with my eyes, drinking in the sharp line of his jaw and the peacefulness that softened his otherwise battle-hardened face. I couldn't wrap my head around it—why someone like him, a God among men, would show any interest in someone like me. Maybe it was fleeting. Perhaps it was something deeper. Whatever it was, I'd take it for as long as I could.

He shifted in his sleep, brow furrowing faintly before his eyes fluttered open. For a moment, we just looked at each other—no words, no breath. Just warmth and something I didn't have a name for yet.

Ahem.

The sharp sound of a throat clearing broke through the quiet, startling us both. Eldrake shot upright in an instant, flames licking at his palms as though his body was already prepared for battle. I reeled at the sudden absence of his warmth, clutching the bedroll for stability as I sat up. My heart sank as my eyes landed on Felix standing at the tent's entrance, arms crossed and shaking his head.

"Sleeping in, are we?" Felix tapped his foot in exaggerated annoyance, his golden gaze darting between my disheveled gown and matted hair. His lips twitched like he was holding back a grin. "Honestly, you two make sneaking around look about as subtle as a parade."

"Fuck," Eldrake muttered under his breath, extinguishing the flames as he stood. He cast Felix a dark look, but Felix only flicked his curls dramatically and muttered something about "Godsdamned dragons and their timing."

Eldrake turned back to me, his expression somewhere between sheepish and amused.

"This was... nice," he said with a crooked smile, leaning down to press a kiss to my forehead. The soft gesture sent my heart racing all over again. Before I could respond, he slipped out of the tent, leaving me alone with my thoughts.

Nice, I thought to myself. It was more than nice. I pressed my fingers to my forehead where his lips had been, the ghost of his touch lingering. I'm falling for him—hard.

Before I'd get hurried along to pack up, I scrambled to my satchel, dragging out the old index I'd packed in haste. My hands trembled as I flipped through brittle pages, my eyes skimming desperately until they caught the word that had burned itself into me last night.

Dragonblood

Classification: Beast – Draconic Hybrid
Rarity: Extremely rare
Threat Level: High

Appearance:

Dragonbloods are humanoid in form, bearing a striking resemblance to men and women but with unmistakable draconic features. Although primarily human in shape and size, they are distinguished by patches of iridescent scales on their shoulders, hips, chest, and throat—remnants of their ancient ancestry. These scales often shimmer in hues of emerald, onyx, or sapphire, and their patterns are as unique as a fingerprint.

Most Dragonbloods possess Star-Glow eyes, which seem to pulse with inner fire, and many have slightly elongated canines, adding a subtle but unmistakable predatory edge to their otherwise human faces.

Temperament:

Known for their fiery intensity and unyielding passion, Dragonbloods are as feared as they are revered. Loyal to a fault, they will defend those they consider kin or bonded with a ferocity unmatched by any other Riftborn. Their emotional range is vast—and explosive. Love and hatred burn equally deep, and once sparked, their fury is nearly impossible to extinguish. Their loyalty is not easily earned, but once given, it is lifelong. Just as true: betrayal cuts them deeper than any blade.

Abilities:

Dragonbloods retain formidable elemental magic, particularly tied to fire. Flames often respond to their emotions without conscious command. In battle,

MANY EXHIBIT ENHANCED STRENGTH, SPEED, AND AGILITY AND CAN WITHSTAND INJURIES THAT WOULD INCAPACITATE MOST RIFTBORN. RARE INDIVIDUALS HAVE ALSO BEEN RECORDED AS POSSESSING LIMITED TELEPATHIC OR EMPATHIC ABILITIES WITH DRAGONS OR OTHER DRAGONKIN—SUGGESTING A LINGERING PSYCHIC BOND TO THEIR ANCESTRAL BLOODLINE.

WEAKNESSES:

WHILE PHYSICALLY RESILIENT, DRAGONBLOODS ARE EMOTIONALLY VOLATILE. THEY ARE PARTICULARLY VULNERABLE TO HEARTBREAK, BETRAYAL, OR LOSS, OFTEN SUFFERING PSYCHOLOGICAL EFFECTS FAR GREATER THAN MOST. THIS EMOTIONAL VOLATILITY CAN LEAD TO DANGEROUS IMPULSIVITY-ESPECIALLY WHEN PROVOKED. PROLONGED EXPOSURE TO HEAVY RIFT MAGIC MAY ALSO WEAKEN THEM TEMPORARILY, AS THEIR HYBRID BLOOD WAS NEVER MEANT TO CHANNEL THE FULL POWER OF DRAGONS.

NOTES:

TO ENGAGE WITH A DRAGONBLOOD IS TO STEP INTO THE FIRE. THEY ARE CREATURES OF HEAT AND HUNGER, DEVOTION AND DESTRUCTION. TO WIN A DRAGONBLOOD'S TRUST IS TO GAIN AN ALLY—OR LOVER—OF MYTHIC LOYALTY. BUT TO BETRAY ONE...

...IS TO SUMMON WRATH AS FIERCE AS DRAGON FIRE.

I carefully folded the corner of the page, marking it for later reference. I knew I'd want to return to it, to study every word. Dragonbloods were known for their passion—for their intensity, their fire, both figuratively and literally. And Eldrake? He embodied that passion in every look, every word, every deliberate move. I closed the book, running my fingers over the scaly cover as my thoughts swirled. He was devoted to the uprising and his cause with a fervor that was almost contagious. But it wasn't just his mission that stirred something inside me.

Packing up camp was a quiet, tense affair. Felix seemed intent on avoiding eye contact with either of us, clearly irritated. Drake, for his part, kept shooting me apologetic looks as if to say, This isn't your fault. I tried not to smile every time he caught my gaze.

Once we were all mounted, I fell into the middle of the group, sandwiched between Felix and Drake. The awkward tension stretched into hours of silent riding, the rhythmic thud of hooves doing little to distract me from my racing thoughts. Finally, I couldn't take it anymore.

"So," I began, breaking the awkward silence, "you said you knew my mother?"

Drake slowed his horse to match my pace, his expression softening. "Not personally," he admitted. "But our Commander, Julian, did. They were close. Your mother saved his life on multiple occasions, or so the stories go."

He glanced at me, his chestnut hair catching the breeze and revealing more of his angular features. "In fact," he continued, "that's how they met. Your mother had the same vision every night for a month. She saw a man—always the same—dying in an alley. Sometimes poisoned. Sometimes his throat slit. But always dead."

I listened, captivated, as we turned a bend in the road.

"She finally recognized the alley in Castle City's market district. Rode three nights and four days without rest until she found him. When the assassin made his move, she intervened, killing him before he could strike. The man she saved was Julian." Drake's voice was steady, but there was a quiet reverence there.

My heart swelled with a mixture of pride and disbelief. My mother—the woman I thought I knew—was a hero—a Riftborn leader.

"But if she was so powerful," I asked, my voice cracking slightly, "how did she die in something as mundane as a house fire?"

Felix finally chimed in from behind me, his tone softer than usual but still distinctly his. "No one knows. And believe me, we've asked every question you're about to ask yourself. It's haunted us for a decade. Doesn't add up. A Seer who saved generals and kings brought down by a stray candle? Please." He gave a little shake of his head, golden curls catching the light. "None of us buy it."

Drake's expression darkened. "There were whispers of sabotage," he said, his voice low. "But no proof."

Silence settled over us again as I processed this new piece of my mother's story.

"Why now?" I finally asked, unable to keep the bitterness from my tone. "If Julian knew about me, why did you wait so long? Why didn't you come sooner?"

Drake looked away, guilt flickering across his features. Felix answered before the weight could strangle the moment completely. "Because the King is getting close," he said simply, though his voice was clipped in a way that suggested even he hated the answer. Then he gave me a quick sidelong glance, his mouth quirking just slightly. "And believe me, love, if it were up to me, we'd have fetched you ages ago. But Julian likes his timing dramatic." he said, his voice clipped. "He knows the Uprising exists and is working with one of our own—a Riftborn traitor," the weight of those words hung heavy in the air.

Drake cut him a look, but Felix only shrugged, unbothered. "What? She deserves honesty."

"A traitor?" I asked, my stomach twisting.

"Vyper," Drake growled, his fists tightening around his reins. "A warlock. He's powerful and ruthless, and he can see through our wards and disguises. He's been picking off our people one by one."

"And now we're desperate," Felix added quietly. "Your mother wanted you hidden, safe, for as long as possible. But the time for that's over." His eyes softened as they met mine. "The world's uglier than it was when she left it to you. You don't get to stay buried anymore. And I'm sorry for that."

Drake met my gaze then, expression blazing with emotion. Despite the hardness of his features, there was a vulnerability there that stopped my breath. He wasn't just a soldier; he was a man carrying the weight of a thousand losses. At that moment, my path became clear. This was my destiny. This was my fate, and maybe he was a part of that, too. The Uprising needed me, and I wouldn't fail them.

We rode for hours the next day beneath a shifting sky, the sun bleeding into gold before giving way to bruised twilight. The landscape changed with every mile—the forest gave way to open fields, then back to thickets dense with tangled roots and shadow. The conversation was sparse. Drake kept close, his presence a steady pulse just behind me, while Felix hummed tunelessly from the rear, his voice scratchy from disuse.

By the second night, fatigue tugged at my bones. I could feel it in the tightness of my thighs from riding, the ache in my shoulders, the way my head swam when I finally dismounted. We made camp in a hollow ringed by towering oaks, the ground littered with leaves that whispered underfoot.

Drake didn't say much as he settled near my tent; he just gave me one long look—the kind that said more than words could. When I turned in for the night, I wasn't surprised when I heard the soft rustle of the tent flap and the familiar weight of him settling beside me. No heat this time. No fire. Just the quiet comfort of his arm slipping around my waist and the soft exhale of breath against my neck.

The third night was colder. Rain threatened but never came. My cloak wasn't enough to chase away the chill, and I found myself scooting back until I felt his chest against my spine. He didn't hesitate. He just pulled me closer and sighed like he'd been holding his breath all day.

"You're warm," I murmured, my voice muffled against the crook of his arm.

"Dragons run hot," he said simply, but there was a faint smile in it.

I turned slightly, enough to glimpse the outline of his face in the dark. "Is that your way of saying you're useful for something after all?"

His chest rumbled against my back, the hint of a laugh. "Maybe."

For a long moment, there was only the steady cadence of our breathing, syncing without effort. His hand brushed my arm—hesitant at first, then firmer, rubbing slow circles into my sleeve as though easing the soreness from the day's ride. The touch was careful, almost reverent.

"You're tense," he said quietly.

"I'm always tense."

"Not with me." The words were simple, almost careless, but they settled over me like a vow.

Silence settled between us again, but it wasn't awkward anymore.

My breaths slowed, my body still pressed tight to his. After a moment, I whispered, softer: "I... usually have terrible dreams."

His hand stilled against my hip, fingers curling just slightly. "Dreams?"

"Well... nightmares, really. Since I was a kid. But..." I swallowed hard, realizing how much I was admitting. "Not when you're here."

His breath shifted against my hair, and the quiet stretched long enough that I wondered if he'd fallen asleep. But then his arm pulled me closer still, his lips brushing the crown of my head.

"Then I'll stay," he murmured.

The words weren't grand, weren't heavy—they were simple. Steady. And they settled into me like an anchor, rooting me in place.

For the first time in years, I wasn't afraid to close my eyes.

The next evening, after another endless day in the saddle, my legs throbbed with every step. By the time we crawled into the tent, I dropped down with a groan, rubbing at my thighs.

"Hurts?" His voice came from the dark.

"Like hell," I admitted, massaging at the sore muscles.

There was a rustle, and then his hand nudged mine away, broad and warm against my leg. He kneaded gently at first, then firmer, finding the knots in the muscle. I sucked in a breath.

"Gods," I muttered. "You missed your calling as a healer."

"Don't tell Felix," he murmured. "He'd never let me live it down."

He worked lower, down to my knee, then back up again, slow and steady. I relaxed under his touch—until his calloused fingers brushed a ticklish spot just above the back of my knee. My whole body jolted.

"Drake!" I yelped, stifling a laugh as I wriggled away.

He froze, then deliberately pressed his thumb there again.

"Stop! Gods—stop!" I tried to shove his hand away, but he grinned—actually grinned—and kept at it until I was laughing helplessly into the blankets.

"Mercy," I gasped, breathless, half-laughing, half-pleading.

He pulled back at last, smug satisfaction glinting in his silver eyes. "Noted. You have weaknesses."

I swatted at his arm, still breathless. "You're insufferable."

"Maybe." His smirk softened. "But you're smiling."

And I was. My cheeks ached with it.

That night, I didn't roll away from him. I shifted until I was facing him, our noses close enough that his breath brushed my lips. His arm came around me again, but softer this time, like he was afraid I'd vanish if he held too tightly.

It became routine. He never asked if he could come. I never told him not to. And when sleep took us, it was deep and still and dreamless—no visions, no whispers, no shadows pulling me under. Just his warmth, wrapping around me like a heavy blanket, steady and grounding, until even my restless mind finally surrendered to peace.

By the fourth morning, the rhythm of travel had dulled into something almost meditative — the creak of leather, the crunch of hooves, the hush between heartbeats. But unease stirred beneath the surface. We were getting close. The terrain had begun to change, the air thickening as if the land itself were holding its breath.

We entered a narrow gorge, the sheer, jagged cliffs towering over us like stone sentinels. The path between the walls was a mere ten feet wide, flanked by ancient rocks that seemed to hum with silent menace. Overhead, the brilliant blue sky stretched peacefully, a cruel contrast to the tension that suddenly gripped the air.

A screech pierced the stillness, echoing ominously. It wasn't the call of any bird I'd ever heard. The sound carried a guttural edge that made my stomach twist. Drake's posture stiffened instantly, his hand instinctively moving to the hilt of his dagger, his piercing gaze scanning the cliffs. Felix, riding close behind me, seemed to close the gap, his presence feeling both protective and anxious.

"What was that?" I asked, my voice barely above a whisper. Before anyone could answer, a dark, winged shape darted across the sky above us, casting a fleeting shadow. My heart leaped into my throat.

Another screech, this one louder, and then— THUD.

The most awful creature I'd ever laid eyes on landed before us, sending a plume of dust into the air. Wenna reared, her ears flattened in terror as I struggled to calm her. I froze as the thing fixed its glowing red eyes on me. It stood over seven feet tall, its leathery wings spread wide, tipped with gashes and tears. Its canine face twisted into a horrifying grin, revealing jagged, yellowed fangs. Talons glinted wickedly in the sunlight, and a guttural growl rumbled deep in its chest.

"What the hells is that thing?!" I shrieked as Drake leaped from his horse.

"Vyrmin!" Felix hissed, notching an arrow. "Get back, Evandra!"

Drake charged without hesitation, his greatsword gleaming as he unslung it from his back. His boots pounded against the earth, a primal force in motion. The beast lunged, its massive claws slicing through the air. Felix loosed an arrow that buried itself deep in its shoulder, throwing its strike off-course. The talons missed Drake by inches, raking the ground with a sound that made my skin crawl.

Drake roared, a sound both human and bestial, as he swung his sword overhead. The blade came down with deadly force, cleaving into the creature's wing. Black, sticky blood sprayed, hissing as it hit the ground like acid. The Vyrmin screeched in fury, rearing back.

Above us, more shadows appeared.

"There's more!" I shouted, pointing as two additional creatures dove from the cliffs.

They landed with deafening crashes. They surrounded us. Felix aimed at the nearest beast, his hands steady despite the chaos. His arrow streaked through the air and embedded itself in one of the creature's glowing eyes. It howled, stumbling back before collapsing in a convulsing heap.

Drake faced the first beast again, his sword raised high. He brought it down with all his strength, splitting the Vyrmin's chest from shoulder to gut. The creature crumpled, its black blood pooling beneath it. But before Drake could retrieve his blade, one of the newcomers pounced. Its talon-like claws jutting from the end of its bony fingers raked across his back, tearing through his leathers and leaving deep, bloody gashes.

"Drake!" I screamed as he hit the ground, clutching his side, his blood gushing between his fingers and staining the earth.

Felix fired another arrow, narrowly missing the third Vyrmin. "Move, Captain! Godsdamn it—don't just lie there and bleed!" He shouted.

The remaining beast advanced on Drake, its wings flaring wide in a display of dominance. My chest tightened as panic seized me. He was vulnerable, unarmed—and about to die. Something inside me snapped.

I closed my eyes, willing myself into the creature's mind. It felt like plunging into ice water, the Vyrmin's chaotic, alien thoughts clawing at my own. But I pushed deeper, gripping its weak will like a vice.

"*YOU WILL NOT HURT HIM,*" my voice thundered inside its mind, echoing with fury.

The beast hesitated, its glowing eyes dimming slightly as it stood upright. Drake, bloodied and bewildered, stared at the creature—and then at me with disbelief.

Felix's voice was distant, horrified and awed all at once. "Eva—what in all the hells are you doing?"

"*Take the sword,*" I commanded. The Vyrmin shuddered but obeyed, stumbling toward the corpse of its fallen kin. "Good." It grasped Drake's greatsword in its clawed hands, black blood dripping from the blade as it pulled free.

"*Fall on it,*" my voice was relentless. The beast trembled, its resistance weak but persistent. Rage flooded through me, hotter than anything I'd ever felt.

"*FALL. ON. IT.*" With a final, anguished screech, the Vyrmin plunged the blade into its own chest and collapsed forward, the sword impaling it completely. Black ichor gushed from its wound as its glowing eyes dimmed and faded.

I released the connection, my consciousness snapping back into my body like a rubber band. My vision blurred, and the world tilted. The last thing I saw was Drake's bloodied face as he scrambled toward me, shouting my name.

Then, everything went black.

Chapter Seventeen

Felix

The wind was cruel at this altitude.

I hunched deeper into my cloak as we descended from the ridge, my pony carefully picking her steps down the slope. Drake rode ahead, Eva's limp form cradled in his arms like something breakable. He hadn't said a word since the Vyrmin fell. Not when I called his name. Not when I checked his wounds. Not even when I told him she would live. He was holding her like silence might stitch her back together.

I tried not to watch too closely. Gods knew I wasn't the sentimental type, but something about the way he moved—coiled and barely holding it together—made it impossible to look away. He didn't look like a man returning from victory. He looked like a man who had lost something vital and hadn't figured out how to breathe without it.

We reached the edge of the valley and found a narrow cave tucked behind a thicket of thornbrush. Shelter. Privacy. Drake dismounted with a fluidity that shouldn't have been possible for someone bleeding from three places. He carried Eva inside like she weighed nothing. Like she was a memory already fading from his grip.

I followed, my palms already glowing with warmth. He laid her down so gently it almost broke me.

"She's stable," I said softly, kneeling at her side. "No broken bones. Rift burn. She just needs rest."

Drake didn't answer. He was crouched beside her, blood drying on his hands, his brow furrowed like he was waiting for her to vanish the second he blinked. His eyes were the kind I'd only seen once before—on a mother who lost her child and hadn't yet accepted it.

I reached for a salve, giving him a moment. "She's breathing, Captain," I said after a beat. "You can stop holding your breath now."

He didn't laugh. Didn't even blink. Just dragged a shaky hand through his hair and muttered, "This wasn't supposed to happen."

"You getting clawed in the back or her puppeteering a monster into stabbing itself?"

His jaw clenched. "She nearly died."

"But she didn't."

He finally looked up at me then—and I saw it. That thing beneath the anger. The fear. The... depth of it. I'd known him a long time. Known what he was like under pressure, in grief, in rage. But this?

This was new.

I shifted, lowering my voice. "You okay?"

His answer was immediate. "I'm fine."

"Bullshit," I said simply.

He turned away, standing like he could shake it off with motion. Pacing. Clenching and unclenching his fists.

"She's strong," I said after a moment. "You've seen it. I've seen it. You don't have to shoulder it all."

He stopped pacing. "It's not about that."

"Then what is it?"

He hesitated.

Something in him wanted to answer. I saw it—right there in the silence between breaths. But whatever it was, he swallowed it back like it might poison us both.

He crouched near her again, watching the rise and fall of her chest like it was the only proof the world hadn't ended.

"She's just... different," he finally said. "It's not what I expected."

I nodded slowly. "You mean how she somehow made a fucking Vyrmin kneel like a trained dog?"

His lips twitched, almost a smile. Almost.

"No," he murmured. "I mean... how I can't think straight when she's around. And how that fucking terrifies me."

A beat of silence passed. *There it was.*

I sat back on my heels, studying him. Watching the lines in his face that hadn't been there a week ago. The way he looked at her—not like she was beautiful, though she was—but like she was gravity and he was fighting not to fall.

"Drake," I said gently. "I've seen you flinch through broken ribs. I've seen you stand between a child and a burning field. I've never seen you look at someone like that."

He stiffened. "Don't start."

"Start what?"

"Whatever you're thinking."

"I'm thinking," I said, keeping my tone even, "that maybe something's happening you don't understand. And maybe instead of fighting it, you should—"

"Drop it." His voice cracked like a whip, sharper than intended.

I didn't flinch. Just nodded. For now.

But I watched him settle beside her again, not touching, just... anchoring himself near her like proximity might make sense of all this. He didn't know what he was feeling. I wasn't sure he could name it. But I could see the shape of it forming.

This wasn't mission loyalty. This wasn't lust. This was something ancient. Something patient and possessive and quiet as a knife in the dark. And it was going to wreck him.

Chapter Eighteen

Evandra

"Of all Riftborn, only gnomes possess the gift of true healing—a rare blessing that allows them to mend wounds, restore vitality, and even stave off death's advance. Yet, this power is tempered by the Rift's demands; each act of healing leaves a mark upon the gnome, a reminder that even life-giving magic carries a price." —Magic of Edralis: An Introduction to Magical Creatures and Riftborn, p. 120

I floated in the black lake behind the veil, lost in its dark embrace. Voices called to me—muffled, distant, and distorted—but one stood out, growing louder with every passing moment. Drake's voice. His deep timbre became my anchor. I let the sound pull me closer until, with a gasp, I broke through the surface. My eyes flew open as I sat upright, my breath rushing out in a gasp.

The world slowly came into focus: the soft sway of motion, the creak of leather, the golden light of late afternoon. I was atop a horse—

Drake's massive black steed. I felt the solid warmth of his body behind me, one strong arm wrapped protectively around my waist, holding me steady in the saddle.

"Are you awake?" His deep voice rumbled softly, the sound just above my ear. I tilted my head back to look up at him, ignoring the throbbing ache in my body, and the concern etched across his features made my heart flutter. The sight of his handsome face so close to mine sent a rush of warmth through me. Then, the memory hit me like a gale-force wind—the beasts, the blood, Drake falling, clawed, and bleeding.

"You were hurt!" I exclaimed, twisting in the saddle to check his injuries, but his hands tightened around me, holding me steady.

"Relax," he murmured. "Felix already took care of it," there was a flicker of amusement in his voice, but I could hear the exhaustion beneath it.

"Damn it," I muttered, sinking back against him. "Did I pass out again?"

"Only for a little while," he said, his tone indulgent.

"I swear, at this rate, I'm going to develop a reputation."

He huffed a quiet laugh against my temple. "Could be worse."

The tension eased out of my shoulders as I let out a breath I didn't realize I'd been holding and let myself relax. I sank back into him, letting the rise and fall of his chest reassure me.

"You didn't have to save me," he said, his tone softer now, his lips just brushing my temple. "But I'm flattered you did."

My cheeks burned at his words, the memory of taking control of the Vyrmin flashing through my mind. The raw power, the fury, the desperation to save him—it all felt surreal now, like a dream.

"Is she awake?!" Felix's voice cut through my thoughts. I turned to see him riding up beside us, Wenna trotting along behind his sturdy gray pony. His golden hair was windswept, and his face bore the lines of exhaustion, like keeping us all patched together was dragging him thinner by the day. "Eva, how did you do that?! You made that beast kill itself!" he exclaimed, eyes wide.

"I..." I hesitated, the memory still sharp but impossible to explain. "I don't know exactly. I was angry—terrified, really—and I thought if I didn't do something, Drake would..." I trailed off, not wanting to say it aloud. "The next thing I knew, I was in its head, screaming at it."

"Well— that's fucking terrifying," Felix said bluntly. Then, softer, with a tilt of his head: "Brilliant, but terrifying. Please don't ever do that to me, love. My heart couldn't take it."

Drake chuckled, the deep sound reverberating through his chest against my back. The warmth of his arm still around me was a comforting weight, and though I could have asked to ride Wenna now, I didn't. He didn't suggest it either, and the thought made me grin.

"What were those things?" I asked, my mind flashing back to the grotesque creatures with glowing red eyes and bone-chilling screeches.

"Vyrmin," Drake answered, his voice dark. "They're henchmen of Vyper's creation. He played God, breeding beasts to serve as his personal killing machines. They're built for violence, easy to control, and hard to kill."

"Gods..." I whispered, horror curling in my stomach at the thought of something so unnatural being brought into the world.

"I suspect Vyper got word that we found you," Felix added grimly. "If he sent them, it means he sees you as a threat. If the King knows we've located a Seer..." He didn't finish the thought. He glanced at me again, his golden eyes gentler this time. "Eva, you scared the shit out of me back there. But you should know—you scared the shit out of them, too. And that? That's power. The kind that changes wars."

The weight of their words settled heavily on my chest. I had expected danger, but this was bigger, darker than I had imagined. Still, there was no room for regret. I had made my choice. This wasn't a grand adventure or escape from monotony. This was a battle for survival, and I was a key piece on a dangerous chessboard.

The steady rhythm of hooves against the dirt path was the only sound for a long while. I sat cradled in front of Eldrake, his arm wrapped securely around my waist, guiding the horse with one hand. The warmth of his chest at my back, the rise and fall of his breath, grounded me—but it couldn't still my thoughts.

I'd taken over a creature's mind, not just glimpsed through its eyes, not just felt its emotions. I'd commanded it, told it to die.

The image flashed again—my voice thundering through its skull, the way it had jerked like a puppet, sword in its claw, eyes dull with submission. My stomach turned. *Was that really me? Was that what the Rift had made me?* I'd never felt power like that before. It had poured through me like fire in my veins.

Addictive. Terrifying. Necessary.

A cold sweat formed at the back of my neck, and I shifted slightly in the saddle.

"You alright?" Drake asked quietly behind me.

I hesitated. "I don't know."

He didn't push. His silence said he understood.

I stared at the horizon, trying to calm the thoughts that wouldn't stop spinning. You did what you had to. You saved him. But that didn't quiet the part of me that whispered: *What if next time, you lose control?*

A strange tension built in my chest—dread and wonder coiled together like a snake about to strike.

Winshire was behind me. I could feel it like a door closing, growing smaller with every hoofbeat. Papa. The inn. The familiar rhythm of a quiet, simple life. That chapter was over.

Ahead was something else entirely. I exhaled slowly, my fingers tightening around the saddle horn. I'd dreamed of seeing it my whole life—the glass towers, the paved streets, the shops full of silk and books. Now, I was riding toward it not as a visitor but as a fugitive with a power I didn't understand and a target on my back.

I wasn't ready. But I wasn't turning back.

"We're getting close," Drake said, his tone lightening slightly. I glanced up and saw both men adjusting their cloaks, their shining dragon-wing emblems gleaming faintly in the sunlight. I followed his gaze to the horizon, and my breath caught.

As we crested the final hill, the city unfurled before us like a storybook come to life. Castle City shimmered beneath the late afternoon sun, its spires glinting a pale blue against the horizon. Even from a distance, the scale of it stole my breath.

Massive stone walls cradled the city like a fortress, with iron gates tall enough to swallow entire wagons. Towers speared the sky, their tips aglow with gilded metal, banners snapping proudly in the breeze. But it wasn't the grandeur that struck me most—it was the movement.

The road leading into the city was thick with life. Merchants hauling carts stacked high with fruit and dried herbs, riders wrapped in patterned cloaks, families shouting to one another across the din. I'd never seen so many people in one place. It was overwhelming—beautiful and dizzying.

The smell hit me next. Warm bread. Manure. Roasting meat. Perfumed oil. Smoke. Life. A thousand different lives tangled together, heavy and cloying in the humid air.

Drake's hand on my hip tightened slightly.

"Stay close," he said low. It wasn't a suggestion.

I glanced up to see him pulling a pair of worn leather gloves over his hands, tugging the cuffs high enough to hide the faint shimmer of scales. He adjusted his cloak's collar, then pulled the brim of his hat low over his eyes.

Only then did I notice the way his entire posture had changed—shoulders tighter, jaw set hard, eyes scanning every face. I followed his gaze to a pair of guards stationed by the outer gates: gleaming black armor, golden lion sigils, halberds resting at attention.

My stomach dropped.

Felix rode slightly behind us, his hat pulled low as well. His usual chatter was gone. He was watching, too, watching everything. We weren't just travelers. Not here. We were prey.

I swallowed hard and sat up straighter in the saddle. My dusty dress clung to my legs, suddenly too plain, too rural, too Winshire. Every pair of eyes we passed seemed to glance our way.

Do they know? Can they tell what I am? What WE are?

The guards didn't stop us as we approached, but one of them gave Drake a second glance as we passed. Just a flicker of interest—but I saw Drake's hand drift near the dagger strapped under his cloak, just in case.

Drake swung off his horse with practiced ease and moved to my side. He reached up and gently eased me down from the saddle, his large hands steadying me like I weighed nothing at all. My boots met the ground, but my mind didn't follow—I was already spinning, reeling as I stared up at the colossal gates looming above us.

They were unlike anything I had ever seen. Cast iron and towering, each bar the width of my arm, the doors stood like sentinels between worlds—one I'd known all my life and one I'd only imagined in dreams. Every hinge, every bolt, every glinting crest told the story of a kingdom that had the power to endure and the pride to flaunt it.

Drake led the horses toward the stables while I stood, rooted to the spot, utterly enchanted. A stable boy emerged, and Drake handed him a small pouch of gold after a brief, hushed exchange. The boy nodded and disappeared with the horses around the back. When Drake returned, I barely noticed at first—I was still drinking in the details like the view could disappear at any moment. He approached, his visage catching the faintest glint of amusement as he took in my wide-eyed wonder.

"This is going to be a long day," he said with a quiet chuckle. "Come on," he placed a warm, guiding hand on my lower back and gently steered me toward a narrow doorway set beside the gate.

The moment we stepped through it, the world exploded.

Inside the gates, the city exploded around us. Shouts. Music. Bells ringing from some far tower. Children darted through legs, laughing as they chased a wooden hoop. Stall vendors barked prices in three different languages. Everything glinted—metal, teeth, jewelry, glass. It was chaos, but it had rhythm—a pulsing heartbeat. Castle City was alive.

And I'd never felt smaller.

I pressed my hands to the glass of a nearby shop window, unable to resist the display of gowns inside—gowns dyed in blues and violets so deep they looked conjured from the night sky. Across the road, the scent of freshly baked bread hit me like a spell, warm and golden and entirely too inviting.

Musicians strummed lutes and piped flutes at every corner, their melodies threading through the din like silk threads through armor. Children shrieked with laughter, dogs barked, and a merchant tossed a shimmering apple from one hand to the next, calling out prices as if he were reciting poetry.

I turned in a slow circle, overwhelmed. This wasn't just a city—it was a living tapestry woven with life and sweat and dreams. I had imagined Castle City so many times, but nothing could have prepared me for the reality of it. I wanted to take every detail and tuck it into a pocket, just to keep it with me forever.

A smile bloomed across my face before I even realized it. “I love it,” I whispered, half to myself. When I looked over at Drake, he was already watching me with an expression I couldn’t quite place. There was pride there and something quieter beneath it—something reverent. Like he’d waited years to see this exact look on my face.

“Enjoying yourself?” he asked, his voice low and warm.

“I love it,” I admitted breathlessly, spinning in place to take in as much as I could. The city was alive—chaotic and beautiful. For the first time in days, the weight in my chest lifted slightly.

But then, like a shadow slipping behind the light, a change crept in.

It started with Drake’s hand at my elbow. Not forceful, but firm. Anchoring. I glanced up and caught the flicker of tension in his eyes—how they scanned the crowd even as he smiled. Felix was doing the same; his head lowered, hat pulled low, shoulders tight with restraint.

My senses, once wide open with wonder, began to narrow. Beneath the laughter and music, I noticed things I hadn’t before: the hard glint of steel at a guard’s hip, the wary glances from cloaked strangers, the distant clang of a gate closing behind us.

“We should keep a low profile,” Drake murmured. The smile on his lips didn’t quite reach his eyes.

I nodded slowly, the magic of the moment still humming under my skin—but now tempered by something sharper. The city was beautiful. But it was not safe.

We turned abruptly into a side alley, and the charm of the city shifted into something entirely different. The golden glow of shopfronts gave way to dim, uneven light spilling from narrow windows. The cobblestones here were slick with grime, and the buildings leaned together as though conspiring to block out the sun. I felt the energy shift immediately. This wasn’t the Castle City of fables and dreams. This was the underbelly, a labyrinth of shadows and whispered deals.

A man dressed all in white, his too-long fingernails tapping idly on the pommel of a dagger, leaned against a crumbling wall. His feathered hat bobbed as he tipped it toward me.

"Evening, lass," he drawled, his eyes glinting with something I didn't care to name. I shrank closer to Drake, who shot the man a cold, warning glance. Felix was at my other side in an instant, and we moved quicker, weaving through the maze of alleys.

Every corner of this place seemed to tell a story. Scraps of colorful fabric hung limply from cracked windows, hints of a life that persisted despite the oppressive gloom. The air was thick with the scent of damp stone, rusted metal, and something faintly medicinal—likely from the apothecary we passed with its chipped sign swinging precariously in the breeze. I barely had time to take it all in before we stopped in front of a shop that looked more like it belonged to the alley than a respectable business.

The building stood alone, its weathered facade sagging against the walls of taller structures. The sign above the door read "Lea her Goods," the missing "T," giving it a vaguely ominous air. The boarded-up window to the left seemed deliberate as if the shop were trying to remain unnoticed.

"This... looks welcoming," I muttered under my breath, earning a quiet snort from Felix.

Drake stepped forward, pushing open the creaky door. A bell jingled overhead, and the sharp, unmistakable scent of tanned leather hit me like a wave. The small, dimly lit shop was cluttered, with piles of hides and scraps spilling over workbenches. The walls were lined with shelves holding boots, gloves, and satchels in varying states of completion.

"Ah, Captain! Doctor," a round man waddled out from a back-room, his thick spectacles magnifying his watery eyes to comical proportions. He wore a grease-stained undershirt beneath a leather apron that was patched in places as though it had seen decades of use. He beamed, his face creasing into a smile. "Who's the lass?"

"She's none of your concern," Drake said in a low, commanding tone. His shift into "Captain mode" was immediate and palpable. I felt a shiver run down my spine.

"Aye, aye! Don't know a damn thing about ya, Cap, other than your pant size," the old man laughed, revealing a missing tooth. He gestured to Drake's boots and gloves. "Made those beauties myself. What can I do for you today?" he asked, still grinning.

"Candelabra," Drake said, his voice firm but calm.

The man's expression shifted immediately, his smile falling into a serious neutrality. "Aye, aye, Captain," he shuffled back behind his desk and gestured for us to follow.

Drake and Felix motioned for me to come along, and we slipped past the counter into a narrow backroom. The space was barely large enough for the three of us. Shelves lined every wall, stacked with leather scraps, bolts of fabric, and tools. The air was close, and the faint smell permeated.

Without a word, Drake stepped to one of the shelves and ran his hand along the edge. His fingers moved deftly, tracing a series of symbols that glowed faintly red before disappearing. A soft click echoed through the room, and the shelf shifted inward with a low groan, revealing a hidden staircase spiraling downward into darkness.

I felt my eyes widen. "Woah."

Felix smirked, and even Drake's lips twitched into the faintest smile. "Stay close," he said, leading the way into the depths below. He conjured a sizable flame in his palm to light the way.

"What is this place?" I breathed, the question tumbling out before I could stop it. The shelf sealed with a final click. The noise echoed like a coffin lid closing. For a moment, I couldn't breathe. We were now sealed off from the leather shop above and left in damp, dimly lit quiet.

"This is the entrance to Riftreach," Drake said, his husky voice echoing softly off the moss-covered walls. His tone held pride, and the faint reverberation only added to its weight. "Our base."

A shiver rippled down my spine, the sound of him alone threatening to undo me. I forced my thoughts away from his closeness and focused instead on the surroundings, noting how each of our footsteps sent ripples of sound along the stone corridor. The tunnel walls curved overhead in perfect, arched symmetry, damp and alive with the scent of earth and the faint tang of something else... sulfur.

I wrinkled my nose. "Oh Gods, is your base in the sewers?" I couldn't help but jeer as I realized the dampness now seeping into my hole-ridden shoes.

Felix snorted from behind me. "What, did you think a rebellion would have a castle?"

"Don't worry," Drake added, glancing over his shoulder with a faint smile. "You'll see."

The path seemed endless, the descent carrying us deeper and deeper until my ears popped with the pressure. It felt as though we were walking forever downward into the bones of the earth itself—so far that by the time we stopped, the weight of the world could have been pressing over our heads. At last, we stopped at what seemed like a dead end. My heart sank, only for Felix to lift his hand. He made a slow motion from left to right, and the solid stone shimmered and dissolved into a wide doorway.

I expected another cramped tunnel.

Instead, it was the opposite.

On the other side was sheer magnificence. I lost my breath as I stepped forward, one trembling hand brushing the doorway for balance as the space swallowed me whole.

We stood at the mouth of a massive cavern—no, a *chasm*—that stretched upward farther than I could see. The ceiling was lost to shadow, but soft golden light spilled from glowing lanterns strung like constellations across the vast dome. A waterfall—no, a *geyser*—burst from the far cliff wall, its mist catching the light as it rained down into a lake that glowed faintly turquoise at its base.

Wooden walkways crisscrossed the open space like spider webs. Structures clung to the walls like swallows' nests—homes, shops, outposts, balconies—all suspended by magic or stubborn engineering. Vines and flowers bloomed in the impossible dark. I caught the scent of woodsmoke, wet stone, and something sweet... baking?

The hum of life rolled out in waves. Laughter echoed from above. Children with wings darted between hanging walkways. A horned man sat on a porch, carving something with intricate precision. Music drifted faintly from somewhere deeper in the city.

My knees nearly gave out.

I wasn't just looking at survival. This wasn't a hole in the ground where rebels cowered. This was... civilization. Defiant, hidden, thriving. A rebellion with roots. I blinked hard, eyes stinging. I didn't know if it was the mist or the weight of what I was seeing.

"This," Drake said quietly beside me, "is Riftreach."

Far across and high up the cavern wall, something caught my eye—and stole my breath. A massive wooden ship jutted out from the rock, sails unfurled as if caught mid-voyage. It perched there impossibly, halfway between air and stone, as though frozen in time. The wood gleamed with age and care, anchored into the cliff like it belonged to both sea and sky.

"Is that a ship? How did you even—"

Drake chuckled beside me. "It's been here since the beginning. A remnant of a forgotten age, repurposed into our council hall and chambers," his pride was palpable. I realized I was gripping his sleeve, my knuckles white with the force of my astonishment.

Embarrassed, I let go, glancing at him. He was already smiling.

"Welcome home," he said, softer this time.

He guided me onto one of the wooden walkways, and I found myself moving in a daze. The closer we got, the more details emerged. Each home clinging to the stone walls was alive with color and personality—hanging baskets overflowing with vines and flowers, wind chimes made from old metal scraps, stained-glass lanterns casting soft rainbows on the planks. The city didn't just exist—it expressed itself.

And its people... They were beautiful. A woman with translucent wings fluttering like silk passed us, nodding politely. A man with shimmering blue skin and gentle eyes offered a warm wave. Horned children chased one another in laughing loops across a nearby bridge. I waved back, awkward but genuine, and felt Drake's warmth at my side as he returned greetings by name.

It felt like stepping into a fable. A dream. But it was real. A city carved from hardship and still somehow—miraculously—still full of joy.

"Pinch me," I whispered to Drake, still overwhelmed.

"Where?" he murmured back, low and teasing. I flushed, laughing despite myself.

We passed a cluster of Riftborn who paused to watch us. Their gazes weren't cold but curious—assessing, even *hopeful.*

"Were they expecting us?" I asked, trying to shake off the weight of all the attention.

Drake's tone shifted. "We're not the only ones who know you're our last chance," his words sank deep. I looked around again—not just at the homes, or the flowers, or the lights—but at the people. Their eyes. The way they looked at me, not with fear or resentment… but with hope. They weren't just living. They were waiting. For something. For someone.

For me.

I swallowed hard and clenched my hands into fists. I let the air fill my lungs. If they believe I'm their last hope…

Then I will be.

We crossed the wooden footbridges, each creaking plank a testament to the craftsmanship of the Riftborn people, and wound our way higher and higher through the cavern. The pathway seemed to rise endlessly, giving me glimpses of the bustling city below. At last, we arrived at the doorway to the massive wooden ship embedded in the wall. The structure was breathtaking, an impossible feat of engineering and magic combined. It jutted outward from the rock as though it had crashed into the cavern mid-sail and somehow remained frozen in place. Its great bow seemed poised to tip forward, teetering over the abyss of the city below, but it held firm.

"This… this is incredible," I breathed, my voice barely above a whisper.

"It was the first Riftborn vessel to escape the King's fleet during the Change," Drake said, his voice tinged with reverence. "It carried our ancestors to safety, where they found this cavern and built Riftreach. The ship was their salvation, and so it remains—our meeting hall, our place of counsel."

Stationed on either side of the entrance to the ship's top deck stood two men, imposing and stoic. They both shared Drake's commanding presence, their tall and muscular frames clad in long woolen cloaks adorned with the same silver emblem I'd come to recognize. Though they lacked some of his rugged charm.

The man on the left had cropped black hair and a patch of shimmering blue scales that crawled up his throat, catching the golden light of the cavern. Another Dragonblood. The other bore tall, spiraling horns that jutted proudly from his forehead, polished to a sheen. Hellwrought. Their swords hung at their sides, the hilts glinting faintly in the lantern light, and they carried themselves with the kind of quiet authority that suggested they were Riftreach's equivalent of palace guards.

As we approached, both men inclined their heads slightly in acknowledgment.

"Captain," one of them greeted in a deep, steady voice.

Drake gave a curt nod, his back straightening as he walked past. The men stepped aside to let us through, their watchful eyes lingering on me momentarily before resuming their vigilant stance.

When we stepped onto the main deck of the ship, my breath hit my throat. It wasn't just a ship—it was a masterpiece of art and magic. The warm glow of lanterns illuminated every inch of the space, bathing it in a soft, golden light. Silken tapestries in vibrant shades of crimson and gold flowed gently in the cavern's breeze, strung from the towering masts. Golden statues stood sentinel along the deck, their craftsmanship so fine that they seemed almost alive.

Each piece was unique—one depicted a warrior mid-battle, their blade raised high, while another captured a serene Goddess with flowing robes. The largest statue, a towering winged Goddess in gleaming gold, commanded attention near the bow. Her sorrowful expression seemed to carry the weight of ages; her slender hand was raised and pointed solemnly toward the distant geyser cascading down the cavern wall. Around her feet sprawled an intricate garden, lush and vibrant despite the lack of sunlight. Planters brimming with flowering vines, herbs, and miniature trees turned the deck into a verdant oasis.

The floor was adorned with richly patterned rugs, their intricate designs hinting at distant cultures and histories, and benches carved from dark wood lined the edges, inviting quiet reflection. It felt like a royal garden from some ancient legend, but there was something more to it. This place carried the heart of a people who had poured their souls into it—a labor of love and survival.

Where the captain's quarters once stood, there now rose a grand wooden archway carved with ornate knot work that shimmered faintly with enchantments. The craftsmanship was extraordinary. Twin staircases flanked the archway, winding gracefully downward into the ship's depths.

"You must be Evandra!" I jumped as a loud, enthusiastic voice echoed through the space, and a man hurried toward me with outstretched arms. He was about my father's age but much leaner, with long, lanky limbs and an energy that seemed to fill the entire room. His attire was immaculate, far more refined than I expected for someone leading a rebellion. He wore a suede navy tailcoat adorned with golden buttons, striped pantaloons tucked neatly into polished leather boots, and a handlebar mustache that wiggled with every word he spoke.

Before I could react, he cupped my face in his long-fingered hands and planted several kisses on each cheek. His mustache tickled, and I fought the urge to pull away. Out of the corner of my eye, I noticed Drake's jaw feather as he clenched it tightly.

"Wonderful, marvelous, spectacular!" he declared. "Our Lady of the Hour, in the flesh!"

Felix leaned close, his voice dry at my shoulder. "Brace yourself. He does this to everyone. Even me."

Julian pulled back, blue eyes gleaming. "Drake, Felix, welcome home!"

Drake took a slight bow, his voice steady as he introduced the man. "Evandra, this is our Commander and fearless leader, Julian."

"It's a pleasure," I managed, dipping into a polite bow, but Julian stopped me with a gentle hand on my shoulder.

"No, no, no," he said warmly. "We bow to kings, not to one another. Here, we raise one another up!" His words carried weight even through the flourish. "Anything she desires," he added, his gaze sweeping the hall, "she shall have."

Anything she desires? *Even Drake?* I wondered mischievously but kept the thought to myself.

Julian clapped his hands together and gestured grandly toward the archway. "Come, Lady Evandra. Let me show you what we fight to protect."

Intrigued, I followed him into the dining hall that had replaced the captain's quarters and immediately gasped. The room was an opulent masterpiece. Ornate vases brimming with fresh, fragrant flowers lined the walls, and expensive-looking rugs covered the polished wooden floors. Original paintings hung between the wooden beams, each one depicting scenes of Riftborn history, their vivid colors illuminated by the flickering candlelight. It was breathtaking... and forbidden. Gods, half of this room could get someone executed. And yet... it was the most beautiful place I'd ever seen.

At the center of the room was a long table set with an elaborate feast, the likes of which I had never seen. Platters of colorful fruits, juicy roasted meats, and a dazzling array of cheeses and breads were arranged in an artistic display. The sight was enough to make my stomach growl audibly.

I gasped, unable to contain my excitement. "Are those grapes?! Oh my gosh, what is that?! And what's this cheese?!" I darted around the table, pointing at various delicacies like a child in a candy shop.

Julian chuckled indulgently while Drake and Felix exchanged amused glances.

"Please, sit," Julian urged, pulling out a chair for me. I didn't need to be told twice. I dove in, filling my plate with as many foods as it could hold. I bit into a cranberry-studded cheese, savoring the tangy sweetness, and nearly melted when I tried a slice of salty-sweet raw meat. The wine was like nothing I'd ever tasted, its rich, velvety flavor warming me.

I was mid-bite when someone cleared their throat. Startled, I looked up, cheeks full, to see Fen and a group of unfamiliar faces entering the room. My face flushed as I quickly swallowed, and Fen rolled her eyes dramatically.

"Starving already? We've barely put the saddle down." Fen drawled.

Julian's gaze sharpened. "Fen." One word, low but commanding. She quieted instantly.

Felix leaned toward me, stage-whispering, "That's him being polite."

"Allow me to introduce the rest of our court," Julian gestured to a younger man with dark skin and a lean, wiry build. Two small nubs protruded from his forehead, the remnants of horns that had clearly been clipped or filed down. Despite his imposing appearance, his smile was warm and inviting.

"This is Avod, our weapons master. He will be assisting you in choosing your weapons and training you to wield them."

"Pleasure to meet you, Avod," I said, nodding politely. He grinned, his sharp teeth glinting faintly in the candlelight as he found his seat at the table.

"And this," Julian continued, gesturing to a plump, curly-haired figure seated to Avod's left, "is Ness, our archivist. They are responsible for preserving Riftborn history and recovering texts destroyed during the Change. They've been studying Seers extensively and will help you hone your Rift."

I offered Ness a warm smile, feeling instantly at ease in their presence. Their round features, cherubic faces, and kind eyes were reminiscent of Felix, though they exuded an aura of quiet wisdom.

"It's an honor to meet you," I said sincerely.

"The honor is ours, Lady Evandra," Ness replied softly, adjusting their round spectacles. "You're already making history by being here." I could have sworn I heard a sigh come from Fen's direction.

Captain Julian stood at the head of the table, lifting his wine glass high. "I'd like to propose a toast," everyone raised their glasses, the glow of the lanterns casting a warm light over the gathering.

"First, to the squad I assigned to retrieve our most prized asset, Lady Evandra," there it was again—retrieve. My stomach turned, but Julian's sincere tone helped to soften the sting.

"Drake," he continued, "proving himself to be a passionate and level-headed captain time and time again."

Felix coughed. Drake glared at him, his jaw ticking.

"Felix, for being one of the few healers of the Rift we have left, selflessly using his power to heal and protect us. Fen, for riding through the night to warn us of the information leak, securing the safety of Riftreach," his gaze then settled on me, his sharp blue eyes softer now. "And lastly, Lady Evandra. She left her home, her family, and everything she'd ever known to help a group of strangers, purely on the chance she might save some lives. On her first day, she has a vision and saves us all. I think I speak for everyone when I say thank you, Lady," the group murmured their agreement as Julian's eyes lingered on mine, his genuine gratitude impossible to ignore. "To Lady Evandra."

"To Lady Evandra," the others echoed before sipping their wine, Drake's eyes simmering with something that almost looked like pride. Julian's warm smile broke into a grin. "Let's eat!"

The rest of the meal passed in a blur of chatter and indulgence. I peppered everyone with questions about Riftreach—how the plants grew, how the lights stayed so bright, how on earth an enormous ship ended up lodged in a cavern wall. Most of the answers were the same:

The Rift. It felt like magic I could barely comprehend, but that only made me more fascinated.

Julian finally dismissed the others, leaving just Drake, Felix, and me seated at the long table. The warmth of the feast faded as Julian's demeanor shifted, his expression growing stern and commanding, the air thickening with the weight of responsibility.

"I heard you encountered Vyrmin on the road?" Julian's sharp gaze pinned Drake and Felix, waiting for their response.

"They ambushed us in Finnegan's Pass, Commander," Felix said, the fatigue from days of healing etched into his face. "There were three of them. We each killed one."

"Eva included," Drake added, voice edged with pride.

Julian raised a brow, surprise flickering across his face. "She killed one?"

"She commanded it to impale itself on my sword, sir," Drake said.

A long pause. Julian nodded once, deliberate. "Remarkable. Dangerous. Both can serve us, if you learn control." His gaze softened briefly. "Your mother would be proud."

Felix leaned back, lips twitching. "Also mildly horrified."

Julian ignored him. "You'll have tutors, Evandra. Weapons. Records. Whatever you need."

"Please, call me Eva," I said quickly, stopping myself just short of bowing again.

Julian chuckled softly. "For now, rest. Rae! Ren!"

The door at the back of the room swung open, revealing two women who bore a striking resemblance to each other. One had shoulder-length raven hair, the other's flowed down her back, but their pointed, pale faces were identical, like statues carved from ivory.

"This is Rae and Ren. They've been appointed as your handmaidens for your duration here," Julian announced with a sweep of his hand.

I blinked at the two women as they beamed at me. "Oh, really, t-that's not necessary," I stammered, heat rising to my cheeks. Their smiles faltered into expressions of pure disappointment.

"Please, we insist," said the shorter-haired one, her voice warm but resolute.

"It's a great honor, Lady Eva," the longer-haired one added earnestly. "There aren't many opportunities for new things down here, and—if I may say so—you'll break our hearts if you say no."

"I—uh..." Their expectant smiles tugged at me, and I found myself nodding. "Okay."

The women instantly brightened, each looping an arm through mine. "First thing's first—we'll get you clean!" the shorter-haired one chirped.

"Yes, you're filthy, madam," the other added with a mischievous grin.

"Wait, you're going to bathe me?!" I exclaimed as they began to tug me toward the door, their enthusiasm utterly unrelenting.

I glanced back at Drake, my eyes pleading for rescue, only to see him stifling a laugh. Felix wasn't even bothering to hide his amusement. Their chuckles echoed behind me as the twins pulled me out of the dining hall and toward what I could only assume would be the most mortifying experience of my life.

My room was... breathtaking. I stood frozen in the doorway, barely able to believe that it was mine. Until now, opulence had been something from stories, something that existed for princesses and queens in faraway lands, not for a barmaid from an unknown village. Yet here it was, sprawling before me like something from a dream.

The room was situated at the bow of the ship, and a grand window framed the geyser and the shimmering city below. Thick, red velvet curtains hung on either side of the window so I could close out the world with a simple tug if I ever wanted, though I doubted I ever would.

At my feet lay ornate rugs so plush and detailed that they seemed like tapestries laid out to be walked on. Bookshelves lined the walls, crammed with volumes that looked older than the rebellion itself, their spines gleaming gold and silver in the candlelight.

And the bed. Gods, the bed. It was larger than any I'd ever seen, piled high with silken pillows and a quilt that looked like it was made from clouds. I bit my lip at the thought of what Drake and I could do in that bed. Images of his hands on me, his breath against my neck, flashed through my mind. Heat rose to my cheeks as I shook the thoughts away.

I darted toward the wardrobe, unable to contain my excitement. Throwing the doors open, I gasped at the sight of gowns more exquisite than anything I could have imagined. I couldn't even picture where someone would wear half these gowns—unless they were planning to seduce a king, duel him, and then seduce him again. I grinned, unable to stop myself.

I'm dreaming. I'm dreaming. I'm freaking dreaming.

The bath with Rae and Ren was even less weird than I thought. What I'd expected to be awkward had been anything but. With my injured shoulder, their help had been a blessing. They'd eased me into the tub—already filled with warm water, which I assumed was heated by one of their Rifts—and scrubbed the grime of the journey from my skin. Their gentle care as they washed my tangled hair and even massaged my sore muscles nearly moved me to tears. For a moment, it felt like having a mother again. I swallowed hard at the memory, both painful and comforting.

I glanced around the room again, trying to take it all in. The beauty of it, the luxury. It was fit for a queen, and yet it was mine. A simple girl from Winshire, whose entire wardrobe had once fit into a burlap sack. That thought made me wonder where it had gone until I spotted it sitting on a foot bench near the door. I rushed to it and pulled out my pillow. It was old, flat, and dusty, but I pressed my face into it and inhaled deeply. It smelled of home. Of the inn. Of Papa.

And that was when the tears came. They slipped silently at first, streaking down my cheeks, until a small sob escaped my throat. I didn't want to go back. I didn't regret leaving. But oh, how I missed him. I missed the strength of his hugs and how he would tell me stories by the fire. I imagined him finding the note, sitting alone at the hearth, tears in his eyes. Did he have anyone for comfort, or had the villagers turned their backs on him, believing I was a murderer?

The thought twisted my heart. I wiped my tears quickly, determined not to let my guilt consume me. I couldn't change the past, but I could change the future. For him. For my mother. For all of us.

I unpacked my things, carefully placing my battered hairbrush next to the beautiful mahogany one already on the vanity. The contrast was almost comical. I hung my threadbare dresses beside the gowns of queens, wondering if I'd ever dare wear them. Then I strode to the window, gazing out over the sparkling lights of Riftreach below.

It was mesmerizing—a new home, a new life, waiting for me to discover it. The view stretched endlessly, a reminder of how far I'd come—and how far I still had to go.

A sudden knock on my door startled me from my thoughts.

"Yes?" I called, my voice barely steady.

"Drake."

"Oh—" I quickly wiped the tears from my cheeks, hoping the redness wouldn't give me away. "Come in."

The door opened, and Drake entered hastily, closing it behind him. His gaze swept over me, and I felt the weight of his attention settle on every inch. For the first time since we'd met, I felt...presentable. Clean and cared for, with my thick red hair brushed and falling over my shoulders. The silk nightgown Ren and Rae had chosen clung to me in all the right ways, its hem cutting off mid-thigh, leaving little to the imagination.

I couldn't stop myself from looking at him in return. His tight, white tank stretched across his broad chest, revealing glints of crimson scales that caught the lantern light. He didn't need to hide them down here, and the confidence suited him. His long, clean hair flowed freely, and the ever-present leather pants hugged his form in a way that made me bite my lip.

"Good evening," he said softly, his smile warm. He stepped closer, but his expression changed as his sharp eyes caught the faint sheen of tears lingering in mine. Concern darkened his features instantly, his jaw tightening. "What's wrong?" His voice was low and edged with a protective anger. "Did someone hurt you?"

"No, no." I laughed softly, touched by his concern. "I found my pillow," I said, gesturing toward the bed.

He looked at me, confused. "Your pillow?"

I smiled at his perplexity and walked over to sit on the edge of my bed. "It still smells like home. Like the inn. Like my papa," my voice wavered slightly as I spoke. "It just... made me miss him."

Drake stayed silent for a moment, his presence grounding. "I get it," he said simply, his voice carrying a quiet sincerity.

"I'm okay," I added quickly, not wanting to seem ungrateful or weak. "I just... Thank you for checking on me."

"I wanted to show you something. Maybe help with the sore muscles after the ride here." He gestured for me to follow him.

I followed Drake through a narrow hall cut into the cavern wall, unsure if I was more sore from the journey or overwhelmed by everything I'd seen since arriving. My body ached in places I didn't know could ache. My excitement pulsed under my skin like a restless second heartbeat, and my mind buzzed with questions I wasn't ready to ask.

I'd expected a lecture. Or perhaps a short tour. I hadn't expected... *this.*

The bathhouse was empty when we entered. It was carved into the cavern wall, a quiet sanctuary veiled in steam and flickering light. Bioluminescent moss clung to the stone ceiling, casting the space in a soft, dreamlike glow. The main pool stretched wide and natural. The air smelled of minerals, lavender, and something older—clean and ancient. Smooth ledges lined the water, and baskets of mismatched towels and herbal soaps sat in corners.

Drake paused just inside the arched stone doorway, scanning the space. He glanced at me. "You first."

I raised a brow—then immediately questioned if it looked too confident. "Afraid I'll stare?"

His mouth twitched. "Afraid you'll enjoy it." Gods. He was impossible.

My heart was thudding far too fast as I stepped behind one of the stone dividers. My hands trembled just slightly as I peeled off my bathrobe and the nightgown—slowly, deliberately, *hoping* I looked confident. The fabric whispered down my skin, and I tried to breathe past the thrum in my chest.

It's just a bath, I told myself. *You've seen him shirtless. You've touched him. You've had his fingers inside you.*

But he hadn't seen *me*—not fully. Not like this. Vulnerable. Bare. The real kind of bare.

Still, I stepped into the water without flinching, letting the warmth rise to my shoulders. I exhaled as I sank in, tilting my head back, hair floating like a question waiting to be answered. The heat on my sore muscles felt divine, like like a hundred knots being untied at once.

Then I heard footsteps. His.

I turned.

He stripped without ceremony, as if being naked was no more notable than breathing. His shirt was gone in a blink—fine, I'd seen that much before—but when his trousers slid low over his hips, my brain started short-circuiting.

I hadn't *meant* to look. Truly. But there was a moment—just one—when the mist parted, and I *did.* Gods, I looked. And then I *looked harder.*

He was... impressive. Thick, long, and hanging heavy between his thighs with the kind of quiet confidence that suggested he had *never* once worried about living up to expectation. My mouth went dry.

No one had warned me that desire could feel like panic. Like *how* was that going to *fit*? Was this a dragon thing? A warrior thing? A *him* thing?

The worst part? He didn't even seem aware of the devastation he caused just by existing. Calm. Collected. Beautifully carved like a war God and *fully aware* of his power—or worse, *not* aware, which was somehow even hotter.

I forced my gaze away so fast I nearly gave myself whiplash, cheeks blazing. Focus on the water. Focus on literally anything else.

But the image was already seared behind my eyes.

And when he slid into the pool, all clean lines and slow strength, I knew one thing with absolute certainty:

I was in so much trouble.

He slid into the water without breaking eye contact. Across from me. Just far enough to be polite. Just close enough that I could cross the pool in three strides and—

Gods. My skin felt too tight.

"Cozy," I said, voice slightly higher than intended. I forced a smile and an awkward giggle.

He huffed a laugh. "You think this is safe?"

"No," I said. "But it feels good." We sank into silence. But not comfort.

My knee breached the surface, and his eyes tracked it like a predator. I stretched, hoping it looked natural—but I was *painfully* aware of how my breasts lifted just above the waterline. His gaze lingered. Controlled. Starved.

I leaned my head against the stone edge of the pool, trying not to squirm.

"You're watching me."

"You want me to."

"Maybe," I said, trying to sound casual. "Would that be so bad?"

Drake's jaw ticked. He looked like a man holding back a dam with nothing but his spine.

"We're already close," I said. "You know that."

His voice was low. "Too close."

I drifted closer. The water lapped around me, warmth soaking into my limbs. My body wanted this. Gods, it wanted *him.* But my stomach fluttered with nerves, and my fingers fidgeted just beneath the surface. What if I wasn't enough? What if—

"You could stop me," I said, breath catching. "If I came over there. You could push me away."

He swallowed. "Don't test me."

"I'm not," I said—*but I kind of was.* I bit my lip.

"Why do you always do that?" I asked quietly. "Pull away right when it's about to be good. You act like you don't care. Like none of this affects you."

"I care," he said, low and rough. "That's the damn problem." He stared at me like I was a storm he'd already decided to drown in. "Because I want too much," he said. My breath caught. "I want to take and not stop. I want to mark you where no one else will see. I want to bury myself in you so deep the Rift forgets where I end and you begin."

My whole body flushed. A coil of heat wound low in my belly—and tightened.

I moved closer. Still space between us. Still time to retreat. But I didn't.

"You think I wouldn't let you?"

His jaw clenched. "If I touch you again, I won't let go."

I stared at him. At the man who refused to say what we were, but still looked at me like I was everything.

"You've already touched me," I whispered. "You've already taken me." He opened his eyes. Slow. Lethal.

"I know."

"This is cruel, Drake."

"You think I don't know that?"

"I think..." I hesitated, pulse fluttering like a rabbit's. "I think you want me to snap first. So you don't have to break your precious self-control."

"I'm trying to *protect you*," he growled.

"From what?"

"From *me*."

I should've been afraid. But all I felt was want.

"Then why do you look at me like I'm the thing that could end you?"

His hand twitched on the stone. White-knuckled.

I reached forward, slowly, and touched his thigh under the water. Just above the knee. My hand shook—but only a little. His skin was hot, tight with tension. He didn't flinch. But every muscle in his body *locked.*

"You want me."

His voice cracked. "Eva—"

"I'm not asking." I leaned in, my mouth brushing the shell of his ear.

"I feel you when you're not in the room. I ache when you're near. And you keep pretending, but I know what I feel."

The space between us thrummed. His breath ragged. My lips close to his cheek. My hand drifting higher.

Then—he turned. Our mouths brushed. Not a kiss. Not quite. But it stole my breath.

"I want you," I breathed. "But I won't beg."

He looked at me like he was already shattered.

Then he whispered, "Don't."

I blinked. "Don't what?"

"Don't stop." For a heartbeat, neither of us moved.

Then he did.

Drake surged forward, his control breaking like a snapped tether. One hand found the back of my neck—firm, commanding. The other slid down my bare back beneath the water, pulling me into his lap in one smooth, hungry motion.

Chapter Nineteen

Eldrake

It hit me in the chest like a blade when I saw her slipping beneath the surface—bare, confident, fucking radiant. Steam coiled around her like a shroud, and she didn't flinch. Didn't hide.

She let me watch. And Gods help me, I did.

I stood at the edge of the pool longer than I should've, pretending I wasn't staring. Pretending I wasn't burning.

Her back was to me, but I could see the slope of her waist, the line of her spine, the way her hips moved through the water as she sank lower, arms resting on the lip of the stone like she owned it.

Like she owned *me*.

My clothes felt like they were choking me. I stripped silently, jaw tight, folding each piece with military precision. Like order could save me.

It wouldn't.

I stepped into the water. Heat licked up my legs, then higher. Too hot. Not hot enough. She turned to face me. *Gods.*

Her hair clung to her shoulders, her red curls wet and wild. Her breasts rose above the surface with every breath. Her lips curved—not mocking. Inviting. And then her gaze dropped. Just for a second.

Her eyes flicked lower—*there*—and widened. She looked away fast, like the steam might save her, like maybe I hadn't noticed.

I had.

My cock twitched in response, heavy and already aching, and I bit back a groan. Her blush bloomed like wildfire across her cheeks, and I almost smiled—almost. But it wasn't funny. It was *devastating*. Because she was looking at me like I was something to want. Something worth wanting, and I didn't know if I could survive that.

I sat across from her. The space between us should've felt safe. It didn't. The Rift inside me thrummed like a wire pulled too tight. My magic pulsed in time with hers—I could *feel* her. Even across the water. Even without touching.

She smiled. Slow. Dangerous. "You're watching me."

"You want me to," I said, before I could stop myself.

"Would that be so bad?" Her voice was silk wrapped around something sharper. Something *hungry*. She drifted closer, gliding through the water like it belonged to her. Every ripple, every shift of her body—a provocation.

I didn't move. Couldn't.

She stopped just a few feet away. My heart pounded like I was walking into battle. Except I wanted to lose.

"You could stop me," she said, voice low. "If I came over there." My hands clenched against the stone.

"Don't test me," I said, but it came out too soft. Too close to begging. She came closer.

The distance between us was nothing now. A few breaths. A single decision. I held still. If I moved, I'd reach for her. If I spoke, I'd confess everything. She kept going. Relentless. Beautiful.

She reached out and touched my thigh under the water. Just above the knee. It was the gentlest thing in the world. Bare skin to bare skin. No pressure. No expectation. And it nearly destroyed me. My entire body went rigid. Every muscle screamed to move—toward her, into her, around her.

Then she leaned in. Her mouth brushed my ear.

"I ache for you," she whispered. "And I know you feel it too."

I clenched my eyes shut. Her fingers moved slightly. Higher. Not enough. Too much.

"I want you," she breathed. "But I won't beg." I cracked.

Completely.

I turned my head. Our mouths brushed—barely. A tremor. A spark. My voice came out like gravel.

"Don't."

She froze.

"Don't what?" she whispered.

I looked her in the eye, hand twitching toward her but not touching. Not yet.

"Don't stop."

One hand found the back of her neck—firm, commanding. The other slid down her bare back under the water, anchoring her as I pulled her into my lap in a single, hungry movement.

She came willingly. Eagerly. Her thighs parted, wrapped around my waist. Her arms curled around my shoulders. Her breasts pressed to my chest like they belonged there, like they were *made* for this contact. Her skin was hot silk, slick and electric.

I was already so far gone, I didn't know how to come back. I crushed my mouth to hers, desperate, deep. She kissed me like she was starving, and Gods, I fed her everything I had.

She shifted against me, hips gliding forward in the water, bare heat pressed to hardness with nothing between us. Her moan vibrated straight down my spine.

My hand slid lower, dragging across the curve of her ass, anchoring her tighter to me. Her nails bit into my shoulders. I hissed. She bit my bottom lip. I growled.

I broke the kiss only to trail my mouth down her neck, tasting salt and steam and skin. Her head tilted back, lips parted, eyes half-lidded and dazed.

"Drake," she breathed, the sound like prayer.

I pushed her back against the stone, my hands braced beside her shoulders, our bodies locked beneath the water. Her legs stayed around me, tightening. She rolled her hips with slow, devastating purpose.

I was shaking.

Literally shaking.

She kissed me again—slower this time, deeper, tongue flicking just enough to make my vision blur. I slid one hand up between her breasts, to the column of her throat, fingers spread against her pulse. She was *racing*. Her magic buzzed beneath her skin, tangling with mine.

Then I felt it. *Snap.*

Like a thread had been tugged taut between us—subtle, then seismic. A shift in the room. In the Rift.

Ours.

That was the only word I could find. Ours.

My breath hitched. My body *froze*. Eva stilled, sensing it too. Her eyes opened. Searching.

"What is it?" she asked, voice soft, still dazed. I didn't answer. I looked at her—bare, flushed, water dripping down her collarbone—and I knew if I kept going, if I sank into her now, it would be forever.

Not just pleasure. Not just release.

Bond.

Claim.

Fate.

And Gods help me, I wanted it. I wanted it so bad I ached. But— "I can't," I said, voice hoarse.

Eva blinked. "What?"

I pulled back slightly, hands still on her hips. Not letting go. Just holding her like she might vanish.

"Not like this," I said. "Not... not just because we're alone. Or because we *can*. I want to take you to dinner, Eva. I want to make you laugh. I want to walk into this with you on purpose."

She stared at me, breathless. Her lips were kiss-swollen. Her thighs were still around my waist.

"I want to fuck you," I said, low and raw. "*Gods,* I do. But not before you know this means everything to me."

Silence.

Then, a shaky breath escaped her lips.

"I was afraid you were going to say you didn't want me," she whispered.

I rested my forehead against hers.

"I want you more than I've ever wanted anything in my life."

Her hands curled tighter into my shoulders.

"But I want all of you," I said. "Not just your body. Not just tonight."

Her thick lashes fluttered. She nodded. I kissed her again—soft this time. Just once. Just enough to promise *later.* Then I lifted her from my lap, hands steady, heart absolutely fucking shattered with restraint, and set her gently back on her side of the pool.

We stayed there, naked, panting, aching.

Fuck. Fuck. Fuck.

I stormed down the corridor outside the bathhouse, jaw locked, breath ragged, hands twitching like they were searching for her in the air.

Which—they were. Gods help me.

I still felt her.

Not just remembered—*felt.* Like her touch had seeped beneath my skin and rewired everything. My chest burned. My limbs trembled. My magic was humming beneath the surface like a live wire.

No—*not* humming. *Pulling.*

My body wanted to turn around. Wanted to go back. Not for another kiss. Not for another moan.

For *her.*

This isn't normal. This isn't—

I veered into a dark corridor and slammed my back against the stone, fists clenched at my sides. The wall didn't ground me. Nothing did.

That wasn't just desire in that water.

It *snapped.*

Something snapped.

My magic had surged the moment she came apart in my arms—when her body arched, when her breath hitched in my ear. It wasn't just the way she held me. It was the way the world had gone *quiet.* Like the Rift *stopped to watch.*

No. No, it couldn't be.

Bonds like that—Riftbonds—they were myths. Ancient. Dangerous. Gone. They didn't happen anymore.

I dug my nails into my palm, breathing hard. *It wasn't a bond. I'm just obsessed. That's all this is. Just lust. Just—*

But my magic had *recognized* her. The first time I even saw her, I felt it. Reached for her like it already knew her name. And her magic had answered.

Gods.

I wanted to fuck her.

I wanted to worship her.

I wanted to lose myself in her so completely there wouldn't be a *me* left to mourn. And the worst part? I didn't know if I even cared anymore. I bit down on the inside of my cheek until I tasted blood. Still not enough.

She'd smiled at me like I was hers. Touched me like she knew I wouldn't stop her. Kissed me like she *belonged* to me. And maybe—just maybe—she did.

No.

I couldn't think like that. Couldn't *want* like that. That kind of bond *consumes.* It ruins. It *kills.* And I'd already killed enough for one lifetime.

I pressed my palm flat to the wall, trying to hold onto something. Anything. But all I could feel was her. Her voice in my ear. Her thighs around my hips. The sweet, fucking *madness* of her.

'I want to date you first.'

What kind of lunatic says that while fighting off a full-blown magical hard-on and *breaking reality* with a kiss?

I was going to burn for this. And not just from want. From the *truth*. This wasn't going away.

I tried the battlefield trick—imagining carnage. Vyrmin corpses. Torn flesh. Stinking hot guts.

Nothing.

I clenched my jaw harder and conjured Fen's voice:

"Well, well. Commander 'Control' just left the bathhouse looking like he got edged by destiny."

That did it. Barely.

I forced my pulse to slow, willed my cock to *fucking behave*, and straightened.

No more improvising. I needed a plan. Something structured. Controlled.

Take her to dinner. Woo her like a rational adult. Then maybe ruin her in a bed with a door and at least one candle lit.

I adjusted myself—because *fuck*—and stalked down the hall like a man on a mission. Noble. Official. Important. I marched through the ship, already rehearsing the speech in my head. For the benefit of the cause. A personal mission of utmost importance. See to her every need. Yes. That sounded official. Noble. I made my way up the stairs, crossed the deck, passed through the dining hall, and burst straight into Julian's chambers without knocking.

Julian nearly launched out of his chair, the book in his hand flying like a startled bird. "Drake! Saints preserve us, must you *always* enter like the Angel of Death kicking in the gates? A knock, a cough, even a delicate tap—any of those would suffice!"

"No time for formalities, Commander." I gave a hasty bow and launched into my well-prepared spiel. "With all due respect, I demand to be reassigned. Effective immediately, my sole mission should be as Lady Evandra's personal watchdog and protector. As our most valuable ass, she is crucial to the success of the Uprising. Someone of my particular skill set guarding her at all times is not only prudent—it's necessary."

Julian blinked. "Did you mean *asset*?"

"That's what I said."

Julian leaned back in his chair, long limbs folding like a marionette at rest. He steepled his fingers, lips quirking. "So let me see if I understand: you wish to abandon your squad—your finely tuned, well-oiled squad—to play nursemaid to our Seer? To *hover* about her skirts like a lovesick mastiff? That's the proposition?"

I paused. "Yes."

He tapped his chin, eyes sparkling with mischief. "Remarkable. I always assumed it would be Fen who snapped first, not you."

I glared.

Julian chuckled, waving a hand. "Relax, Captain, relax. You've made a sound argument. Aberdeen would give his crown to see her captured, or worse, and you *do* make an impressive wall of muscle. Intimidating. Broody." His expression sharpened. "And you're right: we cannot afford to lose her. Not to him. Not to anyone."

I straightened. "So you'll approve it?"

He ignored me, twirling his mustache thoughtfully before speaking again. "Fine. You're reassigned. From Squad Captain to... Captain of Lady Evandra." My heart stuttered, but I kept my face neutral.

"Thank you, Commander. I believe this is the wisest decision for the movement." I bowed lower this time, suppressing the grin tugging at my lips.

"Yeah, yeah," he waved dismissively, already turning back to his book. "And for fuck's sake, knock next time before I die of fright."

I exited like a man on a mission. Once alone in the hallway, I pumped my fist in triumph and tried not to look like I was skipping. Captain of Lady Evandra. Gods, that had a ring to it.

Now, the hard part: *telling Felix and Fen.*

I didn't find them right away. I wasn't sure what I would've said anyway. *Hey, I accidentally bonded myself to a Goddess in a bath—want to grab a drink?*

I wandered for a couple hours instead, letting my pulse finally settle, letting my head catch up to my body.

But the Rift still hummed under my skin.

There was something different in me now. Subtle, but real. A pressure in my chest. A presence. Like I was no longer entirely alone inside my own mind.

Like a part of her had come with me. Gods, I was so far gone.

The smell hit me before I reached the end of the hall—garlic, onions, and something sweet beneath it. Apples. Cinnamon.

Gods. She was trying to kill me.

I slowed at the kitchen doorway, leaning my shoulder against the frame like I had any intention of walking away. Like I wasn't already burning from the memory of her wet skin pressed against mine. Like I hadn't spent the last two hours spiraling through a cold shower, a sparring dummy, and three near-bond-induced panic attacks.

Eva stood at the counter, sleeves pushed up, hair knotted high and already unraveling. She stirred something in a battered pan like the fate of the world depended on it.

I should've walked. Should've turned around the second the Rift pulsed in my chest the moment I smelled her. Instead I watched. Like an idiot. Like a man addicted.

There was flour dusted along her cheekbone. A smudge of jam on her wrist. Her mouth moved as she muttered to herself—soft, focused, unbothered by the way my entire body was short-circuiting.

The Rift stirred again—low, steady, *waiting*. Not aggressive. Not demanding. Just a tether. A heartbeat syncing with mine like it belonged there.

I gritted my teeth. *It's not a bond.* It's proximity. Shared trauma. Bathhouse stupidity. Any man would feel like this. Any man would imagine her stirring soup in *his* kitchen. Wearing one of *his* shirts with nothing underneath. Looking at him like she did in the water.

She turned slightly, slicing into a pear with slow, confident strokes. And something twisted deep in my chest.

That image hit me again—her barefoot, humming, sunlight on her skin. Our kitchen. Her laughter. A kiss at the back of her neck as I passed by. I squeezed my eyes shut, willing it away. *No.* I didn't get a future like that. And she—she deserved more than a damaged man that doesn't even know how to love.

The Rift pulsed sharper this time. Like it knew I was lying to myself.

I cleared my throat. She jumped slightly and turned. Her eyes lit up. *Fuck.*

"Didn't hear you sneak up," she said, smiling. "You want some?"

My mouth opened to say no. What came out was, "What is it?"

"Apple-garlic tarts," she said proudly. "It's a Winshire thing. They look ugly but taste divine. Like me."

I snorted before I could stop myself. *She's Lethal.*

I stepped forward. She held one out. Our fingers brushed—barely—and my whole arm went tense from the contact.

The tart was warm. Flaky. Savory-sweet and somehow nostalgic in a way that gutted me. Eva leaned beside me, waiting for my verdict, eyes bright. I didn't say anything. Just took another bite and groaned. Her grin widened, smug as hell. Then she licked sugar off her thumb.

And I almost dropped the Godsdamned plate.

"I used to make these with my mom," she said softly. "Ya' know. Before." I nodded. Didn't trust my voice. "Before" was enough.

"I like cooking," she went on. "Makes me feel like I'm in control of something. Like I can take chaos and fire and make something incredible."

I glanced at her. Did she know she was talking about me?

"You're good at it," I said.

"I'm good at chaos, too," she smirked. "But this smells better."

I huffed a laugh. Then silence settled heavy in my throat. Warmth spread across my skin. I set the plate down. Too loud.

"I'll come get you before training tomorrow. I'll... show you around Riftreach," I managed. I looked down at her. *Gods,* that was a mistake.

She was still smiling. Still radiant. Still a little flour-dusted and wild. Still everything I wanted to devour and everything I don't deserve.

"I'll look forward to it," she said. Then—teasing—"Unless you disappear on me again. Should I bring tarts to keep you from bolting this time?"

My throat worked. "It wasn't you," I lied. "Just... too hot in there."

She raised a brow. "That a compliment?"

I didn't respond. Just turned and left, fast, like something might snap if I stayed another second.

Because it might.

The next day I woke before the lanterns lit, practically buzzing with anticipation.

I'm going to keep it together. I told myself.

I bathed, brushed my hair, and rubbed my mother's spice salve into my scales—a generations-old recipe to keep them smooth and flexible. The scent of honey, beeswax, and clove clung to my skin. I pulled on my best leathers and pinned my wing emblem at my breast. I looked good.

Confident. Ready.

By the time I reached her door, I was standing at perfect attention, heart pounding. The door creaked open, and my composure crumbled. My jaw slackened before I could stop it. She stood there, wearing the standard-issue leathers, yet looking anything but standard. Good Gods, who in the rebellion thought that outfit was appropriate?

Her red hair was down, cascading in waves around her shoulders and framing her striking face. But it was her figure that knocked the wind out of me. The leather corset-style top hugged her in all the right places, cinching at her waist and emphasizing her generous curves. The laces pulled snugly across her chest, pressing her breasts together just enough to be a distraction. The outfit flared out slightly at the hips before giving way to tight leather pants that clung to her thick thighs like a second skin. The pants disappeared into tall, knee-high boots that looked devastatingly practical.

Focus, Drake. Gods.

"You... you look..." *Say something coherent, idiot!*

She shifted. "Ugh, it's too much, isn't it? I told the girls—"

"No!" I blurted too fast. "No. It's good. You look good. It's, uh... practical," *Great. Flawless delivery, really.*

Her cheeks flushed faintly, and she fidgeted with the laces on her top. "You're sure? I feel like I might pop out of this thing if I move too fast."

Don't imagine that. Do not imagine that.

"Trust me. It's functional. And... flattering." I held out my elbow. "Shall we?"

She looped her arm through mine, her touch light and warm. "We shall! You look dashing, by the way,"

I nearly blushed from the simple compliment. Gods help me; I was falling for her harder than I'd ever fallen for anyone. And today, I'd get to show her the world I'd sworn to protect—and hopefully the place where she'd finally belong.

"Alright," I said, eager to distract myself before my thoughts strayed further. "First stop is Avod's workshop. He'll get you fitted with some weapons. Then, we'll visit Ness to learn more about Seers and see if they've uncovered anything useful about your abilities. After that, we'll swing by Henry's for a proper cloak and hat. And finally, dinner tonight."

I couldn't help the grin spreading across my face as I outlined our plans. Her eyes lit up in response, and I caught her looking at me with a soft, admiring smile.

"What?" I asked, genuinely curious.

"You're just so... passionate," she said, her voice warm. "Whenever you talk about something that matters to you, it's like your whole face lights up. It's... refreshing."

I swallowed, caught off guard by her words. No one has ever took note of me that closely before. Before I could respond, she tilted her head, her expression turning curious. "Can I ask you something?"

"Of course."

She nodded toward my chest. "What's the silver crest you always wear?"

I glanced down at the pin on my cloak and fondled it absently. "Oh, this? It's my Wing Pin. It dates back to the earliest days of the Uprising. Back then, it was a way to identify each other. If someone recognized the pin, they knew they could approach us for asylum," my voice softened as I spoke, memories of the rebellion's struggles stirring in my chest. "Now, it's more of a tradition than anything, but it still carries the weight of what we stand for."

She studied it with quiet admiration. "I see... It's beautiful."

We stepped carefully across the swaying boardwalks suspended high above the cavern floor. Each creak of the planks echoed into the expanse below. I could feel Eva's hesitation through the light grip she maintained on my arm. Her steps were tentative, and her wide eyes darted down to the abyss below us. I had walked these paths so often that the movement of the bridges was as natural to me as breathing, but for someone new to Riftreach, I imagined it was nerve-wracking.

The citizens of Riftreach began to notice us, their curious gazes lingering on Eva and, more specifically, on her arm looped with mine. I could almost hear the whispers. Drake, the lonely grump... with her? Sure, I'd been seen with women before, but they never lingered beyond a night, and I certainly never escorted any of them through the city like this. It stirred something strange in my chest—a mix of pride and protectiveness.

We reached the rocky outcropping where Avod's forge stood, carved into the jagged stone and glowing with the orange light of the roaring flames within. The sharp clang of metal rang out as we approached. I spotted Avod, his broad back turned to us, hammering with precision on the glowing blade laid across his anvil. The heat from the forge warped the air around him.

Avod and I had been through hell together—literally, in some cases. We'd been young scouts together, causing trouble and getting into more than our fair share of fights. Now, though, things were different. The stumps where his proud horns had once stood were a stark reminder of the time he'd spent as a prisoner of Aberdeen before his escape. Those bastards had taken more than just his horns; they'd taken pieces of his soul. He never spoke of what happened, but his silence said enough.

A grin spread across my face, and I couldn't resist. "Ay, tits for brains." Avod froze mid-swing and slowly turned, fixing me with a mock glare from the corner of his eye. Then, with zero hesitation, he hurled his hammer at me. I dodged easily, laughing as it clanged harmlessly against the stone.

"You're the fool, troll fucker!" he barked back, grinning as wide as I was. We closed the distance and pulled each other into a fierce hug, the kind you only share with someone who's saved your life more times than you can count.

"I missed you, brother," he said, clapping my back.

"Missed you too." I stepped back and gestured toward Eva. "Avod, meet Lady Evandra. She needs to be armed—and you're the only one I trust to do it right."

Avod turned to her, his straight-toothed grin lighting up his rugged face. "My Lady, welcome," his voice carried a warmth that disarmed most people. I caught the subtle way his eyes flicked to mine, his eyebrows lifting mischievously. He knew me and my fondness for redheads too well.

Eva, ever the embodiment of humility, bowed slightly. "Right, I saw you at dinner yesterday. It's a pleasure to see you again, Avod." I nearly choked. She bowed-- to a blacksmith. This woman didn't have a pretentious bone in her body. I loved that about her.

Avod, clearly charmed, recovered quickly. "And you've got good manners, too. I like her," he looked at me again, the glint in his eye now outright teasing.

I cleared my throat, suppressing a grin. "Eva needs blades. Can you help her?"

"I think I can manage," Avod said, smirking. "What's your style, Lady? Long sword? Rapier? Cutlass?"

She hesitated, her brow furrowing in thought. "I... uh... I'm pretty good with butcher knives?"

Avod and I exchanged a look before he stifled a laugh. "Alright, let's start small," he walked over to a rack and retrieved two matching daggers. They were utilitarian—simple leather-wrapped hilts and sharp, polished steel blades. No frills, but they were deadly and effective.

"Here," he said, flipping the daggers expertly and offering the hilts to her. "Try these."

Eva took them gingerly, testing their weight and balance. She sliced the air a few times, mimicking the motions of chopping vegetables. I couldn't hide my grin.

Avod arched another eyebrow at me. "She's a natural."

"She'll need proper training," I said, still watching her with amusement. "But these will do for now."

Avod fetched two thigh sheaths and knelt to strap them on. He was all business, but the sight of his hands brushing her thighs made my blood stir. I clenched my fists at my sides, forcing myself to relax. He's my friend. Calm down, Dragonblood.

"All set," Avod said, standing and giving me an apologetic glance after catching sight of my flexing jaw.

"Thank you, friend." I clapped his shoulder, letting him know we were good. As we turned to leave, I caught the subtle smile playing on Eva's lips as she tested the daggers. I couldn't help but think how natural she looked with blades strapped to her thighs.

"Oh, one more thing." Avod shifted on his feet, his usual confidence giving way to a rare flicker of insecurity. "Uh, how's Fen?" His voice was careful, almost too casual.

I raised a brow at him. "How should I know?" I replied.

"Right," he nodded curtly, his gaze dropping to the ground. "Thanks. Have a good day, you two."

"Thank you!" Eva chimed in as she admired the weapons now strapped to her thighs. She took a playful step back and struck what she must have thought was an intimidating pose. "Do I look like an assassin?" she teased, tilting her chin and flashing a mischievous grin.

I chuckled, shaking my head. "No, because I could do this." In one smooth motion, I pinned one of her hands behind her back, her startled gasp filling the air. "And this," I murmured as I swept her legs out from under her, catching her weight effortlessly before she could hit the ground. "And this," my hand slid gently to her throat, my fingers brushing against the rapid pulse at her jugular. I loomed over her, my face mere inches from hers. Her wide eyes locked onto mine, and I saw it —a spark of surprise mingled with unmistakable desire.

I wanted to close the gap, to taste those lips that were so temptingly close once again, but I restrained myself. I'm her Captain. The thought hammered against my skull, a poor defense against the heat of the moment.

"Don't worry... we'll practice," I said, my voice low and steady as I eased her upright, releasing her. Her shock lingered; her lips parted as if she wanted to say something but couldn't quite find the words.

I cursed myself silently. *You've really gone and fucked it up now.* But before I could spiral further, she looped her arm through mine once again, a small smile playing on her lips. I couldn't help but grin back.

"Drake," she said suddenly, her voice light, almost teasing. "I think Avod likes Fen." I blinked, caught off guard.

"Why would you think that?"

"Why else would he ask about her?" She looked up at me from beneath her lashes, her grin sly.

I frowned, genuinely puzzled. "Yeah, I guess. But who would like Fen?" The thought baffled me, and I quickly dismissed it, shaking my head. We strolled leisurely through the winding paths of Riftreach. Eva's face lit up with every discovery, her wonder contagious. Little winged children darted past us, their laughter ringing through the cavern. She stopped to admire a cozy cafe on the corner and then a bookshop nestled between two homes. I watched her as much as I watched the city, fascinated by her unbridled curiosity.

"What's that?" she asked, pointing to a glowing lantern overhead.

"A lantern," I said flatly, unable to hide my smirk.

"Well, yeah," she huffed, "but how does it stay lit?"

"One of our Riftborn can project daylight. She lights them in the mornings and puts them out at night."

"Wow," her eyes widened, the gears in her mind visibly turning. "What about that?" She gestured to a vine climbing the side of a building.

"Chasm creeper. Not magical, just a plant." She continued pointing at things—flowers, signs, even a peculiar set of stairs carved into the rock—and each time, I answered patiently. Her insatiable curiosity might have annoyed anyone else, but I found it... endearing. Besides, I couldn't trust anyone else to show her around. Someone less charmed by her might have been more of a dick about her incessant questioning.

We stopped at a self-watering herb garden, Eva marveling at the way droplets cascaded perfectly over the vibrant greenery. A lavender-skinned woman approached us hesitantly, her hands wringing the fabric of her dress.

"H-hello," the woman stammered, bowing deeply. Her dark, inky hair spilled forward like a curtain. "I'm so sorry to disturb you, Lady." She hesitated, her voice trembling. "My husband is missing. He went on a scouting mission last week and hasn't returned. His name is Ronnie. Can you... see him?"

Eva's face fell, her empathy immediate. "Oh, I-I'm so sorry to hear that." she said softly, glancing at me for guidance.

"She wants you to use your Rift," I explained gently.

Eva swallowed hard, taking the woman's trembling hands in hers. "I'll try," she promised. However, doubt churned in her stomach like a storm. She'd never done this on purpose—never summoned the Rift by will alone. Not without fear, not without chaos. And certainly not in front of an audience.

She closed her eyes, forcing her breath to steady. "Come on. Please work," she whispered. An invisible breeze stirred her hair as if the Rift itself was answering.

The lavender woman gasped as Eva's eyes rolled back, leaving only the whites visible. She froze, her expression locked in the eerie stillness I'd come to recognize. The woman trembled but didn't pull away, her knuckles whitening as she gripped Eva's hands.

For a moment, nothing happened.

"Does he have curly black hair?" she asked, her voice distant, almost echoing. Otherworldly.

"Yes!" the woman sobbed, falling to her knees as tears streamed freely down her face. "Yes! That's him!"

"He's okay," Eva assured her. "He broke his leg, but his companions are taking turns carrying him home. It's slowing them down, but they'll make it."

The woman wailed in relief, dropping to her knees before Eva. "Thank you, thank you!" she cried. Eva blushed furiously, bending to help the woman to her feet.

"Really, it's okay," she murmured, clearly flustered by the gratitude. They embraced briefly before the woman bowed to me and departed. I stepped closer to Eva, taking her hand in mine.

"Thank you," I said, brushing my lips across her palm. I relished the way her blush deepened to match her hair.

"Hey," I teased, "you didn't pass out this time!"

Eva grinned, her earlier embarrassment melting away. "Oh yeah!" she said brightly.

I threaded my fingers through hers and nodded toward the eastern corridor, where Rift-lamps pulsed like fireflies trapped in crystal. "Come on—Julian's expecting us. Something about a... special exercise."

Eva arched a brow. "Special how?"

"You'll find out soon enough." I flashed a halfhearted grin, but a knot of unease tightened in my chest. Julian summoned us to the *truth-room*. I'd only done it once when I was a new recruit and what I saw terrified me for weeks. Whatever waited beyond those doors, I wouldn't let her walk into it alone.

Side by side we followed the spiraling hall, the hum of the Rift growing louder with every step, until a round crystal doorway slid open on a whisper of air.

Chapter Twenty

Evandra

"The Rift does not invent. It remembers. It reflects desire, fear, and buried truth, stripped of shame or disguise. Those who enter its gaze must be prepared to see not who they pretend to be—but who they already are becoming."

—The Magic of Edralis, Vol. IV

The chamber was circular, domed like a shallow bowl, the walls faceted crystal. At first glance, it looked empty. But the air shimmered faintly, like heat rising off pavement. Something in the Rift hummed here—alive and watching.

Julian hovered outside the threshold, his expression tight. "This is a truthroom," he said. "The walls react to Rift. Thought, memory, desire. The more volatile the emotion, the stronger the projection. It's useful for training to help prepare for emotional warfare as much as possible."

"Oh, great," I muttered. "So magical therapy. Just what I needed."

Julian didn't smile. "You'll be in there alone."

Before I could answer, Drake stepped forward. "No she won't be."

Julian frowned. "That's not—"

"She's our *Seer*," Drake said, voice flat. "Untrained. If she loses control in there, she could tear the room apart and crumble with it. We also can't afford for her to be terrified for weeks on end."

Julian exhaled. "Fine. But you don't engage with the projections. You don't react."

The Rift was already humming before we stepped inside.

The room was quiet—no wind, no heat, just the low pulse of magic moving like a slow heartbeat beneath the crystal walls. The ceiling arched overhead in mirrored plates, reflecting nothing but soft shimmer.

I felt exposed the moment the door sealed behind us.

Drake was silent. His arms were crossed. His jaw was tight. He hadn't looked at me since we entered.

Then the walls lit up. Not with one image—but dozens. Layered. Chaotic. Memory bleeding into fantasy, into fear, into something else entirely.

The first was harmless: me, walking alone through Winshire's market. I almost smiled. Then it changed.

Drake. Watching me. Always watching. From shadows, from doorways, from behind half-closed eyes. Silent, intense, like I was something dangerous—or sacred.

I stiffened. The next vision snapped into place like a blow.

The bathhouse. Not how it had happened—but how it could've. My mouth on his throat. His hands gripping my thighs. His head thrown back in something that looked too much like worship.

Then: gone.

The image blinked out, replaced by something worse.

My father's death. The ash on his skin. My mother's silence. A girl in the mirror with hollow eyes. Me.

I turned away, but the room didn't stop.

Now it was Drake again—bloodied, kneeling. Holding something in his arms. Me. *Dead*. I gasped. The scene shifted.

Him, alone, sobbing into his hands, repeating my name over and over until it didn't sound like a word.

I turned to him. "Drake—?"

He didn't answer. His gaze was locked on the crystal wall. His shoulders were taut, his breathing shallow. A storm beneath the surface. And I realized with a jolt—he wasn't looking at me.

He was looking at the vision.

A child. Red-haired. Scaled. Gold-eyed. Laughing. Running through a sunlit field.

My breath hitched.

"No," I whispered. "That's not—I never thought—" The child turned to look at us.

Everything shattered. The walls went dark. The air thinned. The Rift surged through me like a wave, too deep to breathe through, too fast to brace for. My knees buckled.

Drake caught me before I fell—but only for a heartbeat. His touch steadied. Then vanished. He stepped back like I burned him. His expression was unreadable. Masked. But the rawness in his eyes gave him away. He looked... *wrecked*. Not from what he'd seen—but from what he couldn't face.

"Drake—" I whispered.

He turned without a word. And walked out. The door sealed behind him with a soft hiss.

I stood alone in the crystal silence, chest heaving, hands shaking, every nerve exposed. I hadn't touched him. I hadn't said a word. But something had cracked wide open between us. And he'd left me standing in the middle of it.

Chapter Twenty One

Eldrake

The Mirror Room door clicked shut behind me, and I didn't stop walking until I hit cold stone and silence. I braced my hands on a table in the archives, chest heaving like I'd just fought something. Maybe I had.

Her. Us. *It. A Riftbond.*

Gods.

I'd felt it snap in that Gods-damned truthroom.

Not during the bathhouse, like I'd feared. That night had only frayed the cord—lit a match near it. But this... this was the fire catching.

The Rift didn't whisper this time. It shouted. Us—laid bare. Not in skin, but in soul.

Every thought I'd buried. Every vision I'd forced down. The things I swore I wouldn't let myself want, not really. They bled out into crystal walls like confessions. Like prophecy. Like punishment.

Her pain. My longing. That field. *That child.*

I pressed my palms to the stone harder, as if pressure could force it all back inside.

It wasn't just desire. That's what terrified me. If it were only hunger, I could survive it. I'd survived worse. But *this*? This was tether. This was soul-threading. This was the Rift choosing—*for us.*

"Riftbonds were rare. Unpredictable. Dangerous." And most of them didn't end well. Some burned out—slowly, over years, both parties drained by jealousy and lust until they were shadows of themselves. Some detonated—one half dying and the other following in a flare of magic too big to control. Some... *changed*. Not just magic. *Lineage.*

Riftborn children born of bonded pairs were said to carry the Rift *inside them*. Not just tethered, but core to their being. Unstable. Unstoppable. Twisted by power they hadn't earned. It was one of the reasons bonding was *forbidden* before the Great Change.

I had read the reports. I'd seen the transcripts.

"He lost her in battle. Two minutes later, the sky cracked open and swallowed the command tent. Nothing remained. She tried to cut the bond. It took half her village with it. Their child disappeared at three years old. The Rift flared for weeks, killing anyone that came within ten miles of the village." I looked down at my hands. They were shaking. Not from fear of death. From fear of what I might do to her. Eva didn't know. She couldn't know.

To her, the vision had been erotic. Embarrassing. A magical slap in the face from her own subconscious. She had no idea what it *meant.* That the Rift doesn't show you what you *fantasize*. It shows you what you're already building. Quietly. Permanently.

And in the bathhouse, when I pulled her into my lap, when I kissed her like I needed her to live—that's when it snapped into place. I had already felt it then. The pull. The thrum. But I'd lied to myself. Told myself it was control unraveling.

It wasn't. It was us becoming something I couldn't undo. And now? Now I was standing in an empty room, trying to breathe around the weight of it. Part of me wanted to stop fighting. To let the Rift drag us under together and call it fate—because I wasn't scared of loving her. I was scared I *already did.* And that loving her meant I could destroy her—just by existing.

I looked down at the table. At my reflection warped in the polished obsidian. My eyes were wild. My skin pale. My lips still tasted like memory. I couldn't tell her. Not yet. Because once I did, it would be real for her too. And then we wouldn't be two people in want anymore. It would just be taking away another one of her choices that she deserves to make.

We'd be two halves of something the Rift *designed*. And nothing good ever came from letting it choose for you.

After hours combing the archives for anything—*anything*—that spoke of a Riftbond ending well, I came up empty. Every account ended in ruin or madness, every warning repeated until my head throbbed. Sleep would serve me better than chasing ghosts.

I trudged back through the tunnels toward the ship, the damp stone dripping overhead like a clock counting down. When I pushed through to the mess hall, I found something worse than exhaustion waiting for me.

"Eldrake." Fen's voice wasn't sharp. It was cold. And that was worse.

She and Felix sat at a shadowy table in the corner of the mess hall, twin expressions of "we know what you did" carved into their faces.

Shit.

I stopped three steps away, bracing for the hit. "Evening," I said carefully.

Felix didn't return the greeting. "When were you going to tell us?"

"Tell you what?" I asked, even though I already knew.

"That you left our fucking squad over a chance to get laid," Fen snapped, low and vicious. "Seriously, Eldrake? You ditched us for a girl?" Her words weren't loud—but they carved straight through my chest.

"Julian told us this morning," Felix said, his hand moving to Fen's shoulder like he could temper the sharp edge of her glare. "We thought it was a joke."

I exhaled slowly. "I was going to tell you—"

"You should've told us first," Felix cut in, his warmth sharpened by hurt. "We've followed you through fire, Drake. And you vanish to play house without a word? Not your best moment, love."

"This isn't just about Eva." I sighed, preparing.

Fen leaned forward, eyes blazing. "Then what the hell *is* it about?"

I hesitated. Because this was the part that changed everything. I sat down, the guilt sinking in like cold water. My voice came quiet, but heavy.

"I think my Dragonblood finally… chose someone." Felix stiffened. Fen blinked once. "I think… I bonded."

Silence.

"You *what*?" Fen said, like she'd misheard.

I nodded once. Slow. Felix's face went blank. Not calm. Not composed. Just emptied.

"You don't mean—" Fen started.

"Eva," I said. Another silence. This one louder than shouting.

"She doesn't know," I added quickly. "She can't. Not yet."

"Of course she doesn't. Because you've been too busy sneaking around, too busy letting her curl up in your lap and forgetting the rest of us exist."

"Julian thinks I'm pretending to seduce her for the mission," I said. "If he finds out it's real—if he finds out I'm bonded—I lose her. Pulled off her protection detail. I'll lose everything. I'm not letting that happen."

"You bonded," Felix repeated quietly. "Drake… that's not a feeling. That's a fuse."

"I know."

"This could blow everything wide open."

"I *know.*"

Fen leaned back, arms folded like armor. "And what then? You marry her? Pop out little Dragon-Seer kids who torch the curtains?"

"*Fen—*"

"You *bonded,*" she snarled. "Without telling us. Without thinking. And now the Rift owns you."

I met her eyes. "You think I don't hate that? You think I wanted this to happen?"

"That's the problem," she said flatly. "You *did.*"

Felix sighed, rubbing his temples. "Look. I get it. She's fierce, she's beautiful, she makes soup. You're a goner. But lying to us?" His voice softened, almost sad. "That's what stings, big guy."

I dropped my head into my hands. "I'm going to tell her," I said.

"When?" Fen demanded.

"Tomorrow."

Felix arched a brow. "Tomorrow as in actually tomorrow, or the Drake-special brand of 'tomorrow' where you mean never?"

"I'll ask her to dinner," I said.

Fen's mouth twisted. "Oh, great. A *date.* That fixes everything."

"I don't know how else to do it. I want to tell her in a way that matters."

Felix's golden gaze softened, though his words didn't. "She's already bonded, love. She'll hear it whether she wants to or not."

They were both quiet after that. The worst part? They weren't wrong.

"I'm sorry," I said at last.

Fen didn't answer. She shoved back from the table and stalked off, boots echoing sharp against the stone.

Felix stayed. He watched her go, then turned back to me with a sigh. "You're lucky we love your dumb ass," he said.

I huffed out a bitter laugh. "Doesn't feel like it."

"It's not supposed to," he said. "Not when you've fucked up this badly." He clapped my shoulder and left me in the echoing silence.

My hands still trembled.

If we can't be apart, we might as well be together.

The thought settled in my chest like a weight I hadn't asked for—but couldn't put down. I reached into my pocket and pulled out a scrap of paper. A single line was all I had the nerve for. More than that would betray the quake still running under my skin.

Tomorrow. 7pm. Date?

—D.

I folded the note and stuffed under her door. One message, one promise. Now all I had to do was live up to it.

Tomorrow couldn't come soon enough.

Chapter Twenty Two

Evandra

"Most Riftborn possess an innate ability to wield basic magics, often referred to as thaumaturgy. These small spells, requiring minimal effort, allow them to light fires with a gesture, purify water, mend torn fabric, or even summon a faint breeze. While seemingly mundane, these abilities are a testament to their deep-rooted connection to the Rift— blending practicality with magic." —Study of Riftborn and Every Day Magic, Introduction

---

I was pacing the room like a madwoman, wringing my hands and glancing at the clock every other minute. *A date? With Eldrake? Good Gods, what have I gotten myself into? What would I wear? What would I say?*

My thoughts spiraled until I gave in and called for Rae and Ren. As soon as I explained my predicament, their eyes widened, and then they squealed in unison. Actually squealed.

"You're very lucky, Lady Evandra," Rae said with a knowing smile.

"Yes, incredibly lucky," Ren agreed, practically bouncing on her heels. "I've never seen him this way. Did you see how he looked at you in town?"

My cheeks flushed as I recalled the way Eldrake had kissed my palm, the pride in his smile as he led me around Riftreach. I could still feel the warmth of his hand in mine. I told the twins I needed their help—desperately—with my hair and picking a gown. Their excitement was instantaneous.

"We'll make you look perfect, Lady Evandra!" Rae proclaimed, clapping her hands.

"More than perfect," Ren added. "He won't know what hit him."

They set to work with giddy determination. First, they helped me into a bath infused with rose petals, the warm water soothing my nerves. Ren meticulously filed and shaped my nails while Rae pinned my hair into an elegant updo, accenting it with pearl pins. A few soft red curls were left to frame my face, and they gently brushed my eyelids with a pale taupe shadow before adding a touch of rouge to my cheeks.

I was feeling more like myself, albeit a slightly more polished version, until Rae approached the wardrobe and pulled out a floor-length red gown.

"No," I said immediately, shaking my head at the plunging neckline, the shimmering beads, and the daring slit. "Absolutely not."

"Lady, with all due respect... That man is going to combust when he sees you in this." Rae grinned mischievously.

"You'd look so hot in this dress," Ren chimed in, laughing.

I gave them a skeptical look, but their excitement was infectious. Reluctantly, I tried on the gown. As I looked in the mirror, my breath caught. The dress didn't clash with my hair as I'd feared—it complemented it, pulling out the rich crimson tones and making my green eyes pop.

The chiffon sleeves draped off my shoulders, connecting to an intricate, lace-covered bodice that hugged my curves in all the right places. The tulle skirt flowed elegantly to the floor, with a single slit revealing just enough leg to feel daring. I stepped into matching red heels, and the transformation was complete.

"See?" Rae said smugly, her hands on her hips. "Told you."

"You're stunning, Lady Evandra," Ren said with a grin. "He'll be speechless."

I couldn't help but smile at my reflection. For once, I looked... beautiful.

"So, Miss," Ren started, blushing slightly. "Tell us... is it true?"

"Is what true?" I asked, glancing at her through the mirror.

Rae elbowed her sister in the ribs, but Ren pressed on, her cheeks turning scarlet. "You know... what they say about dragons. The, um, size of their— ya know."

"Ren!" Rae exclaimed, smacking her on the arm. Both of them burst into laughter, and I immediately turned beet red.

"Oh my Gods," I spluttered, covering my face. "I mean, I wouldn't know—I've never..."

Their laughter faded as they realized my embarrassment was genuine. "You've never...?" Rae asked more softly, her teasing replaced with curiosity.

"I've never been with a man in that way," I admitted quietly, my voice barely above a whisper. My hands twisted in my lap. "I—I mean, I may have... seen... something in the bathhouse" I stammered. "But it was dark, and the water—and I've never, so I can't exactly... compare." Gods, my face felt like it was on fire. "But if it was what I think it was, then—well—" I buried my face in my hands. "It was... big."

The twins squealed, their laughter bubbling back up, while I wanted to melt straight into the floor.

"Well, surely this dress will get you wherever you'd like to go, milady," Rae said with a wink. The implications made my cheeks burn. Not that I didn't want that, I did want that, more than anything, actually. To be with him in that way. I just... I wouldn't know what to do. What if I disappointed him? I realized my palms were sweating.

I was pacing again, my heart pounding in my chest. A date. With Eldrake. Was I excited? Terrified? Both? Probably both. I glanced at my reflection in the mirror for what felt like the hundredth time, smoothing the crimson gown that clung to my curves. The twins had outdone themselves. The dress was breathtaking, with a plunging neckline, delicate beadwork that caught the light like stars, and a daring slit that revealed just enough leg to make me feel both bold and vulnerable all at once.

Right at eight o'clock, a knock sounded at the door. Of course, he'd be perfectly on time. Taking a deep breath, I whispered to myself, *You don't look ridiculous. You look fine. The girls said so.*

When I opened the door, time stopped. Or maybe it just felt that way because the sight of him stole every last breath from my lungs. Eldrake stood there—tall, sharp, devastating. A vision in tailored black, every line of the suit sculpted to his form like it worshiped him. I suddenly understood why people use the word 'swoon' unironically. The jacket gave way to an obsidian vest and tie, the faintest hint of his crimson scales peeking over the high collar. His hair, free of its usual tie, framed his sharp features like a warrior prince.

His silver eyes found mine and stayed there, wide and stunned. His mouth opened slightly, then closed again like he'd forgotten how to speak. "You look..." he finally breathed, "beyond incredible, Evandra," his voice was low and husky as his eyes roamed over me, lingering on every detail of the gown. He stepped forward, cupping the back of my neck, and pulled me into a deep, urgent kiss, making me dizzy in the best way. When he pulled back, his gaze was darker, more intense. "Gods, woman. Looking at you all night in that dress is going to be torture," he licked his lips ever so slightly, making my knees weak.

I smirked, teasing, "Should I change?"

"Gods no," he said, nearly breathless. "Please don't," his arm slipped around my waist, pulling me firmly against him. My heart fluttered at the sheer strength of him, yes—but more than that, it was the look in his eyes. Like I wasn't just the only thing in his world tonight—I was his world.

We crossed the ship deck arm in arm, the sound of my heels clicking against the wood. Descending into the glowing city, I felt like royalty, the Riftborn stopping to watch us as we passed. Their gazes weren't unkind, more curious, and it made me feel... important. Special. Eldrake's pride was palpable as he led me down the winding walkways toward the private dining room he had prepared.

When we arrived, my breath caught. The restaurant was built into the cavern wall, with a vine-draped terrace overlooking the geyser that sparkled in the lantern light. The private dining room was secluded and cozy, with a table adorned with flickering candles and a vase of flowers—bright orange and yellow blooms that seemed to glow softly in the low light. I approached the flowers, brushing my fingers over their delicate petals.

"Sunfire lilies," he said softly behind me. "They only grow down here. I thought you might like them."

"They're beautiful," I whispered, touched by the thoughtfulness. "Thank you."

He pulled my chair out for me, his hand brushing mine as I sat, sending a jolt of warmth up my arm. As he took his seat across from me, the candlelight caught his silver eyes, making them shimmer like molten metal. We ordered wine—red, smuggled from above—and an assortment of small plates. As the first glass was poured, Drake raised his glass. "To you, Eva," he said simply. "For everything you've done so far... and for everything I know you'll do."

Blushing, I clinked my glass against his and sipped, savoring the smooth warmth of the wine. "So," I began, trying to shift focus, "how long have you lived in Riftreach?"

"Since I was seventeen," he replied, his gaze drifting over the distant shimmer of the geyser. "My mother stays above ground... in hiding."

"Why?" I asked, leaning in.

He hesitated, swirling the wine in his glass as if it held his answers. "The hold she guards has been in our family for generations. It's one of the last places the King's forces haven't touched. Abandoning it would mean letting history be erased." His voice softened, a flicker of pain threading through. "My mother's human, so she isn't hunted the way we are. But she's known to shelter Riftborn when I visit—or when someone needs refuge. If the wrong person discovered that..." His jaw tightened. "It would be enough to see her hanged." Something in his tone shifted then, lighter for just a breath. "She's stubborn. Eccentric. Talks too much when she's nervous and collects stray cats like they're jewels. But she'd give the cloak off her back to someone freezing in the snow—and Gods help you if she catches you with mud on her carpets." His lips curved faintly, almost fond. "She's survived this long because she's clever. But it's still a risk every time I go." My heart squeezed at the quiet weight of his words. I reached across the table, laying my hand gently over his. His eyes met mine, and there it was—that flicker of gratitude beneath the steel of his expression.

"What of your father?" I asked after a moment, though I wasn't sure I wanted to know.

His jaw clenched. "He was murdered," Drake said flatly. "When I was seven. He... exposed his scales in public. Just a glimpse. That was all it took," he looked down into his glass, his knuckles whitening around the stem. "They made an example of him," he took a long, bracing drink, but the haunted look in his eyes remained.

The silence stretched between us like a thread pulled too tight. I couldn't bear the hurt radiating off him, so I offered the gentlest lifeline I could find. "What's your favorite color?" I asked, my voice lilting with forced lightness.

That devilish grin returned, but slower this time, like he had to will it into existence. "Red," he said, glancing deliberately at my dress. "Obviously."

I laughed, grateful for the shift. "Of course it is. Mine's green. Like the forest after a storm."

He leaned in, the tension finally starting to ease. "Favorite flower?"

"Dogwood," I answered without hesitation. "You?"

He gestured to the vase. "You're looking at them."

I smiled, letting the conversation flow more freely now. We left grief behind for a while, letting laughter and memory fill the space instead. He didn't know it, but I admired the way he'd trusted me with that story. And he'd never know how much I needed that smile he gave me right after.

He told me stories about his time as a scout, and I shared funny memories from the inn. The lanterns flickered in the warm glow of the dining room, their soft candlelight reflecting off the red gown that I was starting to feel more at ease in. Drake's gaze had barely left me all evening, and his rare, genuine smiles only made my cheeks flush more. As I sipped my wine, he leaned back in his chair, his expression growing more serious.

"Well," he began, his deep voice tinged with hesitation, "I wasn't lying when I said I had something important to tell you."

I tilted my head, curious. "Go on."

He set his glass down and shifted in his seat, his hand moving to grip his napkin nervously. "How do I say this..." He exhaled, his confidence from earlier replaced by something more vulnerable. "I've been assigned to... you."

My brows knit together. "What do you mean?"

"Well, er..." He rubbed the back of his neck, avoiding my gaze. "As you know, you're the Uprising's—"

"-greatest asset," I finished flatly, rolling my eyes. "Yes, as everyone likes reminding me."

His expression flickered, entertained by my sass. "Eva, it wasn't a decision made about you. It was mine. After the Vyrmin attack... I asked Julian to assign me as your protection detail. I didn't want anyone else watching your back," the air felt heavier for a moment, the flickering candlelight throwing shadows across his face. He looked vulnerable. Uncertain.

My stomach twisted—but not in the way I expected. It wasn't fear. It was something else. "So," I said, trying to force levity into my voice, "you're like my full-time bodyguard now?"

He chuckled nervously. "I guess we could call it that," his gaze flicked to mine, gauging my reaction. "You're not mad, are you?"

I leaned back in my chair, letting a playful smile cross my lips. "Why would I be? Extra security and you're not bad to look at."

His face flushed, and I was struck by the unexpected sight of this towering, confident warrior blushing like a schoolboy. *Gods, I made him blush.* My heart thudded loudly in my chest.

Am I in love? No. No way. Maybe?

He laughed a deep and genuine sound that felt like music. "Fair enough," he said, his voice softer now.

"For the record, I remember being the one saving your ass from those Vyrmin." I said jokingly.

His grin widened, "And I'll never forget it," the tension seemed to melt away as we finished our meal. The conversation drifted to lighter topics, but my mind kept circling back to his earlier admission. He'd chosen this assignment—chose *me*. That thought lingered as we stood to leave.

As we walked side by side through the streets of Riftreach, his hand brushed against mine—tentative at first, then deliberate. His fingers laced through mine like it was the most natural thing in the world. Electricity surged at the contact, warm and steady. I didn't pull away. I didn't want to. Instead, I squeezed his hand gently, grounding myself in the moment, in him.

"Can I ask you something?" I said, my voice quieter now.

"Of course."

"What makes you smell the way you do?" The words tumbled out awkwardly, and I instantly winced. "I mean—um—it's not bad! Gods, no, it's just... unique. I quite like it, actually."

He raised a brow, clearly amused but a touch self-conscious. "Probably my scale salve," he said, brushing the back of his hand where crimson scales shimmered faintly. "It's a blend my mother makes. Keeps them from drying out. Helps with flexibility, too." He flexed his free hand open and shut as a demonstration.

"That's... actually fascinating," I said, marveling at the glimpse into his heritage. There was so much I didn't know about him, so much I wanted to learn.

By the time we reached the ship, the cool cavern air nipped at my skin, but I barely noticed. My focus was entirely on him—on the way his hand stayed entwined with mine, his thumb lightly tracing lazy circles against my knuckles. Each step up the stairs to my chamber felt impossibly long and far too fast all at once.

At last, we stood before my door. The hush of the ship deck was almost deafening, broken only by the distant murmur of the geyser.

"I had a lovely time tonight," I said softly, turning to face him fully.

Each step up the stairs to my chamber felt impossibly long and far too fast all at once.

"As did I."

I smiled nervously, then blurted, "Well... better than my last date, at least. You didn't kill this one."

For a split second his silver eyes widened, and then—Gods help me—a startled laugh rumbled out of him. Joy flooded my chest, dizzy and reckless. I wanted to make him laugh forever.

The laughter faded into something quieter, something heavier. His gaze lingered on mine, dipping to my lips and back again. My heart stuttered, and before he could decide, I did. I leaned in, arms sliding around his shoulders, and kissed him. His hands found my waist instantly, pulling me against him like he'd been waiting for this all night. His lips moved with mine—slow at first, then deeper, needier. And I thought about what the twins had said earlier… not just about the… reputation… of Dragons, but the dress, too—how it would get me wherever I wanted to go.

I broke the kiss breathlessly, fingers trailing down the firm line of his chest to catch the knot of his tie. With a tug, I whispered, "Care to come in?"

His pupils flared, jaw tight with restraint, but his voice was low and hoarse. "Gods, yes."

I smiled, stepped back, and pulled him through the door.

"I want you. Now," I whispered, my voice trembling with raw, unfiltered need. His eyes widened—just for a moment—before darkening with something primal.

"Oh, thank fuck," he growled, his voice ragged as his shoulders hunched like he was preparing to strike.

And strike, he did.

In one fluid motion, he lifted me like I weighed nothing, his strong hands gripping my thighs as he pressed me against the door. My back met the wood with a soft thud, and I gasped as his hips pinned me there. I could feel his growing arousal firmly against me. His mouth found the curve of my throat, his lips grazing the skin before he bit—just enough to make me shudder. He kissed and nipped his way up to my jaw, and I melted beneath him. His hands—large, warm, insistent—cupped my breasts, his thumbs brushing over my stiffened peaks through the fabric of my gown. Each pass of his touch sent sparks rippling through me, heat building with every breath.

I moaned as his teeth grazed my earlobe, my fingers threading into his hair and tugging gently. A low growl rumbled from his chest, vibrating against my skin. "You have no idea what you do to me," he murmured, his voice thick with hunger.

"Drake," I gasped, breathless beneath the intensity of his touch. His scent wrapped around me—warm, spicy, utterly him—and I needed more. My hands slid down the broad line of his shoulders, gripping his jacket. "Off," I commanded, my voice shaking with urgency.

With a groan, he set me down carefully, his hands lingering on my waist as if reluctant to let go. His jacket slipped from his shoulders and hit the floor. I fumbled at his tie, fingers clumsy with need, until he smirked and undid it himself with practiced ease. I barely registered him crossing the room, but I watched as he yanked the velvet curtain closed over the grand ship's window, plunging us into intimate shadow.

Then he was back—his hands finding my shoulders, spinning me gently in place. I shivered at the first tug of the laces down my back, the chill of air kissing newly bare skin. One by one, the ties came undone. The gown loosened... and fell in a whisper to the floor, pooling around my feet like spilled wine.

I turned to face him, bare and trembling, my heart pounding like a war drum. His gaze devoured me—slow, reverent—as if I were something sacred. "Gods," he breathed, his voice thick with hunger. He shed his vest and shirt in one fluid motion, revealing a body that looked as if it had been carved from stone. The crimson scales along his shoulders caught the low light, glinting like molten metal. He reached for my hand, guiding me toward the bed with a tenderness that belied the heat in his eyes.

As I lay back against the silk sheets, he followed, pressing a kiss to my lips—deep, searing—before trailing downward. His mouth skimmed across my collarbone, then down to my breasts, his tongue circling one nipple before drawing it into his mouth. I gasped, arching into him as his teeth grazed just enough to make me whimper. My fingers tangled in his hair, clutching him closer.

He continued his descent, slow and deliberate, lips brushing fire along my ribs and stomach. When he parted my thighs and knelt between them, my breath caught. I flushed, vulnerable under his gaze—but before doubt could creep in, he spoke.

"You're perfect," he whispered, hoarse with awe.

Then his tongue found me. He moved with purpose, drawing a long, slow stroke up my center. I cried out, hips jerking as he worked me with maddening control—alternating between soft flicks and firm pressure, reading my body like a language only he could speak. Every nerve buzzed under his mouth. My hands clenched the sheets, my breath coming in desperate gasps.

"Drake," I moaned, his name escaping in a broken whisper.

He gripped my thighs, holding me open as he buried his mouth in me. His tongue slipped inside, coaxing a sound from my throat that barely sounded human. The pleasure was sharp, relentless, curling tighter and tighter inside me.

Just as I felt myself teetering on the edge—he stopped. I whimpered, the sudden absence almost painful, my body trembling with need.

When I opened my eyes, he was standing over me, his molten gaze fixed on mine. His hands moved to the buttons of his pants, and with agonizing slowness, he pushed them down.

His cock sprang free—bare, heavy, and unmistakably divine. A body carved by the Gods.

The girls were right.

"That look on your face..." He chuckled a low, throaty sound. I realized my mouth was hanging open, taking in his size. "Would flatter any man."

I swallowed hard, unable to speak, my cheeks blazing. He stepped closer, his confidence mingling with a gentleness that made my heart flutter. He reached out to stroke a strand of hair from my face, his calloused fingertips grazing my cheek. Then, suddenly, he froze.

Before I could ask why, he turned and walked away. Naked. Entirely, gloriously nude—his back broad, his thighs corded with muscle, the faint gleam of scales catching the dim light.

"Um... Drake?" I stammered, sitting up as he crouched by my dresser and started pulling drawers open like he owned the place. "What are you doing?"

"Rules," he muttered, rifling through folded linens. "Made myself a promise—first time had to be after a proper date... and with a candle lit."

My jaw dropped. "You're serious? *Now*?!"

He glanced over his shoulder, silver eyes gleaming, mouth curved in a wolfish grin. "Rules are rules."

Finally, with a triumphant grunt, he held up a stub of wax and set it on the nightstand. He flicked his fingers; a flame sparked, catching the wick. The candlelight spilled over his chest, shadows dancing across the red scales on his shoulders.

"There," he murmured, voice low, thick, dangerous. He leaned over me again, his eyes burning like molten silver. "Now I can ruin you properly." The bead of moisture glistening at his tip betrayed his restraint.

I nodded, breathless. He leaned down, chestnut hair falling like a curtain as he kissed me—softly at first, then deeper, hungrier. His mouth trailed to my throat, and I gasped as his body pressed against mine, heat radiating from every inch of him.

His hand slipped to my hip, steadying me. The moment his tip brushed against my slick entrance, a gasp escaped my lips—and he paused, meeting my eyes with searing intensity.

"You're so wet, Evandra," he said, voice reverent, like he was barely holding himself back.

He entered me slowly—inch by thick, aching inch. My breath caught as my body stretched to take him. I whimpered, clutching the sheets, the pressure exquisite. He sank deeper, and deeper, until he was fully sheathed inside me.

He groaned, low and guttural, and began to move—grinding into me with slow, deliberate thrusts that made me cry out. The stretch, the fullness, the pace—it was too much and not enough. I wrapped my arms around his shoulders, pulling him closer, needing every part of him.

His rhythm quickened, restraint slipping with every thrust. His lips found my breast, his teeth grazing my sensitive peak. One hand slid between us, his thumb circling my clit in perfect time with his hips. I moaned, the pleasure cresting fast. It built like a wave—higher, sharper—until it broke.

"Oh, *Drake*!" I screamed, back arching as my climax tore through me, my body pulsing around him.

"F-fuck," he growled, voice hoarse and primal. With one last thrust, he buried himself deep and stilled, twitching inside me as he spilled into my core. His body trembled, every muscle taut. Then he collapsed beside me, pulling me close. His chest rose and fell against mine, and a low laugh rumbled through him.

"What's so funny?!" I asked, breathless.

He grinned, planting a kiss on my temple. "I've wanted to do that since the moment I met you," he kissed me again, slower this time. "And Gods, it was worth every second of the wait."

I smiled, heart still racing. "You don't have to say all that. I mean, you don't have to pretend."

He blinked, confused. "Pretend?"

I hesitated, running a finger over the scales on his chest. "The sweet talk. Like... saying what I want to hear."

"Eva," he said, more serious now. "What do you know about Dragonbloods?"

I blinked. "Um, they're known for their rage, their passion... their intensity."

He nodded. "Exactly. We don't do anything halfway. When we care about someone, we care with everything we have. It's not something we fake. Even if we wanted to."

"Oh." was all I managed to say, my throat tight.

"I'm not saying anything has to get serious overnight," he said, gently cupping my cheek, his thumb brushing my lower lip. "But I'm not just going to fuck you and leave. I like you, Eva. A lot."

Oh Gods. How did I get this lucky?

"Well," I teased, trying to lighten the moment, "you're assigned to be my bodyguard. It'd be awkward if you ran off now."

He chuckled and leaned forward to kiss me. His lips were soft, a gentle contrast to his powerful frame. When he pulled away, he rested his forehead against mine for a moment, and the world shrank to just us.

We stayed like that for a while, wrapped in each other. Eventually, I slipped into a nightgown, the silky fabric cool against my flushed skin. Drake pulled on his pants and started gathering his things.

We'd slept curled around each other every night on the way to Castle City — out of comfort, exhaustion, necessity. But since arriving, we hadn't. As if sharing a bed in a real room made it too official. Too real.

"W- where are you going?" I asked before I could stop myself, hating how small my voice sounded.

He paused, rubbing the back of his neck. "I was going to get changed and, uh, guard your room from the hall." A beat of silence passed.

He didn't turn around—but his voice shifted, low and uncertain. "Eva... there's something I should probably tell you."

My heart stuttered. "Okay?"

He stood there a moment too long. A shadow of conflict crossed his face—like he was weighing whether to drop a sword or swing it. Finally, he shook his head and exhaled through his nose, offering a weak smile. "Later. Doesn't matter right now." I frowned, about to press him—but the hesitation passed like fog, and his smile firmed into something steadier.

"Couldn't you... more effectively guard me... from my own bed?" I asked nervously, my voice barely above a whisper.

He froze. His expression didn't change—not right away—but I saw the shift. A flicker in his eyes, the twitch of a smile he tried very hard to suppress. He cleared his throat, and nodded. "I mean... yes. Logistically, that would be the soundest tactical move."

He didn't even bother pretending after that—just dropped everything and climbed under the covers like he'd been waiting for permission since the day we arrived. His arms wrapped around my waist, warm and solid, his breath steady against my skin. I rested my head on his chest, listening to the steady thrum of his heartbeat as he kissed the crown of my head.

He held me tighter than I expected. Not possessive. Not even protective. Just like he was afraid I'd disappear. As we drifted off together, I felt invincible in his arms.

Chapter Twenty Three

Eldrake

I CLOSED the door behind me quietly, but the memory of Eva—bare skin, sleepy smile, soft breath—still burned in my mind. My chest felt too full, like something alive and fluttering had taken up residence there.

Gods, is this what love feels like?

I caught myself grinning. Actually grinning. It felt foreign on my face, so wide my jaw ached. My boots hit the planks too loudly, my stride bouncing between a march and a... skip. Fucking skip. I cleared my throat, tried to settle into my usual prowl, but two steps later I realized I was humming. Humming. I cut it off immediately and glanced around, as if someone might've heard.

I passed a porthole and glimpsed my reflection. Tousled hair, shirt buttons uneven, face flushed like a boy after his first tumble in the hay. I groaned. The great Captain Eldrake—stoic, feared, commander of a dozen missions—looked like some tavern drunk who'd just been kissed for the first time.

I should've gone straight to my quarters. Rest. Plan. Brood properly. Instead, I found myself veering toward the kitchens. I actually stood there, staring at a basket of muffins like an idiot, wondering if I should sneak one back to her room. Breakfast in bed. Like some doting husband. I ran a hand over my face and muttered, "Gods, you're pathetic." Still... I took one. Just in case.

By the time I made it to my chambers, I was buzzing too much to sit still. I tried to sharpen my dagger, but after three strokes I realized I was just smiling at the whetstone. Tried to shine my pauldrons and dropped one on my foot because my hands wouldn't stop shaking with adrenaline. Muttered a curse, laughed at myself, then collapsed backward on the bed, staring at the ceiling with the goofiest fucking grin.

And still, through all of it, I felt her. Like a second heartbeat. Her calm. Her warmth. Her soft, post-sated glow.

And for a moment, I almost told her.

After dinner, after the kisses and laughter, when she looked at me like I was something good—like I was hers—I nearly said it. Nearly admitted what was happening.

But I couldn't.

Not yet.

Not when she was finally happy.

Not when I'd seen the way joy lit her up from the inside out. I didn't want to burden her with something she didn't choose. Not yet. I just wanted one night where everything felt simple. Where it was just a date. Just a girl. Just a man.

Even if it was a lie.

I shook off the thought. Focus. I wanted nothing more than to crawl back into bed beside her, but duty called.

Julian would be waiting.

After changing into my fighting leathers, I headed toward the strategy room on the upper deck of the ship. The air inside was heavy with ink, dust, and the residue of long-standing tension. Julian stood hunched over a table of maps and reports. Fen was reclined in a chair with her boots up on the table, smirking. Felix sat nearby, his chin in one hand, clearly bored. And Avod—of course—was inspecting the edge of a dagger-like he was appraising a work of art.

"Good morning!" I said far too cheerfully, startling them all.

"Clearly," Fen said, raising a brow.

Avod grinned at me, still flipping the dagger. "Someone got laid."

Julian didn't even glance up from his notes. "Good date?"

"Uh..." I scratched the back of my neck, grinning like a damn fool. "Yeah. You could say that."

"You dog," Julian muttered, still not looking up. "What, she fall for the captain routine that fast?" That landed wrong. Like she was an assignment. A tool. A mission. She wasn't. She never had been. My jaw clenched.

The corner of Fen's mouth twitched like she was trying not to laugh. Felix, for once, had the grace to look away. Avod didn't say anything, but I caught the flick of his eyes toward Fen, unreadable.

I opened my mouth to say something — anything to shut Julian up — but nothing came out. Not without sounding defensive. Not without giving too much away. So I moved to the table and pulled out a chair. Let it stew.

At least Fen and Felix got it. Avod, too, maybe. This wasn't a strategy. This was real.

"So," Julian began, his sharp eyes scanning the group, "as you all know, Fen and Felix have been reassigned. They'll be working as a duo on a retrieval mission. A Riftborn orphan has been located south of Market Street, living in an abandoned building. Since you were their captain, I figured your input would be beneficial for strategy. Even though," he added with a smirk, "I had to pull you from your post."

"Oh, don't worry, he'll have plenty of time to use his post," Fen bit, her icy grin wide as she leaned back in her chair. "We'll think of you fondly while we're crawling through moldy alleyways."

Felix snorted. Julian even chuckled.

Avod tapped his dagger against the edge of the table, eyeing Fen. "You could take the clean route through Market East, but the alleys off Crag Street have better rooftop access. Just don't twist your ankle trying to out-parkour the orphan."

Fen rolled her eyes. "I'll try to keep my grace intact."

"That'll be a first," he muttered.

She kicked his leg under the table—not hard, but with intent. He grinned wider.

We got to work. I laid out the plan: approach the child gently during the day, show the wing pin, and build trust. If they don't come willingly, back off and return at night with supplies or healing—something tangible, something human.

"Keep your hands low and visible," I added. "No sudden movements. One of our last rescues bolted because someone reached for their satchel too fast. Took us three days to find them again."

"Riftborn kids don't run from blades," Avod added, tone even. "They run from kindness they don't trust yet. You've got one shot to look harmless. Don't waste it."

I could see Felix mentally cataloging the suggestion, nodding slightly.

But my mind kept drifting—back to her skin under my hands, the heat in her eyes, the sound she made when she came apart beneath me. The moment I felt the Rift press deeper between us—tightening the knot. I felt guilty that I hadn't told her. Not yet. I Couldn't. If I did, she might look at me differently. Like I'd stolen her choice. *Because I had.* Even if I hadn't meant to.

I didn't realize I was white-knuckling the edge of the table until Julian dismissed the room. I stood fast enough that my chair scraped loudly against the floor. Fen raised an eyebrow.

"Tell her we say hi," Felix said enthusiastically.

"Speak for yourself," Fen muttered.

Avod only gave me a look. Not smug. Not judgmental. Just knowing.

I didn't respond. I had more important things to do. Or maybe— I just couldn't sit still anymore. Not until I understood what was happening to me. What this was. What we were. Because if what I thought was happening was happening... It could mean danger for both of us.

"Drake. A moment," Julian said, gesturing toward the darker end of the war room as Fen, Felix, and Avod filed out.

I followed, pulse still ticking hard from the meeting. Julian waited until the others were out of earshot, then leaned back against the map wall with his arms crossed.

"You've done well," he said. "The mission. Bringing her here. Keeping her safe. But..." He hesitated, eyes narrowing slightly. "You're getting a little... *immersed* in your role, don't you think?"

I froze. "What are you talking about?"

"The way you look at her," Julian said. "It's... convincing. Maybe a little *too* convincing." He gave me a pointed glance. "She trusts you. That's good. But don't forget what this is. You were supposed to make her feel safe. Invested. Not..." He gestured vaguely. "Enamored."

"I haven't forgotten," I lied.

Julian studied me a second longer, then shrugged. "Look. I get it. She's sharp. Brave. It's easy to start blurring lines. Just make sure you're still seeing them."

I didn't answer. I couldn't.

"We can't afford complications," he added, quieter now. "Not from you. Not from her. Not from the Rift."

I nodded tightly. "Understood."

He clapped a hand on my shoulder—affectionate, but heavy. "Good man."

As he turned and walked away, my breath felt caught somewhere in my chest. I stood in the quiet war room, heart pounding like it was trying to outrun my skin.

He still didn't know.

I wasn't acting. I didn't know when the pretending stopped—but it had. I wasn't pretending I hadn't completely fallen for her anymore. And if this was what I feared it was... I needed to know. I needed to be sure. Before I became a threat to her.

Before I lost her completely.

The archives were mostly dark, save for the glow of a single lantern swaying gently above the reading table. Most of Riftreach had gone to sleep, their laughter and music fading into distant hums. The city felt hushed now, like it was holding its breath.

I shouldn't have been here. Not this late. Not for this reason. But curiosity was a dragon of its own—one that sank its claws into your ribs and refused to let go.

The stone floor was cold beneath my boots. My breath fogged faintly in the air. I sat alone at the end of a long wooden table, the weight of ancient texts pressing down from the shelves like silent sentries. The shadows between the stacks stretched long, and the silence buzzed.

Ness had left the texts on a back shelf for me without asking any questions, though I could feel their quiet curiosity echoing down the corridor as I passed. They always knew more than they let on. I told myself it was purely academic, just another tactical inquiry. Understanding the Rift was part of my job, after all.

The book in front of me had no title. Just a cracked spine and curling corners, as if it had been read a hundred times by hands more desperate than mine. I turned the brittle pages slowly.

Descriptions of Riftbonds were worse than I remembered. Consuming. Corrosive. Two minds fused together in a storm of magic and emotion. Lust mistaken for loyalty. Madness mistaken for love. In most recorded cases, one of the bonded didn't survive. Either the Rift unraveled them, or their partner did.

I rubbed a hand over my face. My stomach turned.

But then, near the end—half-buried between a diagram and a warning—there was something different. A few brief paragraphs. Written in a different hand. The ink lighter. Newer.

IN EXCEEDINGLY RARE CASES, A RIFTBOND DOES NOT FORM THROUGH SURVIVAL, TRAUMA, OR PRIMAL FORCE. IT FORMS THROUGH LOVE. NOT LUST. NOT CONVENIENCE. NOT COMPULSION. LOVE. THESE BONDS ARE GENTLE IN ORIGIN BUT NO LESS POTENT. THE RIFT RECOGNIZES THE SOUL'S RESONANCE AND ANSWERS NOT WITH CHAOS, BUT WITH A GIFT. SUCH BONDS DO NOT CONSUME—THEY DEEPEN. THEY DO NOT BURN— THEY WARM. BUT EVEN LOVE CAN BE DANGEROUS. WHEN ONE HEART BREAKS, THE OTHER DOES NOT ALWAYS SURVIVE.

My eyes lingered on that last line, my chest tightening. My thumb traced the margin. Someone—Ness, maybe—had underlined it once. Beneath it, scribbled faintly in the margin:

Shared heartbeat. Dreaming together. Glimpses through the other's eyes.

I leaned back slowly, staring at the domed ceiling above. The silence was thicker now. Heavier. Like the archives themselves were waiting for me to break.

A bond born of love? Could that be what this was?

Eva wasn't a fever. She wasn't a distraction. She was… something steady. Something that pulled me back from the edge when I didn't even know I was near it. She didn't just stir my blood—she calmed it. When she touched me, it didn't feel like losing control. It felt like *coming back to myself.*

And still… a knot sat stubborn in my gut.

What if I was wrong? What if my love—this thing growing too fast, too hot—wasn't a gift, but a spark waiting to devour us both?

I didn't know what love was supposed to feel like. I'd seen it twisted, used, corrupted by power and desperation. Was this different? Or was I just fooling myself—letting the Rift whisper sweetness in my ear while it built something fatal between us?

I closed the book carefully, my fingers resting on the final line like it could somehow answer me. The silence pressed in again, familiar now.

I didn't want to tell her yet. Not about the bond. Not about any of this. On the date, I'd just wanted to make her laugh. I wanted to see her eat something stupid and delicious and watch her eyes light up. I wanted to forget the weight. Forget the future.

Just… be with her. But now I knew. And I didn't know what scared me more—the idea that the Rift had chosen us because of love…

Or the possibility that even *that* might not be enough to save us.

Chapter Twenty Four

Evandra

"There are moments when magic binds without a word. Not through spells or oaths, but through shared breath, through closeness—through touch. The Rift listens most closely when hearts are open and defenses are down." —The Magic of Edralis, Vol. III

I awoke sprawled across the bed, sunlight pouring through the velvet curtains and warming the plush fabric beneath me. My hand instinctively reached for the other side of the bed, but Drake was nowhere to be found. I sat up, rubbing the remnants of sleep from my eyes, and winced slightly at the dull soreness in my thighs and hips—a testament to last night's... activities. A wide smile stretched across my face as memories of his hands, his mouth...

The scent of fresh flowers drifted toward me. I turned to see a bouquet resting on the vanity across the room, lit by the morning sun spilling in from the window. The same Sunfire Lilies from our date—

fiery orange and golden blooms so vivid they looked lit from within. Beside them sat a folded piece of parchment.

I swung my legs over the side of the bed, my bare feet sinking into the thick rug as I padded to the vanity. Lifting the bouquet, I inhaled the spicy-sweet scent. They felt wild yet elegant—just like him. I set them gently down and opened the note. His handwriting was unmistakable: legible but absolutely not tidy.

Eva-
I have a strategy meeting this morning. You were sleeping too peacefully to wake. I
will see you this afternoon for training.
P.S. I'll be thinking about how you taste the whole time.

Yours,
Drake

My cheeks flamed as the heat rushed to my face. Gods, that man. I traced the edge of the note with my fingertips, grinning like a fool. How was he both utterly indecent and genuinely thoughtful in the same breath?

A knock startled me, and moments later, Rae and Ren entered with their usual quiet efficiency. I'd finally learned to tell them apart: Ren wore her hair cropped stylishly short, while Rae's long stick straight hair framed her face like a painting. Rae carried a breakfast tray heavy with tea, fruit, and pastries. Ren swept past me and into the adjoining bath without a word—already running the water.

"Good morning!" I greeted them a bit too cheerfully.

"Good morning, Lady," Ren replied, bowing slightly, though the grin she flashed me was anything but formal. She glanced at Rae, and the glance they exchanged said everything: they knew.

"So..." Ren began with mock innocence, "how was your date?" Rae stifled a giggle behind her hand.

I groaned, though I couldn't stop the ridiculous smile spreading across my face. "It was... incredible," I admitted, hoping that would be enough. It wasn't.

Rae leaned in, eyes bright with anticipation. "Lady Evandra, you must give us more than that!"

"Well..." I hesitated, then laughed and threw my hands over my face. "You were right. About the dress. And the... size." They squealed. *Actually squealed. Again.*

"Was he gentle?" Ren asked, softer now, her eyes sincere.

Rae grinned wickedly. "How big?"

"Oh, Gods!" I said through laughter, my face in my hands.

Rae nudged me with her shoulder. Her playful tone melted into something softer.

"Drake is a good man, Lady. I'm glad he's treating you well."

"He is," I said softly, glancing at the flowers on the vanity. "He really is."

The twins resumed their routine: Rae fetched a vase and placed the lilies with great care while Ren disappeared into the bathroom to finish preparing the bath. They left with knowing smiles and strict instructions to enjoy my breakfast before it went cold. I sank into the warm, rose-scented water, letting the steam loosen the knots in my body and the last of sleep from my mind. My fingers trailed lazy patterns over the surface, but my thoughts moved fast.

I thought about who I'd been just mere weeks ago—a barmaid with no legacy, no plan, no real future. Now I was here. In this extraordinary city, and surrounded by people who believed I could be something more.

The idea of training no longer scared me. I was excited. The Rift, the visions... they weren't just strange or dangerous anymore. They were mine. And I wanted to understand them. I wanted to earn my place—not just as the Uprising's "greatest asset," but as someone who mattered for more than what she could do.

Someone who belonged.

The archives did not look like any library I'd ever seen.

I had imagined shelves, perhaps a few old tomes, maybe a stack of parchment scrolls tied with twine. But this... this was something else entirely.

The cavern stretched wider than Riftreach's great hall, its ceiling arched high overhead like the ribcage of some buried beast. Riftlight glowed faintly at the seams of the stone, veins of silver-blue running through the walls so that the air itself seemed alive, pulsing like a heartbeat.

And the shelves—Gods, the shelves. They rose floor to ceiling, carved directly into the cavern walls. Ladders leaned against them at impossible heights, and perched walkways bridged shelves across the open space like spiderwebs of stone and wood. Books jostled for space, their spines cracked and faded; scrolls stuck out of pigeonholes like reeds. And scattered between them were artifacts: a mask carved of bone, a dagger whose blade shimmered like water, a set of beads that pulsed faintly red as if remembering a heartbeat.

I stopped in the doorway, overwhelmed. "This is..."

"Sacred," Ness interrupted, bustling past me with an armful of parchment that looked one step from collapsing. They dumped it onto a side table and straightened their round spectacles. "Yes, yes, I know. Do close your mouth, Lady Evandra. The moisture can deteriorate the parchment."

I shut it quickly, cheeks warming.

Ness gestured impatiently for me to follow. "Now that you are sufficiently settled, we begin. Instruction, study, comprehension. You will attend me here every morning before your physical training in the afternoon."

Their voice carried the sharp precision of a commander and the overlong cadence of a scholar who lived half inside their own mind. I trailed after them, weaving between long stone tables piled with maps, open books, and artifacts half-wrapped in cloth.

Ness stopped at one of the central tables, swept a space clear with alarming efficiency, and pulled a leather-bound tome from a nearby stack. Its cracked cover looked older than I was, and the air around it almost hummed.

"*An Introduction to the Rift and Magical Beasts,*" Ness announced with a flourish, sliding it toward me. "Anonymous author, First Cycle. The foundation text for all Riftborn studies. You will begin here."

I froze. Recognition jolted through me. My fingers brushed the cover reverently. "I've read this one already."

Ness blinked, thrown off their script. "You... what?"

"My father gave me a copy," I explained quickly. "For my birthday this year, actually. It was my mothers."

For a moment, Ness simply stared at me, spectacles glinting in the Riftlight. Then they exhaled through their nose, muttering something that sounded suspiciously like, "A whole lesson plan out the window."

"You should have told me," they said at last, voice clipped.

"I didn't know it mattered."

"It matters," Ness replied, their tone softening almost imperceptibly. "He prepared you, then. More than most." Their eyes flicked to the book in my hands, then to my face. "And you understood it?"

"As much as I could," I admitted.

Ness gave a sharp nod, already scribbling notes in the margin of a parchment with furious precision. "Very well. We shall accelerate. No sense in plodding through material you already know. But you will reread it regardless, cover to cover. Context changes comprehension. What you skimmed before understanding the Rift existed may strike you differently now."

I nodded, trying to hide the swell in my chest. My father had given me this book. *He knew.* Maybe not everything—but he had wanted me to have this, to carry it even when I didn't understand why. Maybe my mother instructed him to.

"Then where do we start?" I asked.

Ness tapped the edge of their quill against their ledger, eyes narrowing at me as though recalibrating a complex equation. Finally, they turned and strode toward one of the taller shelves, muttering under their breath about "rearrangements to the syllabus." Their stubby fingers trailed over spines, pausing, then darting higher up the ladder in an agile scramble that seemed almost inhumanly precise.

When they descended, they carried a different volume—this one slimmer, its cover plain save for a faded insignia stamped in gold. They set it on the table before me with far more care than the last.

"Then we start here," Ness said. "Records of the early ambassadors. The Riftborn who chose not only to survive the purges, but to speak for us. To plead, negotiate, and—on rare occasions—persuade."

They flipped open the book, the pages brittle, edges darkened with age. In neat script, names and accounts marched down the columns. But my breath caught when I saw it.

Her name.

My mother's name.

Ness's voice gentled, though their diction remained exact. "Here—Lady Morwenna. Notorious for reckless bravery. Acclaimed for her success in saving dozens of Riftborn lives during the Great Change. Do you see?"

Their finger hovered above the passage, underlining the words without touching.

I leaned in. The letters swam. I had never seen her name in ink like this, set down as though she were legend.

"She—she's in here?" My throat ached around the words.

"Repeatedly," Ness said, already flipping further. "Here she is again, negotiating with the miners of Trevain. Here, smuggling a half dozen horned children across the border disguised as monks. Here—" Ness's eyes flicked up at me, sharp behind their spectacles. "Lady Morwenna was no mere sympathizer. She was the spine of our cause when others bent or broke. It seems... fitting that you carry her gift."

The swell in my chest was almost too much. "She never told me."

"Of course not," Ness said briskly. "To protect you. To protect all of us. It is possible your father may not even have known."

I touched the page, careful not to smudge the fragile ink. My mother's name. My mother's courage. Not in lullabies or half-told stories—but here, in the rebellion's bones.

"She was an ambassador," I whispered, half to myself. "She saved people."

"She *chose,*" Ness corrected firmly. "When faced with fear, she chose defiance. That is the pattern you should study, Lady Evandra. Not just beasts or visions. The will behind them. The choice."

The cavern seemed to hum around me, Riftlight glimmering like stars caught in stone. I closed my eyes for a moment, seeing her more clearly than I ever had: not just a mother bent over garden baskets, but a woman standing before soldiers with her head high, carrying secrets that would have burned anyone else alive.

"Then I'll learn," I said, opening my eyes.

Ness's lips twitched in what might have been approval. "Good. That will save me the trouble of scolding you further."

Chapter Twenty Five

Eldrake

It was finally the afternoon and time for our first bout of training. I knocked lightly on Eva's door.

"One second!" she called, and even her voice made my chest ache.

When the door opened, I nearly forgot how to speak. She stood there in her training leathers, somehow managing to look both battle-ready and heartbreakingly soft. Her red hair was braided in twin plaits over her shoulders, and her daggers were strapped to her hips like she was born with them.

"Good Gods, woman," I muttered.

She launched into my arms and kissed me full on the mouth. I groaned into it.

"I loved the flowers," she murmured, her lips still brushing mine. "Thank you."

My hands slid down to her waist, then her hips, then firmly cupped her perfect, round ass. "Fuck. You're going to make it impossible to concentrate today."

"And what kind of training will we be doing today, *Captain*?" she asked, her voice dripping with seductive playfulness as she batted her lashes at me.

"Don't tease me, Eva. I will take you right here in this hallway,"

I growled. Her lips curved into a mischievous grin, her teeth grazing her bottom lip as her eyes dared me to make good on my threat.

"No, no." I flicked her nose, earning a scowl. "We have to train. I have to do my job, but *fuck* you make it hard."

"I know," she quipped. "I felt it last night." She winked and licked her lip. I groaned, peeling her arms off my neck before I lost all semblance of self-control.

"Succubus," I muttered, grabbing her hand and dragging her down the hall. If I had stayed there another second, training would have been out of the question.

We wove through Riftreach's winding walkways and over footbridges, passing curious onlookers and the scent of warm bread drifting from morning stalls. When we reached the training hall, Eva's excitement faltered.

The cavernous room loomed before us—shadowed and echoing, its stone walls lined with racks of blades, staves, and practice gear. Torches flickered in wrought-iron sconces. In the center, the sand-covered sparring ring waited.

Eva stepped inside, her boots crunching softly on the ground. I followed, trying very hard not to stare at the way her leathers hugged her curves.

Okay, focus Drake. Don't look at her butt. Pretend she's just another soldier. A soft, squishy red-haired soldier with great tits. No! Fuck. Just pretend she's a guy. Wait-

"Where do we start?" she asked, dropping into what I could only assume was her version of a fighting stance— feet too close, shoulders stiff, chin too high.

"Today is an assessment," I said, circling her slowly. "We'll test your strength, balance, reflexes. How likely you are to stab yourself."

Her eyes followed me warily. I tapped her foot with mine. "Left foot back. Shoulder-width. Bend your knees."

She adjusted, brow furrowed in concentration. "Like this?"

"Close enough." I pressed a hand to her shoulder. She immediately toppled.

"Hey!" she flailed, catching herself.

"You're welcome." I smirked. "Again. This time, flex your thighs and brace your core. Pretend you've got something to prove."

She grumbled under her breath— probably rude— but resumed the stance. When I nudged her again, she barely wobbled.

"Better." I raised my hand. "Now, reflexes."

She blinked. "Like—"

I smacked her ass.

"Drake!" she yelped, spinning to swat me, cheeks flaming.

"You should've deflected that."

"Tell me, *Captain,*" she said, narrowing her eyes. "Do you smack all your trainees on the ass?"

"Yes." I deadpanned, then quickly twisted, moving behind her in a blur, and pressed my hand mockingly to her throat. "And they all block better than this."

She shoved my arm away with a huff, but a smile tugged at her mouth. "You're insufferable."

"Look, this is how you deflect. Try to hit me," she hesitated, then threw a half-hearted punch. I caught her wrist easily, twisted it behind her back, and pinned her arm with a flick.

"See?"

"Unfortunately." She tugged free, cheeks pink with frustration now.

We ran the drill again. She missed. Again. And again.

"Your hips are ahead of your fist," I said. "You're swinging like you're stirring soup, not trying to kill someone."

She growled under her breath and lunged at me, this time aiming for my ribs. I sidestepped easily and tapped her forehead.

"Boop."

She groaned. "You are the worst."

"I'm better than your footwork!" I said smugly.

But the next strike was sharper—instinctive. Her balance improved. She ducked faster. By the third round, she blocked my jab and nearly swept my leg.

"That's better," I said, breathing a little heavier. "Try again."

She did. And this time, when I twisted to grab her wrist, she beat me to it—twisting my arm behind my back with surprising strength.

She grinned up at me, breathless. "Did I just beat you?"

"I let you." I lied.

"You did not."

We moved on to strength training. I showed her how to squat correctly, then stood close behind her as she mimicked the motion. Too close. Her ass brushed my thigh on the way up, and my restraint nearly snapped in half.

She faltered. "You're standing way too close."

"That's to check form," I said flatly. "Totally professional."

Her smirk said she didn't believe me.

After a round of planks and pushups, she dropped onto the mat with a groan, sweat glistening on her brow. "I need a bath. And a new spine."

I sat beside her, my arms resting on my knees. "Not bad for your first day."

"Not bad?" She looked at me incredulously. "You insulted my soup skills and threw me around like a sack of potatoes."

"Yeah, but you kept getting up." I shrugged.

Her breathing slowed, her lashes casting shadows on her flushed cheeks.

I stood and offered my hand.

The bathhouse was ours. Steam draped the chamber like silk, curling against, soft light spilling from lanterns set into the stone. It smelled of eucalyptus, sharp and clean, like someone had thought to burn it for us.

Eva hesitated at the threshold, hands on the tie of her robe. "There's no firewood," she said, a half-complaint, half-dare.

Eva hovered at the threshold, fingers worrying the tie of her robe. Then she smiled—nervous, daring—and let it fall to the bench. Her skin pebbled instantly, gooseflesh rising over every inch the steam hadn't yet kissed.

"Remember the last time we were here?" she teased, stepping into the pool.

I crouched at the edge and pressed my palm to the water. Heat bled from the shimmer of scales at my wrist, running up my arm in a low, steady thrum. The pool warmed with a shiver, steam lifting in a sudden breath.

She sighed, low and helpless. "Show-off."

"Practical," I said, standing. "Now, in."

She sank beneath the steam until only her shoulders and the line of her throat showed above the surface. Her head tipped back, hair slick against her neck. The sound she made—small, almost indecent—went straight through me. "That's... Gods. That's perfect."

"Turn," I said before my courage thought better of it.

She blinked, then obeyed, scooting forward until her back was to me and the water lapped at her collarbones. I rolled my sleeves, set my palms to the knots braced beneath her shoulder blades, and pressed. Her breath caught. Then I felt her loosen—bit by bit—under my hands.

"You're... good at this," she murmured.

"Professional necessity," I said. "People keep swinging sharp things at me. I figured out how to repair the mess afterward."

My thumbs found the places combat had taught me to find—the stiff ridge where tension hoards itself, the roped line along her scapula that locks when you've been wielding a blade too long. I worked slow. When she winced, I eased. When she breathed out, I followed the breath with my hands. She relaxed so completely that I caught myself smiling—helplessly, stupidly.

"Drake?"

"Mm?"

"Is this a trap?"

"Define trap."

"You say 'bath' and 'ten minutes,' then proceed to make me melt."

"That would be a lure," I said. "Traps snap. Lures *invite*."

"Gods," she whispered, and the word came out like laughter.

The sound undid me. I leaned in, and with the barest brush of my lips I kissed the corner of her damp shoulder, a single point of heat amid the steam.

She froze. Then turned, knees rising onto the seat until we were face to face. Her fingers found my forearm, nails brushing just above the shimmer of scales.

"You're... still dressed," she whispered.

"Technicality," I said, and stepped straight into the pool. Boots, shirt, everything. The heat hit like a slap. My boots filled; my trousers grabbed my thighs; my shirt went heavy and immediately transparent.

She gasped—more laughter than shock—and clutched my collar as I sank in front of her. "You absolute menace."

"Accurate," I agreed, nodding enthusiastically.

Her hands dragged me closer, until our foreheads touched. "Ridiculous," she whispered.

"Ridiculously into *you*," I corrected, and kissed her.

The pool muffled the world. Her mouth was heat and honey, her hands twisting in my shirt. I curled an arm beneath her thighs and lifted, setting her onto the warm stone lip. Water poured down her ribs, her stomach, her throat.

"Drake—" she whispered, uncertain.

"Say stop," I told her. "Just one word, and I'll stop."

Her lips parted. Curved. "Don't."

So I didn't.

I kissed her knee. Then her thigh. Then higher, careful first, reverent. She trembled, biting her nails, trying to keep the sounds inside—but I felt them in the way her hips shifted under my hands.

"Eva." I lifted my eyes to hers and held. "Say it and I stop."

Her lips parted, trembled—and curved. "I know," she whispered.

The steam made the rest of the chamber a myth. There was only the warm stone under my hands and the trail of water down her ribs and the hitch of her breath when I kissed the inside of her knee. Only the slow, reverent path upward, my mouth learning her the way a thirsty man learns a spring—careful first, tasting the shape of the edges, and then bolder when her fingers knotted in my wet hair and urged me where the ache lived.

After that there weren't words, or if there were I didn't recognize them; there were only her hands guiding, and the way her spine arched when I found the right pressure, and the uneven rhythm of her breaths—too quick, then held, then released on a sound that made my knees go weak. I anchored one palm to the small of her back and let the other steady her thigh, and I forgot—gladly, gratefully—everything I had ever known about restraint.

My own hand found my cock beneath the water before I even thought about it, strokes keeping pace with her rhythm. She lay back on the stone, spine curved, breath trembling as her completion rocked her. I held on through it, forehead pressed to her thigh, every muscle in my back drawn taut with the ache of wanting more. Every flick of my tongue, every quake of her hips pushed me closer, until I was groaning against her skin, completely undone. The water took the proof, swirling away into steam.

I pressed my forehead to her knee and breathed until the shaking left both of us. The lamplight swayed and went still again. Her fingers loosened in my hair, drifted down to cup the edge of my jaw. She tugged, gentle. "Come here," she whispered.

I rose, the pool tugging at my clothes, and she welcomed me back into the heat of her. She caught my mouth with hers, slow now, grateful, and the thank-you in it nearly undid me. When my soaked shirt dragged cold against her stomach she shivered and laughed into the kiss. "You're going to catch your death."

"Impossible," I said against her lips. "Too stubborn."

We laughed into each other's mouths. I pulled her back into the pool, into my arms, her legs around my waist, her hands at the small of my back like she'd always belonged there. I kissed her again until there was nothing left but steam, heat, and the certainty that I would burn for her as long as the Rift let me breathe.

The following day after a well deserved night of sleep, I escorted Eva back to her chambers after training. Once inside, she excused herself to bathe, leaving me alone in the warm ambiance of her room. The enchanted lanterns throughout Riftreach cast a soft, golden glow, illuminating the space. Her honeysuckle scent lingered in the air, weaving itself into the room like an invisible thread. It was intoxicating and comforting.

I drifted over to her desk, where the worn tome on Riftborn creatures lay open.

Unable to resist, I picked it up and flipped through the pages, the parchment crackling faintly beneath my fingertips. The illustrations and scrawling text reminded me of my younger years, poring over maps and old manuals while training for the Uprising.

Curiosity tugged at me as I searched for a particular entry. Then I saw it: the folded corner, dog-eared with precision. I opened to the marked page.

DRAGONBLOODS

A slight grin tugged at my mouth. *She bookmarked me.* I skimmed the entry until my eyes snagged on the weaknesses section.

WEAKNESSES:

ALTHOUGH DRAGONBLOODS ARE PHYSICALLY RESILIENT, THEY ARE HIGHLY SENSITIVE TO BETRAYAL OR EMOTIONAL WOUNDS, OFTEN SUFFERING DISPROPORTIONATELY WHEN THEY LOSE SOMEONE THEY CARE FOR. THEIR INTENSE NATURE CAN LEAD THEM TO IMPULSIVE ACTIONS, SOMETIMES TO THEIR DETRIMENT. ADDITIONALLY, PROLONGED EXPOSURE TO POWERFUL MAGIC CAN WEAKEN THEM TEMPORARILY, AS THEIR BLOODLINE, THOUGH STRONG, CANNOT BEAR THE FULL WEIGHT OF DRAGON MAGIC.

NOTES:

DRAGONBLOODS REPRESENT A UNIQUE FUSION OF HUMAN ADAPTABILITY AND DRACONIC FEROCITY, MAKING THEM AS ALLURING AS THEY ARE DANGEROUS. THOSE WHO ENGAGE WITH A DRAGONBLOOD SHOULD DO SO, WITH CAUTION, FOR TO WIN A DRAGONBLOOD'S LOYALTY IS TO EARN A LIFELONG ALLY—OR LOVER—BUT TO BETRAY ONE IS TO SUMMON WRATH AS FIERCE AS DRAGON FIRE.

Great. I slammed the book shut with more force than necessary, the sound echoing through the room. Essentially, it was a written warning not to get involved with me, and she highlighted it. My chest tightened as irritation flared in my gut. I wanted to chuck the stupid book out the window.

I sighed heavily, trying to push down the frustration, when a muffled thump came from the adjoining bathing chamber. My head snapped up.

"Eva?" I called out, already crossing the room.

Silence.

"Evandra?" No response. My pulse spiked. I shoved the door open, and the sight punched the air from my lungs.

She was crumpled on the tile floor, completely nude, her soaked red hair fanned around her head like spilled blood. Her back arched slightly, muscles twitching, convulsing. Her eyes—Gods, her eyes—rolled back in her head, showing only white. Not drowning. Not fainting.

A vision.

"Eva!" I dropped to my knees beside her, panic clawing at my throat. Gently but swiftly, I scooped her into my arms, pulling her trembling body onto my lap. Her skin was freezing despite the warmth of the steam-filled room.

"I'm here," I whispered against her temple, my voice raw. "I've got you." She shook in my arms, shallow breaths stuttering from her parted lips. Her whole body was locked like the Rift itself had reached up and taken hold of her spine. I could do nothing but hold her through it—no training, no flame, no sword could stop this.

I tightened my grip, anchoring her. "Come back to me," I whispered, brushing damp strands from her forehead. Her face was pale, her body trembling. My chest ached with helplessness. All I could do was whisper her name and wait for the storm to pass.

Finally—*finally*—the tension in her body began to ebb. Her convulsions slowed, and her breaths deepened, though her eyelids remained fluttering. I loosened my hold slightly, enough to look down at her face.

"Eva?" I murmured. Her eyelids fluttered, then opened slowly. Green eyes met mine—dazed, unfocused, but there.

"Drake," she whispered, hoarse and breathless. She clutched weakly at my shirt. Her hand was trembling.

"I'm here," I said again, more softly this time.

Tears welled in her eyes. "I saw him."

Her voice cracked on the last word.

My blood turned to ice. "Who?"

But her strength gave out. Her body sagged against mine, her head resting on my chest as her breath evened into sleep.

I didn't move. I just held her.

Whatever she saw—it wasn't just a vision.

It was a warning.

Chapter Twenty Six

Evandra

"Among the most powerful Rift-wielders, there exists a rare ability to perceive the Rift as it manifests around others, appearing like a shimmering aura. This "Rift Sight" allows the wielder to discern not only the presence of Riftborn but also the magnitude of their connection to the Rift." — An Introduction to the Rift and Magical Beasts, Chapter 16

I felt the suffering of the kind of chill that seeps into your bones and scrapes at your soul. The air clung to my skin like damp velvet—heavy, silent, suffocating. When I blinked, the darkness peeled back slowly, revealing the chamber.

Cobblestone walls encased me, slick with age and shadow. Ornate golden frames hung in crooked rows, each housing a painting of catastrophe. Soldiers drowning in blood. Cities burning. Creatures towering above broken bodies. The oil-shined brushstrokes shimmered as if moving—like they were mid-scream, mid-collapse, eternally caught in a loop of destruction.

Desks cluttered with parchments and ancient tomes filled the space, their paper edges curling and yellowing with age. Strange artifacts—glinting metals, jagged crystals, and bone-carved totems lay scattered across the surfaces. The air was thick with the scent of old ink and damp stone. I turned slowly; each step was muffled as if the room itself absorbed sound.

For some inexplicable reason, it felt as though the room was alive—watching me, studying me. A pull, faint and insistent, tugged at my senses, drawing my attention to the left. My breath caught. There, standing alone in the gloom, was a mirror. It was massive, at least six feet tall, its thick silver frame twisting and writhing into the shape of a serpent. The serpent's scaled body coiled along the edges, its head poised at the top with its mouth open, fangs bared.

But it was the glass itself that made my stomach churn. The mirror was black—not just dark, but a void that seemed to drink in the faint light of the candles flickering in the chamber. The flames bent toward it, their glow diminishing as they neared its surface, as though the mirror were consuming them. I couldn't look away. The longer my gaze lingered, the more the air grew heavy and suffocating. A primal dread began to build in my chest, clawing at my sanity. The mirror wasn't just dark—it was wrong. It exuded an ancient malice, an intelligence that felt older than the stones around me. I couldn't shake the feeling that it was watching me, appraising me.

I took one step forward. Then another. And then a face lunged out from the void. It slammed against the glass in silence—a shrieking maw of rotted flesh and hollow eyes, its mouth a wound that stretched too far, too wide. The skin peeled and wept shadows as though the creature was made of nightmare and ash.

I stumbled backward with a cry—but the mirror held me. I felt it reach for me. Not physically—but through something deeper. Through the Rift. It knew me. Then, the world shattered like glass, and I was yanked back into my body with force.

I gasped violently as the vision spat me out. Air surged into my lungs like fire. My chest heaved. My entire body trembled as if I'd been plunged into icy water. The pain in my skull throbbed in tandem with the pounding of my heart. Drake's hands were on me—firm, steady, grounding.

"A mirror," I choked out, clutching at the damp fabric of his shirt. My head ached. My skin prickled with residual fear. Only then did I realize I was dripping wet, the cold tile leeching what little warmth remained in me.

"You're hurt," he said, one hand cradling my scalp as he checked for injury.

"No," I whispered. "I don't think so. I—I laid myself down. The vision started to hit while I was still standing." Drake crossed the room swiftly, returning with my robe. His movements were fluid, but I saw it —tension in his jaw. Worry in his brow. As he wrapped the robe around me and helped me to the bed, the cold slowly began to recede. But the memory of that mirror didn't.

"What did you see?" he asked, his tone both cautious and curious.

"It was... pure evil, Drake," my voice cracked as I struggled to find the words. My fingers twisted in the hem of my robe. "It was unlike anything I've ever experienced. The room—the place—where the mirror was... It felt alive. Dark. And the mirror, Gods, it saw me. I swear it saw me."

He furrowed his brow, his protective nature flaring visibly. "What do you mean it saw you?"

"I don't know how else to describe it. It wasn't just enchanted—it was malevolent, Drake. There was a face... twisted and terrible. It was only for a moment, but I can still feel its presence," my hands trembled in my lap, and I pressed them together to still them. "What do you know about magic items? Artifacts from before The Change?"

He shook his head, his expression grim. "Not much. They were all pretty much destroyed. Anything imbued with Rift energy is contraband now. There maybe something about it in the records. Ness would know."

Desperate for answers, I stood and rushed to the books lining the shelves of my chamber, my eyes darting across their spines. Fiction.

Romance. Tales of adventure I'd already devoured in my youth. Nothing that could explain the overwhelming darkness I'd seen.

Frustrated, I let out a sigh and returned to Drake's side, my shoulders slumping.

"The room around the mirror was so dark, Drake. It was suffocating, like it wasn't meant to exist. And the mirror—it was staring at me. It felt... alive," my voice cracked, and I dropped my gaze to my hands. "Gods, what am I doing? I feel like I'm wielding a magic so much bigger than I can comprehend. So much bigger than me." I couldn't hold back the panic any longer. Tears blurred my vision, spilling down my cheeks as my hands shook. Drake's hand, warm and steady, rested on my knee.

"We'll ask Ness about it tomorrow," he said firmly, his voice soothing and certain. "We'll find answers, Eva. I'll never let anything happen to you."

His words held a gravity that pulled me out of my spiraling thoughts. I met his eyes and saw the same protectiveness that had made me feel safe since the moment I met him. It reminded me of Papa, of the way he shielded me from the world's harshness. The thought sent a fresh wave of tears cascading down my cheeks.

"What's wrong?" Drake asked urgently, brushing a tear from my face with his thumb.

"I-I guess it's all finally sinking in," I stammered. "I've left everything I've ever known—my home, my father, my *entire life*—to risk it all. I'm terrified, Drake. This world is... *insane!* I miss my inn. My kitchen. My garden. It was easy. I was all so *easy*," the words tumbled out between sobs, raw and unfiltered.

Drake pulled me into his arms without hesitation, enveloping me in his warmth. His muscular arm wrapped securely around my shoulders as I buried my face in his chest, my tears soaking into his soft linen shirt. His free hand stroked my arm in slow, comforting motions, and his lips pressed a soft kiss to the top of my head. I cried until the ache in my chest began to ease, my sobs softening into sniffles. My breaths slowed, and I wrapped an arm around his waist, clinging to him like an anchor in a storm.

"Sorry." I muffled as I wiped my nose. "Thank you. For everything," I whispered, my voice thick with emotion.

"Always," he replied simply, his tone carrying a depth that made my heart swell. He held me a while longer, his presence a balm to my frayed nerves. Eventually, he helped me settle into bed. I reached for my old, familiar pillow, the scent of home still lingering in its fabric. It carried me back to my little attic room, to the days when life was simple, and the weight of the world didn't rest on my shoulders.

Drake stayed close, his steady breathing lulling me into calm. I pushed the terrible face in the mirror out of my mind and let the safety of his presence wrap around me like a shield. In his arms, I finally drifted into a deep sleep.

I was back in that room. *Godsdamnit.*

The same damp chill sank into my skin, coiling around my ribs. The air pressed against me, thick and wet. War paintings screamed silently from their golden frames. The mirror waited, coiled in silver serpents, its black surface still consuming every flicker of light.

But this time, I wasn't alone.

Three figures loomed—two monstrous, misshapen men flanking a table, where a third stood hunched over a parchment covered in twisting glyphs. His skin was gray. Gaunt. Cloaked in shadow. Though, he didn't move like a man. He moved like something decayed that was somehow still thinking.

Vyper. The name formed in my throat before I even recognized him. Then his head snapped up.

"She's here," he hissed. My blood turned to ice. His lifeless eyes swept the chamber, searching—seeing.

"Sire?" one of the wretches rasped.

"The Seer," his smile stretched too broad, too sharp. He turned toward me, reaching with long, gnarled fingers—-

I gasped awake, bolting upright. The room tilted around me in the dark. My heart pounded like a war drum. Something shifted beside me.

"Eva, it's me." Drake's voice—calm, steady—cut through the noise in my head.

I whipped toward him, clutching the blanket. "He saw me," I choked out. "Drake—he saw me. Vyper."

He blinked once, and I watched the sleep vanish from his eyes. "Vyper? Are you sure?"

"I'm sure," I whispered. My voice trembled like my hands. "He looked right at me. Said, 'The Seer is here.'"

Drake sat up, pressing a firm hand to my back. "We need to tell Julian."

He was already moving, conjuring a small flame in his palm. Shadows leaped across the room.

I rose, legs unsteady, tugging on my robe with shaking fingers. My breath caught in my throat again—not from fear this time, but from how real it had felt. The chill of that chamber still clung to my skin like a curse.

Julian's quarters were modest, cramped, and cluttered with relics of another life: faded maps, a brass compass, a tangled net hung like a tapestry. A ship's wheel leaned in the corner, long since detached from any vessel. The whole place smelled faintly of salt despite being buried under a mountain.

He didn't sit behind his desk—just dropped into an armchair with a sigh, then motioned at me. "Talk."

I hesitated for only a moment before the words spilled out: the cold chamber, the paintings, the mirror, how it pulled at me. How it saw me. And then Vyper—how he turned. How he spoke. How his eyes locked onto mine like he'd reached across the veil and touched my soul.

Julian listened, half-shadowed by the flickering lanterns. For all his flair, he didn't interrupt once, not even with a quip. When I finished, he rubbed his face with both palms and let out a gusty exhale. "Well," he said at last, mustache twitching. "Are you quite sure it wasn't symbolic? Visions are tricksy things—sneaky little bastards. They rarely play fair."

"It wasn't a dream," I said, more forcefully than I intended. "It was... contact. He knew I was there. He said, 'The Seer is here.' He felt me."

Julian's good humor dimmed. His mustache twitched downward as his eyes sharpened, weighing my words.

"I've seen what she looks like after a vision," Drake said, arms folding. "This was different. Her Rift was... crackling. I could feel it before she woke up."

Julian tilted his head, his gaze narrowing like a hawk sighting prey. "Why were you in her bed, Captain?"

The silence that followed was brutal. My face flushed hot. Drake's jaw flexed once, twice, but he didn't answer. He didn't need to—the slip was already hanging between us.

Julian leaned back slowly in his chair, steepling his long fingers as though he'd just won a hand of cards. "Interesting. I don't recall 'bedside watchman' being one of the duties I assigned you." He shot a dark look at Drake.

"Commander—" Drake began, but his voice came low, tight.

Julian cut him off with a single raised hand, his tone cool and clipped. "Another time. We don't have the luxury." He leaned forward, gaze sweeping the table. "Whatever this mirror is, we need to find it. Now."

Minutes later we were inside the archives, the sconces flaring to life with a soft thrum as Ness traced an intricate sigil in the air. Golden light spilled across the cavernous space, illuminating the vast cathedral of stone and memory.

Stone shelves rose like canyon walls, their edges carved with ancient lettering. Mineral veins shimmered faintly in the dark rock, like stars trapped underground. The scent of wax, parchment, and cold stone hit me all at once—rich and grounding. Even so, something about this place felt... unsteady tonight. Like the air was thinner. Or maybe I was just different now.

"I almost forgot how massive this place is," I murmured, my voice hushed.

Ness gave a faint smile. "Most of our history lives underground now. Like us."

We passed glass cases holding ancient weapons, glowing vials, and strange tools I couldn't name. One mirror caught my eye—just a little too silvery, its surface rippling like disturbed water. I looked away quickly.

"Are all of these magical?" I asked, brushing my fingers along the edge of a nearby shelf.

"Some," Ness said. "Others are cursed. Some are just… waiting. We keep what we don't dare destroy," the way they said it made the hair on my arms rise.

We reached a wide, circular table nestled deep within the archive's heart. Tomes and scrolls lay scattered across it; their edges curled from age and use. Ness wordlessly climbed a stepladder—fast and practiced despite its sway—and pulled a black leather-bound book from the very top shelf. Its cover was cracked and ridged like dried skin. I didn't know why, but I held my breath.

They flipped through the pages with the care of someone defusing a bomb. And then—stopped.

The page looked back at me. I froze.

A silver serpent coiled around the edge of an obsidian mirror; its fangs bared, its tongue forking through the frame. But it was the reflection that paralyzed me: that face—the same one I'd seen in my vision. Mangled. Hollow-eyed. Grinning with sharp, jagged teeth as if it knew I was there.

My stomach dropped. I stepped backward, nearly tripping over my own feet.

"That's it," I whispered. My voice cracked like splintering ice. "That's the mirror."

Drake moved instantly, placing a hand on my back. Julian leaned in. Ness's voice turned grave.

"I believe this to be the Vessel of Azh'raim."

Julian's brows furrowed. "What is it?"

Ness laid the book flat on the table, smoothing the edges with reverent fingers. "Azh'raim was said to be the God of decay, darkness, and dominion. No temples, no worshippers—just rumors. Fear. This mirror… it was crafted to reach him. Or something that *claimed* to be him. We don't know. All we have are scraps—burnt records, fragments of history. But if Vyper has it—"

"He's listening," I said, my voice hollow. "He's communing. That's how he sensed me. That's how he looked right at me."

Julian's face tightened. "It would explain a lot. The unnatural beasts. His uncanny timing. The King's unnaturally long life."

"But why would The King risk keeping something so powerful around?" I thought out loud.

"He needs him." Julian answered simply.

Drake frowned, arms crossed tight. "Needs him for what? The bastard's half demon already."

"Exactly," Julian said. "Vyper's the only one who can see through our wards. He's the only one who can create beasts strong enough to match us in battle. That kind of skill keeps the King's throne safe when his soldiers can't. As long as Vyper keeps feeding him victories, the King doesn't care where his magic comes from."

Ness adjusted their spectacles, voice clipped but thoughtful. "We suspect the arrangement is transactional. Vyper offers the King intelligence, wards, and his beasts. In return, the King offers Vyper legitimacy, protection, and access to the court. To everyone else, he looks like a loyal servant—when in truth, he's working a much darker bargain."

"Darker how?" I asked quietly.

Ness's gaze flicked to me, then back to the parchment. "Azh'raim. Souls bartered for favors. Power traded like coin. He builds his army from the dead and the damned, and the King... allows it, because the King only sees results."

Julian leaned back, a humorless smile tugging at his mustache. "So here's the truth: if we get to Vyper, we get to the King. Cut off his warlock, and he loses the eyes that keep him in power. But don't mistake this for loyalty. Vyper doesn't serve the King. He uses him. One day, he'll tire of playing the servant—and then we'll see which master he truly serves."

Drake's voice cut through the silence. "Can it be destroyed?"

Ness hesitated. Their gaze lingered on the face in the illustration. "Most relics of this scale defy destruction. They twist the very laws of magic around them. But this one... this one was forged with malice. Its only purpose is to serve something that should never have been reached. If there's any artifact that can be unmade—this is it."

Julian frowned. "Plainly, Ness."

Ness looked up, voice flat. "If this mirror still exists—and if Vyper has it—it *must* be destroyed. Or it will destroy us."

Silence followed, heavy as stone. I stared at the face on the page. Its inked eyes seemed deeper than before, as if it could see me again.

Drake's hand slid into mine. "Then we do it."

I nodded slowly, nausea still coiled in my gut. "Destroy the mirror... destroy Vyper... get closer to the King."

Julian exhaled, quiet but resolute. "Then we plan. At first light. Dismissed."

I slept deeply and, mercifully, didn't dream. When I woke, Drake was gone, but a note waited for me on the desk:

Didn't want to wake you. I'll fill you in later—bringing lunch.
—D

I smiled faintly, but the quiet gnawed at me. The silence felt too large without him. Trying to shake it, I sat at the vanity and opened my mother's book. Her signature—bold and looping—marked the first page, faded but unmistakable. My fingers traced the ink. I still couldn't wrap my head around it. You started a rebellion? You, with the soft hands and lullabies and garden baskets?

But something wasn't right.

The rebellion started over a century ago.

In my lesson with Ness only days ago, they said the rebellion had begun more than a hundred years ago. Riftreach itself was over a century old.

And you—you only lived into your forties.

The math hit me like a blow. My breath caught. Gods... that means you must have been—who knows how old when you died! The realization clawed through me, cold and impossible, and I stared at the page as if the ink might rearrange itself into an explanation.

I slammed the book shut and stood, pacing. My heart was hammering. Had my father lied to me, too? Had they both?

The door creaked open.

Drake stepped in, balancing a tray. "They had blueberry muffins—"

"How old are you?" I blurted.

He froze mid-step. "What?"

I crossed my arms. "How *old* are you, Drake?"

"Uh—twenty-nine," he said slowly, setting the tray down. "Eva, what's going on?"

"Ness said my mother started the rebellion. With Julian. That was over a hundred years ago. She died in her forties. Explain that."

Understanding dawned across his face, followed by a quiet wince. "Shit. Eva—I thought you knew."

"Knew what?" My voice cracked.

"Riftborn age slower than humans," he said gently. "A lot slower. It's not something we talk about openly—there's a reason. If people catch on, figure out what you are— you get hunted."

I sank into the chair, my pulse roaring in my ears.

"She must have hidden it," he continued. "So did your father. Probably even from you, to keep you safe."

The weight of it settled like a stone in my chest. I'd spent my whole life believing a version of the truth so carefully built that I hadn't seen the cracks. My breath hitched. A tear slipped free before I could stop it.

Drake crossed to me in two strides, brushing the tear away with his thumb. "You and I will age slower, too," he said quietly.

More tears followed—hot, frustrated, aching. "I'm so tired of being lied to," I whispered. "Of being kept in the dark. I think... I think my father hiding the truth finally broke something."

He knelt in front of me, voice low and certain. "I won't lie to you. Not about this. Not about anything."

I nodded, but the ache didn't fade. He kissed my forehead and pulled me into his arms without another word. Just held me. No pressure. No questions. It felt warm- but my hurt wouldn't fade.

That evening, training passed without incident—sword drills, footwork, the usual patterns—but my mind wasn't in it. Every strike, every parry felt dulled, my movements weighted with the secrets burning behind my eyes. Dinner was much the same: the table spread wide with food, rich and fragrant, yet every bite tasted hollow on my tongue.

Later, when the lamps dimmed and quiet took the ship, Drake fell asleep curled around me, one arm slung over my waist, his hand twitching faintly with dreams. His long hair draped over his eyes, and he let out the occasional soft snore—quiet and strangely comforting. Gods, even unconscious, he was trying to keep me close. But I couldn't stay still. My thoughts wouldn't stop unraveling. Every time I closed my eyes, I saw my mother's handwriting. I saw the lie I'd lived wrapped in love. I saw how easily it had become a truth.

Slowly, I slid out from under Drake's arm. He muttered something, shifted, then sprawled dramatically across the bed like he'd always owned it. I bit back a smile.

"Sleep well, Captain," I whispered, brushing a strand of hair from his forehead. I laced up my boots, wrapped my cloak around my shoulders, and slipped out the door.

The fire had burned low. The sheets were tangled. My mind felt louder than the silence around me. I'd flipped my pillow three times, hunted the cool side, and begged sleep to come. But how could I rest when my entire life had just tilted on its axis?

Not only had my mother lied about who she was—what she was—but suddenly nothing felt safe. I'd been thrown into this strange world with the fate of thousands pressing down on my shoulders, every step dictated by choices I hadn't made.

The corridor greeted me with its usual hush, the ship deck thunking beneath my boots. The two guards stepped aside without questions. It made me grin just a bit, at least I'd earned their trust and respect.

Outside, Riftreach slept, but it wasn't dead. Its silence pulsed, alive and listening, as if the cavern itself breathed with me. I stepped into the stillness and felt it wrap around me—not oppressive, not hollow, but vast, reverent. The hush of Riftreach wasn't absence; it was a presence, a watchfulness, as though the city had been waiting for me to notice it properly. I'd realized I'd been so wrapped up in every detail of Drake, I hadn't given the city nearly enough of my attention.

I followed the main causeway, the hanging bridge leading to a cobbled path dipping gently downward before curving between two towering stalagmites. What had once been natural rock columns had long ago been coaxed and hollowed out into towers. Balconies jutted outward like ribs, each marked with ironwork railings in intricate patterns—spirals, knots, the outlines of wings. Ropes of ivy and flowering vine cascaded from them, the plants bioluminescent, glowing with a pale green-gold as though moonlight itself had decided to root here. Tiny blossoms opened despite the darkness, their petals catching and reflecting Riftlight with a delicate brilliance.

I continued down the path marveling at the Riftborn engineering. Lanterns swayed in unseen drafts, suspended from carved iron hooks and rope pulleys. Their light was warmer than the coolness of Riftlight —amber and gold, pooling across flagstones polished smooth by generations of feet. Here and there, the lantern flames flickered against mosaics pressed into the walls, shards of broken glass salvaged from the surface world and arranged into scenes of nature or windows looking over landscapes. I slowed, letting my fingertips graze one of the visages, its surface uneven and cool.

The very bones of the city were beautiful—an underground forest of stone and light, grown not by nature alone but by countless hands who had insisted on survival. Drakes pride made so much sense to me now.

I wandered past closed doorways tucked into stone alcoves, their archways softened with curtains of woven reed or dyed wool. From behind some came the muted hum of life: a child's giggle, stifled quickly; the scratch of a chair against stone; a lullaby sung low in a language I didn't recognize. Warmth seeped beneath one door, carrying the scent of bread baked earlier in the evening, lingering even now. A market stall stood shuttered on my right, its awning rolled tight, but baskets of fruit still glistened faintly under the lantern glow, guarded by nothing more than trust.

Trust. The word curled in my chest.

A pair of guards leaned against a low wall farther ahead, their spears resting lightly at their sides. When they saw me, they didn't stiffen or demand an explanation as to why I was wandering around the alleys at night. They only inclined their heads in subtle acknowledgement—enough to say, *we see you, you belong here.* My throat tightened unexpectedly, and I returned the gesture before continuing on.

The air shifted as the passage widened, opening into one of Riftreach's many plazas. It spread before me like a cathedral: high stone ribs arching into a vaulted ceiling where vines dripped down like chandeliers, with hanging blooms that were each faintly glowing. In the center of the plaza lay a pool and fountain, its water impossibly clear, fed by some hidden spring. Riftlight shimmered across its surface, casting ripples of silver across the surrounding buildings.

I sank onto the edge of a bench nearby, breathing in the space. The cavern ceiling soared so high it was easy to imagine it as a sky, the vines as stars frozen mid-fall. The realization came slowly, as though the city itself whispered it into me: *This is home now.*

Not because I had chosen it yet, but because something in the stone and Riftlight had chosen *me.*

I pressed a hand to my chest, steadying myself. Not only had my mother lied about who she was, about what she was, but every memory I thought anchored me had shifted, cracked and then reformed. Nothing felt safe anymore. Nothing felt simple. Instead, I had been thrust into this strange, glittering underworld, feeling as though the fate of thousands rested squarely on my shoulders. I hated it. I feared it. But beneath all of that... I felt alive here.

At least I had been given one choice. *Him.*

I rose again, continuing through narrower alleys, where staircases spiraled up stalagmites into dwellings perched high above. Gardens hung in tiers, overflowing with herbs and flowers grown in troughs of soil hauled from the surface. I caught the scent of lavender, thyme, wild mint. Somewhere, a cat mewed softly, its silhouette darting between shadows. A laundry line stretched overhead, pale cloth fluttering like ghosts in the cavern breeze.

Everywhere, life had been carved into the stone. Life insisted on staying.

I passed another guard, who offered me a faint smile. I returned it, realizing with a start that I didn't feel like an intruder anymore. A visitor, yes. But not unwanted. Not unwelcome.

The path climbed, winding toward one of the upper balconies that overlooked the cavern. My breath came short by the time I reached it, but when I stepped out, the view stole whatever I had left. Riftreach sprawled below me like a kingdom reversed, its towers rising downward from stalactites, its lights blooming upward from roots and vines. The cavern walls pulsed with veins of Riftlight, turning the entire hollow into something that felt less like stone and more like a living body. And in its heart, I realized, I stood not as a trespasser, but as a piece of it.

The silence here wasn't silence at all. It was belonging.

I leaned against the railing, tears pricking hot at the corners of my eyes before I could stop them. Home had always been a cramped inn, a life of tending rooms and pouring ale and never quite fitting into the lines my father drew for me. Here, among stone and Riftlight and strangers who trusted me enough to nod instead of question, I felt something I had never let myself imagine before.

I belonged. For the first time, I wasn't running from the lies of my past—I was stepping into something I wanted. Belonging didn't erase the weight on my shoulders, but it gave me the strength to bear it. Now, I knew where I was going. Back to *him*. Back to Drake. My *choice*. Whatever lay ahead, I would face it with him—not as a frightened girl clinging to borrowed strength, but as a woman who had found her place, and was finally ready to claim it.

By the time I returned, the fire had burned down to soft embers.

Drake was still asleep—on his back now, arm slung over his face, mouth parted just slightly in the quiet rhythm of sleep. The blankets were halfway off the bed, one large foot dangling over the edge. My chest ached with something I didn't have a name for.

I stood there in the doorway, heart still bruised, eyes still raw, and realized I didn't want to sleep.

We still didn't have a plan. Not for the mirror, not for whatever it wanted from me. But I was tired of running. Tired of waiting. For tonight, I just needed to feel something solid.

I stepped softly across the room and lowered myself onto the edge of the bed beside him. He stirred at the movement, eyes fluttering open, squinting toward me.

"Eva?" he rasped, voice thick with sleep.

"Hey," I whispered. "Sorry to wake you."

He reached out blindly and found my hand. "You okay?"

I nodded. "I just... wanted to see you."

His thumb brushed across my palm, gentle and grounding. "You're seeing me," he said, smiling lazily. "Unless I'm dreaming. In which case, don't wake me up."

I leaned down, pressing a kiss to the corner of his mouth.

"Not a dream," I whispered. "Just me. Choosing this. Choosing you."

He sat up slowly, eyes clearer now, searching my face. Whatever he saw there must have quieted whatever question had been forming on his lips.

I looked down at him—this warrior who was both shield and fire—and something in me cracked open.

I leaned forward and kissed him.

He rose with me, his arms wrapping around my waist, the kiss deepening. It wasn't hungry—not yet. It was sweet. Soft. My fingers brushed his jaw. His stubble scratched my palms.

"To win a Dragonblood's loyalty is to earn a lifelong ally," I murmured, quoting my index. Then, softer, almost daring him: *"Or a lover."*

His breath caught.

"Which one am I?" I whispered, brushing my lips against his throat.

He inhaled sharply as my fingers slid beneath his waistband.

"You don't have to—" The protest already fading from his lips.

"I know," I said, voice steady as I kissed the hollow of his throat. "I want to."

Drake's chest rose under my touch, his muscles tensing like he was holding back a storm. I dropped to my knees before him, my palms grazing the crimson scales that curled along his thighs—warm, supple, nothing like I'd imagined. He shivered as I ran my hands over them, reverent.

I pulled gently on the hem of his shorts and tugged them low. He sprang free. My breath caught. Even having felt him inside me, the sight of him like this made my mouth go dry.

I took him in hand, slow and teasing, my thumb brushing along his flushed head. He sucked in a breath, his hand slipping into my hair, fingers gentle but taut with restraint. Then I kissed him—softly, deliberately—before trailing my tongue along the length of him in a slow, sinuous motion. His groan was deep and low, guttural. Primal.

I looked up. His silver eyes had gone molten, his mouth slightly open, and for once... he looked completely undone. Encouraged, I took more of him into my mouth, my hand stroking what I couldn't reach. He twitched in my grip, his thighs flexing under my palms.

"Fuck, Eva..." His voice broke around my name. I hollowed my cheeks, letting my tongue swirl with each motion, savoring the taste of him, the heat, the sounds he made. One hand slid up his chest, nails grazing over his ribs. He hissed, his hips jerking forward—and I didn't stop him. He hit the back of my throat, and I gagged slightly but held him there, breathing through my nose. He whimpered. Actually whimpered.

"Gods, I'm gonna—" I squeezed the base of his cock and pulled back just enough to look up at him again, my voice low, breath hot. "I want you to," his restraint snapped. Both hands cradled my face, thumbs brushing my cheeks as he fucked into my mouth in slow, controlled thrusts. His groans came louder now, every breath ragged.

His head fell back. I watched his throat work, the sweat on his brow, the way his body trembled as he held on. I moaned around him. That did it. With a strangled cry, he came hard, hips stuttering as he spilled into my mouth. His fingers clenched in my hair, not pulling, just holding. Grounding.

I swallowed. Slowly. When I looked up again, he was staring down at me like he couldn't believe what had just happened.

"Eva," he said, breathless. "You're going to be the death of me."

I rose, laughing softly, and wrapped my arms around his neck, pressing myself to his chest. "Is that all it takes?" I teased, my voice light and playful.

He groaned again, dragging me into a kiss that tasted like desperation and awe. His hands found my waist, and I melted against him, basking in the buzz between us.

"I don't think I can walk straight," he muttered against my hair.

I smirked into his collar. "Good." I leaned into his embrace, nuzzling into the warmth of his throat and breathing in his scent.

The days in Riftreach began to take on a rhythm, though nothing about them was ever dull. Each morning started with training sessions with Drake. He was relentless, pushing me to my limits and then just a little further. It was grueling—my muscles burned, my lungs screamed for air, and I often left the barracks drenched in sweat—but I relished in every moment we spent together.

"You're improving," he said one morning, sounding almost surprised as I blocked one of his strikes during a reflex drill.

I smirked, out of breath. "You're just going easy on me."

"Don't flatter yourself," he grinned, and then he swept my legs out from under me.

I yelped, but before I could hit the mat, his arms caught me in one fluid motion, holding me suspended against his chest like I was nothing.

His lips were way too close to my ear when he murmured, "That's twice now. You'd better start paying attention."

"Stop being so distracting," I muttered, trying not to notice the way his arm flexed beneath me. Completely unhelpful. We reset. Again. Jab, block, pivot. He moved like a shadow—fast, controlled, impossible to predict. Still, I watched him closer this time. Not just to win. I wanted to impress him. I wanted that look in his eyes again—the one he gave me when I got it right.

When he was proud of me.

I narrowed my eyes. "Okay. Let's try something different."

"Oh?" His smirk deepened. "Finally bored of losing?"

Now he's gonna get it. I dropped into a low stance, feinted left, and then shot toward his centerline. He blocked my first strike—but I pivoted, hooked my foot behind his, and dropped him square on his ass. There was a moment of stunned silence.

Drake blinked up at me from the mat, brows raised. "Did you just trip me?"

I grinned, breathless. "Sure did."

"I must be concussed," he muttered, rubbing the back of his head. Then, almost too casually—like the words slipped out before he could catch them—"Or maybe I'm in love."

His eyes flicked up to mine, quick but loaded, as if testing how much of himself he'd just given away. My blood surged, a dizzying rush, like the floor had dropped out beneath me.

"You're definitely something," I managed, shoving my hand toward him, trying to keep my voice light. "But love? That might be above my pay grade."

He didn't take my hand. Instead, he yanked—swift, effortless—pulling me down until I landed with an "oof" on top of him.

"Cheater!" I laughed, wriggling.

"You tripped *me!*" he said, his arms tightening around me. "That's a violation of the rules. And you know what happens when you break the rules."

"You tripped me!" he said, his arms tightening around me. "That's a violation of the rules. And you know what happens when you break the rules."

"I'm having trouble imagining this scenario on a battlefield," I said, nose-to-nose with him, his hands placed on my low hips.

"Anything can happen," he smirked. And then, wickedly, his hand darted down to the back of my thigh—the exact ticklish spot he'd found before—and pressed just hard enough to make me squirm. "Especially when I know your weak points."

I yelped, laughing despite myself as I twisted against him. "That's not fair!"

"War never is." His grin widened, though his grip on me stayed firm. "But now I'm highly motivated to see what other moves you've been hiding."

I huffed, determined not to let him win, and quickly managed to pin his wrists above his head, straddling him. "Careful, Captain. I'm a fast learner."

His eyes darkened just a little. "Yeah," he said softly. "You are."

And the way he said it made my heart skip a beat. I hesitated, my gaze fixed on his handsome features. I needed to get off of him before the mood got entirely out of hand.

Also, Ness would definitely kill us if I showed up late to the archives with a less-than-legitimate excuse.

"Alright," I said, brushing myself off. "Back to it. Stop distracting me." I shot him a glare.

Drake propped himself up on his elbows, looking way too pleased with himself.

"Don't threaten me with a good time."

Afternoons were for Ness.

They had a way of making learning feel both like an honor and a punishment. Their sharp gestures, their clipped diction, their absolute refusal to "simplify" anything made my head spin more often than not. Yet beneath all the prickliness, I caught flashes of warmth—the way they would shove another book into my arms the moment I finished one, or the meticulous notes they scrawled in margins so I wouldn't lose my place.

"Lady Evandra," Ness said one afternoon, adjusting their spectacles with one precise finger. "You are progressing, though still at a rate I would categorize as... cautious. I understand the Rift manifests irregularly, but irregularity itself can be mapped, if one applies sufficient rigor. Today's exercise will test whether you can create repeatable results under controlled conditions."

They deposited a heavy tome into my hands. Its cracked leather binding looked as though it had survived more centuries than any human had a right to. "This," Ness said, "charts the ebb and flow of Rift surges recorded during the Third Cycle—what some historians call the Dawn of the Riftborn Age. If you can recognize the patterns of resonance, you may find a way to predict your own visions. And if prediction is possible, control may follow."

"Control," I echoed, the word sticking in my throat. "I didn't realize that was possible."

"Anything is possible with discipline and knowledge," Ness replied briskly, already pulling scrolls from a higher shelf. "The Rift responds to order—or chaos. You must decide which you will embody."

Across the table, Drake had been pretending to read for the past hour. His boots were kicked up on a chair, his broad frame sprawled in a way that made him look both careless and predatory. Every so often I caught his eyes drifting toward me, his smirk deepening when I noticed.

"She's already more competent than half our recruits," he drawled, his silver gaze glinting with mischief. "Let her figure it out her own way, Ness. She doesn't need a lecture every time she sneezes wrong."

Ness snapped their head toward him. "Captain Eldrake, if you insist on trivializing a discipline older than the Kingdom itself, I will have to ask you to leave." Their hands flapped in agitated emphasis. "The Rift is not a tavern brawl. It cannot be mastered with muscle and luck."

Drake lifted his hands in mock surrender, though his grin didn't falter. "Forgive me. Carry on. I'll just sit here quietly and... observe."

"You never sit quietly," I muttered, flipping open the tome.

He winked. "I'm *observing*."

Ness huffed and muttered something that sounded like, "impossible men, all brawn, no sense of reverence." Then they launched into another explanation, their words spilling fast, tangled, like a dam loosed of its river.

"This passage—here, see the glyph along the margin? This refers to the principle of emotional resonance. Emotions are not merely influences; they are the very currency by which Riftborn access the Rift. Joy, grief, rage—they are catalysts. If you can learn to center yourself, your visions may sharpen. Emotional chaos produces chaotic manifestations."

I bit my lip. Emotional chaos. My gaze flicked toward Drake. He was leaning back now, watching me with lazy amusement, and my pulse betrayed me instantly. Emotional chaos, indeed.

"I'll... work on that," I said, trying to focus on the glyphs.

Ness gave a curt nod. "Good. Then let us test it."

They cleared the table with a sweep of their hand, scrolls and loose pages stacked with almost alarming precision. From a shelf, Ness pulled down a glass sphere, faintly clouded, its surface rippling with a subtle inner light.

"This," Ness explained, setting it before me, "is a minor Rift vessel. It responds to psychic resonance. A harmless instrument, but it will serve to gauge whether you can channel at will."

"Harmless?" I asked, narrowing my eyes.

"Entirely. Unless you happen to shatter it, in which case shards of crystal may embed themselves in your hands and face."

"Encouraging," I muttered.

Drake chuckled. "Don't worry, Eva. I'll catch the shards before they touch you."

"Captain Eldrake," Ness said sharply, "you are not helping."

Drake only smirked wider.

I pressed my hands to the sphere. It was cool, smooth, deceptively simple. "What do I do?"

"Breathe," Ness instructed. "Summon a thought. A memory. Anything that stirs the Rift within you. Focus on the emotion, not the image. Let the feeling bleed into the sphere."

My throat tightened. I thought of the fire that consumed my home. Of my mother's lullabies, turned suddenly to lies. Of Colin's hands pinning me down. My skin crawled, my chest tightening—

The sphere glowed, faint and trembling.

"Better," Ness said softly. "But chaotic. Too much fear."

I closed my eyes. Fear twisted. But there was something else—something warmer. I thought of Drake's cloak around my shoulders, his laugh rumbling against my back, the way he had held me that night when the dreams finally stilled.

Heat bloomed in my chest. The sphere flared bright.

My eyes snapped open. The glass throbbed with inner light, pulsing in rhythm with my heartbeat.

Drake leaned forward, his smirk faltering into something else—something raw.

"Fascinating. Emotional resonance, yes, but... anchored. Your Rift is not only feeding from your own core—it is tethered to another." Their eyes flicked quickly from me to Drake before their quill scratched furiously across the page, notes spilling faster than their mouth. "Something potentially dangerous. Not a typical bond, no."

My stomach lurched. Bond? Tethered? Our magic was *tethered*? What did that even mean? And why did Drake suddenly look like he'd seen a ghost?

He'd gone still, unnervingly so. The lazy smirk was gone, replaced by something shuttered and sharp. He stared at the sphere like it had betrayed him.

I forced myself to breathe, dragging my palms off the glass before it could flare again. "Not… a typical bond?" I repeated, the words tasting foreign. "What do you mean?"

Ness hummed distractedly, still scribbling. "Rare. Very rare. But possible." They ignored my question. They didn't even look up.

I looked at Drake. And Gods, he looked strange—too rigid, like he was trying to disappear into the chair. My pulse thudded painfully in my ears. Why does he look so fucking weird right now?

Without thinking, I reached across the table, brushing the back of his hand with my fingertips. "Are you okay?"

He blinked, once. Twice. His jaw flexed, silver eyes snapping up to meet mine with a force that almost knocked the air from my lungs. "I'm fine," he said, too quickly. Too tight.

Ness cleared their throat as though the room hadn't just shifted. "Something potentially dangerous," they repeated, more to themselves than to us. "But also very promising."

The lesson trudged on—Ness droning about mitigating variables, about emotional resonance as if nothing earth-shattering had just happened. But my head wouldn't stop spinning. Bond. Not typical. Tethered.

And Drake…

Drake hadn't let go of my hand.

Chapter Twenty Seven

Felix

I WASN'T SNOOPING. Let's just get that clear right now.

I was walking. Taking a break. Stretching my legs. The healer's equivalent of a palate cleanse. You patch up three bruised ribs, mend a dislocated shoulder, and then talk a Hellwrought boy out of sawing his own horns off because he thinks they're "uneven"—tell me you don't need air.

So no—I wasn't snooping.

I just... happened to walk past the archives.

And I just... happened to see Eva.

She was sitting at the big oak table with Ness, her copper hair glowing in the lamplight, her brow furrowed as she concentrated on the glass sphere between her palms. Riftlight shimmered faintly inside it, pulsing in time with her breath.

And Drake? Drake was pretending to read in the corner like the world's worst spy. He wasn't even subtle about it—boots up, arms crossed, staring at her like she'd invented the concept of air.

The sphere flared. Bright. Too bright. Eva gasped, but didn't let go. And in that moment, I felt it: not just her Rift, but his. Tangled. Anchored. Ness's quill scratched furiously as they muttered something about "bonded resonance" and "not a typical bond."

And Drake—oh, he froze. Like someone had nailed him to the floor. Silver eyes locked on her, jaw clenched, the picture of a man who'd just been caught with both hands in the Rift jar.

Eva, Gods bless her, just looked confused. Tired. Like she was trying to puzzle out a riddle that no one had given her the answer key for. She even touched his hand, whispered, "You okay?"

And the bastard lied.

"I'm fine," he said, voice all tight and brittle.

I nearly barged in right there. Instead, I kept walking, because I knew I'd find him later. And sure enough, I did.

I caught him in the corridor an hour later, pacing like a caged wolf, running his hand through his hair hard enough to pull strands free.

"Careful, Captain," I said, leaning against the wall. "At this rate, you'll be bald before thirty."

He scowled. "Not now, Felix."

"Now is exactly the time." I pushed off the wall and stepped into his path. "What the fuck was that in there?"

He stiffened. "I don't—"

"Oh, don't give me that," I cut in, jabbing a finger into his chest. "Bonded resonance, Drake. Ness said it clear as day. Eva's magic tethered itself to yours in front of three witnesses, and you just sat there acting like you ate something sour."

His mouth opened, then closed. For once, the great Captain Eldrake didn't have a comeback.

"Does she know?" I asked.

Silence.

"Godsdammit," I groaned, dragging a hand down my face. "You haven't told her."

"It's complicated," he muttered.

"No, it's not!" I snapped. "You're bonded. She deserves to know. Every second you keep it from her, you're digging yourself deeper into a hole you won't be able to crawl out of. And guess who's going to have to patch your sorry scaled hide back together when she finds out you've been lying?"

He glared, but I didn't flinch. "You don't understand."

"Oh, I understand just fine," I said, softer now. "I've seen the way you look at her. Like you finally found something worth living for. And I've seen the way she looks at you, like she trusts you with the whole Godsdamn world. She already *loves* you, you idiot."

His throat bobbed, but he didn't speak.

I sighed, clapped him on the shoulder. "Drake. Brother. You've fought armies without flinching. Don't be a coward now."

He dropped his gaze, jaw tight. I could feel the storm building in him, all tangled guilt and longing.

"Do it," I said. "If you don't tell her, I will."

That got his eyes snapping back up, molten silver, furious. But beneath the fury? Fear.

Good. Maybe fear would get through to him.

I smirked, stepping back. "Lucky for you, I love your dumb ass, and I'm leaving for a mission for a few days. Otherwise, I'd let this whole mess blow up in your face just to watch it happen."

"Felix—" he started, warning in his tone.

I cut him off with a grin. "Nope. Don't *Felix* me. Go get your shit together, Captain Bonded. I'll see you at dinner."

And with that, I left him standing there, bristling and silent, while I whistled my way toward the kitchens. Because Gods help me, I'd go mad if I didn't find a pastry soon.

The kitchens were half-empty by the time I made it down. A few night-shift guards hunched over mugs of broth, a scullery boy was elbow-deep in suds, and the ovens glowed low, their heat bleeding into the stone.

I made a beeline for the pastry basket, muttering a little prayer under my breath. The Gods, apparently, favored me tonight—there were still three honey rolls left. I took two. Drake stresses me out; I needed both.

I tore into the first, the glaze sticking to my fingers. Sweet. Comforting. Predictable. Exactly what I needed after lecturing a seven-foot dragon-man about his feelings.

And then—voices.

Fen's. Low. Edged, even when she wasn't trying.

Avod's. Warmer. Laughing at something she said.

I froze mid-bite, ears pricking like a nosy cat.

They were at the far end of the hall, leaning close over the long counter where the knives were kept. Fen had her blade out, rolling it between her fingers with casual menace. Avod said something I didn't catch, and she smirked—actually smirked—before giving him a shove with her shoulder. He didn't budge. Just grinned at her like she'd handed him a treasure.

And here's the thing: Fen didn't bite his head off. She didn't scowl, or snap, or storm away. She just... let him look at her like that.

I stuffed the last of the roll in my mouth, chewed, and leaned against the doorframe, pretending to be very interested in the brickwork.

Gods, I hoped she'd let him in someday. Avod had the patience for it—he'd wait as long as it took. But Fen... Fen was all blade and iron. She didn't know what to do with warmth. Not yet.

I licked the glaze from my thumb and sighed. That's what made me ache, I think. Watching someone I loved keep herself locked up when the key was right there in front of her.

Maybe that's why I was rooting so hard for Drake and Eva. Because sometimes, the Rift didn't just tear things apart—it stitched them together. And maybe, just maybe, it would do the same for Fen.

I pushed off the wall, grabbed another honey roll for the road, and headed back toward my quarters. Tomorrow, Fen and I would be riding out together. And if she caught me looking at her like Avod did, she'd probably stab me for it.

Still. I'd take the risk. Because someone had to keep loving her until she figured out how to love herself.

Chapter Twenty Eight

Evandra

"Magic is not sustained by power alone. The Rift stirs most strongly in spaces of connection—shared meals, quiet hands, laughter around a hearth. Where bonds are built, the Rift listens. Where warmth is offered freely, it remembers."
—Excerpt from Foundations of Rift Harmonics, Vol. II

The kitchen wasn't much—a mismatched set of cast iron pans, dull knives, and an oven that needed persuasion to stay lit. But it was mine for the afternoon. And for the first time since arriving in Riftreach, I felt like I could really, actually breathe.

At the very end of the hallway, just beyond Drake's and my chambers, the kitchen opened into the ship's hull where it jutted out from the cavern wall. A line of lanterns kept the shadows at bay, their glow glancing off copper pots and polished counters worn smooth by years of use. This was the rebellion's private kitchen—quiet, well-kept, with just enough space for a few people to cook without bumping elbows. The planked floor sloped ever so slightly toward the cavern, a reminder that the whole place was never meant to be anchored here, but somehow was.

A bundle of root vegetables thumped onto the prep table in front of me, and I set to work. My sleeves were rolled up, and my fingers were sticky with garlic and stained with beet juice. Steam coiled from the pot on the hearth, warm and fragrant with the herbs I'd managed to barter from a Riftborn grower. The scent of simmering broth filled the cavern space like a spell of comfort.

For once, I wasn't the Seer, the asset, the spark of a rebellion. I was just... Eva. A woman with a knife and a cutting board and a meal to make.

"Need help?" Felix asked, sidling into the kitchen with the obligatory grin of someone who did not, in fact, want to help.

"Only if you want to peel these potatoes," I said, sliding a bowl toward him without looking up.

He recoiled. "I think I hear someone calling me from... not here."

"Sit," I ordered, pointing my paring knife at him. "Peel."

He sighed dramatically but complied, flopping into a stool with theatrical suffering.

"You're terrifying with that knife, you know."

"I'm more terrifying with a ladle." I winked.

Behind him, I heard footsteps and the telltale scrape of boots. I turned—and nearly dropped the onion I was holding.

Fen stood in the doorway, arms crossed, brow arched.

"I heard you were poisoning the rebellion," she said dryly.

"Maybe just you," I shot back.

Felix choked on a laugh and ducked behind a basket of leeks.

"You're probably picky, right?" I asked, wiping my hands on my apron.

I expected Fen to turn and walk away, but instead, she stepped forward slowly, examining the kitchen like it might bite her.

"Maybe. What is it?" Her genuine curiosity shocked me.

"Vegetable stew. With some... hopefully-edible mushrooms Ness assured me wouldn't kill us."

"Ambitious," she said. She didn't sit, but she didn't leave either.

I stirred. “I used to cook every day back home. The regulars at the inn would get mad if I changed the stew recipe too much.”

“You owned that inn?”

“My dad did. I ran the kitchen. It was small, but... it mattered to people.”

Fen was quiet. Then, unexpectedly: “I get that.”

I looked at her.

“The mattering part,” she clarified, avoiding my eyes. “Being useful. Having a job that... means something.” I thought about what Felix had told me about Fen nursing him back to health when they were young.

Silence fell between us. It wasn’t uncomfortable. Just... tentative. New.

“You want to help?” I offered, holding out a knife.

She eyed it as if it were a Vyrmin. “I’m more of a ‘stab a man in the throat’ kind of girl.”

I smirked. “Then chopping carrots should be no problem.”

A smirk graced the corner of her lips, just barely noticeable. She reached for the knife.

“Fine,” she said, taking the cutting board. “But if I lose a finger, you owe me wine.”

“Deal.” I said with a smirk. This was the friendliest conversation Fen and I had ever exchanged, though it still involved knives.

The three of us settled into a rhythm. I stirred. She chopped. Felix peeled. The fire crackled, and for a while, the kitchen filled with the soft cadence of preparation—the scrape of blades, the bubble of broth, the quiet comfort of shared silence.

As the stew simmered, I pulled out the last of the foraged herbs and tossed them into the pot. I glanced around the kitchen—at the mismatched pots, the chipped dishes, the two warriors peeling and chopping at my side—and something in my chest loosened. I wasn’t just surviving here. I was building something. Contributing something.

“Thanks,” I said quietly in Fen’s direction.

“For what?” She asked, suspicious.

“For not... walking out.”

She didn’t look at me, just shrugged and said, “Felix seems to trust you. Figured I should give you a chance, too.”

It wasn't much. But it was everything.

A long table had been set on the upper deck of the ship, cluttered with mismatched plates, bowls of steaming vegetable stew, a few slabs of roast meat, and wine.

Drake and I slid into our seats—his hand brushed against mine under the table, just briefly, but enough to send a flutter through my stomach.

"Thank you for inviting me," I said, trying to smooth over the awkward silence that followed. "I was excited to cook for you all."

"And it's not even poisoned!" Felix added brightly.

"...That we know of," Fen muttered, already halfway into her wine.

Julian raised his glass with a wry grin. "To our resident Seer, who hasn't died yet. And to our dear Captain Eldrake, who's apparently now also a babysitter-slash-boyfriend."

I nearly choked on my sip of water.

Drake coughed. "Not a—well, I wouldn't say boyf—it's—Eva's safety is critical to the mission, sir."

Julian waved a dismissive hand. "Of course, of course. Seduction for strategy. Classic move. I once spent three months seducing a baron's daughter just to steal his shipping manifest."

"She's sitting right here," I muttered, eyes wide.

"Oh, we know," Fen deadpanned, tilting her goblet toward me without looking. "Hard not to when you fuck each other with your eyes every chance you get."

Drake shot her a look. "You're drunk."

"I *wish* I were drunk," Fen said dryly.

Felix snorted and leaned into me. "To be fair, it is hard not to notice. He stares at you like you're the only woman he's ever seen."

I covered my face with one hand. "Gods, is every dinner this embarrassing?"

"No," Fen said. "This one is special. This is roast-Drake-for-being-a-simp night."

"We've been planning it for days," Felix added, grinning.

"As long as you don't knock her up before we dethrone the King, I don't care how you get her to cooperate," Julian said between slurps of stew.

Drake's hand froze on his wine glass. "That's not—Sir, with all due respect—"

"Relax," Julian muttered. "We're off-duty."

Drake opened his mouth again, shut it, then took a very long drink.

I didn't know whether to laugh or crawl under the table. What was Julian trying to say? Drake was just manipulating me to cooperate?

Across from me, Fen was watching Drake carefully. She'd gone quiet —not sulking, but observant. Her smirk had faded, and something unreadable flickered behind her eyes. She took another slow sip of wine and glanced at me. "You're lucky, you know," she said.

I blinked. "Lucky?"

She shrugged. "I've known him a long time. Never seen him this soft. Not even when he broke his ribs and wouldn't admit it."

"You're exaggerating," Drake muttered into his cup.

"She's not," Felix said. "He got stabbed in the gut once and still showed up for morning drills."

"He was still bleeding," Fen added helpfully.

I looked at Drake, stunned. "Why would you do that?"

He met my eyes, serious now. "Because people were counting on me."

The laughter faded just a little around the table. Not awkwardly, but gently—as if the mood had shifted from teasing to something quieter, something more real. Julian's words echoed in the back of my mind. 'Seduction for strategy. Classic move.'

I looked at Drake again, at the way he smiled at me—soft, sincere. Or at least it looked sincere.

But what if it wasn't?

What if this warmth, this tenderness, was part of the mission? A role he'd slipped into just as easily as his armor? He was loyal to the rebellion. I couldn't forget that. And I was their greatest asset. I forced a smile, pushing the doubts down. Hard. But a cold thread of uncertainty curled in my stomach like smoke.

Felix cleared his throat loudly. "So! Anyone want more of this stew before I polish it off?"

"Yup," Fen said flatly, filling her bowl.

"I'm full," Julian murmured.

"I can make dessert next time!" I offered quickly, eager to distract my mind from the doubt creeping in. "I used to make these tarts at the inn; everyone loved them."

Julian looked up with sudden interest. "If you can cook blueberry muffins, I might just promote you."

"Oh, she's already climbing the ranks," Felix said, throwing an exaggerated wink in my direction. "You should see her fight now. Nearly knocked Drake on his ass today."

"Nearly?" I teased, shooting a look at Drake. "I seem to recall his ass hitting the floor."

"My foot slipped," he said flatly.

"On my boot," I added.

Fen actually chuckled. "Stars help us, she's becoming one of us."

"Stars help us," Drake muttered, but his smile said otherwise.

I laughed—really laughed—and it echoed in the space like something bright and new. I looked around the table at this ragtag group of rebels and warriors, misfits and survivors. I pushed down the doubt Julian had planted, refusing to believe that the laughter and tenderness around me were nothing more than tactics. This was my home now. My family.

There was bickering and banter and far too much wine. But beneath it all, there was something solid. A bond forged not just in duty but in care. In loyalty.

As the weeks passed, we settled deeper into a routine, whatever it was between us growing stronger by the day. Drake became not only my protector but my confidant, my anchor, my partner in everything. We trained together in the mornings, sparred until our limbs ached, and laughed until the sound of it filled the quiet corners of Riftreach. By night, he was a constant presence, whether in my chambers or his—our bodies entwined under the covers or simply resting shoulder to shoulder, finding solace in the steady rhythm of each other's breaths.

In the quiet moments, when we sat together reading or when his fingers absentmindedly traced patterns on my skin, I realized how deeply I had come to depend on him. The life I'd left behind—the kitchen, the inn, the simplicity of home—felt less like a loss and more like a chapter that had led me here.

This was my new home. He was my new home. And with each passing day, as we shared secrets and silences, I found myself falling more deeply in love with the man who had brought me here.

Drake's mischievous smile had my curiosity piqued from the moment he stepped into my chambers that evening.

"Get dressed warmly," he said, leaning casually against the doorframe.

"Why?" I asked, already sensing the thrill behind his words.

"We're going up to the surface."

My breath hitched, excitement mixing with apprehension. The surface had become a memory I dared not linger on, but the thought of seeing it again—feeling the cool air, the vastness of the night sky—was enough to propel me into action. I hurried to pull on layers of soft wool and sturdy leather, lacing up my boots with trembling hands. When I stepped back to him, he offered me his cloak, the familiar scent of his scale salve clinging to the fabric as he draped it over my shoulders.

"This way," he said, taking my hand as we exited my chambers and wove through the winding paths of Riftreach.

The descent into the sewers was quiet except for the faint trickle of water and our footsteps echoing against the stone. The tunnels were dank and dark, and the air was heavy with the scent of earth and decay. I clutched his hand tightly, my pulse quickening as we navigated the labyrinthine paths. Drake moved with purpose, his sharp instincts guiding us through turns and junctions I would have surely gotten lost in.

"Stay close," he whispered when we heard voices echoing faintly from one of the branching tunnels. We flattened against the damp wall, my heart pounding as the shadows of guards patrolling above flickered in the faint torchlight spilling through a grate. When the voices faded, Drake gave my hand a reassuring squeeze before leading me onward.

Finally, we climbed a rusted iron ladder that seemed to stretch endlessly upward. When we emerged, the fresh, cool air of the forest above hit me like a balm. My chest expanded as I took in the pine-scented breeze, and I realized how much I'd missed the air up here. The night sky stretched above us, endless and glittering, the stars like shards of crystal scattered across black velvet.

The forest was alive with the symphony of crickets and the distant hoot of an owl. Moonlight filtered through the towering trees, casting dappled shadows on the ground. I marveled at the sights, every detail sharper and brighter than I remembered. The feeling of open space was exhilarating.

"Come on," Drake urged softly, pulling me forward.

We skirted the edge of the forest until the faint hum of the city reached my ears. Peering through the trees, I saw the outer districts of the city sprawled before us. The streets were bathed in the golden glow of lanterns, and the muffled sounds of late-night revelers carried on the wind. We moved quickly, sticking to the shadows and taking care to avoid the main thoroughfares.

We ducked through a narrow alley, its cobblestone streets slick with dew, and passed shops with their shutters drawn tight for the night. A baker's shop released a faint, lingering scent of bread, while an apothecary's window displayed an array of dried herbs and glass vials.

Finally, Drake led me to a hidden courtyard tucked behind a dilapidated inn that seemed forgotten by time. The building itself leaned with the weight of years, its timber beams warped and its roof sagging in places. Shutters hung askew on the windows, and the once-bright paint on the door had faded to a muted, peeling gray.

Vines of ivy crept up the stone walls, weaving a tapestry of green that softened the inn's age-worn appearance. A faint glow emanated from a single lantern hanging by the back door, casting long shadows over the courtyard.

The place felt like another world—hidden, isolated, protected. The air was crisp, tinged with dew and ivy, the quiet broken only by the steady trickle of the fountain. Fireflies bobbed lazily in the lantern glow.

"This is it," Drake said, spreading his arms like a man unveiling treasure. His smile was unguarded, boyish in a way I rarely saw. "I used to come here when I needed to think."

"It's beautiful," I whispered. The word felt too small for the serenity of the place.

We sat together on the lone bench facing the fountain. The wood was softened by years of rain and sun, but it held beneath us, creaking faintly. Drake leaned forward, resting his forearms on his thighs, and pulled something from his pocket—a small vial that caught the moonlight, glowing faintly gold.

"This," he said, holding it out to me, "is something I made for you."

I accepted it, turning it carefully in my hands. When I uncorked it, a familiar scent curled up to greet me: warm, earthy, laced with spice. His salve—but softened, blended with something floral, violet maybe. It smelled like him. Like safety and warmth. Like home.

A lump rose in my throat. "It's... perfect." A perfume he made for me, his scent married with something just for me.

His eyes searched mine, silver bright even in the half-light. "I thought you might like something to remind you of me. For when I'm not around."

The ache in my chest deepened. He was giving me more than a trinket. He was giving me something permanent. Something personal. A tether.

I leaned against him, resting my head on his shoulder. The fabric of his shirt was rough, but beneath it, he radiated heat, steady as a forge. The night seemed to still around us—the hum of the city muffled, the stars sharpening into clarity. For once, it felt like time had been gentled, slowed just for us.

I thought of all the moments that had led here: that first rushed kiss in my bedroom back home. His thoughtful glances when he thought I wasn't looking. And now this—quiet, simple, almost ordinary. But ordinary was a luxury I hadn't had in so long.

Drake shifted, his arm brushing mine, then settling lightly across the back of the bench. He was close enough that I could feel his pulse, quick and strong, even through the space between us.

"I need to tell you something," he said suddenly. His voice was low, taut.

My heart leapt. I turned toward him, searching his face. "What is it?"

He opened his mouth, then shut it again, jaw tightening. He scrubbed a hand down his face like the words were caught in his throat, too heavy to lift.

"Drake?"

His eyes flicked to mine, sharp and vulnerable all at once. For a moment, I swore he was about to say something monumental—something that would change everything. His lips parted, his breath shaky.

"I..." He swallowed. "Gods—I shouldn't say this."

My stomach twisted. "Say what?"

He hesitated again. And then—like a dam breaking, like he couldn't hold it in any longer—he blurted, "I love you."

Heat flooded my face, my chest, my whole body. My breath caught, stuck somewhere between a laugh and a sob. "You—what?"

"I love you," he repeated, softer this time, as if testing the words on his tongue. His silver eyes locked onto mine, unflinching now. "Gods help me, I love you."

My throat tightened. No one had ever said those words to me before, not like this. Not with such terrifying sincerity.

"I—" My voice wavered, but the truth spilled out without hesitation. "I love you too."

Something shifted in him then. Relief, fierce and raw, cracked his expression open. He leaned forward, forehead brushing mine, and I felt the tremor in his breath. His hands cupped my cheeks, warm and calloused, and for a moment I thought he might kiss me.

But he didn't. Not yet.

Because even as joy surged between us, there was something else—something heavy lurking behind his eyes. Like the words he'd spoken weren't the ones he'd meant to. Like there was more he'd almost said, but couldn't.

I stroked the back of his hand gently, grounding him. "Drake," I whispered. "Are you alright?"

His smile faltered. He nodded, too quickly. "Yeah. Just… Gods, I didn't mean to—"

"You didn't mean to what? Tell me you love me?" I tried to tease, to lighten it, but the weight in his gaze lingered.

"I didn't mean to tell you like that." His thumb brushed my cheekbone, tender. "I wanted it to be… better. Different." He hesitated, then shook his head, dismissing the thought. "Doesn't matter. You know now."

I searched his face. Something still sat unsaid, caught like a fishhook beneath his tongue. I could feel it. But I didn't press—not when his arms closed around me and the warmth of his body enveloped mine. Not when his lips finally found my hair, pressing a kiss there like a benediction.

We sat in silence after that, my head on his chest, his heartbeat steady under my ear. I wanted to believe that this was everything—that love was enough. But a small part of me knew: he had been on the edge of telling me something else. Something bigger. Something that scared him.

And though I didn't know what it was, I knew it mattered.

For now, though, I let myself sink into the warmth of his arms, the glow of the lantern, the dance of fireflies around us. For now, I let myself believe that love was everything.

Chapter Twenty Nine

Avod

Drake's boots hadn't even finished echoing down the hall before Fen let out a long, theatrical sigh.

"Gods," she muttered, yanking her satchel off the table. "I can smell the pheromones from here."

I leaned against the doorframe, arms crossed. "Jealous?"

Her look was sharp enough to peel paint. "Of *that*? No."

"Sure," I said, pushing off the wall. "Come on. Let's check your gear. If you fall off a rooftop, I'm not explaining it to Julian."

She rolled her eyes but followed.

Her stride through the corridor was clipped, too fast, like if she walked hard enough, maybe she could outrun the tightness in her spine. In the ready room she went straight to the weapons rack, shoving blades into hidden sheaths with precision that bordered on violent.

"You're doing the thing again," I said.

"What thing?" She didn't look up.

"Packing like it's a warzone."

"It could be," she snapped, ramming a dagger into her boot. "You think they'll hand over a Riftborn kid with a thank-you note?"

She yanked a strap too tight and cursed. I stepped forward, loosening it for her, fingers lingering on her thigh longer than I should've.

"No," I said calmly. "But maybe you're mad you're not the one kissing someone before battle. So you're making love to your knife set instead."

Her eyes narrowed. "Don't start."

I lifted both hands. "Just saying."

She strapped on her vambrace, knuckles white. Grabbed another knife, shoved it into her belt like it had offended her.

"Or maybe," I said, softer, "you're pissed Drake finally let himself have something good—and it wasn't a version you approved of."

She froze for half a breath. Just long enough to tell me I'd hit true.

"He's not some lovestruck idiot, Fen. He's the most loyal bastard I know. If he's choosing Eva—it means something." I adjusted the strap over her shoulder. "You could go easier on them."

She ignored me, tightening another buckle like she could strangle the thought itself.

"The last time you packed this fast," I said, lowering my voice, "you were trying not to think about me bleeding out."

That stopped her. She sucked in a breath and went still.

The memory flickered hot in my mind too: cold stone, my blood slicking her hands, her voice breaking as she screamed at the medic to move faster. And later, when she thought I couldn't hear—her whisper, *don't you fucking dare die on me.*

I hadn't forgotten.

"You're so fucking full of yourself," she said finally, voice tight, lashes shadowing her eyes.

"You keep not telling me I'm wrong," I murmured. Our faces were inches apart.

A beat. Then another.

"You're in my space," she said.

"Barely." I leaned closer. Her gaze flicked to my lips before she tore it away. She smelled like sweat and leather and Orchids.

She turned sharp, sudden—like she might slap me, or kiss me. Instead, she slowly bent to pick up a fallen strap near my feet, face deliberately close to my crotch as she moved. Rising, she locked eyes with me, smirk curling like a blade dragged over skin. *Evil woman.*

My pulse stuttered.

"Relax," she purred. "If I wanted you, you'd know." Her hand brushed a stray hair off my shoulder—casual, cruel, intimate.

She cocked her hip and reached for her crossbow. The motion was smooth, but her grip was too tight.

"Don't get killed," I said quietly. "I'd hate to lose someone who makes being annoyed this fun."

"Wouldn't dream of it."

She turned, walking out like she hadn't just rearranged my ribcage.

The door clicked shut.

I exhaled, chest tight in the way it always was after she left—like something important had been ripped out with her. My gaze drifted to the gear she'd forgotten. Fen didn't forget. Not unless she was distracted. Not unless she was looking at me like that.

I rubbed the back of my neck, paced once, then collapsed onto the bench, head in my hands.

I'd let her take out every Godsdamned ounce of her rage on me. I'd let her beat me down and build me back wrong. I'd let her fucking choke me, bruise me, cut me—if it just meant I could love her.

She'll kill me one day. And I'll thank her for it.

Chapter Thirty

Eldrake

The golden light from the enchanted lanterns spilled into the chamber, casting a soft, sun-warm glow over Eva's skin. It wasn't real sunlight—not in Riftreach—but it felt like it. Or close enough when you don't remember what real sunlight feels like.

She lay curled in the sheets, breath slow and even, a tangle of red hair fanned across the pillow like a flame. My arm was still draped around her waist, her back pressed to my chest. She looked peaceful. Safe.

I didn't deserve the trust she gave me.

She had cried in this bed. Cried in my arms. Shaken from the truth about her mother, the visions, I'd felt her fear. Her voice, raw and wrecked, still echoed in my head when she told me she didn't know how to trust anymore.

And I hadn't known how to answer. Only that I wanted to be the one beside her while she figured it out. The one who didn't lie, didn't keep secrets. If I can't own up about the bond yet, I could at least tell Julian the truth.

I slipped my arm free, careful not to wake her, and pressed a kiss to the curve of her shoulder before pulling away completely. She sighed softly, adjusting in her sleep. The shape of her lingered on my skin like heat.

A mark on my neck caught my attention in the mirror as I dressed. Deep violet, just beneath my jaw—a souvenir from her lips. I touched it briefly, lips quirking upward despite myself.

The war room smelled of old ink and iron. Maps, missives, and coded correspondence littered the long table like a battlefield. Julian stood at its center, arms braced on either side of a report, handlebar mustache twitching faintly as his eyes narrowed in thought.

"Good morning, Commander," I said as I entered.

"Captain." He didn't look up.

I walked to the table, scanning the spread of intel. "Any word from Fen or Felix?"

"Not yet." He finally lifted his gaze—and paused. His eyes flicked to the mark at my neck, then to the smirk I hadn't quite managed to suppress. A grin spread across his face.

"I see Lady Evandra's acclimating well to life underground."

I ignored the bait, instead pulling a fresh report from the stack and scanning it. "That's actually why I'm here."

Julian snorted, circling the table with a long-legged stride. He poured himself a cup of thick, dark tea, then waved it lazily in my direction. "Don't tell me you're getting attached. That wasn't in your job description, last I checked."

I stiffened.

He sipped once, then spoke again, almost idly. "Just let her down gently. You played your part brilliantly. Pretending to care for her, drawing her here—you've done exactly as we needed."

Something twisted in my chest.

"Julian."

He glanced back, cup halfway to his mouth.

"That's not what this is," I said, more harshly than I intended.

His expression didn't change. "Isn't it?"

"I care about her."

Julian studied me for a long beat, then let out a sigh so theatrical it could've brought the house down in a playhouse. "Godsdamn Dragons," he muttered, pinching the bridge of his nose. "Drake, you were assigned to *bring her here.* Earn her trust. Get her to stay. Not fall in love with her."

"I didn't plan this."

"No one ever does."

The geyser's faint hiss filled the silence. Julian set his cup down and leaned forward, his expression sharper now, his warmth gone.

"I need you to understand something. This isn't a fleeting distraction. I'm in love with her. We've bonded."

The cup rattled as he slammed it down, tea splashing across a stack of maps.

"Bonded?" Julian's voice lost its theatrical lilt for once, dropping into something deadly serious. "Gods help us."

"I thought you'd be the one person who wouldn't act surprised."

"I'm not surprised. I'm *irritated*. There's a difference." He scrubbed a hand down his face. "Do you have any idea what kind of leverage that gives the wrong people? If anyone finds out you've tied your heart—your rift—to her—"

"I don't care."

"You should!" His voice cracked like a whip. "This isn't about your feelings, Drake. It's about her role in all of this."

I glanced at the wall, jaw tightening.

"She's not a pawn."

"She is," Julian snapped. "We all are. Do you think any of us are here by accident? That the Rift gave her visions of the mirror for fun?"

I said nothing.

Julian leaned closer. "Do you even understand what that mirror is?"

"I know it's dangerous."

"It's more than dangerous. It's a *tether*. A Goddamn anchor point between Vyper and *a God*. Him having possession of it—"

"We will stop him."

He laughed, bitter and low. "You say that like it's a promise. But we still don't know where it is. We don't know why it showed itself to her. Or how long before it drives her mad."

I flinched.

Julian caught it and sighed. "Look. I'm not trying to be cruel. But you need to be clear-eyed about this. If you care for her—really care—then don't let your feelings blind you. She's stronger than she knows, but she's vulnerable. Especially now."

I met his gaze. "I'll protect her."

"Good. Because if you don't, I'll kill you before the bond does."

We shared a long, weighted silence. Finally, Julian sat back down and reached for another map.

"You didn't come here just to argue," he muttered. "What else?"

I hesitated. "We need a strategy. For the mirror."

That got his attention. "You think she's ready to go after it?"

"She will be. Soon. Her training is improving, but in combat and controlling her Rift."

"We don't even know where it is."

"I think we do," I said, voice quiet. "Or we're close."

Julian frowned, but he didn't argue. "Alright. Let's talk logistics."

He started pulling reports closer. I leaned in beside him.

Neither of us noticed the footsteps receding in the corridor beyond the cracked door.

Chapter Thirty One

Evandra

"Despite centuries of study, the Rift remains a profound mystery, often defying logic and expectation. Scholars have documented instances where heightened emotions—such as rage, grief, or joy—trigger unpredictable manifestations of Rift energy. These occurrences can range from harmless bursts of light to catastrophic displays of raw power, further complicating efforts to understand its nature." —Understanding the Rift, Chapter 1.5

I stood frozen at the top of the stairs leading to the main deck, my breath caught in my throat like a snare. The quiet hum of Riftreach—the soft hum of the city below, the distant hiss of the geyser—faded to a dull, suffocating silence. And then I heard it. The words that shattered everything.

"Just let her down gently," Julian said, calm as ever. Measured. Unmoved.

As if he hadn't just detonated something inside me.

My fingers locked around the railing. The wooden banister dug into my palm, grounding me only barely. My knees wobbled. My breath hitched.

Then came the next blow.

"I have to commend you, Drake," Julian continued, his voice slipping into something almost smug. "You played your part brilliantly. Pretending to care for her, drawing her here—you've done exactly as we needed."

Pretending.

My vision tunneled. The world tilted; the lanterns along the walls smeared like wet paint across the stone. I staggered back a step, the stair creaking beneath my heel. The sound of it—small and sudden—snapped like a twig in a quiet forest, loud enough to betray me.

But they didn't hear.

They just kept talking, and I—I couldn't.

I turned and fled, boots slamming the steps in a way that didn't even feel like my own body anymore. The air felt too thin. Too sharp. I couldn't breathe. Couldn't think. All I could do was run.

Lanterns blurred past me in streaks of gold and green, the Riftlight warping with the speed of my panic. I didn't know where I was going, only that I had to get away. Away from that voice. Away from him.

Drake.

The warmth of him was still on my skin. I could still feel the weight of his arm from that morning, the way he'd held me like I was something breakable and beloved. The soft murmur of his voice. The way his lips brushed my shoulder like a promise.

A promise built on lies.

My breath broke in ragged gasps. The faces of the people I passed blurred together. A boy with a satchel. A woman lighting a pipe. A pair of rebels laughing near the market bridge. They all looked up as I passed, but I didn't see them. Didn't register them.

Because all I could hear was his voice in my memory.

"I'll never lie to you."

He had looked at me like I was the only thing in the room that mattered. Like I was his. And maybe I had been. A mark to hit. A girl to catch. A pawn to move across a board I never even knew I was standing on.

I stumbled into the sewers before I realized where my feet had carried me. The scent of rot and rust hit like a slap, but I welcomed it. I wanted to choke. To hurt. To feel something that wasn't this twisting, flailing grief burning through me like acid.

I collapsed against a slick brick wall, my legs finally giving up their performance.

Then I bent over and vomited.

My stomach emptied itself into the muck, again and again, until there was nothing left but bile and broken sobs. The pain was a distraction. Almost a comfort. At least it was real.

Unlike him.

The sobs came in heaving waves, echoing through the tunnel like a haunting. I clutched my knees to my chest, trying to hold myself together as if I could press the pieces back into something resembling whole.

But I wasn't whole.

I was never whole to begin with, was I?

I'd built a fragile, desperate thing out of the scraps of my life—my mother's lies, my father's silence, the Rift's whispers—and then I'd given it to him.

I'd let Drake see me. Touch me. I had loved him. Even if I hadn't said the words out loud, I'd felt them thrumming in every glance, every breathless kiss, every soft "goodnight" when we collapsed into each other's arms.

And it was all a game to him.

The ache twisted deeper, crueler. His smile flashed in my mind—boyish, knowing, crooked at the corner like he was always one heartbeat from teasing me. I thought it meant safety. I thought it meant him.

But it was just a mask—a beautiful, practiced performance.

Gods, how had I been so stupid?

I thought of my father—how he had lied to protect me, how I'd hated him for it.

And now Drake—who I had trusted with the rawest pieces of myself—had done the same. But not to protect me. Not to spare me pain.

No.

He'd lied to use me.

'You've done exactly as we needed.'

What had I been? A target? A key to something? Bait?

I pressed my forehead to the wall, letting the cold seep in. I didn't want to cry anymore. I didn't want to feel anymore.

But it was too late for that.

Somewhere, water dripped steadily from a pipe—a quiet rhythm in the dark. I breathed with it, trying to still the shaking in my limbs. I didn't know what to do.

I couldn't go back. Not to that room. Not to that bed where his scent still lingered on the sheets. I couldn't see him. Couldn't look into those silver eyes and hear another word that might be true—or worse, almost true.

I was unraveling—thread by thread.

The Riftborn needed me. That had been true yesterday. It would still be true tomorrow. But everything else—my place here, my worth, my strength—it had all been tied to him. To the way he made me feel like I belonged. Like maybe I was chosen, not cursed.

But I wasn't chosen. I was manipulated. *Used.*

My fists clenched. My nails dug into my palms hard enough to break the skin. Good. Let it bleed.

I don't know how long I stayed there.

Time didn't pass the same way in Riftreach. There were no clocks, no sun—just the steady beat of the caverns and the weight of silence.

I wanted to scream, to punch, to rage at the cruel unfairness of it all. But the only sound that came from me was a ragged sob as I gasped for air. My thoughts swirled and tangled, choking me. I barely heard the sound at first—the faint, deliberate echo of footsteps on the sewer stone.

My heart lurched. Drake. Of course he'd followed me. He found me. "Go away, Drake!" I shouted, my voice hoarse and breaking as I buried my face in my hands. But the footsteps didn't stop. They grew louder. Heavier. Not like his usual stride. And then I heard something else—something that didn't belong.

Whispers. Raspy, too fast. Like words spoken backward, layered over themselves. Wrong.

"Drake?" I called again, my voice now trembling. Silence.

Then: "What do we have here?" A voice slithered from the dark, cruel and rasping, like rot come alive. Another voice followed, whispering over my skin.

"She reeks of the Rift. She's dripping with it."

I scrambled to my feet, my knees wobbling. My hands fumbled at my hips—only to grasp at air. Empty sheathes.

No blades. I'd left them behind.

Two figures emerged from the shadows, their eyes glowing crimson. One hunched grotesquely, his body twisted into something barely human.

The other was rail-thin, bones jutting from his tight, gray skin like a walking corpse. Vyper's cronies. The ones I'd seen with him in my vision.

A jagged grin split the hunchback's face. "A Seer... alone. What luck."

"The master will be most pleased," the skeletal one hissed, fingers twitching like claws.

"Don't touch me!" I shouted, trying to force my will through the Rift, to push into their minds like I'd practiced. But panic clawed at my focus, and the connection failed.

"Where's your guard, little bird?" the hunchback sneered. "I can smell him on you. Dragonblood," he snuffed the air crudely. "You let him mark you."

I took a step back and slipped, falling hard. My shoulder struck the stone, sending a bolt of pain through my chest.

The skeletal one crouched beside me, his lips curling. "So much power in one so small. It will make a lovely offering."

"Please!" I screamed. "DRAKE!"

The hunchback chuckled. "He can't save you now."

He reached into his pouch and pulled out a fistful of something noxious and powdery.

Before I could react, he brought it to his cracked lips and blew it into my face. And just before the darkness took me, I saw it again. Not their faces—but the mirror. Glinting behind their shapes like a watching eye.

The serpent curled in silver. The void beneath the glass. It was here.

I awoke to the sharp ache of my body suspended, my vertebrae grinding painfully against a cold, unyielding steel frame. My breath shook as the memories surged forward—the sewers, the grotesque men, Drake's betrayal—all of it crashing down like a wave.

The heartache in my chest solidified into an icy wall, shielding me from the rising tide of despair. I tasted bile and bitterness, the lingering flavor of broken trust.

I blinked, my left eye creaking open, though the right refused to comply, swollen shut and throbbing with dull pain. Someone had been rough with me. My vision adjusted slowly to the dim torchlight flickering across rough stone walls, casting jagged shadows like specters watching from the corners.

Chains rattled softly above me as I shifted, testing my restraints. My wrists were encased in cold, jagged manacles, biting into my skin and leaving raw, bloody tracks. The steel cross I was bound to kept my arms stretched painfully high, my shoulders burning with every breath. My toes grazed the ground, just enough to prevent full relief, leaving my weight to drag heavily on my wounds. Each movement sent a sharp, stinging reminder of my captivity.

The room around me was small, suffocating, and reeked of damp stone and old blood.

A table sat to the side, splattered with crimson stains, its surface littered with tools of cruelty. A metal-tipped whip coiled like a serpent. A bone saw rusted at the edges. A scalpel, its blade gleaming in the dim light, still bore traces of its last victim. My stomach churned, bile rising in my throat, but I forced it down.

Fear clawed at me like a living thing, but the bitter emptiness in my chest smothered it. I was tired of feeling small. I'm tired of being a pawn in someone else's game. My hands clenched into fists, my nails digging into my palms. I would not be weak. Not again. Not this time.

I closed my eyes and reached for the Rift the way Ness had taught me—slow inhale, center, open the door. The ache of my body, the raw burn of my wrists, the fury in my chest... all of it sharpened into focus. Power flickered at the edges of my thoughts, the familiar swell of something vast and dangerous pressing against the walls of my mind.

But the moment I pushed—nothing. Just a hollow thud, like the air itself recoiled. A ward. Layered thick, iron and ash and something older woven into the stone. The Rift slid from my grasp like water through cupped hands.

I sagged against the chains, my chest heaving. Gods, they knew. They had built this room to keep me powerless. To cage me like a beast in a menagerie.

The sudden creak of a heavy portcullis startled me, the sound reverberating off the walls. My breath caught as a figure entered—a walking corpse draped in a deep violet cloak, his steps deliberate and predatory. His skin was ashen, stretched thin over his bones, and his lips curled into a grin far too wide for his gaunt face.

"Look who's awake," he rasped, his voice a chilling blend of mirth and menace. His thick cloak trailed the ground, brushing against the filth-strewn cobblestones. "Fate is a funny thing, isn't it? To have you delivered to me so... effortlessly."

I glared at him with my one good eye, unwilling to give him the satisfaction of seeing my fear. His black, soulless eyes gleamed as he closed the distance, inspecting me like a prize he'd won.

"I've been looking for you, little Seer," he purred, his words dripping with malice. "And here you are. Convenient, isn't it?"

"Go to hell, *Vyper*." I spat, my voice hoarse but defiant.

His grin widened impossibly as he leaned closer, the stench of decay wafting from his breath. "Tell me," he hissed, his voice dropping to a near whisper, "what were you doing snooping around in my study? Did you like what you saw?" I flinched as his skeletal fingers reached up and grazed my cheek, cold and clammy against my skin. "That's right," he continued, pulling back to pace before me. "I felt you there. I could smell your Rift... it was intoxicating. And now?" He inhaled deeply, his grin turning cruel. "Now you reek of *Dragon*." I wrenched against the chains, rage boiling in my veins, but the cuffs bit deeper, sending fresh drops of blood streaming down my forearms.

"Tell me," he whispered, "what did the mirror show you?"

I flinched.

His eyes glittered with amusement. "Did it pull you in the way it pulls all broken things?" His voice dropped to a near whisper. "The Vessel remembers those who stare too long. It never forgets what it likes."

"What do you want with me?" I demanded through clenched teeth.

"Oh, so many things," he mused, his tone mockingly playful. He turned to the table, his bony fingers brushing over the tools before plucking up the scalpel. He examined it with morbid fascination, flicking the blade with a sharp metallic ping. "But first, I need you to tell me where your little rebellion is hiding."

"Fuck you," I snarled again, spitting at his feet.

His smile faltered, just for a moment, before returning with twice the venom. "Such a temper," he said, shaking his head in mock disapproval. He stepped closer, holding the scalpel up to catch the flickering light. "But I suppose we'll work on that."

He brought the blade to my cheek, the cold steel sending a shiver through my body. His black eyes bore into mine, his lips curling into that same sadistic grin. "Cooperate, little bird," he whispered, his voice a razor slicing through the silence. "It would be such a shame to ruin something so... pretty."

I held my breath, refusing to flinch. I might have been broken, battered, betrayed—but I would not let him win.

Vyper leaned closer, his skeletal grin almost brushing my cheek. "All of the power that the Rift has gifted you," he hissed, his voice cold as winter's breath, "and yet, here you are. Helpless," his empty black eyes bore into mine, his grotesque smile stretching too wide as if mocking the very concept of humanity. He lifted the scalpel, the jagged edge glinting faintly in the flickering torchlight. Slowly, deliberately, he turned it in his fingers, savoring the tension. "Helpless," he repeated, the word dripping with venom.

I swallowed hard, my breath hitching, but I forced myself to meet his gaze. "Do your worst."

His rasping chuckle echoed in the small chamber, a sound like dry leaves crushed underfoot. "Oh, my dear," he murmured, "you have no idea how accommodating I can be."

The scalpel's cold kiss met my cheek, pressing lightly, enough to sting but not yet break the skin. I tensed against the restraints, the rough steel cuffs digging deeper into my raw wrists. My body betrayed me with a flinch, but I locked my jaw tight. I wouldn't scream. I wouldn't cry. I wouldn't give him the pleasure of seeing me crack.

"You're strong," he mused, tilting his head as if studying a curious specimen. "But strength without wisdom is so... wasted," his lips curled upward, his teeth bared in a mockery of a smile. "Tell me where the rebels are, and this can all stop. I can be quite generous, you know."

I laughed bitterly, a sound that echoed hollowly in the chamber. "You don't know the meaning of mercy."

The mask of amusement cracked for a heartbeat, revealing something darker and far crueler beneath. "Very well," he said softly, stepping back with the calculated grace of a predator.

Placing the scalpel down with a deliberate clink, Vyper reached for the whip coiled neatly on the table. Its leather cords were tipped with jagged bits of metal, glinting dangerously in the dim light. He snapped it once in the air, the sound a sharp crack that made my stomach lurch.

"This is your last chance," he said, dragging the whip along the floor as he stalked toward me. The sound was slow, deliberate. "Tell me where they are, and I will spare you this... discomfort."

I stared back at him, my good eye blazing with defiance. "You'll get nothing from me," the image of the children peacefully playing in the streets flashed through my periphery.

For them, I thought, bolstering my resolve.

The first lash came without warning, the metal tips tearing through my tunic and carving into the flesh of my back. Pain exploded like fire, sharp and searing. My teeth sank into my lower lip, the coppery taste of blood filling my mouth.

"You've got fight in you," Vyper said almost cheerfully, the whip slithering back to him like a living thing. "I like that."

Another strike. Then another. Each lash sent waves of agony coursing through my body, but I refused to cry out. I forced myself to breathe through the pain, even as the blood began to soak into my tattered clothes. I could smell the coppery tinge.

Vyper paused, his bony fingers trailing over the angry gashes on my back. His touch was as cold as death, sending a fresh shudder of revulsion through me. "You're so loyal," he murmured, admiring the blood on his fingertips. "But loyalty is such a fragile thing, isn't it?"

He circled me slowly, his voice lowering to a venomous purr. "Especially when it's betrayed," at the word, my heart clenched painfully, and Vyper's grin grew. "Ah," he said, his voice soft with mock understanding. "The Dragon. Such a tragic little romance. Tell me, little bird, did he whisper sweet lies in your ear? Did he hold you close, tell you that you were his world, only to shatter it all with a single truth?"

"Fuck you." I ground out a second time, my voice hoarse, but the words lacked strength.

"Oh, I can see it," he continued, his tone almost gleeful. "He played you like a violin, didn't he? And you—" he leaned closer, his cold breath brushing my ear—"you fell for it. Poor, naive little Seer."

Tears burned in my eyes, unbidden and unwanted. I blinked them away furiously, but Vyper saw them. Of course he saw them.

"You thought you were special, didn't you?" His laughter was low and cruel. "That you mattered to him. But all you were, all you are, is a tool—a pawn in their game. And now, here you are—forgotten. Abandoned. Left to rot."

"Shut up!" I screamed, thrashing against the chains, the steel cutting deeper into my wrists. Fresh blood trickled down my arms, but I didn't care. Rage flared, mingling with the anguish, fueling my defiance. "You don't know anything!"

"Oh, but I do," he said, his voice chillingly calm. "I can see it in your memories, feel it in your despair. You reek of betrayal, little bird. And that scent... it's intoxicating. Perhaps that betrayal will fuel you to divulge some useful information?" He prodded. I met his gaze with a look from the hells themselves.

He straightened, his grin fading into something colder, sharper. "Don't worry. I'll break you. They all break eventually." Vyper turned, his violet cloak sweeping behind him as he strode toward the door.

"Rest well," he called over his shoulder, his voice dripping with mockery. "We have a long way to go," the door slammed shut, leaving me alone in the suffocating darkness. My breaths came in ragged gasps, my body trembling from pain and exhaustion until I finally lost consciousness.

Chapter Thirty Two

Eldrake

The warmth of my soul had been ripped away, leaving only a cold, merciless void.

She was gone. My Eva. And nothing would stand between me and getting her back. I didn't know what she'd heard—just that it was enough to break her. The lie... or the truth.

Either way, it was my fault.

"Where is she?!" I roared at the gathered villagers. My voice echoed like thunder off the stone walls, laced with a feral edge I barely recognized as my own. They flinched, fingers trembling as they pointed toward the cavern's exit.

They didn't understand what was coming—what would happen to anyone who dared harm her. White-hot rage seared through my veins, but it wasn't reckless. This was the focused burn of a warrior. Every thought, every breath, every beat of my heart narrowed to a singular purpose: *bring her back.*

I tore through the sewers, my boots slamming into the brick with punishing force. Julian and Avod trailed behind, shouting something I didn't hear. The stink of rot and old blood hung in the air, but I only smelled her—honeysuckle and heat, still clinging faintly to the stone.

My mate. My everything.

I rounded a corner—and froze.

A foul stench hit me. Blood. Sulfur. Magic twisted wrong. Then I saw it: her tracks in the grime, suddenly ending. The drag marks. The struggle.

"No. No!" the words cracked from my throat. I dropped to my knees, my fingers scraping at the filth like I could claw time backward. My breath came in ragged, stuttering gasps.

"What?! What is it?!" Julian's voice snapped behind me.

"Vyper found her." My voice was barely a growl, trembling with fury. I staggered to my feet, my fists clenching until the bones in my hand cracked. "Fuck!"

I drove my fist into the stone wall. It shattered with a deafening crack, shards raining down around me.

"Please, Gods," I whispered. "No."

Tears blurred my vision, but they weren't weakness. They were molten. They were war.

I saw her face—smiling, brave, soft. I remembered how she curled against me in sleep, how she whispered my name like it meant something.

All of it—ripped away.

Julian inhaled sharply. "If Vyper has her... then the King has access to a Seer."

He looked between Avod and me, his voice grave. "He'll exploit her magic to create more Vyrmin. Or he'll kill her to keep her from helping us."

The image of her—dead, alone, afraid—sent a sound ripping from me that wasn't human. A Dragon's grief. A promise of destruction.

"It's okay, Drake. We'll find her," Avod said, placing a hand on my shoulder.

I shrugged it off with a snarl. I didn't want comfort.

I wanted blood.

"I'm going after her." My voice scraped like metal. I bolted toward the surface, every step fueled by purpose.

"At least take Avod with you!" Julian called after me.

I didn't slow, but I heard the thunder of Avod's boots behind me. Good. He knew what was at stake.

Back on the ship, I moved on instinct. My hands trembled slightly as I buckled on my armor, but my focus never broke. Each strap fastened with brutal finality. My blades clicked into place like punctuation marks on a vow. Avod stood in silence. He knew better than to speak. I wasn't the same man I'd been yesterday. That man had smiled. That man had slept.

He was gone.

As I fastened the last strap, a single tear carved a hot trail down my cheek. I didn't wipe it away. "I can't lose her, Avod," I said, my voice low and raw.

"I know," he replied. "We won't."

My Star-Glow pulsed, blazing with a light that belonged to something ancient and furious. The dragon inside me roared to the surface, its rage folding into my very being.

Vyper had taken what was mine. And I would burn the world to get her back.

No one—*no one*—gets between a Dragon and his mate.

The heavy stone door sealed Riftreach behind us, and with it, the fragile peace I'd clung to. The cold bit at my skin as we emerged into the wilderness, but I welcomed it. The chill kept me focused—held back the fire threatening to consume me.

I strode forward with purpose, my shoulders squared, my jaw set. Avod's gaze lingered on me, wary but silent for the moment. The only sound was our boots hurriedly crunching over loose gravel, the silence a taut string between us.

At the city gates, a stablehand met us with a knowing nod, producing two Riftborn-bred horses. Their pale coats shimmered under the moonlight, spectral and silent.

"Drake," Avod muttered, his voice low. "We should stick to the shadows."

"No time for shadows," I growled. "We ride."

As we mounted, Avod shot me a sidelong glance. "You know where we're going?"

"I smelled sulfur and blood in the sewers," I said grimly, gripping the reins tightly. "Vyper's creatures reek of it. I'll follow the trail."

Avod raised an eyebrow. "You're tracking him like prey?"

"He is prey," I said, my voice low and hard.

We rode hard into the wilderness, the rhythmic pounding of hooves echoing through the stillness of the night like a drumbeat of war. The air was crisp, laden with the faint, earthy scent of damp leaves and moss. As we pressed deeper, the forest closed in around us, their gnarled limbs like dying hands. The canopy above was dense, blotting out the moonlight and casting the path in shadow, but our Riftborn horses moved with unerring precision. They were bred for this—fast, silent, tireless—sure-footed as ghosts.

The terrain grew more rugged as we pushed on, the once-firm path giving way to uneven ground littered with jagged rocks and tangled roots. The horses barely faltered, their muscles rippling with each stride as they carried us over obstacles with grace.

The forest seemed alive, watching us with an unseen presence. Every crack of a twig and rustle of leaves made my hand twitch toward my blade. This wasn't just nature's song; something lurked out here, hidden in the shadows, its foul presence prickling the edges of my senses. The deeper we rode, the fouler the air became. Damp leaves, wet stone... and beneath it, the rot of something unnatural.

Avod broke the silence. "You sure we're on the right path?" His voice was low, cautious.

I nodded, scanning the forest floor as we rode. "The stench of sulfur lingers. They passed through here."

Clawed footprints marked the ground. Drag marks. Blood. I crouched, running my fingers through the soil. The scent hit me like a hammer—decay, bile, and a faint hint of Honeydew—her scent.

"Fresh," I growled. "They were here recently." We pressed on, cutting through thick brush until we reached a clearing. The stream that wound through it ran sluggish and dark; its banks clawed with gouges. Bark hung in bloody strips from nearby trees. Carcasses—deer, foxes—lay torn and partially devoured. Dark, congealed blood stained the roots.

"Here," I said, pointing to the carnage. "They stopped. Likely fed," remnants of a meal—raw, partially consumed animals, their carcasses were torn apart in ways that made my stomach churn.

Avod crouched beside the marks, his expression grim. "Vyper's beasts don't kill cleanly. They enjoy the taste of suffering." Hours passed in a blur of relentless pursuit. We encountered more signs of the creatures' passage—another shredded deer carcass, its bones picked clean, a patch of ground trampled into a muddy mess of clawed footprints. I sniffed the air and was met with the rotten scent of the beasts.

"They're close," I said, my voice low. My eyes scanned the edges of the clearing.

"We should move," Avod said, his hand resting on the hilt of his blade.

"No," I said, stepping forward. "They're planning an ambush. We wait."

We led our horses deep into the underbrush, the dense foliage muffling the night's stillness. The undergrowth muffled sound, but not enough. Every breath I drew felt like bait. Every heartbeat landed too loud, too careless. I shifted my stance, weight rolling to the balls of my feet, and let the silence wrap me tight. My senses burned sharp with the anticipation of the hunt. Every snap of a twig, every rustle of the wind through the trees was a warning. Somewhere close, they hunted us.

Avod crouched low, blade drawn now, his gaze narrowing into the dark. "They're watching us," he muttered.

"I know." My fingers brushed the hilt of my sword. The leather grip was familiar, grounding. The longer the silence stretched, the more my body itched to break it. Every instinct screamed at me to move first, to strike before they could. But they wanted that. They wanted us blind, swinging at shadows.

So I waited.

Sweat ticked down my spine despite the chill. I kept my eyes on the tree line, breathing slow, steady, trying to bleed the tension out of my muscles before it made me careless. And then—

Movement.

A shadow peeled itself from the forest floor. Hunched, malformed, limbs jerking with a sick wrongness, like a puppet pulled by uneven strings. Its head lolled, then snapped up too fast. Two burning coals flared in the dark—red eyes, glowing with unnatural hunger.

Another followed, this one gaunt to the point of grotesque, its skeletal frame draped in tatters of fabric that clung to its rotted flesh. The stench of decay rolled off them in waves, mingling with the sharp tang of my fury.

"Stay back," I growled at Avod, my voice edged with an unnatural ferocity. He hesitated but nodded, gripping his hammer.

I stepped forward, my blade sliding free in one fluid motion. The steel glimmered in the faint moonlight. The Vyrmin hissed, crouching low as they prepared to strike. Their movements were quick but not quick enough.

The first lunged, claws aimed for my throat. I met its charge with a roar, my blade slicing cleanly through its arm. A sickening screech erupted as the severed limb hit the ground, black ichor spraying across the forest floor. It shrieked raw and gurgling. The other Vyrmin circled, its glowing eyes watching for an opening. It darted toward me faster than the first, but my rage made me faster still. With a guttural snarl, I spun, catching it mid-leap with a fiery arc of my blade. The force of the strike sent it crashing into a tree, its body crumpling lifelessly.

"Is that all?" I spat, my chest heaving, adrenaline roaring through my veins. But the battle wasn't over.

More figures emerged from the shadows, their twisted forms shuffling toward us with guttural growls. Three. Five. A dozen.

Then the fire inside me snapped its leash.

A surge of heat, blinding and overwhelming, erupted from deep within. Flames licked at the edges of my vision, my rage pouring forth like a tidal wave. I let it consume me.

A guttural roar ripped from my throat as fire exploded from my hands, engulfing the nearest Vyrmin. The flames danced and twisted, their screams filling the night as the stench of burning flesh filled the air.

My skin burned hot, more scales erupting along my arms, my fingers elongated, claws bursting from my knuckles. I felt my jaw stretch, my teeth turn to blades, and my senses sharpen to a feral clarity. I was no longer just a man. I had become something more, something primal.

A Vyrmin lunged, but I caught it mid-air, slamming it into the ground with enough force to crack its bones. Another swiped at me, but my claws raked across its chest, splitting it open and spilling its black ichor.

Then, I burned. Fire erupted from my mouth, a torrent of rage turned flame. The forest lit with screams as my flames tore through the beasts, consuming them in a wall of light and death. The clearing became a battlefield of ash.

When the last screech faded into silence, I stood amidst the carnage, my chest heaving, the scent of charred flesh and blood filling my nostrils. Slowly, the fire in my veins ebbed, and I felt the beast recede. My claws shrank back into hands, the scales receded from my arms, and the world returned to focus.

The fire had barely receded from my veins when my knees buckled. The world tilted sideways. The smell of scorched flesh, blood, and earth clung to the inside of my nose like a curse. My vision narrowed, and the last thing I saw was Avod's face—wide-eyed, cursing—as he rushed toward me.

Then, darkness.

Chapter Thirty Three

Avod

He went down *hard.*

One moment, Drake was all fire and shadow, his body mid-shift—eyes burning, teeth bared, half human and half dragon—and the next, his knees buckled like someone had cut the world out from under him.

"Shit—Drake!"

I caught him before he hit the ground. Just barely. He was burning with leftover Rift, magic crawling over his skin like it still wanted to finish what it started. His body twitched in my arms, heat pulsing under my hands, muscles locked like stone.

I'd seen Riftburn before. Seen it hollow people out from the inside, eat them alive for trying to hold more power than they were meant to. But this wasn't burn. This was transformation. I'd never seen someone shift before. Heard the stories, but didn't know it was actually possible.

He didn't even groan. He just collapsed into me.

I gritted my teeth and pulled him upright, slinging his weight over my shoulders. "Godsdamn your big ass," I muttered, stumbling toward the ravine wall. "You couldn't wait until *after* the fight?"

There was a half-sheltered cave tucked behind a tangle of vines, maybe twenty yards off the trail. I'd spotted it earlier—an old instinct never let me stop mapping exits. I hauled him there, half-dragging, half-carrying, stumbling on rocks as his boots scraped across the ground.

Inside, the air was cooler. Damp and close. I lowered him gently, propping his back against the wall. His chest rose and fell in shallow bursts, jaw tight, eyes shut hard. A tremor passed through his arms. Not cold. Pain.

Or whatever came after it.

I pulled off my gloves and crouched beside him, pressing my fingers to his neck. Pulse: fast but steady. His skin was too warm. His scales glowed faintly. His bones looked like they were trying to shift still. Like his body didn't know what shape it was supposed to be anymore.

"You big dumb bastard," I muttered, yanking off his breastplate. "Really had to try and shift, huh?"

No response. Not even a twitch.

Figures.

I struck the flint and lit a fire in a shallow pit. The cave was cold, and he was soaked in sweat and Vyrmin blood. I hated this part—the waiting. Sitting around with no idea whether your friend is gonna wake up or die, drooling blood into the dirt.

I didn't need to ask why he'd done it. It was written all over him. He'd gone full beast mode for her. For Eva.

She was changing him. That much was obvious. And I think she was changing him for the better. He was softer. Kinder. Happier. Either way, she was there, under his skin. You could see it every time he looked at her like she was the last thing holding him together. It's a dangerous kind of look. The kind that doesn't go away clean.

I leaned back against the wall and wiped my face with the least filthy part of my sleeve. It came away streaked with sweat and ash. Gross.

Drake groaned.

"Easy," I said, leaning toward him. "You're not dying today. Not if I have to drag your half-shifted ass all the way back to Felix myself."

His brow furrowed. His lips moved like he was trying to say something, but all I caught was—

"Eva...?"

Of course.

"Yeah, yeah. She's safe," I lied. "Go back to your fever dream, loverboy."

That seemed to calm him. His breathing leveled out a little, and the tension in his shoulders eased. Even unconscious, he needed to know she was okay. *Gods.*

I sat beside him, shoulder to shoulder, feeling the heat coming off his skin like he was still burning from the inside out. The fire crackled low. The cave smelled like smoke and blood and singed leather. Outside, the wind cut across the hills, whistling in the entrance, but here, we had a little quiet. For now.

I looked over at him. He didn't look like the kid I met years ago. That guy was cocky, sharp-edged, trying too hard to be the one in charge. He always carried guilt as if it were part of his uniform. Now? Now he looked like a weapon someone forgot how to hold. The Rift was carving new rules into him, and he was trying to pretend like he could still live by the old ones.

He'd never admit it, but he was scared. Not of dying—that'd be too easy. He was scared of changing. Of not recognizing himself when it was over. Afraid of turning into something that didn't know how to care.

Which was funny because he still did. Even now, half-dead in a cave, he was thinking about her. He always cared enough to ask me if I'd eaten, even when we were neck-deep in a mission. He made sure Fen had tea when she was pacing like a feral cat. He made sure Felix was comfortable when healing.

"Don't disappear on me," I muttered. "You're the only one in Riftreach who laughs at my jokes." But really, I wasn't prepared to let go of my best friend. He didn't respond, but I wasn't really expecting him to.

I leaned my head back against the wall and shut my eyes for a second. Just to rest them. And, of course—like clockwork—my brain decided to pull Fen's face into focus.

She'd have some smartass remark ready for this mess. Probably something about Drake being a showoff. Or me being a sentimental idiot for dragging his body out of a battle again.

But she'd still have come. She always did.

Fen was... a disaster. Loud, stubborn, and too sharp for her own good. And somehow, she'd made herself permanent in my life without asking. I couldn't even pinpoint when it started. The fights that turned into long looks. The insults that sounded a little like flirting if you tilted your head. The way her hand would linger just a second too long on my arm.

She drove me up the wall. And yeah—if I'm being honest? I'd probably let her wreck me if it meant she'd stay. But she wasn't here. I opened my eyes. Drake still hadn't moved.

"You're not allowed to break," I said quietly. "Not before I tell Fen she was right about you being dramatic." Still nothing. But the glow in his skin was fading. Slowly. Whatever the Rift took, it hadn't taken everything.

I stoked the fire again and stood to check the cave mouth. Nothing out there but wind and rocks. When I came back, I sat beside him again and let the silence settle.

"You better wake up soon, Captain," I said, staring into the fire. "We're not done with you yet."

Chapter Thirty Four

Felix

I woke to dripping.

Not mine, for once. Real water, persistent as a torturer. It counted time into a shallow puddle by my ear—drip, drip, drip—until I considered prying out one of the rusty nails in my bench and hammering it into my skull just to stop the rhythm.

The dungeon smelled like a grave: mildew chewing the air, iron thick as pennies, and the sour aftertaste of blood. Torches burned green with Riftlight, sputtering as the wards drank and hummed beneath the stone. The Vyrmin down the hall shifted now and then, claws dragging a rhythm out of sync with the dripping, a scrape like a blade testing its own edge.

Fen snored in the corner, light and dainty. Most would call it sweet. I called it an insult that she slept like a pampered cat in this pit.

So when I heard a chain scrape next door, I thought maybe the dripping had finally made me hallucinate. Then a muffled curse, raw and low.

"Fuck you."

Ah. Eva was awake.

"Eva?" I rasped, shuffling to the bars despite the ache where a

Vyrmin had tried gnawing my ribs. "It's Felix. Fen and I are here—next cell over."

A pause. Then, sharp as a blade: "You knew."

It wasn't the venom that cut me. It was the pain strung through those two words.

"What did we know?" I held up my hands through the bars, palms open, placating like she was a spooked animal—and she was, wasn't she? A cornered one, bleeding and betrayed.

She limped forward into the torchlight, one eye swollen near shut, wrists torn raw by iron cuffs. She was pale, filthy, furious. "Don't lie to me. You knew about him. About Drake. About all of it."

Fen pushed to her feet behind me, bristling. "Eva, you've been hurt. Drugged. You're not—" Her voice still sounding rough will sleep.

Eva laughed, a sound like shattering stone. "Fuck you. No more lies. No more."

I pressed my forehead to the bars, breathing slow. "Eva, tell me what you think you heard."

Her words tumbled sharp, broken. "Julian, Drake, whispers about what a good actor he was. Every kiss, every touch, all a job. A con." Her breath hitched; her nails cut crescents into her palms until blood welled. "He never wanted me. Not really."

That was the twist of the blade.

I let my head thunk once against the bars. "Eva," I said, flat, "Drake's in love with you."

She laughed again, sharp, ruined. "Don't. Don't say that."

Fen crouched near the bars, voice steady but softer than I'd ever heard. "It's true. I've known him half my life. He's never looked at anyone like he looks at you."

Eva shook her head, trembling. "He was faking it."

"Think," I pressed. "You'd already agreed to Riftreach. What did he gain pretending? Why risk weeks of his neck for a con that makes no sense?" I gentled my voice. "Eva, that pull between you—it wasn't your imagination. The Rift noticed."

Her gaze snapped to mine. "The Rift?"

"Yeah." My throat was tight, words sticking. "It has... motive. Once in a while, it threads two people together so tight neither can shake it. That's a bond."

She recoiled like I'd named a curse. "No."

"Yes. And not the kind you've read about in Ness's tomes. Not a chain. This one's rarer. Stranger. A love bond."

Her lips shaped the word like it burned. "Love?"

Fen's voice was almost a whisper. "It means you chose first. The Rift didn't force you. It followed."

Eva's breath stuttered. Then her face hardened. The stone hummed. Not the wards this time. Deeper. A pulse. A heartbeat that wasn't mine. Wasn't hers.

Eva's body arched. Muscles spasmed as if the Riftlight itself tried to crawl under her skin. Her eyes rolled back, white catching the green torchlight. Chains rattled as she fought both vision and ward.

"Eva!" Fen gripped the bars, but the wards sparked, hissing against her hand.

Eva convulsed, breath torn from her throat. Then, a whisper: "D-Drake... I feel him. He's coming."

The Vyrmin outside hissed, retreating a step. The torches guttered, shadows bending like they knew the name too.

I stared at her, helpless, as the pulse hit again—stronger, closer—and realized whatever truth I'd meant to finish had just been cut off by the Rift itself.

Chapter Thirty Five

Eldrake

I didn't wake up.

I fell—hard and helpless—into a dream that wasn't mine, that wasn't a dream at all.

I stood in a corridor of stone I didn't recognize, but my lungs did. My skin did. The stink of blood and damp rot clung to the walls, heavy as chains. The air hummed with pressure. Torches burned green with Riftlight, shadows twisting wrong, as if they belonged to something else entirely.

Cells. A dungeon.

I wasn't really there. I felt it immediately—like I was pressed beneath glass, only allowed to watch. A memory, a vision.

And Eva... Gods. Eva was there.

She sat chained in the far corner, her wrist shackled to the wall, her body folded in on itself like armor. A Vyrmin stood guard outside her door, claws flexing against the stone, its eyes never leaving her. Dried blood streaked from her lip to her collarbone. She trembled—not from cold, but from something deeper. They weren't just breaking her body. They were crushing her magic, pressing it down until it had nowhere to go.

She looked smaller than I remembered. Dimmed, but not extinguished. She wasn't breaking. But she was wearing out.

Across the hall, in the next cell, movement caught my eye—Fen and Felix. Both chained, both awake, watching helplessly. Fen's hands fisted around her bonds; Felix's jaw was set like iron. They were close. Too close. And still, none of them could reach one another.

"Eva!" I tried to call, but my voice had no place here. I was just a ghost, a passenger.

She stirred. Slowly, her head lifted, eyes half-lidded. And then—"Drake?"

My heart lurched. She couldn't see me. She couldn't possibly know. And yet—our bond thrummed to life, thin as thread but stretching across the distance like a heartbeat. Her pain pulsed against my ribs as if it were my own.

"I'm here," I swore, though I knew she couldn't hear.

Her lips parted again, forming my name, soft and raw. She raised her hand—weak, trembling—toward the space where the bars cut shadows across the floor.

I lifted mine in answer, and though it passed through smoke and stone, the bond pulled tight between us. For a moment, I swore I felt her skin against mine.

The air shimmered. Not magic. Not vision. Something else. Ours.

She felt me. I knew it.

And I—Gods help me—I would tear the world apart to reach her.

The vision began to unravel. The torchlight fractured, shadows melting into nothing. Eva blurred, fading back into the dark.

"No!" My roar broke against the silence. "Not yet!"

But already I was falling. The last thing I saw was her mouth shaping my name again and again, a prayer with no answer—while the Rift between us pulsed, alive, hungry, unbreakable.

I woke gasping, every nerve in my body on fire. My throat was raw. My vision swam. Pain exploded in every direction—my spine, my limbs, my ribs.

I tried to move.

"Stop," Avod said. His voice was firm and steady, a hand pressing gently to my chest. "You're going to tear yourself in half."

"She's alive," I croaked. "Vyper has her. A dungeon. Underground." Avod hesitated. That alone made my stomach bottom out. Avod's brows pulled tight, but I kept going, my voice breaking. "She's not alone. I saw Fen. Felix too. Same cells. Shackled."

That name stopped him. Fen.

For a heartbeat, Avod didn't move, didn't even breathe. His gaze slipped from mine to the fire, to the shadows crowding the cave walls.

"You're sure?" His voice was low, strained.

"I'd stake my life on it."

Silence stretched between us, the fire snapping in the space where words should have been.

When he finally spoke, his voice was raw. "She's always been trouble. Always pushed too hard, talked too much, fought too dirty." He swallowed hard, his jaw tight. "Fen and Felix didn't return from their mission." His eyes met mine. "We suspected they were taken, too." The words hit like a second blow.

Eva. Fen. Felix. Trapped inside that place, suffering.

I scanned the cave—small, firelit, stone walls curving in and stalactites like teeth. My armor lay stripped in pieces across the floor. Cloths soaked with sweat and blood. My limbs twitched with aftershock. My skin itched like it hadn't fully settled back into place.

"Where are we?"

"You blacked out," Avod said. "Almost fully shifted. It took an hour to get you down. Your skin was glowing like a bonfire, and your eyes were..." He didn't finish. "I dragged your heavy ass in here and hoped you'd wake up."

He tossed me a waterskin. I drank until my ribs hurt.

"I saw her," I whispered. "I felt her pain. I couldn't reach her."

"She'll feel you again," he said. "When you get to her."

I stared at the fire. The guilt was loud. Ugly. "Every second I'm here, she's in pain."

"You move now, and you collapse again."

"I'd rather die than waste time."

"Well, I'd rather not drag your smoking corpse through another ten miles of wilderness." That pulled a dry huff from my chest. It almost hurt more than the shifting.

He looked at me. "You bonded." It wasn't a question.

I didn't answer. I didn't need to.

"She's going to be alright," he said quietly. "Because you won't stop. Neither will I." I nodded, barely. "I can't believe you love *Fen*."

"*Shut up,*" He laughed and kicked some dust in my direction.

The fire cracked. My body trembled with leftover power. My skin still buzzed with Rift energy. But the worst of it had passed. Avod was right. He always was. I looked at him—my brother, my anchor—the one who never let me fall alone.

Tomorrow, we'd run again. But tonight, I let myself breathe. Just once. For her.

We had been riding for days, and I still wasn't close enough to kill him. The biting wind howled through the jagged cliffs as Avod and I pressed forward. Each step felt heavier than the last, the weight of my armor and the inferno inside me nearly unbearable. The terrain had grown brutal —scarred and unnatural, as though something ancient had clawed its way through the land long ago. The stench of sulfur clung to the air like rot. It was him. I could feel it. Vyper's scent. His filth.

"Drake," Avod called from behind me, his voice strained but steady. "Tracks. Fresh."

I joined him, kneeling beside the clawed footprints etched deep into the frozen soil. They were wider than before—rushed. Fleeing.

"They're running," I said darkly. "They should be." We followed the trail into a canyon where the trees had long since blackened and died. The air thinned, brittle with frost. My Rift pulsed under my skin. I was nearing my limit, but I wouldn't stop. Not until I saw her again.

The first attack came without warning.

A guttural roar echoed through the canyon, and from the shadows, a Vyrmin leaped from the ridge above, claws extended. I pivoted and drove my blade straight into its chest. Its body convulsed, black ichor spurting across the rocks. Two more lunged from the shadows behind it. Avod was already moving, his hammer colliding with bone and muscle in a blur of force.

"Left!" I shouted.

He was already moving, his war hammer crashing into the skull of one beast, its head caving in with a sickening crunch. He spun, blocking the swipe of another's claws with the haft of his weapon before driving his knee into its chest.

I turned my focus back to the wounded Vyrmin, finishing it with a fiery slash that split it from throat to belly. The flames leaped from my blade as if alive, fueled by the raw, unrelenting fury coursing through me.

But the fight wasn't over.

They kept coming—half a dozen more—twisted, screaming, ravenous. My fury boiled over.

My blade flared. My skin burned. The Dragon surged forward. Unlike last time, it didn't take me by surprise. I welcomed it. The shift came like a breath—scales bloomed across my arms, my jaw extended into a snarl. My spine cracked, talons lengthened. Heat erupted from my core. Controlled this time. Focused.

I met them in a blur of teeth and flame. A Vyrmin lunged. I caught it in both claws and hurled it into the others. I opened my mouth and unleashed a fire that danced along the canyon walls, illuminating the carnage. They screamed. I didn't stop.

When the last shriek died and the air filled with smoke and silence, I stood in the center of the scorched path, breathing hard. The world slowly crept back to itself. My claws faded. My bones reset. The flame within me guttered low but not out.

I staggered slightly. Avod approached, giving me a long, deliberate once-over. "Well," he said, casually slinging his hammer across his back, "You're still standing; that's good."

"It's the second time," I muttered, wiping blood from my jaw. "The shift is getting stronger. I'm holding onto it longer."

"And thank the Gods you're learning how to aim your fire," he gestured toward a simmering log that had just about turned to cinder. "You almost roasted me."

"You were in my way," I said with a shrug.

"I was behind you. And still, my left boot melted."

I huffed something between a cough and a laugh. "Sorry."

He shook his head, eyeing the carnage. "You're a walking natural disaster, you know that?"

"I know."

Avod's grin faded into something steadier. "Whatever's waiting for us up ahead—whatever he's doing to her—we're ready. He won't see us coming."

My jaw tensed. "Oh, he'll see me. But it'll be the *last* thing he sees."

I turned back to the trail, the smoldering ruins of Vyper's beasts behind us. My vision narrowed again, not from rage—but purpose.

Eva was close.

And so was vengeance.

Chapter Thirty Six

Vyper

The chamber lay still—too still. Silence like a patient strapped to a table, waiting for the knife.

I broke it with a hiss. "Ahhh... yes. Time for tonight's test."

The incantation spilled from my tongue in jagged syllables, precise as sutures, venom curling at the edges. The Vessel responded—always hungry, always obedient. Shadows bent closer. Riftlight flared like fever. Each reaction noted, expected. Reliable.

The glass darkened.

First the eyes. Always first. Black fire, twin voids consuming the light around them. Then the body—no, not a body. A seep. A hemorrhage of shadow into space, uncontrolled and perfect.

I smiled as my knees found stone. A prayer performed. Fascination genuine.

"My lord," I whispered.

"Vyper." The voice rasped through my skull, a thousand blades scraping bone. My grin widened. "You call me again. What morsel do you offer this time?"

"Dozens," I said, savoring the word. "Rebellion stock. Riftborn. Their pain is fresh. Their screams... exquisite."

The Vessel throbbed. A heartbeat. His weight pressed down, demanding my spine curve.

"And what do you ask in return, Insect?"

I unsheathed the scalpel, its edge still crusted with dried red. A comfort. "The Seer," I breathed. "Her Rift is... resilient. Resistant. A subject unlike any other. I would probe it, break it, wield it. With her power, the rebellion could be excised. Root and branch. A clean amputation."

"You seek to possess what is not yours." The words slithered sharp. "Her Rift is not a door. It is a weapon. One that chooses."

I flinched. A small tic. Not fear—correction. I drew a steady breath. "Then tell me how to unmake the choice."

The God's laugh made the Vessel tremble, cracks veining the glass like fractures in bone. "Ahhh... eager. Arrogant. The surgeon who thinks himself creator." The smoke pressed closer. "But... yesss. There is a way."

I leaned in, pulse sharpening to a single point. "Name it."

"You must sever her anchor." His tone was almost tender, like a doctor breaking bad news. "Offer me what she clings to most."

I tilted my head. I smelt it in her blood earlier.

The smile cut the dark, all fangs. "The Dragon."

The word slithered down my spine. "Mm. I see. The one called *Eldrake.*"

"They are bound," Azh'raim hissed. "Rift. Body. Soul. Deeper than they know. When he breathes, she steadies. When she bleeds, he burns. They are one incision stitched across two bodies."

My breath shivered out. "Then to sever it?"

"Bring me his soul." The Vessel wailed with the pressure. "Break him—and she will unravel. Her tether will rot. She will yield."

The chamber shook. Light flared like cauterization. His voice coiled tighter, softer. "And as you plot, he climbs. Even now, the Dragon comes. Step by step. Breath by breath. The scalpel will meet the flame."

I stiffened, though I masked it with stillness.

"And she," the God purred, "is not the only ripe vessel. The other female. The one with fire in her veins and grief in her marrow. That one will kneel when I call. You will break her for me."

I cared not of anyone else. The Seer was my key to the throne. The chamber went silent save for the crackle of the Vessel. His presence lingered, then receded like a blade slipping from flesh.

"Fail me," he hissed, "and you are mine."

Then gone. Smoke curling where his voice had been.

I stood, chest heaving, scalpel steady. The diagnosis was clear. The Dragon was her anchor. Her undoing.

I turned the blade in my hand, light catching its edge. "Let us see," I murmured, a grin splitting wide, unhinged, serpent-sharp. "Let us see how strong the bond truly is."

And in the dark, I laughed—clinical, ecstatic, a scalpel slicing silence.

Chapter Thirty Seven

Evandra

"Though it is theoretically possible to commune with the ancient Gods, such interactions are rare, dangerous, and always dictated by the deities' terms. Gods are capricious and immensely powerful, often demanding significant sacrifices in exchange for their attention or favor. Attempts to summon or bargain with them have historically led to disastrous outcomes, including madness, death, or corruption." — Understanding the Rift, Chapter 5

I GASPED as I slammed back into my body.

The dungeon reassembled around me in jagged, overwhelming pieces—stone, rust, blood, mold. It was all too real, too loud. But none of it could drown out what I'd just seen. Not the sickly glow of the Vessel. Not the voice of the God made of shadow and rot. Not the words that had hooked into my chest and refused to let go.

The soul of the Dragon.

The phrase echoed in my bones, vibrating with truth I wasn't ready to face. Vyper asked Azh'raim how to control me—how to *own* me. And the answer was Drake.

My head throbbed. I clutched at my temples, fighting the tide of memory. But worse than the vision was the feeling that had followed it. A pulse, like a second heartbeat—not mine, but *his*. I'd felt it. Not just through memory. Through something more. Something alive. A tether between us, suddenly sharper. Thicker.

My stomach turned.

"Eva?" Fen's voice came through the fog. "What happened?"

I looked at her, and for once, words didn't come easily. "I saw him," I said at last. "Vyper. In the chamber. He was communing with Azh'raim through the mirror."

Even saying the name sent a ripple of nausea through me.

"He asked how to control me. And the God told him the price. He said Vyper would have to offer what I desire most."

A pause.

Fen's mouth tightened. "Drake."

I nodded slowly. "He knows about the bond."

I waited for their reactions—shock, confusion, disbelief. But none came. Instead, they exchanged a look. "Tell me what it means," I said quietly. "The love bond. Tell me more. I need to understand."

Felix looked at me, and for a moment, he hesitated—like he was deciding how much of the truth to soften. Then he sighed and crouched beside me.

"There are a lot of kinds of Riftbonds," he began. "Most of them are... well, trash. They form in battle, in bed, in trauma—pick your poison. Burn hot, burn fast, and usually burn someone alive. But your kind?" He tipped his head, a faint, crooked grin on his filthy face. "Rare. The archives call it a love bond. Not lust. Not obligation. Resonance. The Rift sees two idiots choosing each other completely and goes, 'Oh, sweet, let's immortalize that drama.'"

"And how do you know which one it is?" I asked, voice hoarse.

Felix smiled faintly. "That's the thing. You don't know right away. But there are signs. Emotional bleed, stronger when one of you is being a reckless dumbass. A magnetic pull when you're apart. Dreams.

Visions. Sometimes, if the Rift's feeling spicy, you even get flashes of each other's perspective." He arched a brow. "Tell me you've never peeked out of his eyes?"

I blinked. "What?"

"Some bonds allow flashes of shared perspective," Felix said softly. "It's rare, but it happens."

And I thought of it—Colin's death through Drake's eyes. My fall off my horse, seen not from me but him. Gods. How long had the Rift known? How long had *Drake?*

I looked down at my shaking hands. "Why didn't anyone *tell* me this could happen?" They exchanged another knowing look.

"Wait," I said slowly, cold blooming in my chest. "You *knew?*"

Felix winced. "Eva—"

"You knew." I suppose they must have guessed about the bond. But I hadn't let myself see it—that they knew, and stayed silent. And Gods, that silence hurt most of all.

Fen blew out a breath and dragged a hand through her dark hair. "Drake told us. Before we left."

"You didn't think I had the right to know?" I snapped.

"We didn't know if it was real-real," Felix said quickly. "Drake wasn't sure, and you were still recovering. He said he was waiting for the *right moment.* Which, for the record, spoiler alert—there is never a right moment to tell your girlfriend, 'Surprise, cosmic marriage contract.'"

My pulse spiked. "So instead of letting me decide for myself, you just let him sit on it? Like it wasn't *my* life?"

"Eva—" Fen started.

"No." I pushed myself upright, wincing as my wounds protested. "You don't get to defend this. This bond—whatever it is—it connects *my* soul to his. That's not a small thing. That's not something you keep to yourself."

Silence.

Felix stood in his cell. "You're right," he said softly. "We messed up."

The admission made something inside me unravel just a little. I looked down at my trembling hands. "I felt it," I whispered. "Earlier in my vision. Something pulsed. Like a second heartbeat. Like he was—like he was *there.*"

Felix nodded. "That's how you know. Love bond."

I stared at the floor. "He should have told me."

"I think he was scared," Felix offered gently. "Not of the bond—of losing you. Of what it might mean if you didn't want it."

I let out a breath, shaky and raw. "I don't know if I do."

Fen raised a brow. "You don't want to be bonded to him?"

"I don't know what I want!" I shot back. "I don't know if this feeling is love or if it's *fate*. What if it's the Rift making choices for me?"

Felix gave a little half-smile. "Then let me ask you this. If the Rift didn't exist—if there was no magic, no fate, no bond—would you still want Drake?"

The answer came faster than I expected. "Yes," I said. "Of course I would."

"Then it doesn't matter," Fen said, voice soft but firm. "Rift or not, you already chose him."

I looked at her, then at Felix, the heat in my chest shifting. It wasn't anger anymore. Not fully. It was the weight of knowledge, settling in like a new gravity.

"So what now?" I asked. "Vyper's going to use this. He thinks Drake is my weakness."

"He's wrong," Fen said. "Drake is your *anchor*. You just proved it—by reaching for him across the bond."

Felix smiled. "And if I had to bet on someone turning a bond into a weapon against the Gods, it's you."

I swallowed hard, heart pounding. "Then let's make sure Drake survives long enough to see what happens when the Rift chooses love." I thought for a moment. "I have to warn him," I said, my voice low but urgent. "He doesn't know. He's walking straight into Vyper's hands."

Felix blinked. "Eva—"

"He *doesn't know* what they're planning," I snapped. "He thinks we're just bonded in the usual way—whatever that even means. He doesn't know they're using *him* to get to me."

Felix blinked, then softened. "Eva—look, I love your ambition, but logistics. We're locked in a moldy box. You can't even stand, let alone storm the gates. So how exactly do you plan on warning him?"

"I don't need to stand." I closed my eyes. "I just need to find the thread."

The silence around me sharpened as I pulled inward. The dungeon fell away—the cold, the pain, the stink of old blood. All that remained was the tether. That sliver of silver warmth in the dark. It pulsed like a heartbeat. Not mine. His.

The bond wasn't faint anymore. It had swelled—alive and bright, responding to danger like it could sense something hunting us through the dark. My pulse matched it, syncing to a rhythm that wasn't entirely my own.

Drake, I whispered down the thread. *Please… hear me.*

My fingers curled around the bars beside me, grounding myself in the pain. I clung to the memory: the Vessel's glow, the God's growl, Vyper whispering about "the soul of the Dragon." I gathered the vision like a flame cupped in my hands and shoved it down the tether—hard.

It was like trying to force a letter through the eye of a needle. The wards squeezed tight, crushing the magic until it felt like I was shoving fire through a pinhole. My ribs ached, my throat tore, and still I pressed harder, harder, until something gave.

The surge roared up through me—burning behind my eyes, splitting my skull. Gods, it hurt. But beneath the agony I felt him. Somewhere far away. His breath catching. His mind reacting.

Come on, I begged silently. *Feel it. See it.*

A sound escaped me—half gasp, half sob—as the current slammed back through me like a wave. I collapsed against the stone wall, panting.

When I opened my eyes again, the world tilted sideways.

"I don't know if it worked," I whispered, pressing a hand to my chest. "But I had to try."

Fen crossed her arms and leaned against the bars, her eyes sharp with resolve. "Then we buy him time. However we can."

Felix nodded, rolling his shoulders like he was limbering up for a tavern brawl. "Fine. We get out. We find the armory. And then we make Vyper regret he ever learned your name. Maybe even regret he was born, if we're feeling ambitious."

I pulled myself upright slowly, ignoring the scream of my bruised muscles. Something was shifting inside me—some deeper layer of my

Rift opening like a second skin. Not just to protect myself. To protect *him*. "Fen—tell me more about that pit you saw."

Her expression darkened. "It's near the guard barracks. Riftborn prisoners. Dozens. Maybe more. Some looked too weak to stand."

"We can't leave without them," I said. "We don't just escape. We *liberate*."

Felix frowned. "We'll need weapons. I'm good with my fists, sure, but I'm not *that* good. You try defending fifty half-starved prisoners barehanded and see how long you last."

Fen nodded grimly. "I've been watching the guards. There's a gap in the patrols just after the next shift. If we time it right, we can slip into the supply room and grab enough blades to arm a dozen fighters. It's tight, but it's there."

My jaw clenched as I pushed to my feet again, swaying once before catching myself on the bars. "Then we prepare."

The chains at my ankles clinked softly, like a warning.

I looked toward the heavy door, and for the first time, I didn't feel small. I felt like fire waiting for kindling.

"Vyper thinks I'm something he can own," I said. The metal beneath my palm began to hum. "He's about to learn what happens when you back a Seer into a corner."

Chapter Thirty Eight

Eldrake

The forest seemed unnaturally quiet as we rode; the only sounds were the rhythmic clatter of hooves and the occasional snap of a branch underfoot. The air carried an unnatural chill, one that prickled at the edges of my senses and sent a warning deep into my bones. Vyper's tower was close. I could feel it.

Avod rode just behind me, his silence uncharacteristic, though I knew his tension mirrored my own. We'd been following the faint traces of Vypyr's corruption for days now—claw marks on trees, patches of scorched earth that reeked of sulfur, and the occasional dismembered animal carcass that spoke of the Vyrmin's foul rituals. Each sign drew us closer to the heart of the danger and to Eva.

Her scent had been absent for miles, but I clung to the hope that she was still alive, still fighting. I wouldn't let myself think otherwise. The bond between us thrummed faintly, a distant thread of connection that flickered like a dying ember. I reached for it constantly, trying to pull her closer in my mind, to feel her presence, but the distance or her condition made it impossible.

Then it happened. Something punched me in the chest.

Not a blade. Not a fist.

A *feeling.*

I slumped on my saddle as the breath was knocked from my lungs. The forest ahead blurred, moonlight bending like mist. Avod turned, about to ask something, but I held up a hand, fingers trembling.

"Wait," I rasped. "Just—wait."

The air shifted. Thickened. A scent I knew—honeysuckle and dew—flooded my senses. My vision tunneled. The bond—*our* bond—flared to life like a lit vein through my chest. Hot. Bright. Alive.

Eva.

I felt her panic before I saw anything. Her fear. Her pain. The weight of a name:

Vyper.

And then—like something unfolding inside my skull—I *saw* it. Not a memory. Not a dream. A *message.*

A God in shadow, his eyes swallowing the light. The Vessel's unnatural hum. Vyper, kneeling, whispering *"The soul of the Dragon."* Offering me like a sacrament to break her. To claim her.

My blood ran cold.

My knees nearly buckled under me, the vision crashing over me like a tidal wave—real and unreal, present and distant. My heart raced, but it wasn't just mine. I could feel *hers*, too—ragged and furious. The tether between us buzzed, taut as a drawn bow.

She had *seen* it. She was *showing* me.

And worse—she was *hurting.*

I swore, pressing a hand to my sternum, right over the place where the tether burned beneath skin and bone. It wasn't just magic. It was her. *She'd sent this.* Not some uncontrolled flare like before—this had intent. Purpose.

She was trying to warn me.

Avod moved closer. "Drake?"

"I..." I forced a breath, swallowing the bile rising in my throat. "I think Eva just contacted me. Through the Rift. Through the bond."

His face went still. "You *felt* her?"

"Not just felt." I looked up, eyes wide. "She sent me a vision. Vyper was speaking to the Vessel. Azh'raim was there. He—he told Vyper to offer what Eva wants most."

Avod's jaw clenched. "You."

I nodded slowly. "He's going to try and kill me to break her. And she saw it."

I could still feel the imprint of her—like heat after lightning, like someone had carved her essence across my ribs. My hand curled into a fist.

She'd done that from a cell. Injured. Alone. And she'd *known*. She had to. The way the bond had pulsed—deliberate, tethered to memory, to *me*. There was no more hiding it now. She knew we were bonded. And yet... she'd still reached for me. Still trusted me. Gods, she *chose* me. Even knowing the Rift had bound us. Even knowing the danger. That knowledge hit harder than any blade. It didn't feel like a chain. It felt like... grace. Like a second chance I hadn't earned but had been given anyway.

"She's in danger," I said, my voice sharpening. "Vyper knows what we are. He knows about the bond. He's planning to use it."

Avod frowned. "We don't know how much he understands—"

"He doesn't have to *understand*. He just has to *hurt* us."

For a moment, I couldn't move. Couldn't breathe.

And then something inside me snapped into place.

This wasn't just about saving her anymore. It wasn't even about revenge.

It was about the *bond*. The real one. The thing I'd been denying, avoiding, dancing around in the dark. The thing that just reached across Godsdamned miles to warn me. She'd called to me like I was home.

And now I had to answer.

"We keep moving," I said. "No more delays."

Avod nodded.

But as we rode—quiet and quick through the trees—I kept one hand over my chest, where I swore I could still feel her fingers reaching through the tether.

And in the dark, I whispered back.

I'm coming.

"Drake, couldn't this be exactly what he wants? We are playing into his— " Avod started.

Before he could finish, the air shifted—heavy and wet with the reek of sulfur, ash, and rot. The Rift pulsed beneath my boots, wrong somehow. Twisted.

I turned my head sharply—too late.

The ground exploded in a shower of black stone and bone. A massive shape burst upward, shrieking, its roar shrill and broken like metal scraping against itself.

And then I saw it.

Not a beast. A ruin. A memory defiled.

It had the shape of a dragon—but only just. Its body was warped, dragged out of proportion by something dark and hungry. Tattered wings scraped the sky, shredded and stitched with pulsing red veins of Riftlight. Horns curved back like blades, splintered and blackened at the tips. Its scales were patchy, flaking away to reveal muscle that oozed some thick, tar-like fluid.

Its face— Gods.

It wasn't a dragon anymore. But it used to be. You could still see the shape of one beneath the rot. Like something once sacred, gutted and remade by someone who hated what it used to be.

"Vyrmin," I breathed, but this one was different. Bigger. Older. Familiar.

A long scar split its left side—identical to the kind that used to be carried by trained Dragonblood warriors. My gut twisted.

This thing wasn't born. It was turned.

"Drake," Avod muttered beside me. "Tell me I'm not seeing what I think I'm seeing."

"You are." This was one of us. Once. Now, it was just another weapon in Vyper's collection.

The creature let out a rattling hiss and lunged—faster than its size should allow. I shoved Avod back and drew my blade in one motion. The creature's claws tore gouges into the stone where he'd been standing.

"Ambush!" I shouted, eyes scanning the shadows. They answered.

The lesser Vyrmin poured from cracks in the walls, half-human shapes crawling on too many limbs, their skin sloughing off in ribbons. Their eyes glowed like coals, and their mouths snapped in unnatural angles as if chewing on memories they couldn't digest.

The corrupted dragon reared back, wings flaring wide as the swarm fanned out around it. The sound of its breath—wet, broken, bubbling —echoed like a death knell. I gritted my teeth.

"You take the left!" I shouted to Avod. Before he could answer, the first creature lunged.

My sword met it mid-air, slicing through its neck with a burst of hot, hissing ichor. It screamed as it fell, limbs twitching. Another followed. Then two more. The swarm descended in a frenzy, claws, and teeth tearing at the air, driven by something deeper than hunger—something taught. Trained.

Vyper hadn't just made monsters.

He'd made soldiers.

Avod's hammer swung in a wide arc, smashing through one creature and burying deep into the chest of another. "There's too many of them!" he shouted over the cacophony of snarls and screams.

The Star-Glow surged in my veins, the fire in my chest igniting as my rage boiled over. A roar tore from my throat as flames erupted from my mouth, engulfing the nearest creatures in a blazing inferno. Their screams echoed through the forest as their bodies crumbled to ash. But they kept coming.

The power inside me burned hotter, uncontrollably, as I felt the shift begin. My claws tore through my gloves, my teeth elongating as scales started to ripple across my skin. The transformation was partial, my wings bursting from my back as I slammed into the ground with a force that toppled several of the creatures.

The Vyrmin hesitated, their snarls faltering as they sensed the raw power radiating from me. I didn't give them a chance to recover. My claws tore through flesh, my flames reducing their twisted bodies to ash. I fought like a creature possessed, every strike fueled by the desperate need to get to her.

But exhaustion crept in, my vision blurring as the transformation began to recede. My body screamed in protest, the cost of wielding such power too great, too often. I staggered, my wings folding back into my body as I returned to human form, my breaths heaving.

"Drake, behind you!" Avod's voice was sharp with panic.

I turned too late. The largest of the Vyrmin barreled into me, its massive claws ripping through my armor and sending me sprawling to the ground. My sword skittered out of reach as I struggled to push the beast off, my strength waning.

I reached for it anyway. Pain lanced through my shoulder as the beast pinned me with one claw, snarling hot breath in my face. I thrashed, summoned fire—but all I got was a flicker, a dying ember.

"Get off him!" Avod roared. His hammer crushed into the creature's back with a sickening crunch. It howled—but didn't fall. Another Vyrmin slammed into Avod's side, dragging him down. I caught one last glimpse of his arm swinging, blood spraying across the stone.

We were overwhelmed. For every beast we felled, more crawled from the shadows. I tried to shift again, to summon fire, strength, anything. But my body betrayed me. The fire was gone. My limbs wouldn't move. The Vyrmin's claws drove into my chest, pinning me like prey.

"Eva," I whispered, breathless, and everything went black.

I awoke to the stench of rot and stone, the air wet and sour. My head pounded with every heartbeat. Chains bit into my wrists, my ankles. I tried to move—and immediately regretted it. My back arched against the cold floor, breath coming shallow.

I wasn't alone. I heard the rustle of movement, a grunt. "Avod?" I rasped.

"I'm here," his voice came from somewhere in the dark. Ragged. Tired. "You look worse than me, and that's saying something."

"Where are we?"

"Vyper's lair," he muttered. "Or some basement of it. I blacked out right after they jumped me."

I tested the chains again. No give. My rage simmered low and hot. "I'll get us out," I said, every word a vow. "And I'll kill him."

Avod huffed. "Good. Because if we're dying in a dungeon, I'm haunting someone."

Chapter Thirty Nine

Evandra

"Seers possess the potential for extraordinary mental control. With enough mastery, their powers can grow to the extent that they may permanently dominate another's mind and body, effectively turning the victim into a puppet incapable of independent thought or action. Such acts are considered a violation of individual autonomy and are classified as one of the highest crimes in Riftborn society. even the suggestion of such abuse can lead to a Seer's exile or execution." —Understanding the Rift, Chapter 5

"Are we ready?" I whispered, my voice steady despite the tension coiled in my chest. Fen was crouched near the bars of her cell, her eyes gleaming with determination. "As ready as we'll ever be," she muttered, her knuckles white around the crude bone shard in her hand. Felix knelt beside her, his hands glowing faintly as he whispered a quiet prayer under his breath.

A door creaked open down the hall. My breath caught as the sound echoed through the oppressive silence. A Vyrmin sauntered into view, its hulking, twisted frame illuminated by the faint torchlight. Its horns coiled grotesquely from its forehead, remnants of whatever Hell-wrought it had once been. Now, though, it looked ill, its skin sallow and stretched tightly over sharp bones. Dead, almost. Yet its glowing red eyes betrayed a flicker of life, malicious and unwavering. Its guard was down, not knowing I'd been honing my magic for months.

"This is it." I whispered as we all sank back, feigning sleep as the creature's uneven footsteps approached. My heart hammered in my chest, but I forced my breathing to slow, my body stilling. The metallic rattle of the keys at its hip made every nerve in my body scream.

It stopped just outside my cell, its breath ragged and wet. Now. This was my chance. I willed myself into its mind. The effort was immediate and draining; the creature's corrupted thoughts were like tar —thick and resistant. My temples throbbed, but I pushed harder, letting the urgency of the moment drive me through the resistance.

Keys.

The command lashed out like a whip. The Vyrmin froze mid-step, its claws twitching as its mind grappled with my intrusion. It fumbled awkwardly at its waistband, the jangling sound of keys rattling through the corridor. I pressed harder, visualizing my thoughts clamping down on it like a vice. Sweat dripped down my temple as I forced the creature to pluck the ring of keys from its belt.

Give them to me.

My voice echoed through its mind, sharp and unrelenting.

The Vyrmin's movements were jerky, mechanical, as it shuffled to the bars of my cell. Its claws scraped against the floor as it tossed the keys inside. The moment they hit the stone floor, the creature clutched its head and let out a screeching howl of pain. Black blood began to pour from its nose, thick and viscous, but I couldn't stop. I wouldn't stop.

Rage boiled within me—rage at my captivity, at Vyper, at the lies and betrayals that had led me here. I channeled it all into my grip on the creature's mind, squeezing tighter, harder. Its shrieks grew more desperate, echoing down the corridor, until finally, its body convulsed.

With a sickening thud, it collapsed to the floor, its lifeless form sprawled grotesquely in the flickering light. Silence filled the corridor, heavy and oppressive. I hadn't meant to kill it. But I didn't stop, either. I wondered for a moment if this would haunt me. But I don't have time for guilt.

I turned to Fen and Felix, panting from the strain of what I'd just done. Their wide eyes met mine, a mixture of fear and disbelief etched across their faces.

"Good Gods," Fen muttered, her voice barely audible. Awe lingered there, though unease flickered sharp beneath it. "Remind me never to piss you off."

I ignored her, swallowing hard as I grabbed the keys. My hands trembled slightly, but I forced them steady. The metallic clicks of the locks shattered the silence, and then we were free.

Stepping into the corridor was surreal, the freedom of movement almost foreign after days of confinement. The hallway stretched ahead in uneven stone, its walls slick with mildew and gouged deep where Vyrmin claws had dragged along the surface. Torches sputtered weakly in their sconces, shadows twisting into grotesque shapes that slithered with each flicker of Riftlight. The air was thick—heavy with rust, rot, and the metallic tang of old blood baked into the mortar. We picked our way past the felled Vyrmin's corpse, its body already stinking of rot and sulfur, the silence pressing close as though the dungeon itself resented our escape.

As we neared the end of the hallway, Fen raised a hand, halting us mid-step. Her gaze fixed on a heavy, iron-banded door to the left. "Wait. This is where they put my blades."

Nodding, I hurried forward and fumbled with the ring of keys. Each scrape of iron against iron echoed like a scream in the suffocating quiet, my urgency making the metal clatter louder than it should. At last, one turned, and the lock gave way with a reluctant click.

The door groaned open to reveal a cramped evidence room choked with confiscated weapons and belongings. The air inside was stale, thick with dust and the sour scent of despair—as though the grief of every

Riftborn stripped of their steel still lingered here. Blades dulled with neglect hung on the walls beside battered shields, and crates overflowed with trinkets and tools robbed from prisoners long dead. In one corner, a half-collapsed rack leaned drunkenly under the weight of confiscated swords, their edges kissed with rust. The place felt more like a tomb than an armory—a graveyard of forgotten battles waiting to be claimed by desperate hands.

Fen moved quickly, her eyes scanning the shelves. After a moment, she let out a triumphant huff, pulling out her gem-encrusted daggers. Without hesitation, she dropped to her knees, drawing precise runes on the blades with her finger. As soon as the symbols were complete, the daggers lifted into the air, hovering like sentinels at her side. With a flick of her wrist, they slashed and twisted through the air, their sharp edges gleaming.

I couldn't tear my eyes away. "That's... incredible."

Fen smirked, the faintest glimmer of pride flickering across her face. I turned back to the shelves. Among the clutter, I found a pair of daggers that felt right in my hands—balanced, sharp, deadly. Felix rummaged through another corner, pocketing a few small vials and tools.

Once we were armed, we slipped out of the evidence room and into an adjoining chamber. The walls here seemed to close in, the air growing heavier with the unmistakable scent of damp stone and rot.

"Where's the pit?" I whispered, my voice barely audible.

"Under the tower." Fen's tone was grim. "This way."

We pressed forward, reaching a spiraling staircase at the far end of the hall. The sound of chains clinking in the distance made my heart skip a beat, followed by low, guttural growls that sent shivers racing down my spine. Fen crouched low and held up her hand, signaling us to stop. She peered around the corner before quickly retreating.

"Guards," she hissed.

My pulse quickened as adrenaline surged through me. Fen and I exchanged a glance, unspoken understanding passing between us. We crouched behind the doorway, readying ourselves. As soon as the guards lumbered closer, Fen launched into action.

Her gemmed daggers became a blur of lethal precision, spinning and slicing through the air. The first Vyrmin let out a choked roar as the blades punctured its chest, dark ichor spilling onto the floor. Fen controlled the weapons with an effortless grace, each movement calculated and deadly.

The second guard lunged toward her, but I sprang forward. I drew on the techniques Drake had taught me; I sidestepped its attack and drove my dagger deep into its side. The creature howled, swinging its grotesque claws at me. I ducked and twisted, slashing upward and severing its arm. It fell to the ground with a final, guttural cry.

As the chaos subsided, I straightened, panting and clutching my daggers. My thoughts drifted to Drake, his voice echoing in my mind, guiding me through every movement. His face flashed before me, and warmth flooded my chest despite the carnage around me. I couldn't wait to see him again—to apologize and tell him how I really felt.

Fen's voice snapped me back to reality. "Nice work, Seer," she gave me a curt nod, wiping the blood off one of her floating blades.

I glanced down at the bodies, a chill creeping into my spine. I hadn't ever wanted to take a life, no matter how evil the life was, but there was no choice now. Every step forward took us closer to the pit, to the Rift-born prisoners that needed freeing. I hated that I almost liked it.

We moved cautiously down the dimly lit hallway toward the descending staircase when a sharp, metallic scent hit me, the same one that always preceded a vision. My stomach twisted, and I froze mid-step.

"Not now. Damn it!" I hissed through clenched teeth as a familiar tug pulled behind my eyes. Panic surged—I gripped the wall, bracing myself—but this time, the Rift didn't drag me under. It opened.

Images surged forward, blinding and sharp—but unlike before, I could shape it. I'd trained for this. I focused. I took what Ness had showed me and really tried.

The vision stabilized. Chains. Darkness. The faint, flickering glow of a cracked lantern.

Avod hung from the stone wall like a discarded weapon, head slumped forward, blood crusted at his temple. His breathing was shallow. His wrists were torn raw from the shackles. Every inch of him screamed pain and exhaustion, but he was still alive. Still fighting.

And then— The perspective shifted.

I looked down through eyes—not mine—though they were—and saw Drake's body. My body? His. Muscles straining. Legs limp. Arms yanked over his head, cuffed in iron. His mouth was bloodied—one eye swollen shut. The chains groaned as he shifted slightly, instinctively testing his restraints.

Agony spiked through me, real and distant at the same time. It was worse than I imagined. I forced the vision to stop—pulled myself back, like slamming a door shut. I gasped, staggering against the corridor wall, my lungs sucking at air that felt too thin.

"Eva?" Felix's voice reached me first.

"Drake's here," I managed, my voice raw. "And... Avod is with him."

Fen's head snapped up. "What?" Her voice was more urgent than her usual cool tone.

I met her eyes. "They have him too."

Her jaw tightened so hard I thought she might crack a tooth. "Since when? You didn't see him before—"

"No, this was different. I saw them both. Through Drake's eyes."

Felix stepped closer. "Where?"

I closed my eyes, trying to steady the images that still flickered behind my eyelids. "It's the same place they brought me... before the dungeon. I don't know exactly where—the chamber with the metal wall—the hooks, the drains. I remember the smell. Rust. Blood. Wards." I opened my eyes again. "They're in that same hellhole."

Fen looked like someone had punched her. Her fists clenched at her sides, shaking.

"He's chained to the wall," I added quietly. "Bleeding. Conscious, but barely. And Avod—he looked... worse."

Fen turned away sharply, pacing a few steps as if she had to move the feeling through her body physically, or it might break her.

"Godsdammit, Avod," she muttered, voice cracking with fury and something deeper. "You stupid, stubborn bastard." Then, louder, to all of us: "We need to move. Now."

I lingered for half a heartbeat, still seeing the echo of chains. The way Drake had whispered my name through bloodied lips. We were running out of time. Drake had run right into Vyper's trap.

I nodded, forcing myself to focus. *Just a little longer, love.* I thought, sending the words out into the void, hoping he'd somehow hear them.

"Let's go," I said, squaring my shoulders and motioning toward the staircase. My heart pounded in my chest, a steady drumbeat of determination.

The metallic scent of blood mixed with the damp, musty aroma of aged stone as we crept toward the winding stairwell that descended into the depths of the tower. Each step downward amplified the clinking of chains, a sinister symphony accompanied by low, guttural moans that reverberated off the cold walls. The sounds were enough to make the fine hairs on the back of my neck stand on end.

I was lucky the wards weren't as strong in the dungeon. My Rift had still answered me there—sluggish, but present. Now, the closer we got to the Pit, the more I felt them clamp down like a vice. Smothering. Cold. Whatever power I had left, it wasn't coming through. This time, we'd have to rely on muscle, steel, and sheer will.

As we reached the bottom of the stairs, the full horror of the Pit revealed itself. A massive cavern yawned before us, its vast expanse swallowing the flickering orange light from torches mounted unevenly along the walls. Shadows danced across the space, highlighting the iron cages crudely affixed to the stone. The cages were haphazard and rusted, their bars bent in some places, but they were effective in their grim purpose.

The air was thick with despair, each breath laced with the faint stench of decay. The Riftborn were everywhere, crammed into cages too small to stand in, their pale, emaciated forms contorted in unnatural angles. Some were barely more than skeletons, their wrists, and ankles rubbed raw from the harsh iron manacles that bound them. The deeper I looked, the worse it got.

Some of them lay slumped against the bars, their eyes half-closed, shallow breaths rattling in their chests. Their skin was translucent in the torchlight, veins visible like a map of suffering beneath the surface. Others sat with their knees drawn to their chests, their hollow eyes glaring defiantly at the guards pacing lazily around the cavern.

At the center of the massive cavern loomed an altar, a grotesque and blasphemous construct. Hewn from black stone veined with red, it seemed to pulse faintly, as if alive.

Jagged, uneven edges rose in spikes; each tip stained a dark, coppery brown—evidence of the countless sacrifices it had borne. Runes carved deep into its surface glowed faintly, pulsating with a sickly green light that cast eerie, flickering shadows across the walls of the pit. The air around it was thick, as though the altar itself consumed the oxygen, feeding on the despair that permeated the chamber.

This was no mere altar; it was a throne for cruelty, a stage for corruption. Here, the Riftborn souls had been torn from their bodies, their essence twisted and forced into the monstrous forms of Vyrmin in the name of Azh'raim. It wasn't just a place of sacrifice—it was a crucible of transformation, where innocence was destroyed and darkness was born.

Looking upon it, one could feel the weight of the countless lives that had been destroyed here, their cries of anguish echoing faintly in the oppressive air. The altar stood as a reminder of Vyper's unyielding grip on power, his mastery of manipulation, and the depths of his depravity.

I clenched my fists as I took it all in, my stomach twisting violently. It was worse than I could have ever imagined. These weren't just prisoners—they were survivors of relentless torment. The guards seemed to delight in their misery, their sharp laughter cutting through the moans as they casually prodded the cages with jagged spears or tossed scraps of moldy bread onto the filthy ground.

"We have to move fast," Fen whispered, her voice sharp but quiet. She was crouched beside me, her eyes scanning the room for any sign of an opening. Even she, fierce and resolute, couldn't hide the flicker of disgust that crossed her face.

A grim tension replaced Felix's usually calm demeanor. He muttered a quiet prayer under his breath. "There are so many of them," he murmured, the weight of it sinking in.

My heart pounded as I forced my gaze to the nearest cage, where a young Riftborn girl stared back at me, no more than 10 years old, her luminous eyes wide with fear and hope.

Something inside me cracked, and I knew we couldn't falter.

"We get them out," I whispered, my voice steady despite the storm of emotions churning inside me. "All of them. No one gets left behind."

Fen nodded, her lips pressed into a hard line. "And the guards?"

I tightened my grip on the dagger in my hand. "I can handle one of them," I said, determination hardening my voice.

Fen smirked. "Good. Felix and I will take the others. Once the guards are down, we free as many as we can."

I nodded, steeling myself. The image of Drake flashed through my mind again, fueling the fire burning inside me. I would save him, but first, I had to do this. For the Riftborn. For all of us.

We moved as one, slipping from the shadows and spreading out across the cavern. My target was a hulking Vyrmin near one of the cages; its jagged teeth bared as it snarled at the prisoners inside. I crept closer, my pulse pounding in my ears, until I was just a step behind it.

I struck swiftly, plunging my dagger into the base of its neck. The creature let out a choked growl, its movements frantic as it clawed at the blade, but I held firm, driving it deeper until it collapsed to the ground with a heavy thud.

Across the cavern, Fen's gem-encrusted daggers danced through the air—not with magic, but pure skill. No spectral serpents this time. Just steel, speed, and precision. She hurled a blade at a charging Vyrmin and missed by inches.

"Godsdamned wards!" she snarled, already reaching for another.

To my left, Felix was a blur of motion, his strikes quick and calculated. He spun low, sweeping the legs out from under a Vyrmin before driving his blade into its chest with a force that echoed through the chamber. The creature let out one last rasping breath before falling still.

The fourth guard, realizing its comrades were lost, turned to flee, its spindly legs carrying it toward the shadows. But it didn't get far. Fen's daggers shimmered in the torchlight as they shot forward, their glowing tips finding the base of its neck. The guard crumpled to the ground, lifeless, before it could take two complete steps.

The cavern fell into an eerie silence, broken only by the soft, desperate murmurs of the imprisoned Riftborn. The weight of their collective suffering pressed down on me like a physical force. I exhaled a shaky breath, the adrenaline still coursing through my veins as I wiped the blood from my blade on a scrap of cloth I'd torn from a fallen guard.

I stepped to the first cage, the heavy iron keys I'd taken earlier jangling in my trembling hands. Each turn of the key felt slower than the last, the weight of the prisoners' gazes bearing down on me. When the lock finally gave way, the door creaked open, and the Riftborn inside shuffled forward hesitantly. Their gaunt faces and hollow eyes told stories of unimaginable torment.

"Go," I whispered, my voice low but firm. "Stay quiet and move toward the stairs. Stick together. We'll cover you."

The prisoners began to file out, their movements cautious but determined. One green-skinned woman, her wrists raw and bloodied from the chains, paused to clutch my hand. Her fingers were ice-cold, her grip surprisingly strong. "Thank you," she rasped, her voice cracked with disuse. I squeezed her hand briefly before urging her forward.

Fen stood at my side. Her sharp gaze swept the cavern, ensuring no threats remained. "How many more cages?" she asked, her voice tight.

"Just a few, darling," Felix answered from across the room, already working on another lock. "Apparently I moonlight as a locksmith now," The last cage creaked open, and its occupant—a gaunt Riftborn woman with cracked horns and vacant eyes—stumbled into Felix's waiting arms. "Easy, love—two steps, breathe. I've got you," He murmured, steadying her as she limped toward the stairs with the others. I turned toward the corridor.

I'm coming for you, my love.

But just as I took a step forward, Fen grabbed my arm. Her grip was firm—not cruel, but halting. "Where do you think you're going?"

I blinked. "To find him."

Her jaw clenched. "Eva, we need to keep moving the prisoners. If we leave them here, they'll get slaughtered the moment Vyper sends someone to check on his little zoo."

"I know," I said, swallowing the rising panic. "But he's down there. He's hurt. I saw him—he's not going to last long."

Fen's eyes locked with mine. "I get it. Trust me." Based on the look she gave me I felt like she was trying to tell me something about how she felt about Avod. "But we have forty scared, half-dead people depending on us to lead them out of this place. If we split up now—"

"I'm not abandoning him." My voice cracked. "Not again."

Her expression didn't soften. "And I'm not letting those people die for one man."

The words hit me like a slap. I recoiled, breath shallow.

For a moment, neither of us spoke. The flickering torchlight danced between us, casting long, shaking shadows on the walls.

Then Felix stepped forward, gently placing a hand on both our arms. "We finish what we started," he said quietly. "We get them out—every last one. Then we go fetch our idiots. Both of them."

I stared at them, at the bloodied floor beneath us, at the chain still wrapped around my wrist. Every instinct screamed to run, to sprint down the corridor and tear through the tower until I found him. But I couldn't—not yet.

I exhaled slowly. The choice tasted like ash in my mouth.

"You're right," I said, my voice low. "We get them out," then I turned, eyes blazing with resolve.

Then, we find Drake.

Chapter Forty

Eldrake

The cold iron bit into my wrists, the unforgiving manacles slicing deeper into my flesh with every ragged breath. My shoulders burned from the strain of being suspended, my toes barely brushing the filthy stone floor beneath me.

Blood trickled slowly down my arms, pooling at my fingertips before dripping into the muck below. My head pounded, a relentless drumbeat of pain radiating from the gash above my brow, and the metallic taste of blood coated my tongue. The air was thick with the stench of rot, damp stone, and sulfur—an oppressive mix that clawed at my senses.

Across the dimly lit chamber, Avod was shackled to the wall, his usually defiant expression marred by exhaustion and pain. His face was pale, his breaths shallow as he hung limply in his chains. His eyes flicked toward me briefly, filled with a mixture of anger and grim determination, before he turned his gaze downward, conserving his strength. The faint sound of dripping water punctuated the silence, a morbid metronome to our shared suffering.

Somewhere deeper in the dungeon, the guttural growls of Vyrmin guards echoed, a sinister reminder of the monsters lurking nearby.

I gritted my teeth, pulling against the chains with every ounce of strength I could muster, the cuffs biting harder into my flesh. The ache in my muscles was nothing compared to the searing frustration as I willed my beast to surface. I reached deep into the core of my being, searching for the fire that always burned within me, but it sputtered uselessly.

Pain lanced through my back like a lightning strike. My spine arched involuntarily as heat bloomed beneath my skin—my body trying to shift. Scales erupted along my arms for a split second, the faint crackle of fire rising in my throat… and then everything collapsed inward. Something snapped down like a vice, severing the connection mid-transformation.

The partial shift recoiled violently, leaving my muscles locked and trembling, my breath rasping through clenched teeth. My heart pounded as I tasted copper on my tongue. The fire was there—so close—but every time I reached for it, the magic choked me.

The bitter truth settled over me like a shroud. *Wards.* This dungeon was drenched in them, layers upon layers of magical suppression designed to choke the Riftborn. The air felt heavy, like a weight pressing against my chest, cutting me off from my magic. Cutting off the bond. My Dragon roared within me, straining against the invisible chains, but the wards clamped down harder, snuffing out every flicker of power before it could ignite.

What if I couldn't reach her this time? What if she thought I'd left her?

"Try all you like, *Dragon*," a gravelly voice jeered, cutting through the haze of my thoughts. One of Vyper's henchmen stepped into the dim light, his malformed face twisted in a grotesque grin. His skin was an ashen gray, pulled taut over sharp cheekbones, and his blackened teeth gleamed as he smirked at me. His eyes glowed faintly red, a sickly hue that matched the foul aura clinging to him. He was a grotesque mockery of life, twisted and corrupted into something barely human. He stopped a few feet away, tilting his head like a fox prowling a rabbit. "You won't find your fire here," he taunted, his voice dripping with mockery. "The master was quite thorough in ensuring that little trick of yours wouldn't work."

I glared at him, the heat of my fury rising despite the wards' oppressive grip. If I could have torn free from the chains, I would have ripped him limb from limb with my bare hands. Instead, I spat blood at his feet, the only act of defiance I could muster. His grin widened, his amusement at my helplessness stoking my anger further.

"You're strong." he chuckled, stepping closer. The stench of decay clung to him, making my stomach churn. "But we'll see how long that lasts." His words slithered into my ears, igniting every protective instinct I had.

My mind raced, not with fear for myself, but with thoughts of Eva. What if she was in this same hell, subjected to the same torment? The idea was enough to twist the molten rage within me into something sharper, more desperate.

The henchman leaned in, his rancid breath hot against my face. "Tell me, Dragon," he sneered. "Where is your little haven? Where are the rest of your kind hiding?"

I said nothing, meeting his gaze with a cold, unyielding stare. The bastard's grin faltered for a split second before twisting into something darker, more menacing. He turned away, pacing toward the table lined with cruel instruments of torture. Blades, hooks, and brands glinted in the flickering torchlight, each one promising pain.

"Maybe," he said, picking up a jagged dagger and testing its edge with a gnarled finger. "Your friend over there might be more cooperative." I twisted my wrists against the chains, the iron cutting deeper, but I didn't care.

"Touch him," I growled, my voice low and lethal, "and I'll make you eat your own heart."

The henchman barked a laugh, his amusement genuine this time. "Big words from a man in chains," he turned his attention to Avod, his twisted grin widening. "Let's see what secrets he's hiding. Too bad someone beat me to his horns."

I watched helplessly as the creature approached Avod, his clawed hand reaching for my friend's temple. Avod jerked his head away, but the henchman's grip was relentless. A faint glow pulsed beneath his fingers as he delved into Avod's mind, the magic invasive and vile. Avod let out a strangled grunt; his teeth clenched as he resisted the intrusion.

"Ah," the henchman mused, his eyes narrowing in mock pity.

"What's this? A secret buried deep. A heartache?" Avod's body tensed, his jaw tightening further as the creature pulled something from his mind. I wanted to roar, to lunge, to stop this, but the chains held me fast.

"Fen," the henchman purred, his tone sickeningly sweet. "You love her, don't you? So loyal, so steadfast, and yet... so utterly *rejected,*" he laughed, the sound grating and cruel. "She doesn't care for you, does she? You're nothing but a shadow to her."

Avod's eyes burned with fury, but he stayed silent, his chest heaving with labored breaths.

"Enough!" I barked, my voice echoing through the chamber. The henchman turned to me, his grin widening.

"Patience, Dragon," he said, his voice dripping with malice. "You'll have your turn."

He stalked toward me, the jagged blade glinting in the flickering torchlight as he twirled it lazily between his gnarled fingers. His grotesque grin widened as he stopped mere inches from me, his rancid breath washing over my face.

"Let me tell you, Dragon," he hissed, his voice oily with malice. "Your mate... she's quite the fighter," he trailed the tip of the blade along my arm, not cutting, but enough to make my skin crawl. "Master Vyper knows just how to break them... yet she held."

I locked eyes with him, my fury a molten core, ready to erupt. But I said nothing, refusing to give him the satisfaction of a reaction. He sneered at my silence, calculating his next words.

"Her back," he began, his tone mocking, almost gleeful. "Ah, the deep marks she bore were exquisite. Steel-tipped whips have a way of leaving such... memorable impressions, don't you think? The flesh fell from her wounds in such delicate ribbons..." His words slithered into my ears, each one a venomous barb.

My fists clenched against the manacles, the sharp bite of iron digging deeper into my wrists. My breath came in short, furious bursts, but still, I held my tongue.

"Oh, the way she whimpered," he continued, his grotesque face alight with sadistic delight. "How she bit her lip to keep from crying out. Such determination! She bled so beautifully, crimson rivers soaking into the stone," he leaned closer, his voice dropping to a whisper. "But do you know the most fascinating part? She never gave you up. Never whispered a single secret."

A storm of emotions surged within me—pride, admiration, rage. She had endured the unimaginable, holding fast to protect us, to protect me, even though she hated me. A part of me swelled with pride at her resilience, her unyielding strength. But that pride was dwarfed by the consuming fire of my fury. Someone had laid their filthy hands on my mate and dared to harm what was mine.

My chest heaved, the effort of my beast being caged took everything I had. The chains rattled as I strained against them, my muscles burning with the effort. The wards pressed down on me like a suffocating weight, but my rage pushed back, screaming for release.

The henchman stepped back, his laughter grating and triumphant. "You should be proud, Dragon. She endured so much for you. But I wonder… how much more can she take?"

The words were a trigger, an explosion within me. A guttural roar tore from my throat, the sound reverberating through the chamber. I lunged against the chains, the iron biting deeper into my wrists, blood dripping to the floor. The wards pressed harder, choking my fire, but my rage burned hotter.

"Touch her again," I growled, my voice a guttural snarl, "and I'll rip you limb from limb. I will feed you your fucking entrails!"

The henchman laughed, a cruel, mocking sound. "Perhaps I'll visit her again. See how far she can be pushed."

Something inside me snapped. The air around me seemed to hum with tension, the faintest flicker of heat sparking in my core. It wasn't enough to summon my fire, but it was there—a reminder that my beast was waiting, simmering just beneath the surface.

"You won't survive long enough to see her again," I spat, my voice a promise laced with venom. The henchman's grin faltered, just for a moment, before he turned away with a dismissive wave.

"We'll see about that, Dragon. We'll see." He disappeared into the darkness, his flame the only source of light in the chamber, fading as his steps receded. The flame flickered one last time before disappearing entirely, leaving us cloaked in suffocating darkness. The silence felt oppressive, broken only by the faint sound of dripping water and my own labored breathing. My wrists throbbed where the iron manacles dug into my skin, and exhaustion weighed heavily on me.

We sat in the darkness for a time, my rage simmering hotter with each shallow breath. The silence pressed in on me, thick as the stone walls, broken only by the drip of water and the rattle of chains. Hate gnawed at the edges of my thoughts, anger coiled tight in my gut, pain burning steady in my wrists. I needed to think of something else—anything else—before I drowned in it.

"So," I said, my voice rough and low, attempting to distract myself from the burning ache in my muscles. "You're in love with Fen."

Avod let out a shaky chuckle, the sound brittle and dry. "It would seem that way." His tone was subdued—not the usual sharp wit I'd grown used to. He didn't deny it, but there was a weight to his words, a lifetime of rejection and longing packed tight beneath the surface. I might have teased him further if I wasn't actively bleeding out.

Chapter Forty One

Evandra

> "When a Riftborn reaches their awakening, it is not gentle. It is not kind. The Rift does not ask permission—it tears the truth from your bones and burns it into light. What rises after is not the same soul that entered." —The Magic of Edralis, Vol. VI

The stairwell twisted endlessly upward, the stone beneath my feet worn slick by time and worse. Every step sent a bolt of pain through my thighs, but I didn't dare slow down. Not because of the guards. Not because of the growls echoing somewhere below.

Because of the bond. It had gone quiet.

Not silent—no, I would've felt that like a blade—but quiet. Distant. Like Drake was underwater. Like something was muffling our connection, softening it until it was barely more than a breath brushing across my mind.

We weren't going to make it to him in time. Not like this.

"Eva, hold up." Fen's voice cut through my spiral, sharp and low. I turned on the landing, panting. She wasn't even winded. Of course she wasn't. She tilted her head, eyes narrowing. "You feel that, right?"

I nodded. "The bond. It's—fading."

"No." She stepped closer, lifting a hand toward the wall. Her fingers hovered just above the stone. "This. All of this. The air's thick."

"It's the Wards," Felix muttered behind her. " I think there's a source nearby."

My stomach dropped. "How close?"

"Close enough that I can feel it crawling under my skin."

Fen looked at me pointedly. "We find it. We break it."

The hall stank of mildew and rust. Each step down the spiral staircase was colder than the last, the air thinning with every turn.

"I'm still worried about losing time," I muttered.

"No magic, no chance," Fen snapped ahead of me, torch in hand. "You want to storm the dungeon blind and useless? Be my guest."

I bit my tongue. She was right. But we were losing time. Every second we spent chasing this ward room was a second Drake spent in chains—another second I couldn't reach him. Another second we risk Vyper finding us roaming his tower.

If we didn't take down whatever was suppressing the Rift, we wouldn't just be fighting blind—we'd already lost.

Felix limped along behind us, squinting at the walls. "It should be here. Somewhere low and central. They'd want to anchor it close to the rock itself—keep it grounded."

"Like a root," I said absently.

He paused. "Exactly."

We turned down a narrower passage. It sloped sharply, half-collapsed in places. Vyrmin claw marks scarred the walls. A door appeared at the end—iron, corroded, no light seeping beneath.

"This has to be it," Felix whispered.

Fen kicked it open without ceremony.

Inside was a low, damp room—no guards, no throne of bone and glass, no glowing sigils carved into obsidian. Just stone. And moss. And quiet.

I hesitated on the threshold, frowning. "No one guarding it?"

Felix's voice was low. "Vyper wouldn't have bothered. Not if he believed no one could reach it. Or if he trusted Azh'raim to protect it by sheer fear alone."

At the center—etched deep into the floor—was a single rune. Blackened. Burnt into the rock. A shape that shimmered faintly, like something watching us from beneath the surface.

"That's it," Felix breathed. "The suppression point."

"That one glyph?" I frowned.

"It's not the mark itself—it's what it's connected to. Like a taproot. Everything else—the wards, the dampening fields, the anchors—they all feed into this. Break it, and the rest unravels."

He crouched, pulling a flask from his belt and pouring a few drops onto the stone. Steam hissed where it touched the glyph.

Fen backed away, eyes narrowing. "How long?"

"Minutes," Felix said. "Maybe less. But when it goes—" he looked up, his face grim, "it's going to feel like the Rift is trying to claw its way through your bones."

"Wonderful," I muttered.

Felix drew a deep breath, rolled his shoulders, and pressed both palms to the stone. The second his skin touched the glyph, the air changed.

It got heavy.

Not magically, not exactly—just... wrong. The pressure mounted in my chest like a held breath stretched too thin. Like the entire room was waiting to split open.

Felix's body tensed. Sweat poured down his temples. The glyph pulsed once—then began to hum. Light bled from the stone. First blue. Then white.

Felix's fingers curled into claws, his body beginning to shake. The magic was fighting back.

"Felix," I said, alarmed. "You're burning—"

"Don't—" he gritted. "Don't touch me. Almost—" The glyph sparked. And something broke open inside me.

My knees hit the floor. My body bowed forward as the Rift slammed back into me—power roaring into every cell like liquid lightning. I gasped, clutching the ground. My vision blurred. And then—

The bond. Drake. He was alive. Still shackled. Still hurting. But no longer distant.

The bond flared like a silver tether drawn tight between stars. I felt him stir, somewhere in the depths of the tower. Felt him feel *me*.

A second heartbeat pulsed inside my chest. My lips parted on a soft cry, and my body arched. I reached toward him instinctively— And my vision snapped white.

The magic inside me wasn't leaking anymore. It was *blazing*.

Something cracked in the air around me, and Felix gasped—not from pain, but awe. "Her eyes—"

I could feel it too. Light radiating from me. A burning behind my eyes that wasn't fire or tears or fatigue.

Star-glow.

My heart stuttered.

I looked up—saw the mirrored sheen on Felix's wide eyes. Saw the reflection dancing in the blade Fen instinctively raised. They were staring at me.

No—at my eyes. Burning. Glowing. The Rift had awakened in me completely. My body trembled as the bond pulled tighter. I felt Drake's breath catch somewhere in the distance. Felt his shock, his recognition. He knew. He *knew* I had found him.

A tremor rocked the chamber. The glyph cracked.

Felix screamed—and the stone split in half with a flash of brilliant light.

We dove for the hallway just as the floor gave way behind us, stone collapsing into a spiral of debris and flame. The blast roared up the corridor, but this time the magic didn't burn—it surged.

When it passed, the air felt… different. Brighter. Cleaner. *Alive.* The Rift was no longer caged.

I turned back to Felix. He'd collapsed to his knees, arms limp at his sides, body shaking.

"You good?" Fen asked, not unkindly.

He lifted his head, pale and soaked with sweat. "I'll live. Might puke on you, though."

I helped him to his feet, my own limbs still trembling. The glow in my eyes hadn't faded. It flickered behind my lashes like starlight.

"I can feel him," I whispered, pressing a hand to my chest. "I know where he is now."

"Then let's go," Fen said. "Let's bring him home."

We didn't speak as we climbed. The stairwell twisted upward, air thinner but clearer now—like someone had opened the sky inside the mountain. I could feel every Riftborn in the tower stir. Not literally—but magically.

A hundred smothered sparks had caught flame.

"They'll feel it," Felix said hoarsely. "All of them. Every Riftborn locked up. Every one of us trying to fight. It's ours again."

Fen drew her daggers. "Then we don't waste it."

I touched my chest where the bond thrummed like a vow.

"We're coming for you," I whispered. And this time, I knew he'd hear me.

The stairwell shuddered around us as the last echo of the glyph's death rippled through the tower. Dust bled from the seams of the stone, and the air tasted new—bright as cracked ice, sharp as clean steel. The Rift wasn't a far hum anymore; it was a river just under my skin. I felt *powerful.*

We're coming for you, I whispered into the bond. I felt him hear it—like a hand closing around mine.

We had time to take three steps.

Something roared up from the newly gaping chamber below—deep and wrong, like a cavern clearing its throat. The stairwell shook hard enough to throw us against the inner wall. A rain of debris fell from the ceiling; shards of stone pinged down the steps.

"Ah," Felix panted, bracing with a palm. "Note to self: when you kill the giant ominous glyph, be prepared for the *giant ominous guardian.*" He squinted over the edge of the collapsed floor. "And by 'guardian' I mean 'abomination.'"

"What?" I demanded, pushing to the balustrade.

The chamber we'd just fled had become a bowl of ruin. Where the glyph had split, the floor sank inward into a spiral, fractured slabs leaning like toppled teeth. At the bottom of the new crater, something made of nightmare unfurled.

It was Vyrmin, but not like the guards. Bigger—worse. A body like a centipede crossed with a stag, plated in slick, black chitin. A skull-mask crowned it, horned and veined with dim runes, and beneath that bone face, a mouth of too many glassy teeth clacked and clicked as it tested the air. Eight long legs ended in hook-claws that found purchase on bare stone; a second set of arms tucked close to its thorax, each tipped with delicate needle-talons meant for carving sigils into living things. Under its shell, Riftlight pulsed—faint bands of green and red circling a core in its chest where a web of lines crossed and knotted. A *knot*. The place the wards had once fed. *It's weak point.*

Whatever this was—used to be—it was so far gone, fed with so much evil, it no longer resembled anything natural. The evil had corrupted it beyond recognition. This is beyond the work of Vyper—this must have been a creation of Azh'raim himself. Decay, darkness, dominion, personified.

The Warden of the wards.

It lifted its skull and stared up the stairwell at us. No eyes, just hollow bone and humming runes, but I felt it's heavy gaze anyway. Like rot discovering fresh fruit.

"Back," Fen snapped, shoving me up a step. Her daggers spun into her hands like they'd been waiting.

Below, the Warden gathered itself and leapt.

It hit the lower steps with a crack, stone shattering under its weight. The impact threw a ring of pressure up the stairwell that hit the three of us like a wall. I slammed both hands into the rail to stay upright as another section of the staircase collapsed into the pit.

"Okay," Felix wheezed, eyes bright, mouth a thin line. "New plan. We don't die here."

"Work with what we have," Fen said, which was as close as she got to a pep talk. She planted herself between me and the Warden, blades high, stance low. "Eva. Sight me."

I reached. Drake had trained me for this. The star-glow in me flared, a cool burn under my ribs and behind my eyes. The world sharpened. The Warden's movements slowed a hair, like the Rift itself wanted me to trace its path. Lines lit up—faint trajectories in the air where claw would meet stone, where weight would shift, where an opening would bloom for the width of a breath.

"Left—low," I said. "Joint after the third plate. There."

Fen struck without hesitation. The blade hit home. Black ichor hissed; the Warden shrieked, shaking my teeth.

It retaliated with speed a creature that size shouldn't have had. It whipped its stinger at its rear. Fen ducked; the barb buried in stone. The stair shattered under another slam.

The Warden reared back, lashing blindly, and slammed the stair with enough force to spider-crack the stone. We scattered up the steps. The beast hit again, shaking loose a trough of debris that slid toward us like a small gray landslide.

I was done running.

I stepped into the river of debris and met it with my palm. Instinct took over. My star-glow pulsed. The rolling stones instantly slowed—not stopped, but slowed—like the air had thickened around them. Not just the stones. The Warden's tail, too. The hook claw that would have caught Fen's hip. I didn't know I could do that.

"Go," I said through my teeth.

Fen eyes widened with surprise, but she went. She vaulted, drove her blades deeper, tearing the seam wider. The plates parted for a heartbeat—enough for me to see the knot clearly. Every line of glowing runes carved into the beasts shell fed toward that core. It's power was centralized there.

"Fen! At its center!" I said. "There's a core. Plate seam down the sternum, four hand-widths long."

"Copy!" Fen said. She didn't check if I was right. She believed me. The force of that trust hit my throat like heat.

The Warden came low, fast. Too fast. It slammed the flat of its skull into the steps below us and skated forward on a shatter of stone, raking hooks up at our legs.

I threw my hand down and prayed the beast would stop.

The Rift answered—not with fire, not with wind, not with anything I had a name for. Something like pressure and light; something like a net thrown, not outward, but... between. It webbed the space in front of us in a translucent lattice and the Warden was trapped in it. Hard.

The lattice flexed, popped at its edges—and held.

Not for long. Not enough to stop a mountain. But enough to slow one.

Felix slid in beside me, palms up, breath ragged. "That's very interesting," he said, fascinated. "Do me a favor and keep it up while I do something stupid."

"Define 'something stupid,'" I snapped, sweat burning my eyes.

He picked up a broken chunk of a step and traced a rune onto it with his thumb. He gingerly tossed it to its underside before it detonated.

"Something explosive," he said, backing up in a hurry. "Down!"

We dropped as the runed chunk flared and detonated. The blast blew the stair under the Warden's face into shrapnel and flipped its front half up, exposing the stripe of armor along its chest exactly where I needed. *Nice one.*

"Fen!" I shouted. "Now!"

She launched.

She wasn't magic like me. She was momentum and blades honed into something lethal. She ran three steps up the wall, flipped onto the beast's lifted chest, and drove both daggers into the chest plate protecting the knot with a scream. The plates parted. Under them, the knot pulsed.

The Warden went feral. It bucked and slammed its body into the stairwell wall so hard I tasted copper. Fen held; her foot slipped; she swore with devout sincerity; then the tail whipped around, aiming for her spine and I moved without thinking.

I didn't throw power at the tail. I threw it *through* Fen.

The star-glow snagged on every edge of her—It braided through her every muscle. It filled her lungs with air. It steadied her heartbeat and bolstered her resolve. Her body obeyed like I'd asked, not commanded, and shifted her to the left. The stinger missed its mark and drove into stone instead of her back, and a spray of rock dust erupted like applause.

Fen didn't flinch at the magic in her bones. She welcomed it. She gritted her teeth, set her shoulders, and pulled her daggers outward.

The knot tore open.

The Warden screamed. Piercing. Like a thousand tortured Riftborn screams on the wind. The blast threw Fen off its chest. She curled, landed in a crouch two steps up with both blades still in her hands.

The Warden lay still for moments. We were frozen. It twitched. I looked closer into the knot where Fen had sunk her blades. It was trying to *reweave the knot.*

"Godsdamnit!" I cursed, the bond to Drake tugged hard enough to be pain. He was there. He was waiting. I was sick of delays.

Just then, all of the wounds we had created started to slowly close and patch, stitching themselves back together.

Fen snarled, teeth bared, as the force swept her. "It's fucking healing itself!"

"Of course it is," Felix said shakily. "It's feeding on Rift. there!" He pointed at glowing lines in the wall.

"Do it," I said. "We'll keep it busy."

"Love that for us," Felix said, sprinting. "If you die, I will be so annoyed."

Fen moved back in. I felt where she meant to go before she went there, my Star-Glow mapping her intent like constellations. We weren't just fighting near each other anymore. We were fighting together—a braid of steel and sight.

"Left plate," I said.

"On it," she said, and her dagger bit.

"Mind the tail." I reached, hooked the tail's momentum with a hard yank of power, and pulled it wide. The sting chittered off the wall, skittered, and stuck. For a heartbeat, the Warden was pinned by its own barb.

"Nice," Fen said. Her mouth was a slash. Her eyes were bright. "Don't let go."

I didn't.

The Warden screamed frustration and answer. The runes in its skull flared brighter, and three smaller Vyrmin—scaled-down copies of its skull-masked face on eel-thin bodies with too many legs—spilled out like knives from a sheath. They hit the broken stairs and climbed the walls in a spider-dash, one for each of us.

"Absolutely fucking not," Felix yelled, "Somebody kill my problems!"

I let one leap for me, at the last instant, I stepped sideways and reached into its mind.: *stop hunting, fold.* It collapsed into a quivering knot. Fen cut another mid-air.

The third skitterer lunged for Felix, but a silver thread tugged my hand and I flung it into the wall. He flashed me a breathless grin.

The big Warden's tail ripped free. My net snapped. It swung for me —slow, inexorable.

Left, Drake's voice surged through the bond, steady as a hand on my back. *Now.*

I moved. The tail tore the rail where I'd been. Splinters stung my cheek. *Good,* he whispered, pride and pain bound together.

"Two runes down!" Felix called. "Keep it busy!"

Then the freed Riftborn arrived.

A winged boy dove from above, dropping a firebomb onto the beast's mask. A green-skinned woman lifted her arms; the Warden shrieked, runes in its skull burning as if blinded. An old man tossed flames across its chest.

The surge staggered it long enough for Felix to blow the last conduit. The knot flickered, starving.

"Hold it!" he shouted.

I wove another net, pinning claws and stinger. "Fen!"

She sprinted, blades flashing. The chest plates cracked open again.

"Now," I whispered.

She crossed her knives through the knot.

It didn't burst outward—it collapsed in on itself, imploding like a blister. The Warden sagged, skull-runes guttering. Claws twitched once. Then it fell into the crater, still.

Silence.

We stood panting on what was left of the stairwell, lit by the glow burning faint in our bones.

Felix leaned his head back, laughing breathless. "Updates: one, that was stressful. Two, teamwork is hot. Three, we just killed a house-sized bug."

Fen knelt at the edge, eyes flicking up to mine. "You've got some new tricks," she said, her eyebrows raised.

I huffed a laugh. The star-glow softened. The bond tugged urgent, not drowning. *I'm so proud of you,* Drake whispered.

"We move," Fen said, pushing up. "Before something comes to see what screamed."

"Small wrinkle," Felix added, eyeing the wreckage. "Our staircase is now more metaphor than architecture."

The collapse had peeled the wall, exposing narrow service ledges and swaying chains. I lifted a hand, weaving another net across the gaps. "This will work, hopefully."

At the far landing, the tower still loomed above—a maze, but no longer a grave.

"I'll follow the bond," I said. "He's close."

End of the gallery, Drake murmured in my chest. *Hurry.*

I clenched my daggers. "I'm coming, my love."

Chapter Forty Two

Eldrake

Drake?

Her voice.

So quiet it was almost not there. But it echoed somewhere deep inside me—cutting through the suffocating dark like a blade of light, slicing past the pain and the iron and the silence that had drowned me. I sucked in a sharp breath, my heart lurching in my chest.

Was it real? Or had I finally cracked under the pressure—another hallucination, a flicker of hope conjured by a starved mind?

Then, just beneath the haze of pain and the choking silence, I felt it. A flicker. Magic. Not mine. Not Azh'raim's.

Hers.

It slipped through the cracks like moonlight under a locked door—sharp and sudden, like a breath after drowning. My spine snapped straighter. My heart surged in my chest.

The wards. I felt them fall.

"She's here," I breathed. My voice shook with the force of it. "Gods, she really did it."

Beside me, Avod stirred. "Drake?" he asked cautiously, sensing the change in the air—sensing *me*, maybe, reacting to something only I could feel.

"She's close," I said, and couldn't stop the way my lips curved with awe. "I can feel her. The Rift's back."

The room itself seemed to hum, the pressure lifting from my skin like a second skin being peeled away. The fire I'd been holding inside me —dampened, smothered—suddenly caught a spark. The tether between us flared to life. No longer frayed. No longer faint.

The bond thrummed like a silver wire drawn taut through my ribs. She was alive. Fierce. Moving toward me like a storm. And she knew exactly where I was. Gods, and she felt... *different.*

I pressed my hand against the cold stone, grounding myself against the torrent of emotion threatening to crack me open. A moment later, the heavy iron door creaked open.

Torchlight spilled into the chamber like dawn—and then I saw her. *My love. My storm. My salvation.*

She stepped into the room like a weapon drawn in moonlight. Her hair was a curtain of fire, tousled and wild, her body alive with tension. Her chest rose and fell in frantic rhythm, as if she'd fought her way through every beast in the tower to get here—and I didn't doubt for a second that she had.

But it was her *eyes* that stopped my heart.

No longer just green.

They blazed—not with fire, but with starlight. Emerald and silver and velvet and flame. The Rift danced behind her pupils like it had come awake inside her and was looking out through her gaze. Not a flicker, not a trick of the torchlight.

Star-Glow.

Awe slammed into me like a punch. My breath caught. I'd heard stories—myth mostly, of Riftborn developing Star-Glow rather than being born with it. But seeing it... seeing *her* like this... She was a force. No longer on the edge of her power. She *was* her power. And still mine.

"Drake!" she cried, and in two steps she was in front of me, dropping to her knees. Her hands trembled as they reached for the manacles at my wrists, then froze—her breath catching as she took me in.

Her gaze swept over the bruises, the blood, the burn marks. Her touch was featherlight on my skin, and yet it lit something inside me I thought had gone out.

"You're here," I rasped. My voice was broken glass and wonder.

She looked up, her glowing eyes shining with guilt and love and something feral beneath it all. "I'm so sorry," she whispered. "I should've never doubted. I should've known—" Her voice cracked.

I leaned forward as far as the chains would allow. "You came for me," I said. "That's all I care about."

Then she kissed me. Gods, she *kissed me*. There was no fear in it. No hesitation. Just heat and heartache and the desperate hunger of two people torn apart too soon.

Her soft lips crushed against mine like a promise. Her hands cupped my face, thumbs sweeping across my cheekbones. Everything—every minute of torture, every lost hour in the dark, every second spent fearing I'd never see her again—melted in that kiss.

I didn't even realize I was crying until she pulled back, her forehead pressing against mine.

"I love you," she whispered, her voice trembling. "I love you, Drake. I don't care what the bond means or doesn't mean—I chose you. I still choose you."

Her words shattered something inside me. And rebuilt something else.

"I love you," I said, the truth of it anchoring me more than any chain ever could. "You're my beginning and end, Evandra."

Her eyes welled. "I'm never letting you go again." Her hands went back to the manacles, trembling harder now. "I'll get you out. I swear."

From the corner of the room, a voice cleared his throat.

"Ahem. Sorry to interrupt the literal embodiment of fate or whatever this is," Avod deadpanned, "but could someone *please* unchain me before I bleed out?"

Eva huffed a teary laugh. I did too. But even as I looked toward Avod, I couldn't stop glancing back at her. At her Star-Glow eyes. At the Rift singing between us like it had waited centuries for this moment. For us. And in that moment, I didn't care about the battle outside. Or the tower. Or Azh'raim.

Because *she* was here. And the world had finally tilted in the right direction again.

Avod dropped, his knees buckling. Fen caught him by the arm

before he could hit the stone. For a breath, their weight leaned into each other—Avod's grip tightening instinctively on her wrist, Fen's hand steady at his elbow.

"Fen," he rasped, looking up at her with a mixture of relief and something harder to name. Her eyes softened—just barely—as they met his. The moment lingered half a beat too long before she stepped back, her daggers twirling into place at her sides.

"Can you stand?" she asked, tone brisk, though the faintest flush warmed her cheeks.

"Yeah." Avod straightened with a grunt, brushing himself off. But his gaze held hers a breath longer than necessary, heavy with something unspoken.

Despite the tension pressing in on us, I couldn't help but notice the weight of that silence between them—like a line drawn and never crossed, but never erased.

Eva turned her attention back to me, her hands reaching for the manacles still binding my wrists. "Let's get you out of here."

As the iron restraints fell away, I collapsed forward, my body still weak and battered. I instinctively reached for her as soon as my hands were free, desperate to feel her in my arms again. I held onto her as tightly as I could manage, burying my face in her hair, inhaling the scent of honeysuckle and something uniquely her. "I am so in love with you." I said, my voice cracking with emotion.

Her breath hitched, and I felt her smile against my neck. "You better be," she said with a chuckle. She pulled back, helping me stand as Fen and Avod exchanged another glance. Whatever had passed between them in the silence was left unspoken—but it was there, lingering like an uninvited guest.

From the shadows, Felix cleared his throat. "Lovely reunion. Truly heartwarming. But maybe we could save the dramatic declarations and tongue wrestling until after we're not standing in Vyper's basement?"

Eva shot him a glare; and I wheezed a laugh despite the blood in my throat.

Felix raised a brow. "I mean, I get it—you're both very in love, very shiny with destiny. Just...maybe prioritize survival before romance. Radical thought, I know."

Avod shook his head, still smiling faintly.

"Let's move," Fen cut in, brisk again though her flush lingered. "We've got a long way to go, and Vyper won't stay distracted forever."

Felix fell in behind us with a sigh. "Good. Maybe the next room has fewer chains and less kissing. My delicate sensibilities can only take so much."

Chapter Forty Three

Evandra

"Overusing Rift abilities can strain a user's physical and mental reserves, a phenomenon known as Rift Burnout. In severe cases, this overexertion may deplete the user's life force, leading to symptoms like weakness, seizures, or even death. Practitioners are cautioned to exercise restraint, as mastery lies not in raw power but in sustainable control of one's abilities." - The Boundless Rift: A Study of Magic and Mortality, Chapter 1

The stairwell twisted upward like a spine, its crumbling stones slick with moisture and fresh blood from the battle raging below. The distant roars and cries of Riftborn and Vyrmin filled the air, the sound of clashing blades and guttural snarls reverberating through the tower.

Drake leaned against me as we ascended, his weight pressing heavily on my side. I could feel the trembling in his muscles, a raw testament to the battle he had fought and the punishment his body had endured. His eyes, usually blazing with energy, now carried a flicker of exhaustion. He tried to straighten, shifting his weight to carry himself more fully as if refusing to let me see how much he was struggling. It's clear he got more of the torture than I had.

"I can't believe you're here," he murmured, his voice rough and low, but there was something tender beneath the fatigue. His gaze softened as he looked at me, a brief crack in the armor he was trying so hard to maintain. "You saved my ass. Again."

I tightened my grip on his side, steadying him as he faltered for a moment. My lips twitched into a faint smile, though my eyes flicked upward toward the towering darkness above us.

"Damn right I did," I said, keeping my voice light despite the turmoil swirling in my chest. "Though we do have to talk about you lying to Julian about me at some point. AND hiding a *bond*." I shot him a look, half-serious, half-teasing, as I tried to distract him from his pain.

Drake chuckled softly, the sound strained but genuine. "I'm not going anywhere," he said, his words a quiet promise. But even as he spoke, I could see the tension in his jaw, the way he fought to keep upright and appear strong in front of me.

"Neither of you are going anywhere if we don't keep moving," Fen interrupted from a few steps ahead. Her voice was sharp and commanding, but her eyes softened as they flicked to Avod, also limping.

I glanced at Drake again, noting how he clenched his fists like he could will himself past the pain. Even now, when his body screamed for rest, he was trying to shield me, to carry the weight of this fight for both of us. My heart twisted at the sight, a mix of love and frustration swelling within me.

The staircase seemed to twist endlessly upward, the air growing colder and heavier with each step. Each breath tasted of sulfur and decay, the acrid tang of corrupted magic stinging my throat. I could feel Drake leaning harder against me, his weight pressing into my side, but he kept moving, his determination pushing him forward.

Suddenly, the sound of an explosion echoed from below, sending a tremor through the tower. Dust and debris began raining down from above, stones clattering against the crumbling stairs. Felix acted instantly, raising a glowing hand as a barrier of shimmering light flared to life above us, deflecting the falling rubble.

"Move!" Felix barked, urgency sharpening his usual calm. "The Riftborn are holding the Vyrmin off, but the tower won't hold forever!"

As we rounded another landing, the oppressive air seemed to thicken. The torches lining the walls flickered, their flames bending unnaturally. A shadow flickered in the corner of my vision, and my heart raced with unease.

"Drake—" I started, but his instincts were faster.

"Down!" he roared, his voice a guttural command. With a burst of strength, he shoved me aside just as a hulking Vyrmin erupted from the darkness, its grotesque form charging toward me.

The creature was a nightmare-made flesh—a twisted amalgamation of Riftborn and beast, its body scarred and stitched together with raw sinew and dark magic. Its glowing red eyes locked onto me, and its lips pulled back in a snarl, revealing jagged rows of teeth.

Drake's found blade flashed as he stepped between me and the monster, but his movements were slower than usual, his injuries dragging him down. The Vyrmin swung a massive claw, striking him across the chest and sending him crashing into the stone wall with a sickening thud.

"Drake!" I screamed, scrambling to my feet as the creature turned its attention back to me. His growl reverberated through the room, low and feral. Despite the gash across his chest and the blood dripping down his side, he pushed himself up. The air around him shimmered as he attempted to summon his dragon beast form, but his exhaustion and injuries kept him from shifting.

The Vyrmin lunged at me, its claws outstretched, but Drake was there, intercepting its path with a roar of fury. He drove his blade into the creature's shoulder, the impact forcing it back a step. The effort cost him, his body sagging slightly, but he didn't falter.

"Get behind me," he growled, his voice sharp despite the pain lacing through it. I hesitated, torn between wanting to fight beside him and fearing for his safety.

"No!"

"I said, get behind me!" he barked, his gaze never leaving the creature. Fen and Felix charged forward, their weapons flashing as they joined the fray. Fen's daggers sliced through the air with deadly precision, striking the Vyrmin's thick hide, while Felix summoned a burst of light that seared the creature's twisted flesh. It howled in agony, but its strength was monstrous.

Drake, despite his wounds, fought with a ferocity that bordered on recklessness. He parried the creature's attacks with his blade, his movements fueled by raw determination.

When the Vyrmin swiped at him again, he sidestepped, driving his sword deep into its side. I could see the strain in every muscle, but he didn't let up, his growls echoing through the chamber like the beast defending his mate that he was.

The Vyrmin staggered, ichor spilling from its wounds, but it wasn't finished. With a desperate lunge, it swiped at Drake again, forcing him to his knees. My heart clenched as he gasped for breath, his body trembling under the weight of his injuries.

"Now, Eva!" Fen shouted, her daggers holding the beast at bay for a split second. Seizing the moment, I charged forward, gripping one of the daggers I had gotten from the evidence chamber. I plunged the blade into the creature's exposed neck, twisting it with all the strength I could muster. The Vyrmin let out a final, gurgling roar before collapsing to the ground, its massive body crumpling in defeat. The room fell silent, save for the labored breaths of our group. Drake leaned heavily against the wall.

"Still saving my ass," he rasped, a faint smile tugging at his lips. "What are we, three for three?"

I knelt beside Drake, gently lowering him to the ground as the others gathered around us. Blood stained his tunic, seeping through the fabric and pooling on the cold stone beneath him. His breaths were shallow, each one labored, and the sight made my chest tighten.

Felix stepped forward, his usually steady hands trembling slightly. "Let me," he said, his voice firm despite the exhaustion etched into his features. He knelt on Drake's other side, his hand already glowing with the faint blue light of his healing magic.

"You don't have to—" Drake began, his voice rough, but Felix shot him a look that silenced him.

"Stay still," Felix ordered, placing his glowing hand over the gash on Drake's chest. The light flared brighter than I'd ever seen it, and the magic flowed into Drake's body, knitting torn flesh and staunching the flow of blood.

Drake winced but remained silent, eyes locking onto mine. I placed my hand on his, giving it a reassuring squeeze as Felix continued to work. The healing light pulsed rhythmically, its warmth cutting through the cold, oppressive air of the tower.

"You don't need to fight for me like I'm weak." I said softly. "Its going to get you killed."

He managed a faint smile. "I know you're not weak, Evandra. Gods, I know that. I just don't want you to have to fight. I just don't want you getting hurt. Not if there's a chance I can stop it. Not ever."

"Please. You brought me here to help, Drake." I whispered. "So let me help."

Felix snorted without looking up, shifting to a deeper gouge on Drakes ribs. "For the record, she's underselling it. Her powers are getting fucking terrifying. You should've seen the new net trick."

Minutes passed, each one dragging longer than the last. Felix's breathing grew heavier, beads of sweat forming on his brow. His magic was doing its job—Drake's color was returning, the tension in his muscles easing—but the toll on Felix was evident.

"Felix, that's enough," I said, worry creeping into my voice as I saw him sway slightly. "You've done enough."

"Not yet," Felix muttered, his voice strained. "He's not fully healed."

"You'll kill yourself, brother!" Fen said sharply, stepping forward to steady him. Her gem-encrusted daggers hovered protectively at her sides, but her eyes were fixed on Felix, a rare flicker of genuine concern softening her usual edge.

Felix ignored her, pouring more of his magic into Drake. The light surged once more, brighter than ever, before flickering and fading. Felix gasped, his body shuddering as the last of his strength left him. He swayed, and Fen lunged to catch him before he crumpled to the ground.

"I told you," Fen muttered, her tone more gentle than her words as she eased Felix down. She brushed his damp hair away from his face, her expression unreadable. Avod looked at her with fondness, relishing in her momentary genuineness.

Drake sat up slowly; the pain in his movements greatly diminished. He glanced at Felix, his jaw tightening. "You didn't have to push yourself so far."

"Don't flatter yourself," Fen said dryly, though her voice wavered slightly. "He'd do that for anyone."

I knelt beside Felix, placing a hand on his arm. "Thank you," I whispered, my gratitude immeasurable. His breathing was shallow but steady, and I knew he just needed rest. Fen scooped the tiny man over her shoulder, and we continued upward.

We continued our climb, the sounds of chaos growing louder with each step. Every room we entered was a war zone, the clash of steel against claw, the cries of the wounded, and the guttural roars of Vyrmin echoing off the stone walls. Freed Riftborn surged forward, their desperation and fury driving them against their grotesque captors.

A hulking Riftborn warrior, his skin a mottled blend of bronze and emerald, reminiscent of his draconic ancestry, wielded a stolen sword. He cleaved through a Vyrmin, its twisted form splintering under his sheer force. Beside him, a slender Riftborn woman with translucent, opalescent skin and glowing lavender eyes hurled bolts of energy from her hands, her magic cutting down beasts that tried to flank their group.

Nearby, a stocky Riftborn with fiery orange skin and sharp, obsidian-black horns stood firm, his enormous fists crashing against a Vyrmin's chest. The creature, a patchwork of Riftborn and beast, fell with a gurgling snarl. His fists sparked as he struck, remnants of his molten abilities scorching his enemies. Behind him, a younger Riftborn with pale, shimmering skin and silvery hair darted between combatants, her daggers flashing like quicksilver as she struck vital points with precision.

Drake's eyes scanned the scene, his pride swelling despite the urgency of their mission. These were his people—brave, resilient, and unyielding. But the sight of fallen Riftborn tempered his pride with sorrow.

A young woman with scales like sapphires lay crumpled near the base of a staircase, her bow still clutched in her hand, her quiver emptied in the fight. Nearby, a Riftborn man with bark-like skin and glowing green veins lay motionless; his staff shattered beside him.

I gasped softly as we passed another fallen fighter, her golden-green hair fanned out around her, a jagged spear protruding from her chest. Drake placed a hand on my shoulder, his grip firm and steady. He looked at me with sympathetic eyes.

"These are the risks of war," he said, his voice rough with emotion. "We honor them by finishing this."

Despite the Riftborn's bravery, the toll of the battle was evident. Bodies, both Riftborn and Vyrmin, littered the floors, and the air was thick with the stench of blood and sweat. Each step upward felt heavier, the weight of their losses pressing down on us all.

When we finally reached the top, a vast hall sprawled before us. I froze, my breath catching in my throat. Ahead, the faint glow of the Vessel's energy seeped through the cracks of a heavy door, bathing the corridor in a sickly, pulsating light. It felt alive, a malignant heartbeat echoing through the stones. Drake paused beside me, his hand brushing mine briefly, a silent reassurance.

I crossed and pushed the door open carefully, the hinges groaning in protest. The room beyond was precisely as it had been in my visions. The air was heavy with dark magic, an almost suffocating presence that seeped into every crevice. The Vessel of Azh'raim dominated the space, its shining serpentine frame gleaming faintly in the dim, flickering light of the torches. Its surface rippled unnaturally, reflecting shadows that didn't align with the room's contours. It was far more daunting in person.

The study was eerily quiet. The faint crackle of torches mounted on the walls offered the only sound, their flames casting twisting, living shadows that seemed to shift and writhe across the stone. The air itself buzzed with malevolent energy, prickling against my skin like a warning.

The Vessel stood at the room's center, glowing faintly like the eye of a storm. Its presence exuded an almost tangible malice, a dark authority that sent a shiver down my spine.

Fen and Avod positioned themselves near the door, their movements precise and measured. Fen's daggers floated just above her hands, poised to strike. The gems caught the torchlight and refracted it, casting sharp, fleeting rainbows against the dark walls. Her expression was sharp, her eyes scanning the room for any sign of movement. Avod stood beside her, his frame taut with readiness. His fingers clenched around the hilt of his sword, the tension in his grip visible in the whitening of his knuckles. His eyes darted to every shadow as though expecting Vyper to emerge from the darkness.

"This thing..." I murmured, my voice barely above a whisper as my fingers brushed the Vessel's frame. The cold metal felt alive under my touch, like the scales of a living beast.

Its surface rippled unnaturally, reflecting a warped, twisted version of myself. My breath hitched. "It's watching us."

Drake growled, the low, guttural sound rumbling deep in his chest. His vision was locked on the Vessel, his disdain for it burning brighter than the torchlight. "Then we destroy it. Now."

I nodded, my heart hammering in my chest as urgency surged through me. My mind scrambled to recall Ness's lessons. "We can't just smash it. If it's still connected to Vyper, it'll reform. We need to sever their connection first."

"Then work fast, find a spell or something!" Fen said sharply, her daggers slicing through the air in restless arcs, their edges gleaming like deadly stars.

I moved toward the desk nearest the Vessel, my trembling hands flipping open a few ancient tomes resting there. The pages crackled like brittle leaves, each one covered in spidery runes and faded diagrams. My fingers skimmed the text as I muttered under my breath, searching for anything that might sever the mirror's link to its dark master. Behind me, the others shifted uneasily, their weapons ready, their eyes scanning the room.

The hairs on the back of my neck prickled, and a chill slid down my spine. Something wasn't right. I glanced at Drake, who had gone still, his eyes narrowing, his head tilting as if listening for something in the silence. He knew I sensed something.

"He's coming." I said quietly.

And then I heard it. The soft footfalls against stone, deliberate and slow, sending icy tendrils creeping through my veins.

"Ah, my guests," came a voice as smooth as silk and as sharp as a blade. It was melodic in its malice, cutting through the tension like a knife.

My breath caught in my throat as we all turned toward the doorway.

There he stood. Vyper. His pale, corpse-like skin gleamed under the flickering torchlight. His black eyes, like two endless voids, locked onto mine, and a cruel smile stretched his thin lips. My stomach twisted.

"You're a long way from the dungeon," he purred, his voice dripping with mockery. The taunt was aimed directly at me, and I felt my body stiffen under his gaze. Behind him, grotesque figures began to emerge—his henchmen, their twisted, unnatural forms lurching forward. Their glowing red eyes burned with malevolence, and the low, guttural growls that escaped their mouths sounded like death itself. They blocked the doorway, cutting off our only escape.

"Fen, Avod, take the Vyrmin!" Drake barked, his voice steady despite the chaos. He stepped in front of me, his body a shield between me and danger. "Felix, protect her!"

Felix immediately produced a ward, its faint glow forming a barrier of safety around me. He glanced at me, his face exhausted but resolute.

Vyper's eyes flicked to Drake, and his smile widened. "You? Haven't I already defeated you once?" he sneered, his words laced with venom. "I remember the smell of your blood."

Drake growled low in his throat, the sound vibrating through the chamber. His claws flexed at his sides, and his entire body coiled like a spring ready to snap.

The Vyrmin charged, their grotesque forms lunging into the room with terrifying speed. Fen touched her fingertips to her temples, and her daggers spun through the air like deadly stars, slicing through one beast after another. Avod let out a war cry, his hammer smashing through twisted flesh with brutal efficiency. The sound of clashing steel and inhuman snarls filled the chamber.

Vyper raised a hand, and the air thickened, oppressive magic pulsing through the room. The torches flickered violently, their light casting erratic shadows across the walls.

"You can't win," Vyper said, his tone casual but filled with a terrible certainty. "You should have stayed in your little hiding hole."

Drake didn't respond with words. Instead, his growl deepened, becoming something primal, something ancient. His entire body seemed to radiate heat as his muscles bulged and his shoulders broadened. Scales shimmered across his skin, catching the torchlight and reflecting it in hues of crimson and silver.

I could only stare as his body began to shift, his transformation tearing through the room like a storm. Massive wings burst from his back, leathery and powerful, nearly brushing the ceiling. His limbs elongated, his hands morphing into claws that gleamed like steel. His face twisted, his jaw extending into a fearsome maw filled with razor-sharp fangs. He was enormous now, towering over everyone in the room, his presence both awe-inspiring and terrifying.

What. The. Fuck.

"Drake?" I whispered, my voice trembling with a mix of emotions. Awe, fear, and something else—something primal and electric—coursed through me. He was magnificent, every inch the beast he had suppressed for so long, and yet, I knew it was still him—still the man I loved.

His usually kind eyes, now glowing fiercely, turned to me for a brief moment, and I saw the same unwavering determination I'd always known.

"Stay back," he rumbled, his voice distorted and deeper, carrying the weight of his dragon form. My heart pounded in my chest as I took in the sheer power radiating off him. Part of me was terrified—terrified of what he could do, of the raw destruction he was capable of. But another part of me was utterly captivated, unable to tear my eyes away from him. He was beautiful in his ferocity, a force of nature made flesh.

Drake lunged at Vyper, his claws tearing through the air with devastating speed. Vyper conjured a shield, but it cracked under the sheer force of Drake's attack, the sound of splintering magic ringing through the chamber.

"Drake, behind you!" I screamed as two Vyrmin closed in from his blind spot. He whirled, his massive tail slamming into them with bone-crushing force. They crumpled to the ground, lifeless.

He fought with a single-minded ferocity, every move precise and devastating. But even in his dragon form, I could see the toll it was taking on him. His wounds from earlier still bled, and every swing of his claws or beat of his wings seemed to cost him.

Despite his pain, he kept fighting, his gaze never straying far from me. I realized then that he wasn't just fighting to win. He was fighting for me. To protect me. To save me.

Drake roared, the sound reverberating through the chamber like an earthquake, shaking the very walls with its sheer power. His rage was a palpable force, an inferno consuming everything in its path as he charged at Vyper. Flames erupted from his mouth, a torrent of blazing fury that engulfed the dark sorcerer entirely.

Vyper laughed, his mocking tone cutting through the flames as his dark magic formed a shimmering barrier around him, deflecting the searing fire. "You think fire can harm me, Dragon?" he taunted, his pale lips curling into a sneer as he raised his hand to unleash a blast of dark energy.

Drake's massive tail whipped through the air with lethal precision, smashing into Vyper's shield. The impact sent cracks spidering across the dark energy, and the air around them shuddered with the force of his strike.

"Your death is not just certain," Drake snarled, his voice guttural and raw with fury. "It's inevitable."

The look he wore burned with an intensity that bordered on divine, his molten rage mirrored in every movement of his massive form. His claws carved deep, jagged gouges into the stone floor as he advanced, each step echoing with the weight of his fury. The weakened shield flickered, its dark energy splintering under the onslaught of Drake's relentless assault.

Vyper staggered backward, his arrogant grin faltering as he hastily summoned another spell. Before he could utter a single incantation, Drake lunged. His massive body collided with Vyper, slamming him into the wall with enough force to send cracks racing through the stone like lightning bolts.

Vyper's smile twisted into a grimace of fear as Drake's massive clawed hand wrapped around his throat and torso. The sorcerer's limbs flailed as he was lifted off the ground, his magic sparking uselessly against Drake's hardened, gleaming scales. Drake's grip tightened, and a deep, menacing growl rumbled in his chest like thunder.

"You thought you could touch her?" Drake's voice was a low, venomous snarl, each word laced with unrelenting wrath. "You thought you could harm my mate and escape unscathed?" His claws flexed, puncturing Vyper's pale skin. Thick, black blood oozed from the wounds, dripping to the stone floor in viscous drops. Vyper's lips curled into a weak grin despite the pain, his black eyes glinting with a final spark of malice.

"She... cried... like a bitch..." he rasped, his voice barely audible over the sound of Drake's ragged breathing.

The air in the room seemed to compress, and Drake's roar erupted, shaking loose dust and debris from the ceiling above. In a single motion, he slammed Vyper against the stone floor with earth-shattering force.

The impact sent shockwaves rippling through the chamber, fragments of stone flying outward as Drake loomed over the broken sorcerer. He pressed a clawed foot against Vyper's chest, pinning him like a trapped insect.

"You think Azh'raim's power makes you untouchable?" Drake hissed his voice, a molten growl that sent shivers down my spine. Flames licked at the corners of his mouth, the air around him heating with his fury. "You're nothing. Nothing to the Gods. And now, you're nothing to me."

Drake's rage surged into an inferno, flames roaring to life around him in an uncontrolled torrent of heat and light. The fire illuminated every scale, every claw, every inch of his formidable form as he leaned closer, his voice a chilling whisper. "You will feel every ounce of the pain you inflicted on her. And then you'll feel mine."

His claws plunged into Vyper's side, twisting with merciless precision. The sorcerer's guttural scream echoed through the study, his body convulsing as black blood sprayed across the room. Drake's form seemed larger than life, his presence eclipsing everything else as he tore through Vyper's wards. The magic fractured under his unrelenting assault, each strike a physical embodiment of his need for retribution.

Everyone was standing back as Drake unleashed everything and more on the sorcerer, no one wanting to stand in his way.

"You deserve no mercy," Drake growled, his voice vibrating with the intensity of his anger. "Now, you'll know what it feels like to be powerless." With one final, devastating strike, Drake drove his claws into Vyper's chest. The room seemed to still as his talons wrapped around the sorcerer's heart. With a savage pull, he tore it free, severing Vyper's connection to the Vessel. The artifact dimmed, its pulsating glow flickering like a dying ember as Vyper's final cry strangled in his throat.

The silence that followed was deafening. Drake stood over Vyper's lifeless body, his expression still burning, his chest heaving with each ragged breath. His claws, slick with blood, hung at his sides, and the faint glow of the Vessel finally extinguished, leaving the room bathed only in the flickering torchlight.

The room fell eerily silent for a moment, our collective tension easing as we watched Vyper's lifeless body bleed out onto the cold, cracked stone floor. My chest heaved, my heart pounding in my ears as if it had already sensed the malevolence still lingering in the room. Then, a sound—a low, rumbling laugh—shattered the stillness, and I turned sharply toward the mirror.

Its surface, once a twisted haze of darkness, now glowed faintly, and Azh'raim's shadowy face emerged like a nightmare realized. His glowing red eyes locked onto mine, his serpentine grin stretching too wide for comfort.

"You killed my thrall," he spoke, his voice deliberate, every word weighted with malice. "A wealth of souls sacrificed to me, no longer available. What will you give in its place?"

Before I could react, an invisible force yanked me from my body, and I was plunged into a blinding whirlwind of light and shadow. The abyss swallowed my scream, and when the chaos subsided, I found myself standing in a desolate plain, hellish and unyielding.

The air was oppressive, hot, and thick as if even breathing was a sin here. Ahead loomed a grotesque throne made of bleached skulls, their hollow sockets staring into oblivion. Perched atop it was Azh'raim, his presence an overwhelming wave of power and menace. He was no longer in a shadow form, but now a form my mortal mind could comprehend. He was a devastatingly handsome man with cropped black hair, slicked half back, wearing a tight white suit. His crimson eyes glittered with sadistic amusement as he leaned forward, resting his chin on his clawed hand.

"The Seer," he drawled, his voice a caress and a blade all at once. "Do you know how much trouble you've caused me, my dear? All those sacrifices, all that energy, and you've snuffed it out like a candle," he chuckled, the sound rattling my very bones. "Balance must be restored." He stood and flicked his cane as he tapped his way down the hill of skulls toward me.

"What do you mean?" I whispered, my voice trembling. The weight of his gaze bore down on me, making me feel small and insignificant. His unnaturally sharp features were beautiful. Devilishly so.

Azh'raim's grin widened. "You took from me, Seer. So I will take from you. But I am a generous God. I'll let you choose what I take."

His hand flicked lazily, and suddenly, I wasn't alone. Around me, my companions appeared frozen like statues. Drake, Fen, Julian, Avod, and Felix stood motionless, their eyes wide and unseeing. My heart dropped into my stomach.

"Strike down one of your friends in my name," Azh'raim purred, his voice oozing with malice. "Offer their soul to me, and your debt is settled. Or…" His grin turned predatory, his gaze locking onto mine. "Promise me the soul of your firstborn with your dragon. Such potential in a child born of a bond. That, too, would suffice."

"No," I choked out, my chest tightening. "I… I can't…" My memory flashed back to the Mirror Room. The little red-headed boy.

"Oh, but you must," he said, leaning back on his throne. "Go ahead. Choose. Who will it be?"

My gaze darted frantically between my friends, my mind racing. I couldn't choose. I couldn't kill any of them. Tears blurred my vision as I shook my head. "I won't. I won't do it!"

He sighed, feigning disappointment. "Then perhaps I'll help you decide," his grin turned razor-sharp. "Go on. Look at them."

I squeezed my eyes shut, but it was no use. Some invisible force compelled me to open them. My gaze landed on Felix first, his kind, patient face still as stone.

"The Gnome," Azh'raim said, his voice dripping with mockery. "How noble of you to offer the healer."

"No!" I screamed, but it was too late. The God snapped his fingers, and Felix's body crumpled to the ground. His lifeless eyes stared up at me, and I collapsed, a guttural sob tearing from my throat.

"Your debt is settled," He said, his tone almost cheerful. "But there's a condition, Seer. You will continue to kill in my name, or I will still take your firstborn. A soul for a soul."

I looked up at him, shaking with rage and despair. "Fuck you," I spat, my voice broken.

He smiled, his crimson eyes gleaming. "I'm unfortunately not interested, my dear. I have my eyes on someone else," He winked, and with a snap of his fingers, the hellish plane dissolved, and I was yanked back into my body.

I hit the stone floor hard, gasping for air. Drake was at my side in an instant, returned to his human form again. His silver eyes were wide with alarm. "Eva! What happened?" But I couldn't answer.

My gaze drifted to Felix's lifeless body, and my chest constricted with the weight of what had just happened. Azh'raim's voice echoed in my mind, a haunting reminder of the deal I never made but could never escape. The room was deathly quiet, save for the crackling of the torches on the walls. And then Fen's scream of anguish tore through the air, raw and primal. It sent shivers down my spine. She collapsed beside Felix's lifeless body, clutching at his tunic as if her touch alone could bring him back. Her shoulders heaved with every wracked sob, her face buried in his chest, but even through her despair, her pain was palpable, seeping into every corner of the room.

"Felix," she whimpered, her voice breaking. "You were the only good thing I've ever known. Please don't leave me... you can't. Please."

The sight of her grief was unbearable. Felix, the warm, steady presence we had all leaned on, his golden glow now extinguished like the snap of fingers. Her tears soaked into his clothing, and she gripped him tightly as if afraid the world would steal even his body away from her.

Avod stood off to the side, his face pale and stricken, his usual composure shattered. He opened his mouth as if to speak, but no words came. Instead, his hand hovered near Fen's shoulder, unsure, trembling, before falling back to his side. His eyes glistened with unshed tears as he watched her crumble, the unspoken bond between them now fraying under the weight of her sorrow.

"Fen," he said softly, his voice shaking. "I—"

She whipped her head up, her bloodshot eyes filled with fury, cutting off whatever words he'd tried to say. And then her gaze landed on me.

"You," the single word came out like a hiss, low and venomous, brimming with enough hatred to burn a city to the ground. Her grief morphed into something darker, sharper.

Her cold, wounded heart now beating with fury.

"What did you do?!" she screamed, her voice echoing off the stone walls. Her daggers were in her hands before I could react, their sharp edges gleaming like her unrestrained rage.

"Fen, no!" Avod shouted, but she was already moving.

She sprinted at me, her grief and fury driving her forward like a hurricane. Her daggers glinted in the flickering torchlight, aimed straight at me. I froze, panic and guilt rooting me in place.

Then Drake was there, intercepting her with a powerful clash. His arm locked around hers, the force of his movement sending her daggers clattering to the floor. She thrashed violently against his hold, her screams piercing, her pain rippling through the room like a physical force.

"I didn't choose this!" I cried, my voice trembling as I stumbled back. "Fen, please, you have to believe me!"

"You selfish *bitch*!" she spat her words like daggers of their own. Tears streamed down her face, her eyes wild with agony. "You traded him! You gave his life away!"

She crumpled to her knees, her body shaking with sobs. Drake released her slowly, his movements cautious, and she collapsed into herself, her hands gripping the floor as if trying to hold herself together.

Her sobs slowed, though her body still shook. She buried her face in her hands, and Avod pulled her into an embrace, his arms strong and steady as her fury gave way to broken, guttural weeping. He looked up at me over her shoulder, his gaze heavy with shock and confusion.

I stood there, guilt pressing down on me like a crushing weight. "Fen," I whispered, tears blurring my vision. "I... I'm so sorry."

She didn't respond. Her cries echoed in the chamber, and the pain I felt in my chest was nothing compared to the raw anguish consuming her.

The horrifying truth settled like a stone in my stomach: Felix's death was on me.

The world narrowed to a pinpoint as I stared at the mirror, my blood roaring in my ears like an unrelenting tide. I could still feel Azh'raim's presence, his cruel laughter echoing in my mind. Images flickered within the surface—visions of a small, red-haired Dragonblood boy with molten silver eyes. Our child. My child. The boy smiled up at me, innocent and unknowing, before the image twisted into something grotesque, Azh'raim's face leering back at me.

"No more," I growled, my voice trembling with fury and resolve. My hands gripped Avod's hammer off the ground, my knuckles white against the strain. I felt Fen's quiet sobs reverberating through the room, her grief a physical presence. Every moment of pain, every life lost, every sacrifice culminated in this singular choice.

With a scream of pure rage, I swung the hammer with every ounce of strength I had left.

The impact struck the mirror dead center, and the air seemed to shatter with it. A deafening explosion of sound and light erupted, blinding me as shards of glass burst outward like crystalline stars. Each fragment reflected Azh'raim's twisted visage, his mouth wide in a silent scream that splintered into nothingness as the shards hit the ground.

A shockwave rippled through the chamber, knocking me backward. The oppressive darkness that had suffused the air lifted, replaced by a strange, eerie calm. Around us, the fallen Vyrmin's corpses crumbled into ash, their grotesque forms collapsing in on themselves as if unmade by the very destruction of the Vessel.

I collapsed to my knees, the hammer slipping from my grasp and clattering to the stone floor beside me. My arms trembled with exhaustion, my chest heaving as I fought for breath. The silence in the room was deafening; the absence of the mirror's dark presence leaving a strange void.

Drake's arms were around me before I realized I had moved. He held me tightly against him, his body a wall of warmth and stability in the chaos. His hands were gentle as they brushed over my back, soothing despite his own ragged breath.

Tears welled in my eyes as I buried my face in his chest, the overwhelming weight of everything crashing over me. "I'm sorry," I whispered, the words barely audible through my sobs. Sorry for Felix. Sorry for Fen. Sorry for the innocent child I had glimpsed, promised to a monster. Sorry for everything I had done and everything I had failed to do.

Drake pressed a kiss to the crown of my head, his voice low and steady. "Eva... we're alive. Because of you."

I shook my head against him, the truth of his words doing little to ease the ache in my chest. Deep down, I knew the cost of my choices would haunt me forever. The images of Felix's lifeless body, Fen's broken sobs, and the haunting smile of a child I may never hold would be etched into my soul.

Behind us, Fen's ragged breathing filled the silence, her grief still raw and unrelenting. Avod hovered near her, his hand resting lightly on her shoulder as she knelt beside Felix's body. She didn't look up, didn't acknowledge the destruction of the mirror or the dying embers of Azh'raim's power. Her world had crumbled, and no amount of vengeance or victory could piece it back together.

And it was my fault.

Chapter Forty Four

Eldrake

Hundreds of injured Riftborn had fled Vyper's tower—wounded, starving, disoriented. Some could barely walk. Others were still half-bound in warding cuffs. We'd done what we could in the aftermath, but we needed more than bandages and firelight.

I'd sent a scout on horseback to Riftreach the moment we cleared the tunnels, and Ness with the other gnomes had answered faster than I expected. They met us halfway, exhaustion carved into their bones but fire in their eyes. We stopped in the foothills—remote enough to hide, close enough to keep moving by dawn.

Ness and the others worked without rest, their magic dim and fraying at the edges. They weren't as good at healing as Felix, as they mostly trained as an archivist, and the other in other things, but it was better than nothing. Fen barely looked at them, but Ness didn't flinch. They just kept healing. Quiet. Steady. Like the sun rising behind storm clouds.

The fires around camp were barely more than embers—just enough to warm hands, not enough to give away our position. The woods around us were thick, shadowed, and dead quiet except for the distant rustling of wind through pine needles and the low murmurs of the Riftborn encampment.

We couldn't risk more than a handful of scattered campfires, well-shielded and buried under rock or brush. Even one watchtower scout spotting the wrong shimmer of light could mean the end of all of us.

I shifted on the log I'd dragged closer to Eva's bedroll. She hadn't moved in over an hour.

She sat curled in on herself, her arms wrapped tightly around her legs, face half-lit by the fire. Her Star-Glow eyes stared at nothing—glass-bright, distant, haunted. She hadn't spoken since we stopped moving. Hadn't eaten. Barely blinked.

Shock was a strange thing. I'd seen it before in war, in bloodied men and broken warriors who'd walked away from things their minds hadn't caught up with yet. But I'd never seen it on her. And it gutted me.

I crouched beside her slowly, like approaching a skittish animal. "Eva." Nothing. I brushed my fingers along the back of her arm. "You with me, my love?"

Her gaze didn't change. But her breathing hitched—just once. I offered her a tin cup of broth. She didn't take it.

"You need to eat," I said quietly.

She blinked once. Slow. Then finally—without looking at me—took the cup. Her fingers barely curled around it.

She still hadn't spoken since we left the tower.

Across the camp, a child stirred in her sleep. Someone coughed. A few murmured words passed between two guards who should've been silent. No one laughed.

I stood slowly, stretching the ache out of my spine. The bond tugged behind my ribs like a string still wound too tight. Her devastation was leeching into my every pore. Eva was here, alive, breathing. But part of her was still down there—still locked in the moment she watched our friend die.

Across the fire, Fen sat sharpening her blades with a motion so harsh it sounded like she was skinning the stone. She hadn't looked at Eva since we left the tower. Avod sat beside her, silent and pale. His arm rested on his bent knee, his gaze unfixed.

"Watch her?" I asked Ness quietly.

They nodded.

I stood and crossed to Avod, sitting beside him on the edge of the boulder they'd claimed as a lookout. Fen didn't acknowledge me.

"She's not sleeping," I said, jerking my chin toward Eva.

"Neither is Fen," Avod muttered. "She hasn't closed her eyes since the tower."

We sat in silence for a beat. The fire cracked. A distant owl called. Avod nudged a pebble with his boot. "You remember that outpost in Helwick? The one with the ale that tasted like burnt molasses and rat shit?"

I huffed. "Gods. Don't remind me."

"Oh, I'm going to remind you," Avod said, his grin faint but real. "You challenged the tavern master to a drinking contest. Thought you could win back that dagger you lost in cards."

"I *did* win it back."

"You did. After throwing up behind the stables and declaring your undying love for a goat."

I smirked. "It was a noble-looking goat."

Avod shook his head, laughing quietly. "You tried to name it Commander Hornsworth and demanded we take it with us."

Drake chuckled, the sound low and warm. "Still better company than most of the squad," We sat in the quiet, our laughter fading into a shared silence that wasn't as heavy as before.

Avod's voice dropped. "Feels good. Laughing. Even just a little."

I nodded, staring at the fire.

For a moment, it helped. The grief didn't go away. But it made room for breath.

"Fuck," I said.

"Yeah," Avod said, softer now.

We watched the fire for a while. Eva hadn't moved. Fen was a shadow against the far tree line.

"They're going to need us to hold it together," I said.

Avod nodded. "So we do."

My eyes drifted back to Eva. Her hands were still cupped around the broth like she couldn't quite remember how to drink.

"I don't know how to reach her right now," I admitted.

"Then don't reach. Just stay close." Avod's voice was steady. "That's what Felix would've done."

I nodded once and turned back toward her.

The night deepened. The fire dimmed. And beside the people we loved—flawed and fraying and fragile—we kept watch.

Days had passed since we had arrived back at Riftreach and the dining hall was quieter than it should've been. Not silent—there were still plates clinking and a fire crackling in the hearth—but the sound barely rose above a murmur. Like the whole rebellion was holding its breath.

Evandra sat beside me, close enough that her shoulder brushed mine when she shifted—but she hadn't looked at me once since we sat down.

Julian was talking. Something about the Vyrmin postures he'd seen in the battle, how one of them had turned its head sideways like a curious wolf before launching at him. It should've been funny. Normally, it would've made Eva smile. She loved when he got theatrical. But she just pushed a piece of bread around her plate, tearing it into smaller and smaller pieces like she couldn't stand the thought of eating.

I leaned in a little. Let my knee press lightly to hers beneath the table. I kept my hand close enough that if she wanted to reach for it, she could.

She didn't.

I caught Ness watching her from across the table. There was sympathy in their eyes—and worry. The kind that said they'd noticed the same hollow quiet I had. But even Ness didn't say anything.

Because what do you say?

Fen sat at the far end, her jaw tight, her eyes locked on nothing. She hadn't spoken once. Her plate was untouched. Her knives stayed strapped to her thighs, but her fingers kept twitching like she wanted something to stab. When Ness offered her a refill of wine, Fen waved it off like the sight of it offended her.

Avod looked worse. Pale. Drawn. He'd sat stiffly, nodding when spoken to but saying almost nothing. Every time someone said Felix's name—even in passing—his shoulders tensed like he'd been slapped.

And me? I was trying not to crumble.

Eva looked like grief had turned her bones to glass. Guilt, heavier than armor, was draped over her like a second skin. She wouldn't eat. She barely blinked. She hadn't spoken to anyone since that morning—and even then, it had been in half-sentences.

I reached for her hand beneath the table. Brushed the backs of my fingers over her wrist.

She didn't pull away. But she didn't hold on, either.

Her thumb just kept stroking the rim of her cup. Round and round. The rhythm of a woman trying to convince herself she was still tethered to this world.

Then she stood.

The motion scraped her chair against the floor, a sharp, jarring sound in the low hum of the hall. Her cup tipped, sloshing water across the stone table. No one moved to clean it up.

"I need air," she said. No one stopped her. The door slammed as she exited. It echoed—loud, final, like a blade driven into stone.

For a beat, nobody moved. Then I threw my napkin down and started to rise.

Then Julian glanced at me. "You sure she wants company right now?"

"No," I said. "But I'm going anyway."

I pushed back my chair and stood. My legs ached from the tension of sitting still, of pretending to eat. I hadn't been hungry. I'd only come to dinner because Ness asked me to. Because Julian thought maybe sharing a meal would help us start to feel normal again.

Normal.

Felix was dead.

And Eva—Eva was falling apart right in front of me, and I didn't know how to catch her.

I left the hall. The corridor beyond the dining room was dim, the lanterns low for evening. I passed two rebels whispering by the stairwell, and they both went silent the second they saw me. I didn't care.

Her scent still hung by the exit tunnel, which meant she hadn't gone far. I let instinct guide me—followed the honeysuckle like a thread of smoke through cold stone.

Back to our quarters.
Ours. What a fragile word that suddenly felt.

Chapter Forty Five

Evandra

"When love and magic entwine, the soul does not speak—it demands. The Rift does not bless such unions lightly. To bond in grief is to burn with it. But even ruin can be sacred if both hearts survive the fire." —The Magic of Edralis, Vol. V

The door slammed behind me harder than I intended. Dust rattled loose from the beams, and the echo rang down the corridor like an accusation. I didn't care. Let the whole damn rebellion hear it.

Drake followed me in, silent but close. I didn't turn around. Couldn't. The air in this room—my quarters, now his too—was suddenly too thick to breathe.

"You left in the middle of dinner," he said quietly, like I was some frightened animal he didn't want to spook. "Everyone's worried."

"I couldn't stand it anymore," I muttered, peeling off the outer layer of my cloak with shaking fingers. "The pity. The stares. Fen's silence. Avod's silence. Yours."

"I didn't want to push you."

"Well maybe you should have," I snapped, louder than I meant to. My hands curled into fists, my breath coming hard and fast. "You're all treating me like I'm going to shatter, but guess what? *I already did.*"

Drake stepped closer, but didn't touch me. "Eva—"

"I *killed* him," I said. My voice cracked. "You all want to say it but don't. You want to be kind. But I saw it in Fen's eyes. I felt it when Avod couldn't look at me. I *know* what it cost to win that fight. I watched it happen. I let it happen."

"You didn't choose—"

"Didn't I?" I turned to face him, and he flinched at whatever was on my face. "You weren't there, Drake. You didn't see the mirror. You didn't hear him. Azh'raim *offered me a trade*. A soul for a soul. He gave me the choice. I didn't answer fast enough and he took Felix anyway—and then told me that wasn't even the real price."

His expression shuttered. "What do you mean?"

My voice dropped to a whisper. "He said if I didn't keep giving him souls, he'd take something else. Something sacred."

Drake's eyes sharpened. "What did he mean?"

"He wants our firstborn."

The silence was like a blow.

I forced myself to keep looking at him. "He said a child born from a love bond—between Seer and Dragonblood—would have power he's never seen. That if I didn't obey, he'd claim them instead. Our child. A child we haven't even had yet."

Drake stared at me, his jaw clenched, his hands shaking slightly at his sides. "And you waited until *now* to tell me?"

"What, like you've been such a fucking beacon of honesty?" My voice was bitter. "Let's talk about Julian. About the bond. About every moment you looked me in the eye and lied because you didn't want me to *know*."

"That's not the same—"

"It's exactly the same!" I shoved past him, pacing now because if I stood still I might explode. "You kept it from me. All of it. You decided for both of us. So don't you dare stand there and act betrayed when I'm the one who—" My voice broke. "When I'm the one who had to choose between a life and a God's sick promise."

"I was trying to protect you!"

"From what? From the truth? From your feelings?" I turned back toward him, eyes blazing. "How am I supposed to trust you now? How do I know you're not looking at me the way Fen does? Like I'm a curse? Like you hate me just like the rest of them do?"

Drake's eyes flashed. "Don't you *ever* say that. I could *never* hate you."

"You don't even look at me the same."

"Because I'm trying not to break down every time I remember his face!" he shouted. "Because *I* lost him too! And I'm sick of pretending I didn't!" His chest heaved. His fists were clenched. "You want honesty? Fine. You want to know when I knew about the bond? When I fucking *knew*?"

I stared at him, breath caught in my throat.

"The moment I fucking *met you*, Evandra," he said, voice low and dangerous and trembling with emotion. "The second you looked at me in that tavern like you'd seen a ghost and I couldn't breathe, I knew. I felt it in my chest like a blade. I knew I'd never be the same again."

My throat closed. "Then why *lie?*"

"Because I was scared," he said, stepping closer. "Because I loved you before the bond and I didn't want it to *own* us. Because I wanted it to be *real*."

"It *was* real," I whispered. "And now all we do is bleed on each other."

Something cracked between us then. Not just anger, not just grief—but the unbearable weight of surviving something together and still feeling alone.

And suddenly, we weren't yelling. We were kissing.

Fierce, desperate, clawing kisses. His hands tangled in my hair. Mine pulled him closer by the collar of his shirt. We collided like a storm breaking its own sky. His mouth was hot and furious on mine, and when he shoved me back against the wall, I didn't resist. I *needed* it. The rage, the ache, the proof of him still here, still *mine*.

Our clothes didn't so much come off as vanish. He lifted me, and I wrapped my legs around him like a lifeline. His teeth grazed my throat, and I arched into him with a sound that wasn't quite pain, wasn't quite pleasure.

There was nothing tender about it—nothing sweet. Just need. Just the crash of two people who had nothing left to give but this. His hands moved to my waist, pulling me closer as he deepened the kiss. I felt his warmth seep into me, chasing away the lingering cold.

My lips parted, inviting him in, our tongues meeting in a dance that felt as natural as breathing. A deep sense of urgency overtook me—a desperate, all-consuming need to be as close to him as possible. The fear of losing him still pulsed in my veins, a visceral reminder of how fragile this moment was. I crushed my body against his, kissing him firmly, over and over again, as if trying to imprint the feeling of him onto my very soul.

He moaned softly, the sound vibrating against my lips, and slid his hands beneath my robe. With one fluid motion, the garment fell to the floor, pooling around my feet like forgotten silk. His lips found the crook of my neck, where he buried his face, inhaling deeply as if committing my scent to memory. A soft kiss followed, delicate and reverent, before his hands rose to cup my breasts, his touch gentle yet filled with a palpable hunger.

I pushed him back toward the bed, guiding him down as I moved to straddle him. The firmness of his growing erection pressed against me, sending shivers of anticipation down my spine. Leaning down, I captured his lips again, our breaths mingling in heated, desperate rhythm. My hands moved to the waistband of his pants, tugging them down to free him. The urgency between us was undeniable, but it was laced with tenderness—a shared understanding that this moment was as much about connection as it was about passion.

Lining myself up with his tip, I met his gaze, filled with both love and need. Slowly, I sank down, taking him in inch by inch, a deep moan escaping his lips as he filled me completely. The sensation stole my breath, tears pricking at the corners of my eyes as I moved against him, grounding myself in the reality of his presence. He was here. He was mine.

I began to move, grinding my hips in a steady rhythm, savoring every sensation. His hands found my waist, guiding me as I quickened my pace, each downward motion pulling him deeper inside me. The sound of our breaths mingled with the soft creak of the bed, his low groans matching my own gasps of pleasure. I threw my head back, overwhelmed by the sheer intensity of our connection, my tears now spilling freely, though they were born of gratitude, not sorrow.

"Evandra…" he groaned, his voice rough and filled with awe. He brushed my hair back, studying me with something like reverence. "You're still mine," he whispered. "Even now," his eyes fluttered closed, his head tipping back as I rode him, my body moving with unrelenting purpose. The sight of him—his broad chest rising and falling, his jaw clenched with restraint—only drove me higher, the coil of pleasure inside me tightening with every thrust.

I climbed higher and higher, my body trembling as I reached the peak and slammed myself full weight onto him. Finally, I toppled over the edge, a wave of ecstasy crashing over me with an intensity that left me breathless. I clenched around him, my climax triggering his own as he groaned my name, his release filling me in a warmth that felt both physical and emotional.

I collapsed onto him, our bodies still intertwined, both of us shaking with the aftershocks. His arms wrapped around me protectively, pulling me close as I buried my face in his chest. A few stray tears escaped, soaking into his skin.

And when it was over—when we collapsed together, breathless and silent, skin slick and hearts still pounding—it wasn't peace we found. But it was something close. Truth, maybe. Or the beginning of it.

"I thought it all meant nothing to you," I whispered after a long silence, my voice trembling. "Don't lie to me again."

"I won't," he murmured into my hair, his voice still broken. "Not about anything."

For a moment, that was enough.

I lay there tangled with him in the dim of our quarters, the candles guttering low, wax making small glassy lakes on the shelf. The cavern holds its breath beyond the ship—deep, dark, and studded with far-off lanterns like a night sky pressed underground. The ship hums with its own quiet, not water, not wind—just the old timbers settling and the shy creak of rope where the anchors bite into the cavern wall. We hang here—jutting out like a blade from the stone high above Riftreach. If I look out, I can see the city falling away beneath us in ledges of light and shadow, stairways and alleys braided like ivy, the faint shimmer of heat from cooking fires, the low thrum of voices woven together until they sound like a single breath.

It isn't peace. But we are getting there. His palm is wide and heavy at my waist, my cheek tucked to his sternum to count each steady lift, the bond a quiet, golden wire humming along with our heartbeats.

After a long while, when the candles were breath away from drowning themselves in their own wax, he murmured, "Sleep."

"I don't want to lose this," I said. "If I close my eyes—"

"You won't," he said simply, like certainty was something he could lay over me as a blanket.

My eyes stung. I closed them. When sleep came, it didn't drag. It comforted me.

Morning in Riftreach is the city waking in layers. First the soft clatter of pans in the terraces below, a laugh tossed up a level and caught by someone you can't quite see. Then the hiss of kettles, the tang of smoke and spice rising and thinned by the cave-cool air. Light comes as one lantern switches from moonlight to sunlight. It spills through our large picture window now, slanting across the bed and touching the edge of Drakes broad shoulder, the place where his scales gleam faintly like someone burnished him in sleep.

He's already awake, watching the ceiling. I know the way his thoughts gather; I can feel it, like weather. When I move, his arm tightens reflexively, then relaxes; he lets me go like he's teaching himself that he can.

"Morning," I say, voice soft as featherlight.

He turns his head. That unguarded look—private, helpless—finds me, and the bond hums like a glass rung by a careful finger. "Morning."

I sit up and pull the sheet with me. It smells like warm skin and old beeswax and the mint I tucked in the corner last night to keep the room from turning thick with us. He watches me find my shirt—his, now, because mine is somewhere on the floor and refuses to be located—and the corner of his mouth fights a smile. He loses.

"You're pleased with yourself," I accuse.

"I'm relieved," he says, honest enough to make my breath catch. "That you're still here."

"I live here," I say, and then the rest of it arrives, not as a panic but as a firming in my bones. "We live here."

A flare in his eyes, quick and bright. "We do," he says, and the words stop being scary, and start being solid.

We take a quick bath, splashing one another, relishing in the comfort of being home. Being safe.

"I'm hungry," I say, surprised by it. It might very well be the first time since...

He tilts his head. "Good."

"Come with me to the market. But walk way behind me. If the old man at the flatbread stall sees you he will give us the tough ones out of spite." I say, half joking.

He makes a noncommittal noise that might be agreement.

We step out into the narrow gangway clinging to the hull, one palm on the rope rail because the drop is a real thing, and begin the descent. Stairs zigzag down along the cavern wall, hacked out of rock and shored up with beams older than I am, slick in places with the breath of the cave. Voices float up. Somewhere, someone is singing—a low, work-song that has more humming than words. We pass two teenagers hauling a slatted crate between them; they glare at Drake like he's about to criticize their grip.

"Captain." They nod. He nods back and doesn't say another word, and their shoulders drop an inch.

The higher terraces are quieter—homes and small shrines, chalked marks on stone marking family names, strings of bone and ribbon crossing doorways for luck. The lower we go, the more people, the tighter the air. Familiar faces are nodding at us. Thanking us for saving them or their loved ones from the tower. By the time we spill onto the main terrace, my heart is doing an odd little stutter of happiness I don't recognize in myself. It's not joy, exactly. It's... relief. Maybe everyone *didn't* hate me.

The market spills itself out in ragged rows. Fish dried to sturdy planks. Earthen jars stamped with thumbprints. Piles of mushrooms, some with pale glow still trapped in their gills; baskets of roots shaped like fists; rounds of cheese sweating lightly beneath waxed cloth. A girl with night-black eyes lets me smell a bundle of herbs and tuts when I guess wrong. "Not thyme," she says. "A cousin that grew in the old gardens. Stronger." She presses a sprig into my palm anyway. "For your tea," she says. She means for your nerves. I tuck it behind my ear.

Drake and I argue about bread because it's safe to argue about bread. The round loaf with the blistered crown looks like yummier. The long one looks crusty.

\"“The long one keeps better," he says again, squinting at it like he can shame it into beauty.

"It looks like someone stretched a frog," I say, and he nearly smiles, which means I win, and then the baker laughs and drops both into our arms with a muttered: "Pay or I'll charge you for the air you breathed while deciding."

We buy figs too, and fresh cheese folded into leaves, and a paper cone of sugared nuts we absolutely do not share equally.

Fen is not here. Of course she isn't. I feel the empty place where she would have stood like a black hole. I hear her silence as clearly as a voice. Her absence changes the way people approach me; they aren't sure if I did what she thinks I did.

We climb back up slower, the basket heavier and my legs unaccustomed to carrying anything that isn't guilt. Drake walks half a step down from me, as if he means to catch me if the stairs betray me. He just makes it true by placing himself where the world could break and turning that into a person instead. He insisted on carrying the basket, but I insisted I wasn't weak. I'm just an idiot.

Inside the cabin again, I set the bread on the desk and the cheese on the bed and the herbs in the water glass and every wrong thing in every wrong place because none of this has been practiced yet. He corrects nothing. He pulls his coat off and hangs it on the peg he installed yesterday with exactly the number of taps it took to make the board accept it. He moves around the room with the awkwardness of a bull in a china shop.

I tear a piece of bread and press it into his mouth. He takes it, eyes on mine, and the bond hums in approval.

"I'm wondering... if we should talk to Julian," I say, hesitantly. "About the deal,"

He nods. "Together. He should hear it from you."

"I don't want him to feel like I'm keeping secrets." I took another bite of bread, first dipping it in steaming mushroom soup.

Julian's map room had the familiar smell of ink and damp stone. Vellum sheets lie like shed skins on the tables; lines of charcoal stitch districts to names and names to consequence. Ness perched on a stool, quill tucked behind their ear, watching us without pretending not to.

"We need to speak," I say, as we charged through the door.

Julian's mouth goes thin, not unkind, just accustomed to us barging in at this point. "Then speak."

I don't ask Drake to explain. I don't hand my name away. I tell it myself.

"Azh'raim forced me into a bargain," I say, letting the words be ugly and true. "If I don't feed him souls, he'll take our firstborn for his own. As you know, the child produced of a bond has the potential for great power. And in his hands, that could be..."

Silence opens—clean, cold, merciless. The word firstborn lands like a thrown blade. Drake doesn't flinch. He stands at my shoulder the way a wall stands: not to pen me in, but to keep the room from pushing closer.

Ness inhales sharply. Julian's gaze flicks, once, to Drake, then anchors on me. "You're certain," he says—not doubt, but the courtesy of a final door left to me to close or keep.

"Yes," I answer. "He showed me enough that doubt would be a kindness I can't afford."

Julian's hands settle on the edge of the table. "And you intend to pay?"

"I intend to choose how," I say. "If there's no other way. I won't ignore the threat and let him come for a child that doesn't yet exist."

Ness finds their voice first. "We look for other ways," they say, stubborn as a prayer. "Always. But if none—"

Julian lifts a hand. Not to stop them—just to gather the air. He studies me, measuring something I can't see. Then, quietly: "What if..."

Drake's shoulders tighten.

"You could be... *a blade*," Julian continues, careful, precise. "Not indiscriminately. Not as spectacle. As pressure. As consequence. Your curse could be fed by the worst of them so Azh'raim learns there is a cost to preying on us. If the God demands souls, then let the debt be taken from men who have already sold their own."

The word assassin isn't spoken, but it sits between us anyway, breathing.

"I won't be your monster," I say, and my voice surprises me with how steady it is.

Julian inclines his head. "Nor mine to command. Your choice. Your line. I'm offering a way to turn a noose into a leash—on them, not you."

Drake steps forward a fraction, enough for me to feel the heat of him. "You don't use her," he says, iron laid flat on the table.

Julian meets his gaze without blinking. "I don't intend to. I intend to give her the truth and let her decide what to do with it, with us standing where we said we'd stand."

Ness's voice threads through, softer. "And while we search for a way to break it—the bargain—we can at least decide that if something must be fed, it eats rot, not bread."

I let out a breath I didn't know I'd caged. "General details," I say, half to them, half to myself. "No timetables. No names yet. We don't move in the dark and call it virtue. If I do this, it's because the people truly deserve it."

Julian nods once, as if this was the answer he hoped for and feared. "Then for now, we do nothing but know. We keep the thought. We sharpen it in silence. And if the day comes when we choose to use it, it's because we can't choose anything gentler."

My hands have curled without my permission. I uncurl them. Felix's face rises to the surface too often: the half-smiles he saved for me, his stupid little songs, the way he made even the worst moments feel like they remembered how to be kind.

"I keep thinking," I say, and the words scrape going out, "that I could have saved him. That if I'd been faster, smarter—less... me—he would still be here."

Drake turns toward me, but I don't let him speak yet. I need the words to sit in the air where I can see how wrong they look in the light.

"But I couldn't have," I add, and the admission is small and stubborn and real. "We walked in together. He chose to stand where he stood. He knew the cost and took it anyway because he loved us. Because he loved me. I hate that that's true and I am trying to be grateful for it at the same time."

The ache in my chest shifts, not smaller, but different—like a knot worked loose enough to breathe through.

I set my palm flat on the map, over a blank piece of vellum where no routes are drawn yet. "I won't let Azh'raim collect on his threat," I say. "Not from me. Not from any child of mine. Not from any child of this city. If he wants a debt, he can choke on mine instead."

Drake's hand finds the back of my wrist—light, a single warm point. Ness looks away, giving me the privacy of not being watched.

Julian's voice is very quiet. "Then we agree on this much: we don't rush a single step. We search for a way to break the bargain. We keep your choice yours. And we remember who put the noose around our throats in the first place."

"Azh'raim," I say, and I taste the name like iron.

"For Felix," Drake says.

"For Felix," I echo, and it isn't absolution, not yet, but it is a breath that doesn't hurt to take.

I look down at that blank space on the map. In my mind, I draw a single line—nothing clever, nothing winding. A straight stroke from where I am to where he waits, through whatever halls or nights stand between. I don't need tactics or tokens or code for this part.

I only need the promise.

"I'm coming for you," I whisper to the God who thinks he owns me. "Not today. But soon."

The stone seems to hold the words the way a hand holds heat. I let my palm rest there a moment longer, then lift it. And for the first time since the tower, I feel the tiniest slackening of the rope I tied around my own throat.

Chapter Forty Six

Avod

Something was wrong with Fen.

Not wrong in the way most people meant it—she still moved with that lethal, effortless grace, her knives as precise as ever. She still showed up when she was needed. Still trained harder than anyone else in the caverns. But something had changed since Felix died.

She didn't grieve like the rest of us. Didn't cry or rage or even speak about him. She just vanished. Into the training halls. Into the tunnels. Into herself. I hadn't seen her eat in three days.

I leaned against one of the carved stone pillars near the western overlook, arms crossed, trying not to look like I was watching her. She was down below, where the natural light barely reached, practicing with those blades again—sharp arcs, tight pivots, the rhythm clean and brutal. Her strikes had no waste. No art. Just violence.

The Riftborn gave her a wide berth. Can't blame them.

She didn't look like a soldier anymore. She looked like a ghost. Something barely holding together, and maybe not trying to. Her face was thinner. Her eyes hollowed. Even her movements, as flawless as they were, carried an edge I didn't like. Not rage. Not even pain. Purpose. That was worse.

I'd seen what happened when grief curdled into purpose. I'd buried people like that. Proud, dangerous people who stopped seeing the line between sacrifice and suicide.

A younger Riftborn approached her once—maybe trying to offer help or company—and she turned on him so fast I almost jumped from my perch. No words, just a flash of daggers and a stare so sharp it cut the air between them. The kid fled without a sound. Fen just turned back to the target wall and kept going.

I let out a slow breath. Dragged a hand down my chin. Something gnawed at the back of my mind, something I couldn't name. A weight that hadn't shifted since the battle. And not just because we lost Felix.

I pushed off the pillar and made my way down the steps. Maybe I was a fool, but someone had to try.

She didn't stop when I reached the edge of the chamber. She knew I was there. She always knew. But she didn't so much as glance over.

"Training alone again?" I asked, keeping my voice light.

No answer.

"Riftborn've started calling you the Widow," I added after a beat. "That's not a compliment."

Still nothing. Her daggers sang through the air. One embedded itself in the wood with a heavy *thunk*. The other followed half a heartbeat later.

I stepped closer. "Fen."

This time, she paused.

Turned.

The look in her eyes nearly stopped me cold.

This wasn't just grief.

Her face was unreadable—utterly still—but her pupils were too wide, the whites of her eyes just a little too shadowed. Her hair clung to her sweat-slicked face like vines, and her skin, already pale, had taken on an odd cast in the dimness of the cave. Like moonlight on water. Cold and shifting.

"You're wasting your time, Avod," she said finally. "Go play caretaker with someone else."

"Someone's gotta keep an eye on you."

"I'm fine."

I huffed. "You're not. You haven't been since the tower. You look like you haven't slept in days. You flinch when someone says his name."

"Don't say it," she snapped.

My jaw clenched. "I understand loss, Fen. You know I do. But this thing you're doing—cutting everyone out, treating us like threats—it's not helping you."

She stepped forward slowly. Her boots made no sound on the stone. "I don't need help." The way she said it sent a ripple up my spine.

The shadows behind her shifted. It could've been the torchlight.

Or not.

"You know," I said, testing the ground, "some of the younger ones are scared of you now. They say you've been talking to the walls."

Her eyes flicked to mine. For just a second. And in that second, I saw it. Something watching from *behind* her eyes. Not Riftburn. Not madness. *Influence.*

Godsdamn it.

When she finally looked at me, her voice was barely more than a breath. "What would you do, Avod? If it meant bringing him back?"

I didn't answer. Because I knew the answer. And so did she.

"That's what I thought," she whispered, more to herself than me.

The shadows behind her stirred again. A flicker of motion. I reached for the hammer on my back—not threatening, but ready.

She noticed.

"Don't," she said quietly.

"Then talk to me. Before you do something neither of us can undo."

For the first time, her mask cracked. Her throat bobbed like she was swallowing something hard. The glint of grief flickered in her expression—real and raw.

Then she turned away again.

And the shadows swallowed her.

Chapter Forty Seven

Fen

The whispers started as judgment.

Every step I took through Riftreach carried the weight of eyes and murmurs, of Riftborn pretending not to flinch when I passed. *Widow,* they called me when they thought I couldn't hear it. *The one who lost control. The one who lost her brother.* They didn't understand what I had lost.

Not just Felix.

The way he used to laugh when I burned breakfast. The stupid hand signal we used when we were bored on watch duty. The way he'd hum to calm me down after a mission went bad.

The best part of me died in that tower. I wasn't mourning him. I was mourning the version of myself that only existed because he believed I was good. Everything else now was bone and blade.

I stopped sleeping in the barracks after the first night. Couldn't stomach the way people looked at me. Couldn't stand the way they avoided saying his name. As if silence would make my grief cleaner. As if their pity wasn't worse than their fear.

The caverns below Riftreach became mine. The lowest halls where the lanterns flickered and the stone was cool to the touch. Where the echoes made it feel like maybe—just maybe—someone else was still walking beside me.

Down there, I trained.

Not to get stronger.

To feel something.

The crack of blades against stone. The wheeze of breath in my lungs. The soreness in my shoulders. Pain was honest. Pain didn't ask questions. Pain didn't watch me like Avod did, hovering at the edge of the shadows, pretending not to flinch when our eyes met.

Let him worry. Let them all worry. They should be.

Avod asked me once if I'd heard anything. He didn't say what. Didn't have to. I had.

The whisper had started the night of the funeral, quiet as breath. I thought it was grief at first—my own thoughts turning cruel. But the voice had shape. Rhythm. Intelligence. And every night since, it had grown louder. I didn't seek it out. Not at first. But the nights were long. The silence too sharp. And there was nowhere else for me to go.

Fen...

The voice was like velvet now, wrapped around a blade. It found me again while I sat with my knees drawn to my chest, Felix's scarf clutched in my hands like a lifeline I couldn't let go of. The dark had settled thick around me. The lanterns had long since gone out.

"You've lost everything," it murmured. "Your brother. Your name. You're drifting, unmoored. But you could have it all again. I can give it back." I didn't speak. Not that night. But I didn't walk away, either.

I trained harder the next day. Dug the edge of my blade so deep into the practice wall it stuck, hilt-deep. When a recruit came too close, I didn't threaten—I warned. And when I saw Eva standing at the edge of the shadows, watching me with those wide, green eyes full of *guilt,* I nearly lost what was left of my restraint. She wanted to talk. *Of course she did.* I turned my back on her before I did something I'd regret. Or maybe something I wouldn't.

She didn't belong in the dark anymore.

I did.

That night, I returned to the tunnel. The voice greeted me like an old friend.

"Felix," it whispered, shaping his name like a promise. "Wouldn't you like to hold him again? Hear his voice? Feel him hug you like he used to, when the nightmares came?"

I didn't realize I'd begun walking until I felt damp air brush my cheeks. The tunnel beneath the old shrine curved deeper than I'd ever explored, narrower than a Riftborn should be able to pass. But I did. And the deeper I went, the louder it became.

"You've always known you were more," the voice crooned. "More than soldier. More than weapon. More than sister. But they never let you become what you were meant to be. You loved him. I don't ask you to stop. I ask you to *use it.*"

The tunnel widened into a hollow drenched in pale, silver light. The stone walls throbbed with some unnatural pulse—alive and cold. Azh'raim stood in the center of it, wearing the dark like a cloak. His eyes were endless. Bottomless. A void you could fall into and never stop.

I should've felt fear. I didn't. I felt relief. Like I had finally stopped pretending.

"You are ready," he said, his voice a hiss of wind over steel. "You've already begun walking toward me. Let me show you where the path leads."

My grip tightened on my daggers. They felt small now. Pointless. Like children's toys in the presence of a God.

"What do you want from me?" I asked.

Azh'raim smiled. "Nothing you weren't already willing to give."

The air shifted. Heavy. Binding.

"Say yes."

I should've said no. Should've remembered Felix's voice—*Don't lose yourself, Fen. We fight monsters, but we don't become them.*But he wasn't here. He wasn't the one being haunted. Hunted. Hollowed.

He wasn't the one who'd been left behind.

My throat tightened. My hand hovered at my side.

I whispered the word before I could stop myself.

"Yes."

The shadows closed in like a second skin.

And this time, I didn't fight them. It didn't feel like betrayal. It felt like becoming.

Index

Azh'raim – The Old God of Darkness. Worshipped through sacrifice, often via the Vessel. Demands souls in exchange for power.

Edralis — The ancient kingdom that existed before Aberdeen's reign. A golden era where Riftborn and humans lived openly in peace.

Beasts – Humanoid Riftborn descendants of a lost magical era, marked by traits like wings, horns, and glowing "Star-Glow" eyes. Their powers are innate, woven into their bodies as natural conduits for magic. Beasts are often linked to elemental forces and ancient myths but are distinct for their inherent connection to the Rift itself.

Blade Dancer – A Riftborn combatant class specializing in precision, agility, and telekinetically controlled weaponry—most notably enchanted daggers. Blade Dancers channel their Rift through focused mental discipline, allowing their weapons to hover, spin, and strike independently.

Bonding (Riftborn) – The deepening magical and emotional link that can form between two Riftborn, especially when romantic or spiritual ties are involved. May lead to shared powers or visions.

Castle City – The capital of the human-controlled territories and seat of political power. A walled metropolis governed by the High Council, it represents order, tradition, and magical regulation.

The Change / The Great Change — The era over a century ago when Aberdeen seized power, outlawed magic, and began the genocide and persecution of the Riftborn. This period also saw the burning and destruction of any and all magical artifacts.

Dragonblood – A Riftborn lineage descended from dragons, marked by silver eyes and the potential for partial or full draconic shifts. Drake is a Dragonblood.

Hellwrought – Winged, horned Riftborn hybrids feared for their destructive power and chaotic origins. Their bat-like wings and curling horns evoke ancient legends of demons, though they are Riftborn in origin, not tied to any divine realm.

Magi — The first mortals capable of wielding magic during the age of the Rift.

Nestlers Inn – A modest, crooked inn located in the quiet town of Winshire.

The Rebellion – Present-day organized Riftborn resistance.

Rift / The Rift – A mysterious magical force that grants power to Riftborn. It connects all living things and responds to emotion, especially grief, rage, or love. The Rift is also remembered as the age when Gods walked among mortals, before ascending and leaving their magic behind.

Riftborn – Beings born with a connection to the Rift. Marked by magical traits such as glowing skin, elemental abilities, or other non-human features.

Riftburn / Rift Burnout – A dangerous overexertion of Rift magic, which can result in seizures, unconsciousness, or even death.

Riftreach – The underground sanctuary of the rebellion. A hidden city carved into a mountain and powered by Riftstone.

Rift Sight — Among the most powerful Rift-wielders, there exists a rare ability known as Rift Sight. To those who bear it, the Rift manifests around others as a shimmering aura, revealing not only the presence of Riftborn but also the magnitude of their connection to the Rift.

Riftstone – Crystalline formations charged with Rift energy. Used to power wards, lighting, and other magical technologies within Riftreach.

Seer – A rare kind of Riftborn with powerful psychic abilities. Can see potential futures, manipulate minds, or enter others' dreams and memories.

Star-Glow – A rare Riftborn trait marked by luminous silver eyes that shimmer in low light. Often inherited through bloodlines with ancient magic, Star-Glow is considered a sign of deep Rift affinity and spiritual potential.

Thaumatology — The discipline devoted to unraveling the mysteries of magic. Rooted in the Rift's legacy, it strives to follow the divine threads left by the Gods and comprehend the remnants of their power.

The Vessel (of Azh'raim) – A magical mirror used to communicate with the Old God. Capable of extracting power from sacrifices and channeling dark magic.

Vyrmin – Corrupted Riftborn, mutated through sacrifice and dark ritual. Serve as foot soldiers and guards for Vyper and Azh'raim.

Ward – A magical barrier or suppressive enchantment used to block, dampen, disguise or redirect Riftborn abilities.

Winshire – A small town located the grasslands of the Aberdeen Kingdom.

Wyrm – An ancient, earth-rending creature of legend. Often referenced in Riftborn texts as a primal force, wyrms are associated with massive subterranean power and are ancestors of some draconic bloodlines.

Embers of the Rift
Book Two of the Riftreach Series
Coming Soon

www.ingramcontent.com/pod-product-compliance
Lightning Source LLC
Chambersburg PA
CBHW020916310726
48980CB00011B/907/J

* 9 7 9 8 9 9 9 3 4 7 3 5 0 *